I0706139

RESURGENCE

FRACTURED ORBIT
BOOK 3

HERMAN STEUERNAGEL

RESURGENCE

Book Three of Fractured Orbit

First Edition

Copyright © 2023 by Herman Steuernagel

This is a work of fiction. Names, characters, places, and incidents either are the product of the author's imagination or are used fictitiously. Any resemblance to actual persons, living or dead, events or locales is entirely coincidental.

All international rights reserved. No part of this publication may be reproduced, stored or transmitted in any form or by any means, electronic, mechanical, photocopying, recording, scanning, or otherwise without written permission from the publisher. It is illegal to copy this book, post it to a website, or distribute it by any other means whether digital or printed without permission in writing from the copyright owner.

ISBN: 978-1-990505-14-0 (hardback)

ISBN: 978-1-990505-13-3 (paperback)

ISBN: 978-1-990505-10-2 (ebook)

Cover by Covers by Christian

Edited by Novel Approach Manuscript Services

https://www.hermansteuernagel.com

Hello reader,

If you're here, you've no doubt already read *Eclipse &* *Chimera*. As we get deeper into the Loop and the tragedies it contains the series does grow somewhat darker. However, *Resurgence,* is very much a continuation of *Chimera* and you won't find anything here you didn't find in the last book. As in the previous instalments, *Resurgence* contains death, murder, conspiracy, and violence, as well as themes of kidnapping, suicidal thoughts, human and sex trafficking, as well as non-consensual surgery and body manipulation.

While these topics are part of the story's narrative, none of them are covered in-depth, described in an overly graphic way, or glorified.

Abigail Monroe
The *Redemption*

"I swear, Marvin, this might be the most horrific plan you've come up with yet."

Abigail Monroe paced the bridge of the *Chimera*. She hadn't believed she would ever find a ship she loved more than the *Black Swan,* but this one far exceeded all her expectations. A top-secret military vessel with more capabilities than was even supposed to be possible? She couldn't even have dreamed of being so lucky.

The *Chimera* was so new that she swore there was paint in some quarters that had yet to dry. There were even some holo-screens that had yet to be installed. It left the bulkheads a little bare in places, but it was a detail that would be to her benefit in the days to come.

Abigail's pact with the Resurgence had already paid off. She could have never procured this vessel for herself. But the Resurgence had managed to snag it during their raid of the Syndicate shipyards on Callisto. Even though she hadn't been directly involved, they provided her with part of the spoils—a ship and supplies. In exchange, they received herself as a captain, and authorized a crew of her choosing to man the craft when the inevitable fighting began.

"Your memory's clouded from all that rum," Marvin protested. "Many of my plans have been far worse. And to be fair, I'm not sure you're the best person to be throwing rocks, given how things look for you right now. What are you going to do—keep Jenax hostage until she agrees to give you what you want?"

The holo-projection of Marvin shimmered, reflecting bits of the Chimera's bridge lights throughout the rest of the cabin, creating a light kaleidoscope effect. Abigail presumed Marvin was somewhere on Lunar, but so far, she wasn't trusted enough to be told. But the backdrop that faded in and out behind him suggested he was in an office building like the ones found in Shackleton.

But Abigail knew the resistance movement wouldn't have lasted five minutes if they'd established their base in Lunar's capital, not with the military presence the Syndicate Empire maintained there. No, this hideout had to be somewhere else.

At least he looks better than he had when we first pulled him off that space station, she mused. Some of the color had returned to his cheeks, and it was clear the Resurgence team around him had been ensuring he'd been eating as properly as one could with their bootlegged resources.

Still, it had been a shock to Abigail that those on board the *Eclipse* had been as malnourished as the rest of the

Loop. The damned FLOWs grew the Empire's food, and they still got shafted.

"Don't be ridiculous," Abigail scoffed. "I haven't even told her what I want. Not yet. There'll be time for that later."

"And what *do* you want with her?" the resistance leader pressed. "Or are you still waiting for your teenage eight ball to come up with something?"

Abigail ran a palm over her thigh, absently caressing the fabric of her favourite black bodysuit. The outfit clung to her skin, but she liked the way it made her feel—sleek and covert.

"Relax. She'll be my guest for a couple days at most. Once whatever threat Zee is seeing has passed, we'll let her go on her way. By that time, Jenax will realize the man she's aligned herself with is less man and more monster."

"You know how I feel about your little puppet." Marvin eyed her with consternation. That was the problem with him—always so damned serious. "You're heading down a dangerous path, and I don't like that you're using Syndicate assets to do it."

"Trust me, love, I'm steering us *away* from a path we don't want to be on. It's a slight detour. No harm done."

"I wish I shared your confidence, Abigail, but as far as I can tell, you're poking around at ghosts because of a *kid*. Do you not see how insane that is?"

"Nobody has ever accused me of being sane." She smirked. "Jenax is safe. You have my word."

"According to my sources, she's been in bed with Aries —both literally and politically. I'm not sure 'safe' is the word I'd use to describe her. I'm glad she's in your brig instead of mine."

"Zee says that the Syndicate will not fall without her. But if we don't keep her at bay for a time at least, innocent lives will be lost. More than we can spare. Added to that, Mikka will be set on a path to ruin, and we can't have that. That beautiful woman's redemption is the only hope for this empire."

"What you do with Jenax is up to you. What worries me is the blind faith you put in this child and his short-circuited mods. I really would like you to return to the outpost and await our orders."

"A few days," Abigail reasoned. "That's all I ask."

Marvin Alejandro crossed his arms, the light of his holo-projected body flickering against the backdrop of the *Chimera's* bridge. The Resurgence-issued outfit he wore fit him well. It wasn't technically a uniform, but most of those who were active wore them. It was a simple gray track suit with that double circle emblem stitched in black on the shoulder. Marvin's amber eyes had become both more tired and more determined since Abigail had last seen him. But that old fire had returned as she knew it would. He gritted his teeth as he spoke. "You know you're not even supposed to be flying that thing around yet? If word gets out that it was the Resurgence that stole the prototype fighters, we'll lose our advantage."

"Oh, *please.*" Abigail waved a hand dismissively. "You know these ships can't be detected on standard scans, right? *Nobody* knows we're out here. We're practically invisible."

"Not from a viewport, you're not! All it takes is one Orbital Guard patrol to look the wrong way and it's game over. The *Chimera* isn't exactly a standard vessel, and I'd appreciate it if you didn't end up on every holo-feed from Venus to Ganymede. Plus, I'm not sure how easy it'll be to convince my people to mount a rescue attempt once they find out the only reason you're in the shit is because of your own arrogance."

"Easy now—you've made your point," Abigail warned. "I'll keep under the radar from here on out. No public appearances until you're ready to pull the pin. Besides, Mikka's on board. The crew's getting her quarters ready as we speak."

"I still don't understand what you're hoping to achieve . . ."

"*Patience*, Alejandro. I'm hoping for patience. Wars are lost over rushed decisions."

"They're also lost because commanders wait too long." Marvin moved his hands to his hips. "We've got one shot. That's it."

"You keep saying that, but I don't know that it's true. This is the only shot *you* can see. There will be others—you just need to be prepared to vary your approach. For what it's worth, I have a feeling this plan of yours with the boy will go very badly."

"If you've got any better ideas, I'll hear them, but I'm not interested in vague feelings or whatever your plaything believes the odds to be."

Abigail raised her hands placatingly. "Hey, I'm just playing devil's advocate. Django just got off a FLOW. He barely knows his mouth from his asshole, and you're going to sew the most powerful chip in the system into his arm and send him off to fight an empire he didn't even know existed a week ago? And you say I'm the insane one."

"Django's a good kid. I trust him to do the right thing," Marvin replied.

"That's all well and good, but try seeing things from his point of view. He's being told to get his head around two centuries' worth of misinformation and the death of his family, all while being sent out onto the battlefield. It's a lot."

"Let's not get ahead of ourselves. We're starting small."

"Care to elaborate?"

"Not over these frequencies, I don't. Besides, I'm still waiting on the Table's sign-off on the mission. So, you might still get your wish."

"It's not so much my wish, as it is my *warning*. Zee knows the boy will be involved. He's also predicted things will get a lot worse before they get better. My point is, you call this boy your nephew. I hope you realize the danger you're putting him in."

"Everyone in the Loop's in danger every damned second they're still breathing. He hadn't been off that station for more than a few hours before some PA goon had him smuggled off to the mines. If you ask me, it can't get much worse for him than what I've already brought him into."

Abigail paused and pursed her lips, running an index finger across her crossed leg as she considered Marvin's position. The resistance leader had been out of the game for a while, it was true, but he knew better.

"Oh, love. You've been on that cushy station for far too long. It can get worse. *So* much worse."

Django
    Shackleton City

Django had been outside for mere minutes, and already he hated it. No, 'hate' wasn't the right word; 'terrified' was more like it.

How does anyone live like this?

Artificial lights assaulted his senses from every angle. Neon hues of orange and green reflecting off the glass towers that stood mightily nearby. Several motorized vehicles rushed by him, threatening to run him over if he stepped in the wrong place at the wrong moment. Dozens of people scurrying about their day as though there was nothing wrong with the hellscape that surrounded them.

Yet the worst of it all wasn't the calamity that buzzed around him; it was the reality that stretched above his head that sowed primal fear deep within his gut. Past the tops of the towers, and the hovering drones casting spotlights below, past the ships that traveled to and from the docks, beyond all the dizzying lights was a blackness that shouldn't have been there.

Outside means death. It had his entire life. A space for accidents and the punishment of crime. And now there was nothing but openness, threatening to envelop him.

Pressed against the sides of the buildings, Django's back was nearly glued to the wall. He grappled with an unsettling fear that, at any moment, he might be launched into the vacuum of space, where his lungs would burst and his body would freeze.

Your blood would boil first. Words his uncle Marvin spoke to him long ago reverberated in his mind.

Django shivered. *Not helping.*

As the residents of Shackleton breezed past him, going about their business, Django resisted the urge to yell at them to get inside, to avoid imminent danger. Being outdoors meant death, and he was starkly and distressingly outdoors. No ceilings, no walls—nothing holding him in. Nothing keeping the air flowing, or temperatures moderate, or cosmic radiation from microwaving his insides.

His brain tried to reason with him that there had to be safeguards for all these things. But of course, no one had taken the time to explain to him how it all worked. Instead, Django had been left to discover this new normal for himself—and clearly, at some point in humanity's past, someone had cracked the code to make lunar living possible. Shackleton City was nothing short of a technological marvel, and convincing his brain that invisible forces and science were keeping everything in check was a challenge.

Instead of placating his fears, the towering buildings only intensified Django's sense of vulnerability. How could anything stand so tall without tipping over? Without collapsing? How were thousands of tonnes of rock and metal able to reach so imposingly for the stars?

There was only the Moon's artificial gravity to ground them. Artificial gravity had always made Django nauseous, though he wished he could attribute his queasy stomach to that alone. The stabilization tech probably didn't help, but the more likely cause for the flips in his stomach was the overwhelming sensation that death was imminent.

Every part of him screamed that if there was nothing but an endless sea of stars overhead, it meant he'd been jettisoned out of an airlock and was experiencing the final precious seconds of his life.

Walking on Lunar's surface—through its streets, no less—was exposure like Django had never imagined. Running naked down the corridors of the *Eclipse* would have felt less vulnerable.

Django had stopped several times during his journey to ensure he wasn't gradually lifting from the ground, a second away from being flung into the void of space. Each step seemed too light, as if his feet were barely connecting with the ground; as if the solid rock underfoot would willingly let go of him.

After considerable concentration and effort, Django managed to convince his brain that Lunar's gravity was sound. *This is no different from the high-ceilinged farmscapes of the* Eclipse. He forced himself to focus on his destination and the note from his Uncle Marvin that rested in his pocket.

Django had memorized the address while still in the apartment Commander Aries had provided for him, though it was of little use since he had no idea how Lunar addresses worked. Navigating the *Eclipse* was ridiculously straightforward—torus level, quadrant, room number. Simple.

A person *could* wander around the D-Ring torus for a day, maybe two, but as the main corridors ran in a circle, they would always end up exactly where they started. Here, Django didn't know how far he could go. How would he know if he was reaching the city boundary? He was pretty sure breathable air didn't extend around the entire moon. Would there be a barrier? A sign? Any hint that one minute he would be breathing oxygen, and the next, nothing?

Focus. He had to focus.

He pulled out the slip and studied it again, attempting to extract some hidden meaning from the cryptic message scrawled on the dirtied slip of paper.

Velvet Underground, 9333B Hadfield Ave, Old Artemis District.

The words "Velvet Underground" made Django think he was about to return to the tunnels below the surface. Deep into the belly of Lunar, where he'd become separated from his newfound friends, Rowyn and Wilder. If it hadn't been for them, he wouldn't have made it this far.

It was also where he'd been captured. After that, the guards had dragged him to the surface, where Commander Aries struck a deal with him—a shot at finding Eventide in exchange for intel on his uncle, Marvin Alejandro.

Uncle. Revolutionary. Mercenary. He didn't know what moniker to assign the man anymore. But regardless of who he was, Marvin was his ticket to rescue Eventide. Either through cooperation or betrayal.

And his would-be uncle was the one who appealed for his rescue, giving the Resurgence leaders the push they needed to get him off that trader vessel destined for the mines. Hopefully he could do the same for Eventide, who had been hauled off on one of those so-called 'Domani' vessels.

Django could only hope Marvin would be waiting for him at the location he'd scribbled down before they were separated.

But that would only matter if he could figure out how to make the words and numbers match up. It wasn't as if he could simply travel in a straight line and eventually hope to get there. An endless number of streets, alleys, and sidewalks seemed to lead in every direction.

Holo-screens decorated the city streets. Advertisements and announcements that made little sense to Django practically yelled at him from their larger-than-life positions on billboards and alleyways. Certain words he recognized, but didn't understand the context: Resurgence, Syndicate, terrorists. Reports of turmoil and strife. Negativity that seemed to be a call to arms against threats that might challenge the empire. Other terms were cast in a more positive light: Prefect, Council, Reykjavík. But Django couldn't focus on their messaging now. They only overwhelmed his senses and were making his task that much more difficult.

He had to find his way underground, so he did his best to tune out the noise. Determining exactly where and how he could access areas beneath the Moon's surface was yet another challenge in this maze.

At least he was well rested, no matter how confusing the search. Commander Aries had provided him with a temporary room for the night, complete with a warm shower and a soft bed. Heck, he'd even left the place with a new set of clothes. They were fancier than Django would've liked, but his old outfit reeked of dirt and urine, and he was thankful to be rid of it, despite how unpleasantly soft these new Lunar threads were.

The fabric felt luxurious, reminiscent of something Eventide would have found in—and knowing her, pushed to the back of—her B-Ring closet. The collar crept up his neck, and Django constantly fought to flatten it against his collarbone.

He would have preferred the gray slacks and soiled button-up shirt he'd been wearing when he was taken into custody, but after showering and sleeping in a clean bed, he couldn't bring himself to put on the tired outfit again. It had been dragged across Lunar's walkways, urinated on, bled on, sweated in, hosed off, and then dragged through the regolith tunnels underground.

Even Django, with so little to his name, had a point where he could accept when something had served its purpose.

So, he'd donned the dark gray dress shirt, which, despite being cut from too fine a cloth, didn't look half bad. It fit him well, although he wasn't a fan of the gold stitching and matching buttons.

The pants, however, were a ridiculous electric blue. Why anyone would choose to wear anything that could signal one of the Lunar Police Force officers, from a kilometer away, Django couldn't begin to guess, but they were clean and comfortable.

He'd ran a brush through his hair for the first time in what felt like ages, then left the room and the uncomfortably lofty chambers behind to embark on his search for his uncle.

Django had roamed the streets for hours before finally deciding he needed to ask for help. There were plenty of people around, but they all seemed determined to avoid him. Everyone wore the same fixated stare, doing their absolute best not to make eye contact, which immediately reminded him of the few brief hours he had spent on the B-Ring with Eventide before they'd left the *Eclipse* for good.

When someone did meet his gaze, they would hastily look away, as though he was mere filth in the gutter rather than a person in need of simple directions.

Django wandered a few more blocks before he finally found someone who looked friendly enough to approach. The vendor stood near a cart that wafted a salty-sweet aroma into the air. The man was haggard, with rheumy eyes and a limp that he tried to mask as he shuffled from side to side, but at least he looked up and attempted a smile as Django approached.

Rows of greasy tubular food lined the front of the vendor's cart. Despite the strange appearance, the offerings smelled delicious, causing Django's stomach to growl. He assumed the brown rods were some sort of meat that he watched the vendor slide into a sliced bun.

"Looking for a hot dog?" the man called out to him as he caught Django's gaze. "Family recipe. Passed down from Earth."

Django recoiled. "Dogs? You eat dogs here?"

His question earned a hearty laugh from the vendor. "That's a good one, son. Ain't nobody here *seen* a dog for a couple hundred years, never mind eat one. I hear a few colonists took some over to Mars, mind, but not here."

Django's cheeks flushed, relieved that the mystery meat was not, in fact, someone's lost pet.

The man wrinkled his brow as he sized Django up. "Never heard of a hot dog before? Not from here, are ya?"

"You could say that," Django said, pulling his face deeper into his collared shirt.

"Don't worry about it, lad. We all come from somewhere. Won't find these just anywhere, though. Give one a try?"

Django's stomach growled in response, but he shook his head. "I'm a little low on credits."

Stars, do they even use credits here?

Despite his hospitality, Aries had explained nothing about how this world worked. He'd given Django a place to stay and had allowed him to roam the Syndicate headquarters building freely—or as freely as the armed guards on every level would allow—but he was at the commander's mercy for even the most basic needs.

The vendor looked over Django's outfit. "You sure don't look like the type to be down and out, but I guess bad luck hits us all at one time or another. More so lately, especially with word of this new Prefect. Rumor has it none of us are safe; that he's even more of a hardliner than his father."

He looked at the sky as though it might offer some sense of security, then focused back on Django. "Hate to think you've never had a hot dog, though. Tell you what—

this one's on the house. Tell your friends 'bout me. Just don't be telling anyone I gave you one for free. I'll have beggars lined up from here to Armstrong."

Prefect. Aries had mentioned him, too. Django had figured out the man was a Syndicate leader, but everything else about him remained a mystery—except that the Prefect had only recently assumed their position and that he wasn't well-liked.

The vendor handed Django the thick bun with the dog inside. It was white and pasty—much like the man behind the cart—and the hot dog itself was unlike any meat he'd tasted back on the *Eclipse*, where the only servings to be found was gritty, textured meat from chickens and geese. The dog's texture was smooth and uniform, exploding with spice and oil.

"This is incredible!" Django exclaimed, barely pausing between bites. "If this isn't dog, what type of meat is it?"

"'*Meat?*'" The vendor recoiled, as if the thought alone offended him. He scanned both sides of the street at the people passing by, concern etched into his brow that someone might overhear their conversation. His face tightened as he lowered his voice. "You trying to get me in trouble, boy? You think a lonely cart owner like me would have meat? And that I'd give it away if I did? You won't find anyone outside of the higher-end district restaurants offering it, either—and you definitely won't get anything in one of those places with no credits to your name."

Django raised an innocent palm to the vendor. He had to think quickly; he still needed this man's help. "I'm so sorry. I didn't mean to offend you. I'm new to this city. Everything is so much more modern and fancier than what

I'm used to. This was so good, I thought perhaps meat was something that might be offered everywhere here."

"Hah!" The vendor laughed. "Visiting from the outer colonies, then? Should've known—no local would mistake a hot dog for real meat.

"Listen, friend." The man waved his set of tongs toward Django. "Shackleton isn't as fancy as it looks. Remember that. There's a world beneath your feet that many good folks here would rather forget." He lowered his voice conspiratorially. "Trouble brewing beneath the surface."

Django wanted to ask the man to elaborate, but he figured he should get the directions he needed before he made another ignorant comment. "I'll try to remember that." Django put on the most convincing smile he could muster, took another bite of the hot dog, and mumbled through a half-full mouth, "I appreciate the meal. I'm happy to pay you back once I'm able."

"Bah!" The vendor waved dismissively. "Don't worry about it. What brings you here, friend?"

"I'm trying to find someone," Django said. "But I need some help with the address."

"Well, today's your lucky day, lad. Ain't nobody who knows this city's streets better than me. Comes with knowing where the hungriest crowds are going to be, and sometimes that means heading to obscure streets most people wouldn't think of."

Django permitted himself a wide grin. Finally, a bit of luck. Hopefully, Marvin would be there as promised. He took the note from his pocket and slid it across the counter.

The vendor's eyes widened with horror and he pushed the note away as if it were contaminated. "The Velvet

Underground?" His voice dropped even lower. "What are you, lad? A Syndicate spy?" The vendor eyed him suspiciously while scanning the surrounding street. "Or are you a pirate? Murdered a man for his clothes, did you? No credits? Bah! I should have known!"

Then, as though the vendor realized he'd already said something he shouldn't have, his shoulders hunched, and he gave Django a nervous glare. "What makes you think I'd know where a place like that is? 'Tis a hideout for pirates and thugs. I told you this place has a seedy underbelly, and the Velvet is the heart of it. You might wanna find yourself some new friends. If the person you're looking for hangs out at the Velvet, it doesn't say much for them. And I wouldn't go down there looking for them, neither—you'll find a knife in your back for no other reason than someone likes your belt. *Unless* you're an SF spy. If that's the case, they'll see right through whatever act this is supposed to be. Don't matter what you say you've got in your pockets, lad—you smell like credits, and that will be enough for some." The vendor waved his tongs at Django again, gesturing at his outfit. "And you'll be beggin' for death before they're through with you."

SF spy? Pirates and thugs? What is Marvin getting me into?

Visions of the people Commander Aries claimed his uncle had murdered haunted him. His uncle was a stranger to him, and he no longer knew what to believe.

If what the vendor had said about the Velvet was true, maybe Aries' claims that Marvin had been a mercenary weren't so far-fetched.

Why the hell am I trying to find him?

But what choice did he have? Either trust his uncle and rely on his help, or find him and turn him over to Aries.

Whether benevolent revolutionary or heartless mercenary, the path to Eventide was through Marvin. Finding her was the only thing that mattered. He had to press on. He had no other choice.

"I'm no spy," Django said, fully aware that it was exactly what a spy would say. He decided the best course of action was to stick as close to the truth as he could. "A relative of mine gave me that address. He said that if I ever found myself in trouble, I could ask about him there."

"Relative, you say? What kind of relative sends a well-heeled lad to the Velvet Underground? This might be a relative you want to stay away from."

Django opened his mouth to reply, thinking he might glean some insight into his Uncle Marvin's reputation from a neutral party. It was possible, if he knew the streets as well as he claimed, that the vendor might know whether Marvin was respected or feared.

But he felt an immediate sense of trepidation about what the response might be.

Before he could vocalize his thoughts, the vendor's eyes widened, and he pushed the scrap of paper back to Django. "No, don't tell me anything more. I'm better off not knowing." The vendor heaved a sigh and cast several anxious glances over his shoulder. "Look, I've only heard of the place because a few of my customers go there, okay? You already have the address, so I guess I can guide you there if you've got your mind set on going, but I strongly advise against it. Ain't nothing good comin' out of the Velvet. But if you insist on getting your ass handed to you, that's your own problem."

The vendor relayed a labyrinth of turns, alleys, and stairways for Django to navigate. The man was as good as his claims; he clearly knew Shackleton well. Django echoed them back to confirm his understanding and commit the directions to memory.

Once he'd finished, the vendor squinted at Django, shook his head, and gestured dismissively with his tongs. "Off you go, then. But don't say I didn't warn you."

Feeling the surrounding air grow cold, Django took the hint. It was time to leave.

Turning, he moved from the cart and took his first tentative steps toward the Velvet Underground. So much rested on finding Marvin, on finding Eventide . . . and if that meant entering a place of ill-repute, then Django would need to dig deep and face it head-on.

"Hello, good friend." The vendor's voice interrupted his train of thought. Django momentarily thought he was about to be berated for lingering, but instead, the man was focused on his next customer.

The newcomer was dressed in a uniform reminiscent of the security detail aboard the *Eclipse*, except that instead of pristine white, this suit was composed of rigid gray panels with luminescent yellow at the seams. The guard ordered a hot dog and then swiped his sleeve over a scanner mounted to the front of the cart, a feature Django had previously overlooked.

Django absentmindedly scratched the spot on his forearm that Marvin had traced with his finger several days prior.

A chip that can access any Syndicate system.

Apparently, these chips also served as payment methods. If the chip to be implanted in him was as versatile as Marvin had suggested, Django questioned whether it would grant him credits or if he would need to secure employment to earn a wage.

"Thank you, sir," the vendor said, offering a deeper nod than seemed necessary. "Long live the Syndicate."

The guard raised his hands in protest. "Drop the formalities, Chuck. We've known one another too long for all that."

"Easy, friend. Not everyone around here is as relaxed as you are. Gotta watch our tongues these days. The new Prefect is rumored to be even worse than his father. And there are eyes everywhere."

The last comment seemed directed at Django, who found himself lingering, drawn in by the guard's subsequent words.

"Things might change soon, you know."

"What do you mean?"

The guard shot Django a suspicious glance. Django nodded and shifted slightly, masking his eavesdropping by finishing the last morsels of his meal.

"Aries is working on something. I can't get into it—not here. And it's all rumor, mind you. But if it pans out, the Loop might finally see some good days ahead."

Django knew he couldn't stay any longer. He set out on the route the vendor had given him, moving out of earshot before the guard could expand on Aries' plans. Ultimately, it didn't matter. The Syndicate, the Resurgence, the FLOW stations—they were all irrelevant. The only thing that mattered was finding Eventide. If Django could bring Benson down in the process, as Aries had promised, that would be a bonus, but he harbored little trust that the commander had his best interests in mind.

As a stranger to this world, his only options were Aries or Marvin.

And he didn't trust either one of them.

CHAPTER TWO

Django
    The Velvet Underground

The pounding music and raised voices of its rowdy patrons made The Velvet Underground relatively easy to find. Even as Django navigated the tunnels beneath the city, he could feel the bass pulsing through the regolith. His experience running through the subterranean tunnels used by the Resurgence helped him feel slightly less alien among the hewn-out rock. The Tubes, as they were known locally, seemed to be an extension of those. Nature or human hands—Django had no idea which—had carved out a wide street from the dark gray regolith that descended into darkness.

It hadn't been a difficult journey to get this far. The entrance from surface to tunnel was hidden away at the rear of an otherwise nondescript building, its only purpose seemed to be providing access to the underground. The structure bore signs of past grandeur, with ornate stonework framing the gateway. Rock carvings, now crumbling, once adorned its façade.

The stairs were lined with marble, but the steps themselves had been worn down by centuries of use, revealing the underlying rock beneath. Django got the sense that, once, this place had been important, but it now lay forgotten on a deserted street corner, watched over by a handful of shabby guards.

Django had approached the stairwell cautiously, expecting to be stopped, but instead, the guards appraised his attire, then nodded him through with a tight-lipped stoniness that gave the surrounding regolith a run for its money. The guards were tasked with preventing people from coming *up*, not from entering.

Dim LED lights faintly illuminated the rough rock walls of Shackleton's underbelly, casting shadowy patterns across the gray cavern. Intermittent lights ahead flickered or failed altogether, and it took Django some time before his eyes adjusted to the cavern.

The main road, possibly wider than the streets above, branched off into smaller pathways, housing makeshift businesses in the tunnel's hollows.

Stalls spilled over with rotting fruit and vegetables, along with unappetizing gray and brown slabs of gelatin masquerading as "chicken" or "beef." Even without Chuck's warning about the illegal trade, by the look of them alone, Django would never have believed them to be real meat.

As Django continued to follow the tunnel, the market morphed into a square, the ancient fountains dotted around it having run dry long ago. No longer a place for people to socialize and enjoy the afternoon, it was instead filled with makeshift beds, blankets, and packaging materials strewn out everywhere. Laying out in the open were people with nowhere else to sleep.

The tunnels beneath Shackleton City were filled more with an air of desperation than Chuck's depiction of danger. The people here didn't appear to be a threat.

If anything, they needed help.

Django coughed; the air was stale, reminiscent of an uncleaned D-Ring maintenance bay—a mix of stale, burnt odors, left-over waste, and mold. The grit in his lungs echoed the discomfort he felt in the tunnels surrounding the Resurgence's safe house, as did the hacking and wheezing around him.

The tomb-like catacombs crawled with life, reduced to mere shadows by Django's unadjusted vision. Wide-eyed figures retreated into the alleys, regarding Django with equal measures of suspicion and fear. Most were children, their faces gaunt and expressions haunted.

Django couldn't help the shiver that ran down his spine. How long had these people been suffering?

Ghosts pushed back into the darkest corners, pressing deeper into the shadows as he passed, Aries' words about his life aboard the *Eclipse* ringing in his ears and flooding him with guilt. *"No crime, and nobody goes without food and water ..."*

How can this place exist so close to the wealth of the city above?

The throbbing music had increased in volume with each step until finally he'd reached the destination where he now stood. The Velvet Underground. From the outside, it didn't seem to be anything special. Like most of the structures within the Tubes, it had been carved out of the rock wall. Albeit with more precision, as its walls were smoothed, as though sculpted in place with cinder blocks instead of chiseled out of the regolith.

Dominated by a massive, solid metal door, the entrance resembled the mouth of some ancient lunar beast. The door was aged and battered, scarred with dents and gashes that hinted at a past, or perhaps present, that was no stranger to violence.

There was no sign marking the establishment. Django guessed it was either an effort to be discreet, or perhaps an unnecessary expense—waves of music, and patrons clutching beer steins both flowed out of the entranceway as the door open and shut.

With the music cranked to max volume, maybe discretion isn't their concern.

Like many of the Tubes' other constructs, there had been holes cut in the building's side that looked as though they might have once held glass-filled windows, but now only thick rebar crisscrossed over them.

Patrons steadily flowed in and out, their faces lost in shadow. Others who caught his eye deflected their gaze and hurried off to their intended destination.

Ain't nothing good comin' out of the Velvet.

He braced himself and leaned into the old metal door and into the cacophony of smoke and noise that waited inside.

Inside, the dingy ambiance contrasted with the buildings on the surface, but it was practically a sanctuary compared to the streets outside. Purple lighting cast an eerie glow on the Velvet's patrons, who occupied the tables and booths lined with bright red cushions. Django, in his pristine Syndicate outfit, attracted wary glances.

Pirates and thugs, remember?

The venue was larger and busier than Django had expected. Between the dim interior and the crowded tables, if Marvin was here, it would be difficult to find him. Throngs of people were scattered everywhere, occasionally silhouetted by glancing beams of strobing laser light. Rough cheers and taunts broke through beats in the music, and as Django moved a little closer, he could finally attribute them to patrons arguing over a complicated-looking card game. To their left, a couple of lean, yet fit, men sullenly threw darts at a board fixed to the wall, against a backdrop of unsociable regulars who did nothing but stare at their mugs of beer.

"Are ya lost, son?"

A stocky woman behind a counter to Django's right accosted him, a towel in one hand and a metallic beer stein in the other. The bartender's arms were nearly the size of most of the patrons and Django didn't doubt for one second that she could single-handedly keep a rowdy crowd in line. She set the stein down on a lower tier of the bar and lifted another, drying it for whoever would need it next.

"I'm looking for someone," Django replied.

The barkeep's gaze never left her work. "Most folks here don't want to be found; especially by someone dressed like they walked out of an SF District fashion mall. You tryin' to get mugged, or are you just stupid?"

"I didn't realize . . ." Django started.

"Stupid, then." She cut him off. "I don't think anyone

here wants to be found by you. Better head back to your penthouse . . . though I could use a customer with a few credits for once. That said, I don't want trouble in my bar, and you don't seem worth the risk."

"I'm not here to cause any trouble. I'm just trying to find someone."

"It's not *you* I'm worried about." The barkeep gestured to a group across the bar. "There's half a crew of Saturnian pirates been sizing you up since you walked in. If I were you, I'd watch your back on the way out."

Pirates. Even though Chuck had forewarned him, Django had naively been hoping the vendor had been exaggerating. His only frame of reference for the term was the tales of ancient seafaring adventures down on Earth: men and women sporting bizarre hats, curved swords, and peg legs, pilfering goods across the Atlantic Ocean to and from the Americas. These modern pirates, it seemed, had traded water-borne vessels for spaceships, but he could hazard a guess they were cut from the same cloth.

Django had never been one to crave adventure, especially the lethal kind. For a fleeting moment, he wondered how Eventide was faring in this alien universe. Adventure had always been *her* dream, but he doubted this reality was of the type she'd envisioned.

The quicker they could get themselves out of the Loop's seedy underbelly, the better.

"Ma'am, my uncle . . ."

The barkeep chuckled.

"'Ma'am'? I can tell you don't come down here much—or ever. What's your uncle's name? If he's here, he's here, but don't expect me to share my customers' private affairs."

Django sighed. Evidently, not all of Lunar's inhabitants were as friendly as Chuck, if their earlier exchange qualified as friendly.

"His name is Marvin Alejandro."

At that moment, the song on rotation ended, leaving enough of a gap in the melody for the nearby patrons to hear Django's words. The barkeep's face lost all color, her towel ceasing its circular path around the beer stein she had been drying.

The surrounding chatter also came to a lightning-fast halt as the rest of the bar froze. All eyes were now fixed on him.

"That's a dangerous name to be speakin' aloud." The barkeep lowered her voice as she firmly placed the stein down and poured a yellowish liquid into a smaller tumbler. To Django's surprise, she downed the drink in one gulp. "Especially for the likes of you."

Django regarded the comment, uncertain of his next move. He had braced himself for the possible unsavory deeds his uncle might have committed, but he was now being stared down by a dozen patrons who looked ready to gut him and leave him for dead. Was his uncle's notoriety so extensive that even pirates feared him?

Maybe it's not fear . . . maybe it's hate.

"Last I heard, Alejandro's dead. One more casualty in the *Infinity* 'accident.'" The barkeep lifted her fingers in air quotes around her last word.

Django's heart sank. If Uncle Marvin had been here, this woman wasn't aware of it . . . or she was too afraid to tell him. But Django had a hard time believing there was much that scared the barkeep.

Even though most of the patrons had returned to their own conversations, Django could feel their eyes still glancing toward him, and thought it was best not to announce that she was mistaken. "I'm sorry," he offered instead. "The information given to me must have been outdated."

"Yeah," the barkeep snorted. "By a bloody decade."

"It's okay, Leslie," a confident feminine voice said over his shoulder. "I'll handle this."

A wave of dread washed over Django. Saying Marvin's name here had clearly been a mistake. *Why the stars would he tell me to come here if he's not welcome here, either?* He resisted the urge to glance behind him, trusting the barkeep wouldn't permit anyone to shiv him in the back in the middle of her bar.

Would she?

Leslie grimaced, moving further down the bar to attend to a customer frantically vying for her attention to refill his drink. "I see ya. I see ya."

A flash of red hair shifted to occupy the stool beside Django. "You got a death wish?"

His gaze met a set of sparkling emerald eyes.

Rowyn. Django exhaled in relief. The red-haired woman was a sight for sore-eyes. She had cleaned up well since the last time he'd seen her. Compared to the grizzled men and women who sat in the Velvet, she stood out nearly as much as he did. Although she had the good sense to be wearing more appropriate attire, a brown shawl that she'd wrapped around her beige jacket, pulling it up like a hood over her head.

The last time he'd seen her, Django had dug her out of

a rockslide and diverted a group of guards to allow her and their friend Wilder to escape.

"Marvin told me I'd find him here. How can I do that if I don't ask?" he murmured.

"You use your eyes and not your mouth, like any other man on this rock would do," Rowyn replied. Her tone was stern, but her eyes twinkled in jest.

"Two rums, please, Leslie!" Rowyn shouted over the buzz.

Leslie nodded from her position at the bar and produced a bottle of dark liquid from a shelf beneath the counter.

"Rum?" Django's stomach churned at the thought of alcohol. "We're not leaving? Is Marvin going to join us?"

"Lower your voice," Rowyn warned. "Since you've made our intentions known to the *entire* bar, we'll need to stay here awhile and see if anyone takes an unhealthy interest in us. Marvin's name rarely draws the right kind of attention, and we can't afford to be followed."

"Well, if we're going to be here awhile, maybe you can tell me a little more about my uncle, because I'm really starting to wonder whether I even knew him at all. Why does his name alone make me a target?"

Rowyn accepted the two drinks Leslie had prepared and stood from her stool. She leaned in to whisper in Django's ear, the strong, syrupy scent of the rum in her hand reminding him of his uncle.

"We can't discuss this here." Her cool breath brushed his cheek as she whispered, sending shivers down his spine. Django could smell both the sweetness of whatever perfume she was wearing and the bold, boozy scent of the rum.

Rowyn placed a hand on his arm and directed Django toward the back of the bar, past the gaming tables and dart boards. Several hardened players eyed Django and his attire, but for the most part, they were much more interested in Rowyn.

Regardless of her admonishments, it *was* good to see her—especially back on her feet. Django had been worried the tunnel collapse might have caused her some lasting damage, but the way she strode confidently through the maze of tables told a different story.

"You're walking okay," Django observed. "How's the leg?"

"It's as good as new. The damage wasn't all that bad. Inflammation mostly. The doctor was surprised nothing was broken. But enough talk about me. It appears you've had quite an eventful few days. First of all . . ." Rowyn laughed as she selected a booth and sat down. "What *are* you wearing?"

Django glanced down at his outfit. Among the sea of people around him, he stuck out like a sore thumb. Everyone else's clothing seemed so alien to him. How was he supposed to know that the outfit Aries had provided would attract so much attention?

Guess the bright blue pants should have been a clue.

"This old thing?" he joked, trying to take the embarrassment in stride. "Listen, I didn't have many options. But it beats sitting on the floor of a dank jail cell."

Rowyn squinted at him. "The Syndicate arrested you?"

"They *interrogated* me, actually. Wanted to know about my connection to the Resurgence."

Rowyn's usually playful green eyes turned serious. "And what did you tell them? You didn't tell them anything they could use against us?"

"How could I? I don't know anything!"

Rowyn nodded, satisfied with his answer, though she continued to eye the Velvet's patrons as if expecting someone to ambush them from the shadows.

"Are you going to tell me what's happening? I feel like my feet have barely touched the ground. One minute, I'm risking my neck to get off the *Eclipse;* the next, you and Marvin are putting a rifle in my hands! And now here I am in this dive bar filled with pirates and thieves trying not to say the wrong thing for fear of finding a knife in my back. What's this Resurgence really about?"

"You see these people?" Rowyn gestured to the crowded space around them, the people each clutching their steins of ale. "They're the fortunate ones. They have a few extra credits to splurge on a drink after a hard day. Most of them are shipping crew. Some are pirates; others are fugitives with nowhere else to go, wanted by the Syndicate Front. But aside from the loners drowning their sorrows, most still harbor hope. They're not revolutionaries, and most aren't even bad people, but the Syndicate's taken their freedom away from them. You think it's easy to ascend from the Tubes to the Upper Rim? It's nearly impossible."

"What does Lunar's living conditions have to do with the Resurgence?"

"*Everything.*" Rowyn's gaze held a fierce intensity. "The only way these men and women will have an opportunity for a better life and those living on the streets will get a chance at survival is if the Syndicate falls."

"From what I hear, the Syndicate has a different view. They say the Resurgence would replace order with anarchy. That the power vacuum would cause chaos."

Rowyn scoffed. "Do the children huddled in the alley outside seem orderly to you? Because I can assure you, those kids are better off than those deeper in the Tubes. Did you notice the hordes of displaced people in the port when you landed? The ones that the Port Authority have stopped bothering to drive away? Does that seem orderly to you?"

"I was too busy getting my face scraped along the metal walkway to notice." Django touched his cheek. The memory of the experience still burned his skin.

Rowyn ignored his comment. "There's only order for those on the surface. Nobody cares about any of us wasting away down here. Why would they? We carry out the dirty work they wouldn't even dream of doing! Chaos already exists—under the heels of Syndicate boots.

"The Resurgence doesn't seek anarchy—we just want to live. We want life for those who have been denied it simply because of where they were born. There are more than enough resources in this system to benefit everyone, but eighty percent of the wealth is channeled to the Earth's surface, where only a fraction of humanity lives. How is that 'order?' While those of us below ground and in the outer colonies struggle for survival, fighting each other for scraps, those above us live like royalty!"

This feels like a speech she's delivered before.

"And Marvin aims to change all that?"

"Marvin and the others who started this movement. We thought he'd died almost a decade ago, but his legacy lived on. We've finally grown his vision into the movement he'd imagined and we can only thank the stars that he's alive to see it unfold!"

Without realizing what he was doing, Django took a sip of his rum. As the liquor burned down his throat and hints of vanilla and caramel danced on his tongue, he decided it wasn't quite as awful as the sludge he'd tried on the station.

"What about you?" he asked. "Why did you join?"

"I have my reasons."

Rowyn shot Django a playful smile, as if she was about to tell him a story, but her expression quickly soured when her gaze shifted over his shoulder. She grabbed his hand and yanked him forcefully to his feet.

"Come on," she said. "We need to leave."

CHAPTER THREE

Mikka

The *Chimera*

In her pirating days, Mikka Jenax had taken command of plenty of vessels. Most had been more run-down than her small Delta class runabout ship, the *Redemption*, but there had been a couple times where she had found herself boarding something with a little more class. The pleasure cruisers she'd commandeered had all been owned by affluent Syndicate yes-men and retirees who spent their days drifting through the inner system, with cabins designated for Domani quarters, full-service bars, and infinity pools that looked out upon the stars, all wrapped up in a level of comfort that those in her employ had never experienced.

The *Chimera*, however, was so much more than the architects of those vessels could possibly have dreamed of. Even though its design and weaponry confirmed it was a ship intended for battle, it made the finest luxury yachts Mikka had ever boarded seem like the antiquated shuttles and rockets first used to colonize Mars or deploy pioneering equipment to Io.

Mikka stepped off the *Redemption*, struggling to keep her jaw from dropping as her feet settled on the *Chimera*'s cargo bay floor.

Kiara Ryson followed closely behind her. To her credit, Mikka's navigator did a better job of maintaining her awe—but that could just as easily have been because Kiara was pissed about being on board.

No doubt intended to transport substantial payloads of military equipment and weaponry, the *Chimera*'s cargo bay alone could have housed the *Redemption* five times over. Despite Abigail's insistence for Kiara not to 'scratch the paint' on the way in, there'd been more than enough room for the navigator to maneuver into the larger vessel's hold.

The cargo hold still smelled of fresh paint and newly glazed machinery. Whoever Monroe had seized the ship from had only recently manufactured the vessel. All the strength and might on display suggested it was a military craft and an advanced one at that.

Even the storage facility was lined with vibrant lighting and holographic displays. Their clarity made the technology in David Aries' Syndicate Front office back on Lunar seem outdated. Whatever Abigail and her accomplices were planning, they were pulling out all the stops.

If the engines match the level of sophistication of the decor, Mikka thought, *the* Redemption *had no chance of outrunning this ship.*

She released some of the tension she'd been holding in her chest. She and Kiara had been outmatched and outmaneuvered in a standoff with not just one of these vessels, but *four*. It would have been insane to make any other move than surrender.

There will be a time and a place to escape, she reassured herself, *but it requires finding the right opportunity.*

Abigail Monroe stood on the opposite side of the hold, facing the *Redemption's* loading ramp. The eccentric pirate had changed outfits since their last encounter; she now wore a black cape with gold trim, made from a thin, silk-like material. It was tied loosely at the neck, masking a black bodysuit that accentuated her petite frame in a way that was more than attractive. The synthetic leather clung tightly to her, accentuating her toned, muscular frame. The necklace of bones she wore at her throat was more noticeable, either because of its increased size or the contrast of the pirate's black ensemble. Either way, a chill ran down Mikka's spine.

For someone who claimed never to kill, the ornament was menacingly sinister.

But that was the enigma of Abigail Monroe, Mikka guessed. She still hadn't figured the pirate out, and that made her more formidable than any Syndicate soldier or bounty hunter who might cross her path. There was simply no predicting the erratic pirate's next move.

Monroe's claims not to kill unless in self-defence struck Mikka as an odd code for a pirate, but she knew Abigail manipulated that rule by delegating her dirty work to others. Her tingling spine reminded her to stay alert while aboard the *Chimera*, regardless of what Monroe claimed. This wasn't a safe haven for her—not so long as those on board knew about Mikka's past.

Abigail's skin tone was one of the palest Mikka had

ever seen, and next to her own darker complexion, Monroe could have been a ghost. People who grew up in the Tubes were often paler than those living on the surface, though a wide range of skin tones and races appeared in both places. Pale white skin such as Abi's was said to have originated in the northern regions of Earth's past. Maybe, Mikka supposed, it existed on the Earth's surface.

It wasn't so much Abigail's skin that made the pirate stand out, but her pale eyes, her white brush-cut hair, and the scar that ran down her cheek. Her small stature was further emphasized by the five crew members surrounding her, each of whom stood nearly a foot taller than her.

Abigail had managed to become captain of a crew that was, by all accounts, stronger, more intimidating, and likely more experienced. Each of the men and women at her side was at least ten years her senior, yet they had each agreed to serve the sprite of a leader before them.

Mikka had learned a long time ago never to underestimate a pirate based on appearances—a principle this crew seemed to understand, whether voluntarily or not.

There was something regal about Abigail's pose, like a matriarch awaiting a grand procession. The woman Mikka had rescued from the explosion of her own vessel only days before was gone. This woman held the confidence of a ship's captain. Her eccentricities were still uniquely Abi— the mischievous grin and the unbridled charisma—but the illusion of nonchalance had vanished.

"Welcome aboard the *Chimera*," she greeted, her trademark grin widening.

The two lead members of Monroe's crew approached Mikka and Kiara and stripped them of their weapons. Of course, Mikka had hidden most of her gear aboard the *Redemption*, hoping Abigail might leave the ship alone, but the knot in her stomach told her that was wishful thinking.

The *Redemption* had been ill-prepared. It had never faced off against a top-secret military armada before, and even if Mikka had poured all her resources into arming her ship, it still wouldn't have been enough. There was no black market dealer in the Loop that would have been able to provide her with the parts or enhancements needed to match the *Chimera*.

Mikka had considered trying to seize the *Chimera* by force, exiting the *Redemption* guns blazing in a desperate attempt to overcome the pirate and her crew, but she knew Kiara would never have agreed to it and they would likely have died in the effort. Besides, she didn't know Abigail's true motives for attacking the *Redemption* and singling her out. And there was an infuriating part of Mikka that couldn't help being intrigued by that.

She also had no idea how many crew members Monroe had on board, and there were those three identical ships that would provide backup the moment the first shot was fired. Given that Abigail had brought five crew members with her to the cargo hold, Mikka imagined at least another five were manning the ship, though there could easily be another twenty.

Mikka could take on five lackluster pirates by herself, but two dozen was an entirely different story—especially considering Abigail was no fool. She would have chosen her crew members based on skill.

All in all, this was one of the craziest situations Mikka had found herself in. A pirate interested not in her cargo, but in *her*. As far as Mikka could tell, Monroe wasn't planning on killing her, like a bounty hunter would; she'd merely prevented her from completing a delivery because . . .

Because what? Because a kid with a malfunctioning neuro-implant had told her to? Mikka didn't quite believe the pirate would be so stupid as to follow the advice of a child blindly, but then again, how well did she really know her?. Throughout history, people seeking power often resorted to desperate and crazy things. Nero, for instance, had killed his own mother following the prophecy of an astrologer.

Was this any different? And who would be the victim of this modern-day prophet?

Prophet.

Mikka snorted. Abigail's pet was nothing more than a poor kid who'd had the misfortune of being butchered by some back alley bio-hacker.

The pirates accompanying Abigail made for a motley crew and, like most pirates, had no uniforms to speak of. Each of them, however, excluding Monroe herself, was united by a single element that hung around their necks—two intertwined circles. Mikka swore she had seen that symbol before, but for the life of her, she couldn't place where. It could easily have been a trend started by some Lunar or Martian celebrity; she had always found it hard to keep up with the Loop's latest fads.

One of the crew approached Mikka, clad in a brown patchwork suit padded for combat. The suit's nanostructured fabric was designed to disperse blaster fire, and several burn marks on the suit's surface revealed it had seen more than its share of battle. Energy weapons were typically restricted to Syndicate soldiers or the rebels who stole them.

The crew member herself also appeared to be no stranger to warfare. Her left sleeve, rolled up a few inches, revealed a bionic arm—synthesized flesh covering a nano-carbon appendage. The prosthetic was more noticeable at the hand, which lacked the same deep bronze skin. More fragile than the bionic components themselves, hands were often left bare, as they were more intricate and prone to wear and thus costlier to cover than arms, legs, and other body parts. Besides, the silicon design rarely accounted for nerve endings, so the use for skin was purely cosmetic. For amputees who worked frequently with their hands—mechanics, electricians, engineers, soldiers, and the like—it was more practical to coat the carbon with a protective spray.

Though the bionic arm should have been a surefire giveaway if their paths had crossed before, something about the pirate seemed familiar, but she couldn't quite put her finger on it. The woman's raven black hair was shaved on the left side, revealing the dark skin of her scalp, while the hair on her right was long and thick and was styled into a braid that reached the center of her back. Her eyes were a striking hazel, her lips slightly parted, and the softness of her face gave the impression that she was about to soothe a baby to sleep, though Mikka suspected, given the woman's choice in friends, that the serene look could morph into a menacing one in an instant.

"Have we met before?" Mikka asked in a hushed tone. "What's your name, soldier?"

The pirate had no reason to answer. In the middle of disarming her, she looked Mikka dead in the eye, and her comforting gaze turned haunted. Mikka finally recognized the woman even before she spoke.

"Penelope Martínez." Her accent was thick Northern Lunar—a distinct, uncommon accent that was immediately recognizable. Everyone Mikka knew from the three North Lunar settlements spoke fast, with a tendency to omit words and drop their 'r's. "We've met, but I was only thirteen then."

A rush of memories flooded Mikka's mind. Flames flickered at the edges of her vision and the roar of explosions filled her head. The screams of long-dead ghosts echoed from a time she had tried to forget.

"You're Lex Martínez's daughter," Mikka managed, struggling to remain in the present. The flashbacks had become less frequent over the years, but they always lurked on the periphery, threatening to break free and consume her.

"Yes, ma'am," Penelope confirmed, her gaze unwavering. "The day we met was the last time I saw my pop. And after what you pulled, I swore that day that if I ever got the chance, I'd kill you."

CHAPTER FOUR

How many dead friends are too many?

One. One would have held more weight than one person should bear. Mikka Jenax had lost eight.

All because of her.

Because of her arrogance. Because of her ego.

Jax Luana
Kraken's Fury
Eight years ago

"Captain, there are more security protocols protecting those elevators than I've ever seen."

Lex Martínez was the best hacker Jax Luana had ever had on her team. If he was uneasy about penetrating the system, that should have been enough for her to stop and reconsider her plans.

But the payload on Space Dock Nineteen was irresistible. Too good to pass up.

And far more tantalizing because of the crew she held in her command. If anyone in the system could bypass that level of security, it was Lex.

"Ten *tons* of xenon. Imagine what we could accomplish with a payload that size."

"I understand that, Captain. That's not the issue. The Syndicate realizes the value of what they hold. There's a reason Space Dock Nineteen isn't even on the charts. Technically, the only reason we know it's there is because it's pretty damn hard to hide a station tethered to a *planet*, even a small one."

Captain Jax Luana of the *Kraken's Fury* had been the terror of the Loop for the past decade. She had swiped ships from one side of the system to the other and had always managed to stay one step ahead of the authorities and her enemies. But of all her exploits, *this* payload would be the pinnacle of her career. Xenon was scarce—and processed xenon was even rarer. It was a dangerous gas to mine and nearly impossible to get outside of Syndicate control.

Which meant the reserves they'd discovered would fetch a fortune on the black market. Jax had it on good authority that Space Dock Nineteen was filled to the bulkheads with the stuff, waiting to be shipped to Earth.

"Come on, Lex," Butterfly prodded. "You've always said you're the best hacker in the Loop. Time to prove it."

The five-foot-nothing blonde tucked a stray strand of hair behind her ear. Butterfly had been an integral part of Jax's crew from day one. A loyalist through and through, she was the first to bend over backwards to stand up for Jax and the first to place herself in harm's way if the need arose.

But she was also the first to coax a crew member into a risky situation if she thought the end justified the means.

Which was exactly what Jax needed at the moment.

Camila Montego, known as Butterfly among the crew, had grown up on an experimental farm on Ganymede. She was orphaned after the Syndicate burned the farm to the ground during the Bloody Ganymede Food Blitz, brought about by the colonists discovering untapped nitrogen deposits within the moon's icy crust. The discovery had allowed their farms to double their production, but instead of informing the Syndicate, they distributed the surplus among their own people and sold the remaining reserves to neighboring moons at a discount. When the Syndicate found out, instead of figuring out a way to democratize the additional food stocks, they burned everything. They wanted to both set an example to those who would dare circumvent their protocols, and to ensure they maintained their stranglehold of goods in the outer system. Butterfly lost her family, her home . . . her entire *colony* that day. She only survived herself because she happened to be surveying an ice field when the Blitz rained down on all they had built.

"Screw the security systems," Kenzo stated, crossing his bulging arms as he leaned back, his brown cotton tunic pulling taut across his pecs. "We charge in, guns blazing, grab the payload, get out. Leave no survivors."

"That's *brilliant*, dipshit," Lex quipped, his eyes rolling but never leaving the scrolling code on his holo-feed. "I hope you've prepared a goodbye message for your family."

"*Heh.*" Kenzo grunted. "Joke's on you, nerd. I don't have a family."

Raised on the streets of Mars, Kenzo Bentai survived on his own until he was thirteen, when he'd walked into a dive bar, hoping to find work as a mercenary and nearly earning a knife in his back before Jax had intervened and offered him a job. Kenzo was the *Fury*'s muscle, and he'd intimidated his way through more than one close scrape. He'd lost an eye to cancer as a child, but his brown eyepatch had given him a reputation for being a badass. Not that it wasn't well-earned—he landed the crew in a tight spot nearly as often as he helped to get them out.

"Kenzo!" Jax snapped. "Gear up and shut up! If you can't rein it in this time, you're staying on the *Fury*. We need to get in and out without the SF locking the place down. Copy? Only fire if we're fired upon—and even then, do whatever you can to get everyone out in one piece."

"With all due respect, Captain," Lex cut in, "we have no idea if the goods are actually there."

Jax squared her shoulders. "You think I came all this way based on a rumor? The goods are there, Lex. Just get us in and out without being seen. Where are we with hacking their surveillance equipment? Cameras? Audio? Anything?"

"I can get you a direct feed of the commanders of Space Docks One through Eighteen taking a dump if you'd like, but I'm telling you, Space Dock Nineteen is *different*. It's black ops—stonewalled. I'm trying to establish a link, but I've never even seen encryption like this before."

"Keep working on it," Jax instructed. "Once we get closer, you can confirm. *If* we get a read and the goods aren't on base, we'll abort, but for now, we've got the schematics, so we plan with those. Just like the good old days."

Lex rolled his eyes and shook his head, but the hacker held his tongue.

Undoubtedly, the top specialist at subverting cybersecurity anywhere in the Loop, Álex Martínez, known to the crew as Lex, had the least reason of any of them to be aboard the *Fury*. Not only was he a resident of the Rim, he also had a wife and a daughter. Jax had met Penelope at one of their recent stops. A straight-A student with a bright future on the Rim ahead of her. At only thirteen, she was as old as some pirates.

Lex was always quiet after they came across renegades that young, and Jax knew he was pondering how differently his daughter's life could have turned out. He wanted a better future for his family—and, ever the optimist, for humanity, too. He didn't want Penelope to grow up in a system where people were treated as disposable, so he risked everything to work for Jax.

So devoted to the team that he would follow Jax to his death.

Of course, any of them would.

All of them did.

An hour later, the crew of the *Fury* were suited up, and Lex was still working on establishing a link to the dock's surveillance feed. The hacker was now confident in his ability to get through, but he claimed the *Fury* would have to position itself within a ten-kilometer radius to gain access. Jax would have preferred a greater distance, but this would have to do. Ten klicks was the best he could promise.

The plan was straightforward in theory. There were nine crew members, including Jax. Seven would board the space dock. Lex would monitor and guide the crew via comms. Jax would negotiate a deal with the dock's Admin, while the rest of the crew would transfer several dozen canisters of precious xenon gas from the dock's storage center and into the *Fury*'s hold.

As long as the crew could reach the xenon without triggering the alarm, they would be golden. The Syndicate had designed the docks to keep people out, hence getting in was the challenging part. Getting *out* should be a breeze.

Or at least, that was what Jax was hoping.

Until they could actually lay eyes on the space dock's interior, they were navigating based on patchwork schematics and the word of a former guard. Jax had to hope that would be enough.

Still, she couldn't help but hold her breath as the *Fury* coasted smoothly toward its target. Jax was no stranger to Syndicate fortresses; she'd raided a damn fine number in the past and had always slipped back into the shadows with a full hold. But none of those had promised such an immense payload, nor had they presented such an intensive surveillance challenge.

The quiet enveloping the space dock was ominous. No traffic in or out. The dock's elevator descended to a remote tropical island in the Pacific Ocean, ensuring just enough distance from other FLOW stations and docks to deter casual observers. Space Dock Nineteen also emitted a jamming frequency day and night to further dissuade unwelcome attention.

Yet, the more something was shrouded in mystery, the stronger the allure.

There was, of course, only one way onto Space Dock Nineteen: with a high-value delivery that the Syndicate would want control over.

"You've scheduled us into their receiving calendar?" Jax asked Lex.

Without the hacker, their plan would have been impossible. She'd promised him a sizeable chunk of the earnings to secure his cooperation—and his silence. The last thing she needed was a mutiny over perceived favoritism.

"One canister of dark matter scheduled for delivery, Captain."

Jax retrieved the canister from beneath her captain's chair. Just thinking about the power it held gave her a rush, even if it wasn't real.

A cargo hold full of xenon was incredibly valuable, but a canister of stabilized dark matter would be even more so. There were no current records of ships powered by dark matter, but Jax had connections who were convinced the Syndicate was actively working on developing such technology.

Of course, securing dark matter was no small feat, even for those with the unlimited resources of the Empire. The possibility of a private party stumbling across some from a black-market vendor was almost absurd, but there was no way the Syndicate would risk such potent material falling into the wrong hands. At best, it would be used as a weapon against their regime; at worst, it would become the basis for technology that far outperformed their own.

It was both a legitimate threat and a ridiculous notion. The Syndicate's dominance throughout the system was so pervasive that, barring a sophisticated alien invasion, it would be near impossible for anyone to pose a credible challenge to their supremacy. On some nights, Jax wasn't ashamed to admit she found herself whispering a silent prayer to the stars to send the aliens.

The delivery setup was easy—*too* easy. While dock security would take the canister for examination, the crew would disembark from the *Fury*. The gamma ray tests required to confirm the dark matter's authenticity couldn't be rushed, affording the team ample time to infiltrate the station and retrieve the xenon.

By the time the *Fury*'s crew finished loading the cargo, the Syndicate's analysts would have uncovered that the canister was radioactive, but it didn't contain dark matter, and Jax would apologize for wasting their time. Naturally, no one would expect her to have verified the canister's content; such technology was beyond the reach of most civilians. After contrivedly thanking her for her diligence and for bringing the canister to their attention, the Syndicate officials might inquire about its source in an effort to apprehend the swindler. Of course, Jax would send them on a wild goose chase; she had a long list of indebted merchants who could use a run-in with the Syndicate Front.

After that, the *Fury* and its crew would be on their way.

But, of course, things didn't go anywhere near according to plan.

Mikka

The *Chimera*

The Loop had a notorious habit of taking someone with a future as promising as Penelope Martínez, squeezing their hopes and dreams in a vise-like grip and molding them into a pirate.

The prevailing narrative was that Jax Luana had died on Space Dock Nineteen, along with the rest of the *Fury*'s crew. This was a story Mikka had been willing to accept. Her team had perished because of her own stubbornness. Lex Martínez had warned her that the fortress was impenetrable, but she had turned a deaf ear.

Penelope Martínez's father had died that day. All because of Mikka.

When the news feeds heralded the death of the Loop's most elusive pirate at the hands of Syndicate Front patrols—conveniently omitting mention of the secretive space dock she'd been raiding—Mikka had seized the opportunity to start her life anew.

She'd changed her name, used the last of her stashed-away credits on purchasing body mods and the *Redemption,* and had then sought refuge on Lunar.

To her relief, nobody had connected the dots from Jax Luana to her mother, who had been at death's door, deep within the Tubes. It was only then that Mikka had grasped how critically ill her mother truly was. It was the first time she had visited in years; the first time she had witnessed her mother sprawled in the street, scarcely able to feed herself and hardly functional. Lying in her own filth, waiting for the end.

Mikka's world had crumbled that week, and she'd realized how she had squandered away nearly a decade of her life chasing a foolish dream of making a difference. A life that had only led her to ruin.

Now, standing before her was another repercussion of her past actions, returned to slap Mikka in the face.

A shiver crawled down Mikka's spine. Penelope wasn't exactly threatening her. Not yet, at least. The comment had been a statement rather than a warning; a fact, as if proclaiming the void of space was perilous. But there had also been no humor in the words; no apology for her revengeful craving. Mikka knew she had to be vigilant on board this ship.

She didn't believe Penelope would stab her in the ribs, however. Not yet. Not while Monroe watched, at least.

"Your father was a good man." Mikka fruitlessly attempted to ease some of the tension. There was, of course, nothing she could say that would suffice. "He deserved better than what he got."

Penelope's expression remained unmoved. Icy eyes glared from beneath a pirate's brow, offering neither contempt nor reconciliation. Mikka had enough experience dealing with pirates to know that those who concealed their emotions well were the ones to worry about the most.

"When I first heard you were dead, I was devastated." Penelope's voice held none of her father's warmth; none of the uncertainty of a computer programmer turned rebel. It lacked the gentle, velvety tone of someone raised on the Moon's surface, the rugged South Lunar drawl. Penelope had evidently been a pirate for a long time. She knew her capabilities and harbored no doubts about her ability to square off against those who wronged her. "My father loved you. He admired your vision. All he wanted was to improve the Loop for those who would never be granted a second chance, and for some reason, he saw hope of that in you. But then the whispers started; reports trickling throughout the system that you led my father and the rest of your crew on a suicide mission and then deserted them when the Syndicate outsmarted you. At first, I defended you. I argued you would never do such a thing. Your crew were your family, your friends. But as time passed, more evidence surfaced and, eventually, I couldn't deny the truth. I'd hoped you'd died, but part of me always knew that was a pipe dream. The great Jax Luana wouldn't fade away so easily. You might have deceived the rest of the Loop, but not me. I knew. All the body modifications in the Loop wouldn't be able to disguise you from me."

Mikka was grateful she hadn't brought more of her weapons from the ship. Penelope had drawn Mikka's

Pulsar SC11 pistol from her belt and now pointed it at her chest. Admittedly, she wasn't overly concerned; Mikka knew the weapon wasn't charged when she'd equipped it. Nevertheless, there was something inherently disconcerting about the sensation of the metal barrel of her own weapon being pressed against her.

"I'm deeply sorry for your loss," Mikka said. "Lex was my friend. If I had known . . ."

"I wouldn't bother finishing that sentence if I were you," Penelope interjected. "You're lucky I found my peace years ago—but watch your back. You might have more enemies than friends aboard this station. But if I suspect for one second that you're planning something reckless, I won't hesitate to pull the trigger. There's no way I'll let history repeat itself."

Martínez's hands patted Mikka down roughly. She made a point of being thorough—more so than necessary. Mikka didn't blame her for her hostility, but the intensity of the frisking underscored Penelope's disdain for Mikka and her past actions more than any words ever could.

Penelope turned to Kiara. "You too, navigator. Watch your back with this one around. She might seem like a friend, but you could wake up with a knife in your back."

She stomped back over to Abigail, apparently disappointed that Mikka hadn't fumbled some foolhardy attempt at escape that she could have used as a smoke screen for violence.

"Lovely!" Abigail grinned and rubbed her hands together. "Glad we've got the awkward reintroductions out of the way."

Kiara swallowed. "Are you okay?" she whispered. "What was that all about?"

"I don't want to talk about it," Mikka replied sternly. This certainly wasn't the time or the place. "Not here."

She had secrets she wished to keep, even from Kiara, who was unquestionably her closest friend. Despite their differences, there was nobody Mikka trusted more, but there were some things she had kept to herself. Kiara was aware of part of the story—the parts Mikka could bear to say aloud—but not to its full extent. She needed a navigator, and without any doubt, revealing those parts of herself would have meant kissing that goodbye.

But Mikka was no fool; she knew that Martínez's presence and their terse exchange meant she would have to disclose more of those hidden details. It was a part of her past Mikka wished would have faded with time, but it was only fair to Kiara that she knew exactly why Penelope had spat venom her way.

The event itself wasn't a secret. Half the Loop knew about the botched heist—or parts of it, at least. The true location had never been shared, though: as far as word of mouth knew, Space Dock Eleven had been under siege. The Syndicate had kept their secret surrounding Space Dock Nineteen.

Not that it mattered. The name "Jax Luana" had been thrust into the spotlight, and her crew had met their ends that day. Yet still she lived, confronting the truth of her deeds with each breath she drew—only the lungs they filled now belonged to Mikka Jenax and not Jax Luana.

Mikka had invested a lot in shaking her former life.

Sure, time had dulled the pain, but her past was resurfacing too often for her liking.

The details of her part in the siege were carefully guarded secrets Mikka had maintained over the years. Monroe had alluded to as much upon boarding the *Redemption* when they'd first crossed paths. Mikka hadn't delved into how much the pirate knew or how she'd come by that information, but she couldn't help wondering now.

Had Penelope unearthed the truth behind what happened on the dock? If so, it wouldn't be hard to guess that she had passed that information on to Abigail before the *Black Swan's* destruction. Mikka supposed Monroe learning of her true identity in that way would be a relief. At least she knew the source.

The alternative was more disturbing. *Was Monroe the one divulging secrets?*

If so, Mikka would be forced to accept her anonymity was lost. Mikka couldn't afford even half of Jax Luana's enemies to come looking for her. If Abigail had a mouth on her, half the system likely now knew that Jax Luana was deceased in name only.

Either way, it was unsettling, but Mikka knew she had to atone for her past. Currently, the path to redemption ahead of her was through completing her deliveries to the FLOW stations. Neither Kiara nor Abigail would stop her. David Aries was offering her another chance, and she would be damned if she didn't seize it. First, Aries would free the residents trapped aboard the stations, then he would focus his efforts on usurping the new Prefect, ensuring the Syndicate Empire came under the steward-ship of someone who genuinely cared for its citizens.

And through it all, Mikka would play her part. It was the least she could do to honor the memory of the lives she had been responsible for losing that day.

But first, she needed to escape the *Chimera*.

"I'm pleased you're being reasonable," Abigail said. "It would have been a shame to damage your lovely ship."

"A shame for *you*," Kiara chirped. "Mikka would have tanned that white ass of yours."

Mikka nearly choked on Kiara's spunky comment.

Abigail's eyes twinkled with amusement. "Nice to see you're as feisty as ever, pilot. Trust me, love, this is for your own good."

"Forgive me if we don't see eye to eye about that." Mikka stepped forward, only halting on account of the five energy weapons directed at her chest. She clenched her fists. "You had no right to disrupt our mission. We're out here minding our own business, Abi."

"As I've said, I'm playing the odds. Zee has been incredibly helpful so far."

"So helpful that your ship and crew were decimated by an unknown enemy? If you recall when we first met, the odds hadn't been in your favor then. We helped you minutes before you ran out of air. And *this* is the thanks we get? I should have let Kiara eject you out of the airlock the moment we discovered who you were."

"I think I suggested collecting her bounty," Kiara chimed in. "Still not a bad idea, by the way."

"I misjudged you, pirate," Mikka continued. "I thought you would at least honor the help we gave you."

"Honor's a slippery thing, isn't it?" Abigail mused. "If a starving Martian dog spots a morsel of food on a bustling road in the Syndicate District, is it honorable to let it run out and get it? Or is the true honor in restraining it to prevent harm?"

Mikka held her tongue.

"Most would say the latter," Abigail continued. "But the dog doesn't comprehend your intentions; it merely thinks you're being cruel. Similarly, if someone's about to do something that risks not just their own lives but *thousands* of others, isn't it more honorable to intervene? Despite their inability to see the danger? Despite their belief, you're depriving them of a tasty treat?"

"I'm not a dog, Abigail. This mission was *my* choice. Just because your little fortune teller whispers apocalypse into your ear, that doesn't give you grounds to attack my ship!"

Abigail smiled. "Zee's no fortune teller. He identifies pathways, calculates odds based on unfolding events. That's why we call him the Wayfinder. If not for that assault on my ship, as unfortunate as it was, I would not have found you and we wouldn't have rescued Alejandro from that station, hindering the Resurgence's efforts to topple the Prefect and liberate the Loop from the Syndicate's grasp. Both of you are crucial to how this all plays out, even if you fail to see it. Our skirmish was a means of grabbing your attention—a flirtatious tussle, if you will. It was the only way I could get you to come over."

Abigail extended her palms and pirouetted in a three-hundred-and-sixty-degree turn.

"You could have asked."

"You and I both know you would have refused."

She had a point.

"If you refuse to join us, Mikka, then there's no chance for the Empire to fall. The cycle of Syndicate terror simply continues, so to speak."

"I *am* working to topple the Empire! I've just aligned myself with someone with the resources to actually do it."

"Ah! The boyfriend, yes." Abigail sighed. "I hope you know there's no good way for that to end."

Mikka shook her head. "Fate is what we make of it, Abi. Aries has shown me well enough what his true colors are. The Syndicate doesn't need to be dismantled; it needs to be *reformed*. The infrastructure is already in place. We can shape it, transform it into something new. With the right leadership, we won't have to suffer anymore."

"There are only two flaws in your little fantasy, love. The Syndicate is built on the sweat and blood of others—they're the cogs that keep it turning. There can be no Syndicate without the slaves in the mines, the deluded maintaining the FLOW station farms, the laborers scraping for food and air, those with nothing to live for except to fill the plates and garnish the statues of the elite in their lofty towers. You think Aries will give up his gilded furniture and six-course dinners? His performance to get into your pants is just smoke and mirrors. David Aries is only interested in helping himself."

"You're wrong," Mikka shot back. "But I don't expect you to understand how someone could be driven to help others instead of themselves."

"Oh, you *have* changed, love! And I don't think I like this new look on you. When it comes down to it, we *are* both pirates. We do what we need in order to survive. Enjoy the sex and the fancy meals; just don't get seduced by them. If Zee is whispering apocalypse in my ear, Aries is whispering falsehoods in yours." Abigail turned, her cloak flowing in a flourish around her, and signaled to her entourage. "Penelope, escort our guests to their new quarters."

Eventide
The *Inanna*

Eventide Rossi shot out of bed, her heart pounding as the last tendrils of her nightmare receded. Pain shot through the back of her skull as though someone was trying to stick a fork inside her brain. Sweat cooled on her skin as images of Orin dying invaded her mind. The intensity of her pulse caused her entire body to shake.

She tried to convince herself that it was all a dream; that the haunting, wide eyes of the dying Domani man were part of her imagination. But those nightmares were never just dreams—they were real.

Sensors dotted around the room registered her movement, flooding it with light as her feet touched the plush, carpeted floor. The effect was meant to mimic daylight, she supposed, though the artificial morning held no comfort. Eventide shifted uncomfortably on the expansive bed. It was too soft, too gentle—a mockery considering the horror she had witnessed.

She grimaced, wrestling with the mental image of the previous night's discovery. Orin, lying on the carpeted floor, the blood from a deep gash in his gut saturating the lush fabric. His lifeless eyes, filled with confusion and fear, were forever imprinted in her memory.

Was his death real, or was it woven from the threads of her nightmares?

It was a rhetorical question; her mind still had trouble computing what had happened. It didn't help that her dreams were as vivid as reality.

Eventide wished she could push it away and forget all of it. Her entire life had become a hellish nightmare.

She changed from her nightgown into the blue silk pajama outfit that had been provided to her as a Domani. The damned thing was awful. Nothing more than loose pants held up by two flowing straps over her shoulders that barely covered her chest.

But the indecency of her outfit was the least of her concerns.

As awful as her dreams were, it was the living night-mare Eventide found herself in that was far worse: the ship she found herself imprisoned on, the *Inanna*. Sure, it was aesthetically pleasing and had the most advanced tech she had ever seen, but she had been sold to the ship's owners against her will. Once on board, she had been forced into surgery, both to enhance her physique and make her more susceptible to the whims of the Caregivers who watched over her.

Caregivers? More like wardens.

Eventide touched the nodes at the back of her neck, wishing the implants had been a figment of her nightmares, but, of course, they were still there—feeding stimuli directly into her brain.

A buzzing at the door interrupted her thoughts. Before she could move to answer it, the door slid open, and a pair of light-skinned Domani, a man and a woman clothed in matching yellow pajamas, entered. Despite their wildly different hair and cosmetics, the Domani could have been twins. They even moved in the same way, gliding into the room with their arms outstretched, holding compact cases that could have held anything from tools to cables and wires.

The woman's hair, reminiscent of the octopus tentacles Eventide had seen in old texts, was a mass of dark purple that shifted into iridescent blue at the tips. Her opalescent eyeshadow refracted light into different colors, subtly changing with her movements. Texture paint adorned her temple, giving the illusion of cybernetic implants where there were none.

Eventide had never seen anything more stunning, and she subconsciously touched her own blue hair, wondering if she could ever manage the volume this woman possessed.

The man's shoulder-length silver-white hair, high-lighted with shades of red and gold, was cut at sharp angles, giving it the false appearance of a wig. His makeup, subtler than the woman's, was a blend of pasty white and shimmering silver, catching the light within the room and reflecting it in a shimmering halo all around him.

Like all other Domani Eventide had crossed paths with, these two were the epitome of physical attractiveness. When she had been captured, she had been given the impression that the ship only allowed the most beautiful people to come into service. However, since she had come on board, Eventide had come to believe that the Caregivers molded their captives into the image they portrayed so heavily.

As beautiful and elaborately dressed as the Domani were, Eventide sure as hell didn't appreciate them coming into her room unannounced. A few seconds earlier and she wouldn't even have been dressed.

"Can I help you?" Eventide demanded. "Why are you here?"

"My name is Solara," the woman replied. "This is Phoenix. We're here to prepare you."

Solara seemed to be slightly more coherent than most of the other Domani Eventide had interacted with, though there was still a distant joy dancing in her eyes that betrayed the effects of the signals the Caregivers were feeding into her neocortex.

Eventide crossed her arms. "Prepare me for what?"

"For the day. We are required to do your hair and makeup," Phoenix responded. "So you can look your best."

So, Domani served other Domani. Eventide wondered if these two had styled themselves. If so, she wasn't sure she wanted them anywhere near her.

"Can I refuse?" she asked.

The day before, Yunni, another Domani, had given her a vacant stare when Eventide had confessed that she wanted to leave the ship. Something about the request did not resonate in the Domani's clouded mind. Eventide received a similar look now: one of utter confusion. Solara's brow furrowed, and Phoenix looked so dismayed that Eventide feared she would have to console him if she didn't take the suggestion back.

And that would involve a lot of unnecessary touching.

"I thought so."

The two Domani got to work. They escorted Eventide over to a vanity on the opposite side of the room, where they retrieved the various cosmetics needed to implement Eventide's transformation. They communicated little, merely complimenting each other's skills and praising Eventide's facial features, hair color, and bone structure as they applied the makeup to her skin.

"Where are you from?" Eventide asked. Small talk wasn't her strong suit, but as she was stuck aboard the ship, it was probably in her best interest to get to know some of the others.

"Our past no longer matters," Solara replied robotically as she opened a palette of colors onto the table. "We sought out the *Inanna* and now this is our home. Until we are hired by a client."

"You mean, *sold* to a client?" Eventide corrected.

Phoenix flicked his wrist dismissively. "What's the difference, honey? We work to survive."

It might have been the most coherent thought Eventide had yet heard from a Domani. Maybe collectively, she had misjudged them.

"But what if the *client* requires services you don't wish to deliver?" she pressed.

Another blank stare.

I take that back. No misjudgment here.

"Everyone has to do things they don't want to do," Solara said evenly, lifting one of her hair-tentacles slightly with her palm. "Miners sweat all day. Businesspeople have to wear those *awful* clothes. All of us do unpleasant tasks. We came here because if we are chosen, we'll have the chance to style the hair and makeup of an elite. Whatever the client wishes will be our delight to deliver."

To some degree, Solara had a point, but Eventide knew that wasn't at all the same thing.

"But what if you change your mind? What if you want to leave?"

"'Leave?'" Phoenix looked at her with a squint, his makeup sticking in the creases of his forehead and creating lines. "Why would we ever leave?"

Yunni had expressed a similar sentiment when Eventide had questioned her about it. Something had convinced them all that being a Domani was the greatest privilege they could possibly receive. The transmissions being directed into their skulls evidently reinforced that decision.

Eventide wished she understood how it all worked—something to do with the nodes sticking out of the back of their necks. It was almost as if the men and women on board the *Inanna* were perpetually being brainwashed.

But that still didn't explain why *she* wasn't affected.

Controls your pleasure and your pain . . .

That's what the ship's doctor, Doctor Morales, had said to her after she'd integrated Eventide's implants. The words bounced around her head, wrapped in the haunting vision of Orin's corpse. Morales had explained the Caregivers were using transmissions to affect the Domanis' dopamine and serotonin levels, but there had to be more to it than that. These people acted more like they had surrendered all control rather than being stimulated.

Perhaps it didn't matter. For some reason, Eventide had been singled out. These transmissions—the ones for pleasure, at least—and whatever brain-altering states they stimulated had no effect on her. If she kept her wits about her, she could discover a way off the ship.

She hoped.

Her fingers absently returned to the nodules behind her head. They didn't hurt—not anymore—but they were foreign, as though someone had attached a console control to the base of her skull. They were embedded firmly in place, and trying to tug at them made Eventide instantly nauseous.

"Quite the brilliant accessory, aren't they?" Solara observed. "I only wish we could select different colors to coordinate with our outfits. Black does go with just about everything, though!"

Eventide fixed her with a hard stare. "You realize the Caregivers are using them to manipulate us?"

Phoenix waved a hand. "Don't be ridiculous. The Caregivers mean us no harm. Look at this room! They want nothing but the best for us."

Eventide refrained from commenting further. There was no sense in getting into an argument. Instead, she bit the inside of her cheek as she waited for them to finish poking and prodding her face.

The rest of their conversation was filled with commentary about the makeup they had access to and the structure of Eventide's face. "Fiery corals of the Sun; blues and greens of Earth; the crimson red of Mars; the subdued pastels of the gas giants; and the icy hues of Pluto. The best splashes of color in the system."

Their excitement seemed over the top, but Eventide let them prattle on regardless, somewhat amused by their enthusiasm.

"Your cheekbones, my dear, are like perfectly sculpted marble! Exquisitely angled and as captivating as a breathtaking sunset. No wonder you were considered a prime Domani candidate!"

Eventide did her best to keep from rolling her eyes.

The Domani continued with their preening for the better part of an hour. When they finally finished, they promptly packed away their supplies and left.

Eventide scrutinized herself in the mirror. She had to admit, Phoenix and Solara had done a good job, even though there was a mountain's worth of makeup stacked on her face. The purple eyeshadow accentuated her blue eyes, her blue hair gleamed, and her cheekbones, nose, and eyebrows were perfectly highlighted without overshadowing one another. Never overly concerned about her appearance, Eventide was more invested in learning what made the *Inanna* tick rather than how to fit in with the statistical good looks of the rest of the Domani, but she couldn't deny the result of their work.

The door to her quarters slid open again and Eventide started at the intrusion. Privacy, it seemed, was something she wouldn't be granted on the *Inanna*.

A wide set of shoulders attached to a small bald head with beady eyes and a crooked nose strolled through the door. Lars was claimed to be Eventide's personal protectorate by the purse-lipped Caregiver, Lin. However, this was the first time she'd seen the man outside of Orientation.

Yunni had told her there was no need for security on

board, but this man's sole purpose defied that statement. Eventide couldn't shake the feeling that he had been instructed to watch her rather than protect her. Either way, she put her hands on her hips as the man entered and did her best to keep the snarl from her face.

Any other Domani on board would likely have been intimidated by Lars' imposing figure, but Eventide had dealt with her fair share of bully technicians aboard the *Eclipse*, and she'd learned enough to know that size wasn't necessarily an indicator of skill.

In her mind's eye, she walked through wrestling the man to the ground, grabbing her old magnetic screwdriver, and using it as a blunt weapon at the base of his neck.

"I'm here to escort you to the doctor."

The man's voice wasn't gruff, as Eventide had expected, but instead it was flat and croaky, like how she imagined a frog might sound if it had a voice.

"I feel fine," Eventide said.

Her response earned a derisive snort from Lars. "We'll see."

CHAPTER SEVEN

Eventide

The *Inanna*

"You need to be more careful," Doctor Morales said as she sat Eventide down.

Eventide sat in the doctor's MedLab, perched on the bed amidst the now familiar symphony of beeps and whirs —the very sounds that had greeted her when she awoke to this nightmare.

"'Careful?'" Eventide scoffed. "How can I be any *more* careful? I've done nothing since I got here! I might as well lock myself in my room. Nobody will even give me a straight answer to a simple question."

"Exactly," Morales retorted, analyzing numbers displayed next to a rotating holographic image of Eventide's head. "You shouldn't be asking questions."

When the imagery had been taken was a mystery to Eventide. She could only guess that the stats that circled her image were being relayed to the ship's computer via the implant in her neck.

"Look, I have no clue about what's going on. I don't know where this ship is going, or what to expect when we get there. Hell, before I got here, I didn't even know there *was* somewhere to go to! I'm an engineer. I like to know how things work. If I can't be told a simple answer to the most basic questions about the ship . . ."

"Take a breath," Morales interjected, raising a hand to hush Eventide and nervously scanning the sickbay as if worried about unseen listeners.

Eventide hadn't planned on stopping her tirade, but Morales' gesture pulled her out of her mental spiral. She began to voice another question, but Morales silenced her with a finger to her lips.

"Wait," Morales mouthed, heading toward one of the computer stations.

Beeps emanated from the console, and then, abruptly, all sound ceased. The ship's ambient hum, the monitor's feedback—all gone. The sudden silence startled Eventide, and she raised her hands to her ears, fearing the doctor had meddled with her hearing somehow. But she could still hear her clothes rustling, her joints creaking, the clicking of Morales' nails on the computer console . . .

"I can't keep the barrier in place for long, but it should give me a chance to explain a couple things," Morales said.

Eventide glanced around, unconsciously attempting to identify *what* barrier Morales was referring to.

"Energy field?" she asked. "What kind of technology can create an invisible force field that stops sound waves?"

Morales' eyes narrowed. "Do you want a crash course in quantum acoustics or information about what's happening aboard the *Inanna*? Because we don't have time for both."

Eventide bit her lip. She desperately wanted to know both, but if this was her only opportunity to learn about her situation, she had to prioritize.

"Now," Morales began, "the first thing you must understand is that Domani don't ask questions. Something about your implants didn't fully integrate with your neocortex. The other Domani don't care about engines, quantum entanglements, navigation, or diagnostics."

Eventide sighed. "What am I *supposed* to do, then? I didn't ask to be brought here. You can't expect me just to fall in line."

"Lin expects *exactly* that. Haven't you noticed the others' lack of curiosity? Their inability to process your way of thinking?"

The starry-eyed gazes of the Domani? Yeah, there's no way I could have missed those.

Except for Orin's eyes. His eyes had been lifeless, staring up from a pool of his own blood.

No. She couldn't broach that subject. Not yet.

If there was one thing Eventide knew, it was that she wasn't supposed to have been awake and roaming around the ship when she found him.

But she couldn't shake the fact that there was a killer on board the ship. Maybe all Domani life was dispensable, but Orin's murder seemed to have been more than that. Lin wouldn't have been that sloppy.

She wanted to tell somebody what she had seen . . . But she also didn't want to be the one who was next.

"What the other Domani do, or don't do, doesn't

concern me," Eventide replied defiantly, even though she knew she didn't mean it. She wasn't that cold. The empty stares of the others troubled her greatly.

"If you want to survive, it should."

"Being here is as good as being dead. Everything I've worked for has been ripped away from me."

"Perhaps," Morales admitted, "but where do you plan on going? We're days from Lunar, months from Mars. At substantial risk to myself, I've kept my mouth shut about your faulty implants and I expect you to do the same; I've stuck my neck out too far to have you get your head chopped off. Be sensible. Play the part. Bide your time."

Eventide knew the doctor was right, and she couldn't help but bring to mind the image of the blue and green speck of Earth as she'd seen it through the viewport the night before, hundreds of thousands of kilometers away, a blip in a void of black. Endless nothingness lay between the *Inanna* and another living soul. Eventide had already reached that same conclusion before she'd found Orin's body lying on the recreation room floor, but that didn't mean the thought of staying aboard the *Inanna* for any amount of time didn't turn her stomach. It also didn't mean that she wasn't terrified of becoming another mindless Domani. The thought of succumbing to the pull of the emotions she'd felt before leaving her room the night before, the sense of longing to remain in her quarters and surrendering her independence, filled her with dread.

Most concerning of all, it had been the sense that she was home.

She had to fight it. She couldn't accept that she belonged here. She *wouldn't*.

"The implants manipulate us, don't they?" Eventide asked. "The others, they're not as thrilled to be here as they seem. They're being controlled."

"Some are genuinely happy to be here," Morales replied, her face darkening, "but they're in the minority. Many initiates give themselves to the Domani because it's this or death—or at best, a gruelling life. We offer unparalleled luxury aboard this ship, but it's temporary. The likelihood of being treated well, wherever you end up, is slim. Though, on the *Inanna*, they are bound to end up in the home of a high-ranking official or businessperson. Other Domani ships are a lot less exclusive with their clients. We keep the Domani comfortable for as long as possible. We keep them happy—it's the least we can do."

"So, you keep them under control," Eventide pressed.

"It's really not all that bad. It used to be far worse."

"What do you mean?"

Morales pointed to the back of her neck. "Your implant allows the Caregivers to administer pleasure or pain. Initially, they tried controlling Domani behavior through punishment. Anytime a Domani stepped out of line, varying levels of intense signals would be sent to the pain receptors in the brain in order to quell any further dissent."

Eventide connected the dots, including the stabbing pain she'd experienced when she'd spoken up against Lin. The Caregiver must have inflicted these signals.

"Let me guess, that didn't go so well."

"Not for long. Initiates raised in harsh environments can withstand a lot of pain. Instead of changing tactics, the Caregivers increased the intensity, but this only resulted in outbreaks of violence and suicides. Domani resorted to throwing themselves out of the ship's cargo hold just to make it stop."

Considering Eventide had already thought about ripping the implants out of the base of her skull, she could relate.

Is that what happened to Orin?

Eventide had a hard time dismissing his waxen face from her mind as she listened to Morales explaining the way the Domani were treated. Despite being totally converted to the Caregiver's preferred way of thinking, Orin had seemed like a nice kid.

How much of his demeanor had stemmed from the implants, and how much had been because he was actually happy?

"Would the Caregivers kill a disobedient Domani?" she asked impulsively.

Morales regarded her suspiciously, as though trying to discern if Eventide knew more than she should.

"They haven't had to for a long time," Morales replied.

Eventide studied the doctor intently, trying to gauge her sincerity. She couldn't determine whether Morales believed her own words or whether she was parroting Caregiver propaganda.

One thing was certain, though. Morales wasn't telling the whole truth.

Eventide sensed it was time to move the conversation along. "Pain didn't work, but something did. The others don't appear as though they've been beaten into submission."

"Pleasure," Morales answered simply. She took a hand-held device and ran it across the sensors at the back of Eventide's neck.

"When it became clear pain was ineffective, the Caregivers took a different approach. They sent low electrical stimuli to the subjects' pleasure receptors. This function had originally been intended as a reward system, but it was soon realized that if the men and women experienced a deep sense of satisfaction here, they would be less likely to protest. The deliverance of pleasure is potent enough stimuli for the mind to quickly dismiss any objections."

A wave of nausea washed over Eventide. She gritted her teeth.

"What are you doing to me?"

"Just because the barrier counteracts sound doesn't mean that the cameras aren't watching," Morales reasoned. "I need to conduct tests. The Caregivers want assurance that your implants are functional. Your recent behavior is puzzling. I want to help you, but I need to convince my superiors that I'm working on the problem, otherwise they'll become suspicious. It's going to be challenging enough justifying why I activated the sound barrier. We have little time."

"My implants aren't working?" Eventide thought back to the compulsion she'd felt toward her bed.

"They're not performing as they should," Morales admitted, shifting from the scan to a holographic console, where she began inputting data Eventide couldn't see. "Your brainwaves are interfering with their transmission. The *Inanna* is continually emitting low-level data streams. They're meant to stimulate the nucleus accumbens, gradually releasing dopamine to elicit a constant sense of happiness and bliss."

"You're drugging us?"

Morales sighed. "In a manner of speaking, yes."

"But the brain isn't capable of handling constant dopamine stimulation. You're going to damage the brain's receptors, maybe even cause severe mental illness!"

Morales looked at Eventide with a blend of surprise and intrigue. "You're familiar with brain chemistry."

"I'm a woman of science, but I only have a basic understanding of biology."

And she knew enough to identify the Caregivers' treatment of the Domani was inhumane.

The doctor's look of confusion deepened, but she continued. "We turn off the signal at night to allow the body to regain equilibrium, which is why the urge to sleep is so potent. I'm frankly surprised you resisted it."

"I nearly didn't," Eventide admitted.

"Sleep alone usually isn't enough, but we rarely keep Domani long enough for the bouts of stimulation to cause permanent harm. Once they're handed off to the client, the constant stimulation ends. It's not a pleasant sight when those receptors burn out, let me tell you."

Eventide wasn't sufficiently familiar with biology to comprehend exactly how it all worked, but there still seemed to be a missing piece.

"But that won't be your concern," the Doctor continued. "Your brain is exceptionally well-adapted to sensory input. It seems capable of regulating a vast amount of stimuli, and it taps out before it can become overwhelmed."

"What does that mean?"

"It means you're not experiencing the intended constant state of bliss because your brain refuses to accept more dopamine or serotonin than it needs."

My brain still registers choice. The realization enforced in Eventide's mind that many, if not all, the men and women aboard hadn't remained so willingly. They weren't acting out of desperation; they were being manipulated, stripped of their freedom of choice.

Eventide's blood boiled. It all made sense—the starry-eyed glances, the questioning looks. Whatever mechanism was manipulating their minds prevented them from processing negative thoughts.

Whereas Eventide's mind had thought of nothing but escape since the moment she awoke aboard the *Inanna*.

"There's got to be more to it than that though. Surely simple brain chemistry isn't enough to explain all of this?"

"It's more complicated than that, yes. But it's not worth getting into now."

"But why is my brain resisting the transmissions?"

"I haven't determined the reason yet, but if Lin or the others find out, it won't go well for you."

The doctor made several more evaluations on the MedLab screens as Eventide tried to comprehend the information she'd been told.

"Has anyone else ever resisted before? What happened to them?"

The doctor shook her head. "In my twenty years aboard this ship, you're the first I've come across. The implants integrate with standard brain physiology; in essence, they should *always* work. Initially, I thought it was a problem with the chips or the connection, but something about your brain is limiting their influence."

Eventide swallowed. "When I questioned Lin earlier, I felt a stabbing sensation in my brain. Was she using these transmissions to inflict pain?"

Morales grimaced and glanced at her datapad, seemingly reluctant to meet Eventide's gaze. "I'm afraid that while your brain won't accept more dopamine than it can utilize, the same isn't true for your insular cortex."

"What does that mean?"

"It means your brain is still receptive to the transmissions that induce pain."

Great.

"Our time is nearly up, Miss Rossi."

"Why are you telling me all this?" Eventide asked. "What's in it for you?"

Morales sighed as she looked up from the screen. There were bags under her eyes that Eventide hadn't noticed before, and the light from the holographic screen highlighted the lines that stretched from her lips in a permanent frown.

"I became a doctor to help people. This . . . This isn't what I had in mind. I thought by joining the *Inanna,* I'd be doing good work; that I'd be making a positive contribution of some kind. Most people that come aboard are in poor health. Generally speaking, we do help them; they're malnourished and often suffer from illnesses and conditions that have never been examined by a doctor. I provide them with care they would otherwise never have received. But that doesn't excuse what we do with them: hand them over to the wealthy, who use and discard them. Perhaps it's a better life than they would have had, but it doesn't last, and it's never their own. By coming here, the Domani have little control over their own fate."

Morales sighed again. Eventide could have sworn tears were forming in the doctor's eyes, but she blinked them away swiftly. "I thought that if I could help you, it might atone for some of my sins. There's something about you that's unique from everyone else who has passed through my lab. Putting aside your resistance to the program, you also possess a determination that most of our initiates have lost. You push where others would have surrendered. You calculate your odds, whereas others would have acted rashly—aside from your relentless questioning, that is. Through you, I saw a chance to effect change, and possibly even end all this." Morales waved a hand absentmindedly around the room.

"Why haven't you tried to stop it before?"

Morales' gaze was distant now, as if she were elsewhere, pondering the reason.

"Cowardice, I suppose. As a young doctor, I was pleased to hold such a prestigious position. The Syndicate is responsible for a lot of hardship, and I convinced myself that in the grand scheme of things, this was a minor sin. I was still helping people. But as time went on, I started to question what I was doing. I was too fearful of the consequences if I spoke up. And even if I did, what would change? The Caregivers would simply dispose of me and find a replacement. Heaven knows there are hundreds of doctors who would do anything to trade places with me."

Morales shook her head. "I was terrified for my life and powerless to effect any significant change."

Eventide thought back to the technicians on the *Eclipse,* who were forced to choose between preserving the secret behind Earth's true stability or forfeiting their own lives. She wondered how many people across the system felt like Morales did, torn between hopelessness and death.

Eventide knew the answer.

All of them. Or the ones still alive, at least.

Many of the technicians she'd worked alongside probably believed that by surrendering their silence, they were doing the right thing—but that was only because they had been lied to themselves.

And yet, instead of yielding to the lies, *she* had escaped.

She could escape this, too.

But her defiance was about more than just escaping; in many ways, her roles on the *Eclipse* and the *Inanna* were intertwined. Her escape from the station, had led Eventide here. She hadn't chosen to board the *Inanna,* but she had chosen to risk leaving the *Eclipse.* Her internment on the ship and the horrors that came with it were the reality of the consequences of that choice.

But that didn't mean she had to accept the Caregivers' plan for her. Not only would she escape this place, she would also bring about change.

Somehow.

But could she trust Morales? Aboard the *Eclipse,* helpers had revealed themselves in the direst of circumstances, particularly Django's uncle, Marvin. So far, Eventide hadn't met anyone else on board the *Inanna* she could trust, but given the doctor's efforts at honesty, she guessed now was as good a time as any to double down.

Despite the doctor's admonishments about asking too many questions, she needed to ask one more—and Morales was the only one who could answer the question that had been gnawing at her insides since the night before.

"What about Orin? What happened to him?"

Morales' eyes widened. "How do you know about him?"

"Was he murdered?" Eventide asked, her tone blunt.

Nodding, Morales cast her eyes toward the ceiling, where hidden cameras likely watched their every move, and sighed. "Yes, but not by the Caregivers. Not directly, at least. I'm sorry, but that's the end of our time. For your own safety, please do not mention Orin's name to anyone again. Tugging on that thread will not end well for you.

"Now, enough talk. I must proceed with the tests."

<hr>

"This is going to hurt, I'm afraid," Morales warned, her fingers gliding across her holographic display.

Eventide was bursting with questions, but Morales had made it clear she wasn't going to answer any of them.

Her instructions were clear enough. For now, at least.

Play along. Bide your time.

The problem lay in *what* she was supposed to be waiting for. Escape? Sabotage? An opportunity to shut down the transmissions? And would Morales assist her with whatever scheme Eventide dreamed up? Or would she stand by and betray Eventide if things went awry?

Eventide didn't need to calculate the odds to foresee the outcome of that scenario. Morales had confessed to being a coward. She wouldn't take the fall. Instead, she'd make Eventide get her hands dirty.

If Eventide failed, Morales would survive another day, giving herself a pat on the back for the attempt before proceeding with her work. She would accept no outward risk that would jeopardize her position of favor among the Caregivers.

Finally comprehending the doctor's earlier warning, Eventide asked, "What do you mean it's going to hurt? What are you doing?"

She felt a pinch at the back of her head, akin to the prick of a needle.

"Ow!" The pain wasn't severe, but it was unexpected. She raised a hand to the base of her skull, rubbing the area above the edge of her implant.

There was no needle, and she didn't need to ask to understand what had caused the sensation.

"So, the pleasure transmissions don't work, but the pain transmissions do?" Eventide clarified.

Morales' expression remained unchanged as she evaluated the readouts on her screen. "It appears so."

"Lucky me."

"It's another incentive for you to cooperate until you can plan your next move. Even though it's not their preferred method of attaining compliance, the Caregivers won't hesitate in using it for behavioral correction. But if they realize the pleasure stimuli doesn't work at all, they might choose to terminate you before you present a problem."

"Right," Eventide responded, her voice heavy with sarcasm. "So, I'm just supposed to keep my head down?"

"Correct. That's how you'll survive until you work out a plan." Morales seemed to have missed Eventide's tone as she continued with her work. "Unfortunately, I'll need to conduct more tests before I can release you, otherwise I won't be able to justify maintaining the sound barrier. And I need to make this count. Brace yourself; this *is* going to hurt."

CHAPTER EIGHT

Django
  Shackleton City Tubes

Django and Rowyn had run several blocks and taken multiple turns through increasingly narrow side streets before Django realized they were being pursued. He didn't know by whom, and every time he tried to gasp out a question, Rowyn chided him and barked, "*Just keep running!*"

Django had always considered himself fit. He was accustomed to being on his feet, and the demands of operating stubborn farm equipment meant he was no stranger to heavy lifting. How often had he needed to lift crates of produce or muscle through an equipment issue? Handling wheelbarrows and shovels full of dirt and fertilizer were part of his everyday routine. But running had never been a part of his work regimen, and he was quickly discovering that the skills were non-transferable.

A popping sound erupted from behind him and he instinctively ducked, not pausing to see what was happening in their wake. Sparks on the regolith wall above them reinforced they were taking fire.

It wasn't long before fire burned in Django's legs. The air in the tunnels was dry, filled with the regolith dust that clung to the walls that passed them by. It coated his lungs, threatening to choke him out before their pursuers got a chance to end him with a bullet.

Django cursed under his breath. Ever since he'd arrived on this blasted rock, all he'd been met with was violence.

He shook off the nihilist thoughts. Whoever was chasing them, he wouldn't let them take him. He hadn't come this far to allow Eventide to disappear into the void.

He propelled himself forward with all the strength he could muster, catching up to Rowyn and running in step with her.

Unlike him, she ran with little effort, her movements graceful, even under such intense strain.

Her hand disappeared beneath her jacket and, in one fluid motion, pulled a projectile pistol from her waistband.

Django brought a hand to his ear as the gunshot echoed through the narrow tunnel, erupting amid the sparks from ricocheting bullets that glanced off the regolith behind them.

Rowyn fired two further shots, summoning a cloud of dust in the tunnel behind them as the bullets struck the dirt.

"What exactly are you shooting at?" Django asked.

"Quiet!" Rowyn hissed. "Turn! Now!"

Two small but strong hands landed on his arm and shoved him aside. Django bumped into the wall of yet another alley before being pushed through a green door-way, almost tripping over the short steps that led inside.

The building they had entered was pitch black. Rowyn slammed the door behind them and Django leaned against it, gasping for air.

Rowyn held her petite frame against him as if she were trying to keep him from drifting away from the door. Her breath, ragged and cool, contrasted against his flushed skin, the first sign that she had exerted herself. The vest she wore was surprisingly soft, emphasizing the starchy stiffness of his own Syndicate-issued dress shirt.

His chest expanded as Django struggled to catch his breath, pressing against Rowyn with each inhale. His heart screamed as though it might burst from his chest.

Rowyn's breathing steadied and her hand moved to Django's waist. He found himself bewildered, caught in the moment, until she pushed him aside to press an ear against the door, her hands following suit, leaving the spot on his waist cold and empty.

Was he disappointed that she was trying to get to the door instead of him?

What am I thinking? I can't let myself get distracted.

He was only there because of Eventide.

I don't think this could ever work.

The harsh reality of Eventide's words struck him anew, just as they had the first time she'd said them. Their stolen kiss in the cargo hold of the *Redemption* felt so long ago now, but the emptiness Django felt in her absence had only intensified. He'd dedicated himself to finding her and rescuing her from the traffickers, but perhaps it was time to abandon all hope of the two of them becoming more than friends. Trying to force a romantic connection between them was only setting himself up for disappointment, and if he was being totally honest with himself, Django had known that before he kissed her. Deep down, he'd known it for years, but like a fool, he had still clung to the hope that one day, her feelings for him would change.

Now, though, Django flirted with the possibility that maybe someone else could be interested in him. Someone who was already here.

But it felt as though he was just apt to misinterpreting the actions of the women around him. *Had* Rowyn been flirting with him? Or were their interactions just friendly banter? His experience with women had been non-existent, so he was left questioning and doubting every gesture.

He shook his head. There were more important things to worry about at the moment—like someone bloody shooting at them.

"Okay," Rowyn whispered. "I think they're gone."

A flashlight flicked on in her hand and she waved the light source around the room, confirming they were alone.

The interior of the building was nearly the same gray as the tunnels, but its walls were smoother. Flakes of white paint clung their surface, remnants of a long-forgotten past.

The ceiling was low, barely taller than the doorframes. A small sofa sat in the center of the cramped room, alongside a matching chair and a threadbare oval rug that lay on the floor between the two.

A second, smaller room was separated only by a protrusion in the wall. Inside, a bed and a makeshift nightstand, both made of repurposed boxes and crates, were nestled against one corner.

Bookshelves graced the wall to Django's left, a few dusty tomes still occupying its shelves. Most of the reading material aboard the *Eclipse* had been technical manuals. Some Earth classics still existed, but most physical copies had either been destroyed or were archived in the station's storage center, awaiting transfer back to the planet with the supposed remnants of humanity. Reading was not something Django had ever made much time for, though, in contrast to many of the residents on the agricultural levels, his father had ensured he could read.

Reading was one of Eventide's passions. Even before she began training for the technicians exam, she had devoured everything she could find. The modest collection of physical books on the shelves here wasn't large, but he knew she would love to see them.

"*Now* can I ask who was chasing us?" Django brushed his damp hair from his eyes, the strands clustering over his forehead, shining with sweat. "Was that the Syndicate?"

"Not the Syndicate," Rowyn replied, rolling up her sleeve to press her forearm against a panel beside the door. A light on it flashed green, turned red, then extinguished. "Law enforcement carry energy weapons. Bullets mean mercenaries or pirates."

"*Pirates.*" Again, with the pirates. Django's father had regaled him with stories of pirates hijacking ships in the Caribbean Sea on Earth centuries ago. But Django couldn't imagine what any pirate, regardless of switching the sea for the stars, would want with him. For starters, he had nothing of value, except for the clothes on his back. "What, do they think we've got—buried treasure or something?"

Rowyn flashed him an uncertain grin. "I keep forgetting how sheltered your life has been."

Django scratched the back of his head, flummoxed by his own naivety. "So, what do these pirates do? Why are they chasing us?"

"It could be for a number of reasons. Someone might have a score to settle with your uncle. Or another pirate that's joined forces with us. There are those who covet the progress the Resurgence has made and have designs on taking some of it for themselves. Private Syndicate hires might be after information. The SF would love to find our base. We've established quite a society, and where there's prosperity, people will always try to take advantage." She appraised Django. "Plus, that outfit of yours screams wealth. I can't believe you wore it down here."

"It was between this and being naked."

Rowyn smirked. "You would've blended in more if you were naked. Though I doubt Leslie would've let you inside the Velvet."

"I thought those chips in people's arms controlled everything? How are pirates able to steal and sell goods if they can't access their credits?"

Rowyn rolled up her sleeve, revealing a burgundy armband beneath. Django remembered feeling a shock back when it had touched him in the transition house. At the time, he'd mistaken it for chemistry between them.

"These armbands aren't just decorative. They shield my chip from sensors."

"Is that legal?"

Rowyn shrugged. "Owning one isn't illegal. *Selling* one, though, is a different story."

"Is that how pirates operate, too?" he asked.

"Mostly. They're lawless, but they have their reasons. The Resurgence has been working alongside some of them to get supplies."

Maybe the entire movement had questionable motives. Django recalled the image of his uncle on the holo Commander Aries had shown him.

Django swallowed. *He sought out his targets and killed them in cold blood.*

"And mercenaries? People hire them to kill?"

"For someone who wants a man named Benson dead, I wouldn't think you'd have a problem with that."

Django wanted Benson to pay for his crimes, but hiring an assassin? That didn't sit right with him.

"I'd prefer to be the one to pull that trigger."

"Taking a life isn't as easy as it sounds," Rowyn said, moving from the door to scan the surrounding room. "Every life you take demands a piece of you that you'll never get back."

Her words suggested personal experience.

The dead eyes of the guard Django had killed back on the *Eclipse* haunted him. He tried to swat away the memory as if it were tangible, earning a puzzled look from Rowyn that quickly faded.

"I've killed," he admitted. "I'd rather not do it again if I can avoid it, but I don't think I'd regret ending Benson's life. Not when doing so could save so many others."

"Sounds logical, but our brains aren't wired that way. When it comes to pulling that trigger, it's just you and him. But enough questions for now. We need to get moving."

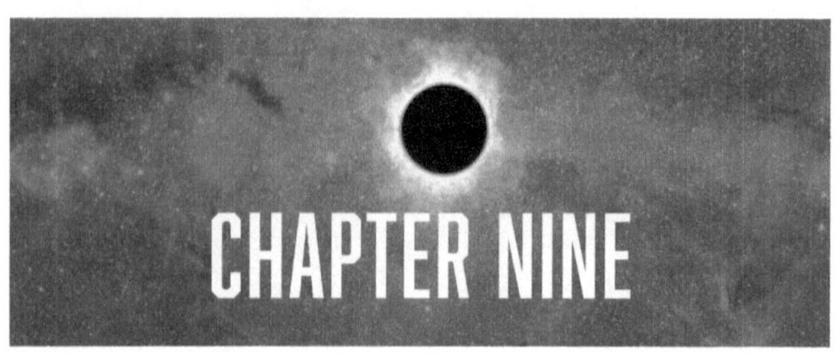

CHAPTER NINE

Django
    Shackleton City Tubes

It took Django several moments to collect himself, brush off his dress shirt, and survey the new location they'd found themselves in. Rowyn had switched on the dim incandescent lighting, emanating from clouded bulbs that seemed more like something out of an ancient tomb than the same advanced civilization that had built the city above their heads. In one corner of the room sat a small countertop with a sink and a hot plate. Next to it, a doorway led, presumably, to the bathroom. A patchwork blanket was draped over the back of a threadbare couch, and a collection of rock samples—each labeled with its moon or planet of origin—accompanied the books strewn across the shelves.

This is someone's home.

Rowyn surveyed the room as well, her vibrant emerald eyes reflecting the yellow lighting with an unspoken sadness as they roved around it. A faint smile spoke volumes about her familiarity with the place. Her posture—straight yet somewhat languid—suggested she was committing every detail to memory for the last time.

She sighed softly before shaking off her reverie and moving further inside.

"You live here," Django observed, stating the obvious rather than posing a question. A family portrait hung on the wall. It wasn't a holographic image like those he'd seen on the surface, but a print. It pictured a mother, a father, a son, and a youthful Rowyn. She couldn't have been more than fifteen.

"I used to," Rowyn replied, settling into a chair in the center of the room. "These days, I spend most of my time with the Resurgence."

"This place seems nicer than what I've seen of the Tubes so far."

Rowyn shrugged. "I guess. I have it better than most."

The living space reminded Django of his quarters aboard the *Eclipse*. It was comparable in size, at least. Apart from the door lock, the place lacked the technological advancements of his former home, but it was comfortable.

"So, if you can own a home like this, why can't others? Why are so many sleeping on the streets? What did you do to afford a place like this?"

"I didn't do anything," Rowyn said, leaning back in her chair and crossing her arms over her chest. "This place belonged to my mother, and to her father before her. My grandfather's family were among the first colonists to settle here. Things were different back then. Few people lived on Lunar. Places like this were built in the Tubes to protect against radiation while the containment zone over the city was being constructed. Over time, as Shackleton developed, the wealthy claimed homes on the surface and costs escalated. Families from Earth began buying homes here as contingency plans as soon as they saw things deteriorating down on the planet. The people who left before the wars were lucky, but it forced those who couldn't afford property on the surface to live underground. At first, it wasn't so bad. People traveled between the Rim and the Tubes every day. But once the Syndicate took over, more and more food was diverted to the planet and to Syndicate families. Prices skyrocketed, and work and resources favored the elite. People living from hand to mouth were priced out of the market, leaving the upper class to snatch up every cubic meter of prime real estate on the Rim. Shackleton was soon divided along the lines of rich and poor.

"Then the Lunar sickness hit, which only added to the Tubes' misery. We were blamed for its origins, seen as vile and dirty, and we were refused any treatment. Those on the surface made it even harder for us to move freely, setting up checkpoints and LPF guards at every exit to the surface, convinced we would spread the disease to them."

"I've heard of this Lunar sickness a few times. What is it?"

"Nobody really knows. It starts as a cough and progressively worsens until you eventually lose your ability to function. If you're lucky enough to have someone to take care of you, Corielus seed can ease the symptoms enough to keep you alive. If you're not, you end up dead on the street, and Sanitation throws your body into the incinerator with the rest of the city's garbage."

Django moved to the sofa and was about to sit when Rowyn raised a hand to stop him.

"What? I'm not allowed to sit on your furniture?"

She grinned. "You can sit anywhere you like, but first, we have to get you out of those clothes."

Django's eyes widened. "Excuse me?"

Rowyn burst into a fit of laughter. It came out as more of a cackle.

"Oh, I see . . . Well, I'm sorry if the thought of me standing here naked is hilarious to you, but . . ."

"Oh, shut it!" Her grin still hadn't faded. "You should have seen your face! Totally worth it!"

Django shook his head. Off-station humor left a lot to be desired. "So . . . I'm *not* undressing?"

"No, you totally are. Take off your clothes. There's a good chance your new Syndicate friends put a tracking device in them. It's bad enough I had to lead you here wearing them. I wouldn't have if we weren't being chased."

On top of everything else, I also have to worry about being tracked?

Considering Aries' intention to find the Resurgence base, it shouldn't have surprised him. Their eagerness to take his station clothes and give him these substitutes now made sense. Django had thought it was because of their stench, the odor clinging to them after his ordeal aboard the slave ship and the assault on the transition house had become offensive, even to him.

There's nothing to say there wasn't more than one motivator.

He wouldn't miss the itchy Syndicate suit, but with no alternative, was he supposed to walk around Lunar nude?

"You . . ." He wasn't sure how to phrase his thoughts. "You want me to undress *here*? In front of you?"

"What? Are you shy?" Rowyn erupted into laughter again. "Okay, okay, station boy—there's a washbasin behind that door. Go in there and undress. I'll bring you some fresh clothes. I'm sure I have something that'll fit you around here somewhere."

Django wasn't sure if he was more embarrassed or relieved, but he quickly sidled to the closet-sized room regardless. There was just enough room inside for him to turn around amid the sink, toilet, and pipes that ran into the wall. He undressed quickly, shivering in the cool underground air. There had to be some kind of heat source in the Tubes, but Django hadn't yet discovered what that might be. He made a mental note to ask.

The door flew open. Rowyn stood on the other side, grinning and holding a handful of clothes.

"Do you mind?" Django asked. He thought about turning to shield his mostly naked body, but it was too late to hide anything.

Rowyn paused, her expression turning serious, and she nodded toward his chest. "Where'd you get that?"

"What? This?" Django grabbed the pendant that hung from his neck, its cool metal adding to the chill in the room. "It was Marvin's. I guess it might still be his if he wants it back. It was given to me when I thought he'd died on the *Eclipse*." He scoffed at the thought. "He tricked us into believing he'd died in a hull breach. I didn't know for sure that he was alive until we saw him at the docks."

Rowyn lifted an eyebrow. "Do you wish he was dead?"

"Of course not! It's just . . ." Django scratched the back

of his head, letting the cool pendant fall back against his skin. "Imagine thinking you'd lost someone, grieving their loss, processing it, only to discover they were never really dead. They're alive, but everything you knew about them was a lie."

Rowyn's lips curled in an empathetic smile as she stepped toward Django and rested a hand on his chest. Her palm was warm against his skin, and surprisingly gentle. His hair stood on end as she traced a line up his pec muscle and her finger came to rest on the medallion.

"I can't imagine how tough it must be," Rowyn said. "But you kept his pendant, so you obviously care about him. You called Marvin uncle for eight years. I've got to know him these past few days, and I don't doubt he cares about you in return. I see how he treats others on the base. I bet he treated you as an equal when the others wouldn't; talked to you like someone who matters. If I were in your place, I'd be grateful to have Marvin in your corner. Someone like him is a rare treasure, especially in the Loop."

Django remained motionless, not wanting to give Rowyn the satisfaction of admitting she was right. But deep down, he knew it was true.

"Marvin Alejandro is highly respected. That's why his legacy has lived on, even after he disappeared for nearly a decade. If he deceived you, he had his reasons. Either he didn't think he could take you with him or he thought you wouldn't want to—but he isn't your enemy. Don't make the mistake of thinking he'll be the one to betray you."

She stepped back, her hand lifting from his chest, leaving a cool absence. Her playful smile returned as she looked him over.

"Underwear, too, station boy," she said, winking and twirling a finger in the air. "I'm assuming those aren't yours."

Django quickly grabbed the clothes she offered him, pushed her out of the small space, and closed the door to the sound of her laughter. Monitoring the door, half expecting Rowyn to burst in as some sort of prank, he removed his underwear and dressed swiftly, his face still burning with embarrassment.

The clothes Rowyn had given him were softer and more comfortable than the ones Aries had provided. He pulled on the khaki pants, which fit well, with a little extra room that he guessed would be useful for running—something he suspected he would be doing a lot more of soon. The black T-shirt was loose across his shoulders, as though it had been worn by someone of a similar height but with a much more muscular build. Rowyn had paired the outfit with a woolen pullover that would come in handy in the chilly passages of the underground.

Django emerged into the living area, clutching his discarded Syndicate attire, and found Rowyn was busy filling a backpack with supplies from the kitchen. She gave him an appreciative glance and a satisfied smile.

"Those suit you," she said. "Much better than those awful blue pants. I'm glad I kept them." She paused momentarily as something caught her attention, then zipped the backpack shut.

Kept them?

"Whose clothes are these?" he asked.

"They're yours now," she replied tersely.

Django waited for her to elaborate, but instead she

slung the backpack over her shoulder, took the pile of Syndicate-issued clothes from his hands, and headed for the door.

He didn't mean to pry, but he couldn't help himself. "They were your brother's, weren't they?"

Aboard the slave ship where the two of them had first met, Rowyn had shared how her brother had drugged her and tried to sell her to the Domani after their parents' death.

Rowyn nodded, glancing back at him, pain swimming in her eyes.

"You held on to them? For all this time?"

"It's only been a few years," she admitted. "And . . . I don't know. He's a bastard, but part of me hoped Gavin would come back; that he would apologize for what he did to me."

Django didn't know what to say. *Would it be possible to forgive someone who had betrayed you so badly?*

"You'd welcome him back, even after what he did?"

Rowyn bit her bottom lip. "Not easily. But growing up, we were inseparable. It's probably just nostalgia talking. You don't get to choose your family, after all.

"Anyway, it's time for us to go." She lifted the Syndicate garments bundled in her arms. "We'll find a place to discard these on the way."

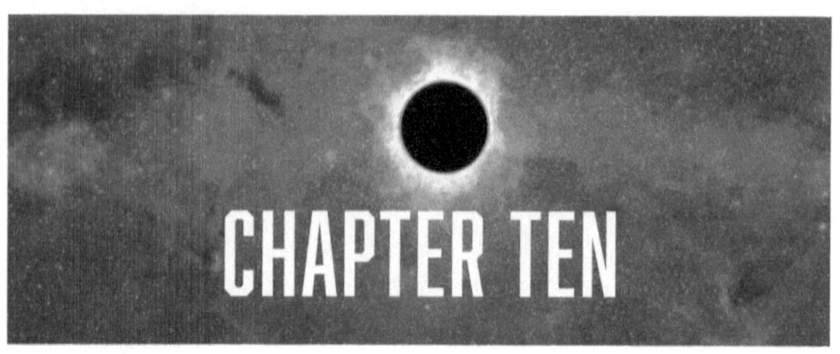# CHAPTER TEN

Django
    Shackleton City Tubes

An endless maze of tunnels.

Growing up on a space station, Django had never imagined he could be so claustrophobic, so uncomfortable, as he was within these narrow, rocky spaces, but the unbroken, low light and the monotonous walls of regolith quickly wore him down. It was the opposite of the endless expanse of space visible from Lunar's surface. Beneath the streets of Shackleton, it was hard to feel anything but oppressed.

Django followed Rowyn for what seemed like hours, plunging ever deeper into the subsurface network. From one tunnel to the next, the Syndicate's neglect became increasingly clear. They passed buildings carved straight from the regolith, ranging from dismal to derelict, the glass from their windows long since shattered or removed, covered over with drab boarding or leaving gaping holes in the exteriors. Since these windows would only have offered views of the suffering in the streets, there seemed little point in maintaining them.

The stench of human waste and disease intensified as they descended. Sometimes, it was hard to distinguish the living from the dead. Lunar sickness left many residents incapacitated, their existence marked only by sporadic coughing, incoherent mumbles, and the occasional scream. Ragged children scurried about, carrying feeble armfuls of food and what Django guessed to be handfuls of Corielus seed to parents who lurked out of sight in the alleyways.

Suddenly, Django's own problems seemed insignificant. Despite losing his family and finding himself penniless on the Moon, he had not one, but two highly influential leaders vying for his allegiance and friends who were watching his back.

His forearm itched. Surely with so many people this far below the surface, with nothing to their name but the clothes on their back and, if they were lucky, a blanket to fend off the chill of the subterranean air, not all of them could have received chip implants.

"Are all these people chipped?" he asked Rowyn, lowering his voice to avoid attracting attention. "I can't believe the Syndicate would bother to go to the effort of tracking them."

It was impossible to tell by looking at them, though Django was sure that beneath the gaunt and feeble arms, he could make out a protrusion where a chip might have been inserted.

"At least those who aren't too sick for the Syndicate to worry about. It actually works in the Empire's interest *not* to know how many of their citizens are dying. Almost all infants are supposed to be chipped at birth, and the LPF conduct regular raids to ensure compliance. Some of the sicker children probably aren't, but to find an adult who hasn't been chipped? If it's not impossible, it's close. Most of the people down here don't live past the age of ten. Those who maintain any semblance of health past that point are shipped to the mines, and most of those don't make it to their twentieth birthday."

"Why doesn't the Syndicate do something more for them?"

Rowyn rolled her eyes. "Because the Syndicate doesn't give two shits about what happens beneath the surface. Most people on Earth would rather forget the colonies exist, and the elite on the surface are more worried about what type of martini to order with dinner than those who work the mines that generate the wealth for all their luxury. That's what the Resurgence is fighting for, Django: a chance for those people who have given everything to satisfy the greed of the Syndicate and received nothing in return."

How much of this is Aries willing to fix? How much will Marvin *be able to?*

"But why chip them at all? It seems like a lot of effort to go through just to allow them to suffer."

"Politics. Lunar cities receive funding based on population numbers—not that the money makes it down to the people who need it most. The Upper Rim hoards it for themselves. The chips also allow the Syndicate to maintain control over the masses. It keeps the people living in the Tubes out of the markets and buildings on the Rim. It ensures they don't get access to the Upper hospitals, schools, and jobs."

Django shook his head. Much of what Rowyn was saying echoed what Aries had told him, but there was more compassion in her version. Still, Django wasn't sure if he was ready to throw Aries to the wayside just yet.

Find Eventide first.

Rowyn stopped in front of a doorway that had been built into the rock face. This far into the Tubes, it appeared the early settlers had stopped trying to replicate buildings found on the surface and had resigned themselves to burrowing modest caves into the tunnel walls.

Rowyn scanned the street behind them, as though expecting someone might have followed them this far undetected, before lifting her arm to the door.

"Another place of yours?" Django asked.

"*Quiet!*" Rowyn whispered. "Not another word until I tell you it's okay."

The request seemed strange in the empty tunnels, but Django bit his tongue.

Dim LED lights flickered to life as they entered a room barely bigger than a closet. An unmade bed sat in one corner beside a small pile of clothes that was covered in regolith dust. On the other side of the cramped room was a descending staircase.

Cozy.

Django followed Rowyn down the stairs, which led to a room not much bigger than the one on the top floor. On one side was an entry to a toilet, with no sink or shower—or even a closing door. Django was used to communal showers on the *Eclipse*, but no privacy on the toilet was something totally foreign to him. Having seen more than one person defecating in the street outside, though, any semblance of plumbing would probably be considered a step up for many.

In the main room, there was nothing but four plastic chairs, arranged to face each other, a set of empty bookshelves lining the wall, and a digital clock fixed above them.

With each step, Rowyn paused to study the room. It seemed like overkill to Django—the room was clearly empty—but after their earlier encounter with the mystery gunman, he could see why she didn't want to take any chances.

Rowyn lifted a finger to her lips, studying the chairs in the center of the room as though she expected a person to materialize in one of them at any second.

Django froze. He dared not breathe as Rowyn stood motionless, her eyes fixated on the center of the room.

Django fought the urge to ask her questions. His fingers itched, and a bead of sweat rolling down his back set his muscles on edge.

A deep rumbling beneath their feet broke the silence. The intensity of the shaking increased, vibrating through his bones with such force that Django thought he was going to topple over. Just as he prepared to brace himself against Rowyn, a high-pitched beeping filled the room.

If the rumble was intrusive, the squeal was downright invasive. His stomach rolled as the noise grated his teeth and tightened his gut. Django moved to lift his hands to his ears, but Rowyn's hand grabbed him and yanked him toward the chairs. He grunted as his butt hit plastic. Rowyn planted herself in a chair beside him and waved an arm at a console beside her. A holo-screen appeared, and she typed a few characters into a holographic keyboard.

What is *this place?*

Between the rumbling and the squeal, there was no point in asking questions, even if he hadn't been under strict orders to remain silent.

A second device rose from Rowyn's console, and it took Django a moment to realize that one had risen from his own console, too.

"What the . . .?"

He couldn't even hear his own words, lost in the surrounding ocean of noise. The clear pane of what looked like a holo-screen flashed a red light in his eyes. Django blinked in confusion and the screen disappeared.

Rowyn nodded as though the process was expected. Django was about to protest when the room started spinning around him. The motion didn't help the unsettled feeling in his gut, and he grabbed onto the chair beneath him with both hands. It took him a moment to realize that the room wasn't spinning—*they* were. The chairs rotated in a circle as though on a disc.

Within a matter of seconds, the spinning slowed, and the room came into focus. It was clear they had descended into yet another room below.

Django fought with himself to orient his focus. The room was still spinning, even once the motion of the platform had stopped. The cavern they found themselves in was much like the rest of the Tubes, but here, the gray regolith had been shaped, squared away to fit a train that rested before them at a smooth platform. It was like a prehistoric version of the transport system on board the

Eclipse. Lights glared with a bright white intensity, but only half of the bulbs were still functional. Old posters clung to the walls, faded and dirtied to the point they were no longer legible. There were so many aspects of Lunar's underground that appeared as though they had once been planned and maintained, but had long ago fallen into ruin.

Django briefly closed his eyes to stop the dizzying lights. When he opened them again, Rowyn stood ten feet away. She turned as if she hadn't realized he hadn't already been following, urgent eyes pleading for him to move.

The rumble was still ongoing, but the high-pitched squeal had subsided. Even that change eased Django's stomach, but his insides still churned.

With no chance to argue, he pushed off from the chair. Behind Rowyn sat the gray and orange gloss of a transit car, not unlike the shuttle that ran between the station rings on the *Eclipse.* The doors to the car were ajar, and Rowyn, despite her eagerness for Django to pursue, still moved toward them.

Django picked up his pace—or at least, he tried to. He stumbled, as though he'd had too much rum at the Velvet Underground; the spinning platform had disoriented his senses, and the ground still wavered beneath his feet.

A rush of air blasted behind him, and Django turned to see the platform he had just been sitting on ascend back into the ceiling above. A large, screw-like mechanism, wider than his arm span, wound the platform back into place.

Wherever it had taken them, there was no going back.

"Let's move!"

Django jumped at the words, Rowyn's return surprising him. Her voice was muffled by the noise of the transport hub, despite her shouting directly into his ear. She grabbed his arm and yanked it toward the train. Django had to sprint to keep up and nearly tripped over his own feet before Rowyn tossed him forward.

Django hit the metal floor, landing on his left arm, which jarred between two plates. The doors closed behind them, as if on cue, and Django pushed himself to his feet as the train started its move.

"Do you mind telling me what the hell *that* was all about?"

CHAPTER ELEVEN

Mikka

The *Chimera*

It was becoming clear that escape was unlikely.

That aside, it wasn't as though Mikka and Kiara were treated like standard prisoners: they were given a surprising amount of freedom aboard the *Chimera*, except for entry to any room that would allow them access to controls, information, or viewports. Which, to be fair, did render most of the ship off-limits. Abigail had effectively welcomed them with open arms, as though bringing aboard a pair of old friends rather than two unwilling contractors who had been kidnapped against their will. Not that her hospitality made their position any more enjoyable—or deviated their plans.

Mikka, for her part, avoided Abigail as much as she could. The space pirate's crop of white hair and the ticking of her ridiculous walking stick made Mikka's blood boil. That hadn't stopped Abigail from seeking Mikka out, however. In fact, Mikka was starting to think the pirate had been intentionally popping in on her quarters just to get under her skin.

Once the *Redemption* had been secured in the ship's bay, Mikka had heard one of the crew say something about heading for the dark side of the Moon. That, in itself, wasn't surprising; it was the bastion of those on the wrong side of the law. It was far less colonized than the side of Lunar facing Earth. Being Earthside made it easier to stay in contact with the planet, and residents wanted a view of their home world rather than the endless void of space.

The dark side, of course, wasn't actually any darker than Earthside; it was just an old Earth term that had stuck through the ages. Its proclivity for harboring pirates made sense, in that the dark side didn't offer a view of the planet and was therefore well suited to hiding from spying eyes. The dark side offered good places to settle, but for the advantages that came with discretion, there were downsides to the isolation. There weren't enough legitimate contractors that needed or wanted to go out of their way to service the smaller, rural populations, leaving those willing to skirt protocol to meet the need.

It was the closest thing to the Wild West that still existed this close to Earth. Io and Enceladus were of a similar mindset. They were harder still to deliver to, but that only meant the runs were more profitable.

The distance between Mars and Earth was also rife with pirate activity, especially at the edges of the Opposition—the point where Earth and Mars were closest in their respective orbits. Haulers who rushed to plow between the planets before this delicate window closed were careless and easy targets. During her pirating days, this was where

Mikka had landed her biggest hauls. With so much empty space, there was no way for Syndicate or private contractors to effectively guard the ships that diverted from the main routes.

Still, despite the pirate's slip, Mikka hadn't yet been able to determine whether the *Chimera* had landed on Lunar's surface, if it was stationed in orbit, or if it had found a space dock to hold up in.

It would be unusual to maintain an orbital position for three days. No pirate worth their salt would want to gain unnecessary attention by hanging out in plain sight, especially with a vessel as exemplary as the *Chimera*. Even though the ship's ability to avoid detection was beyond compare, anyone could still look up and see the damned thing. The Orbital Guard rarely resorted to visual inspection, but they still had eyes. More time in orbit meant more potential for detection.

Be that as it may, Mikka refused to accept that Abigail would run her fuel cells if they were parked at a space dock. No platform would allow them to keep their engines powered up if they were clamped to the hull. Either they were running completely off battery power—which wasn't unheard of—or they weren't in the Moon's orbit at all, and drifting somewhere in space.

Mikka and Kiara were closely monitored to ensure they couldn't see out any viewports. While they were somewhat free to roam the ship, it seemed every effort had been made to keep her and Kiara ignorant about the *Chimera*'s current position.

This also left the two of them with few private moments to themselves. On those occasions where they were alone, usually during meals, they had to assume there were eyes and ears fixed on them, watching their every move—which made executing an escape almost impossible.

Their table was one of a dozen in the ship's mess hall. Other than the detail Monroe had assigned, there was nobody else in the room at the moment.

The two guards, one for each Mikka and Kiara, stood by the mess entryway, engaged in their own conversation in hushed tones.

The hall was spacious for the size of the ship. Mikka estimated it could hold nearly a hundred passengers, which, as far as she could tell, was more crew than Abigail had on board. Like the rest of the ship, the décor left something to be desired. Bare walls were only broken by a single banner bearing that familiar interlocking circle emblem. Otherwise, it was as though the ship had been newly constructed and pulled out of the shipyard before the finishing touches could be added. Large flat spaces with wires dangling from the walls hinted at holo-screens that had either yet to be installed, or recently removed. A small buffet had been set up along the side wall, and had been mostly picked through, leaving only the scrapings of the day's meal behind. Clearly, her and Kiara were only allotted these brief moments alone because the crew was making them wait until everyone else had finished eating before allowing the prisoners their scraps.

"At least they let us have lunch together," Kiara said, picking at her food—a disdainful serving of rice, peas, potatoes, and bean paste.

What Mikka wouldn't give to have a little fat in their diets. It was like she was living in the Tubes again, with a staple of texturized starch and whichever scrap of leftover garbage could be scavenged on the surface. She couldn't really complain, though; at least the food on board the *Chimera* had been grown in the ground somewhere, as opposed to in a lab. Natural plants were a luxury to those who lived underground.

"It'd be nice if they left us a bit of meat." Mikka gestured to an empty plate on the buffet table.

A mound of darkened bean paste sat on her plate. Only those in the highest echelons of society could afford real animals for slaughter, and it had been that way for hundreds of years. As Mikka understood it, global governments restricting livestock production had been one of the catalysts that had sparked the Climate Wars. Millions of farmers had seen their livelihoods crumble overnight. Millions of people believed their right to eat meat was more important than the emissions the industry produced. From that point on, it was impossible to contain the riots.

"Aries is a bad influence on you." Kiara nearly spat the words. "When was the last time you ate actual meat? Have you really become so privileged?"

The words gave Mikka pause. The ship around them was so advanced, part of Mikka felt justified in her statement. If these pirates held enough sway to gain access to advanced weaponry and prototype engines, then how hard would it be to house a few chickens? But she also knew her old self would never have even imagined desiring meat over the simple foods offered. As a pirate, she had relished that slight sliver of luxury when she found a job that she could either skim off a meat delivery or earn enough credits to treat herself. But for the past eight years, she and Kiara and rarely seen the stuff. Growing up, Mikka would have been grateful to have had anything to eat at all.

Stars knew she'd gone long enough without a credit to her name. And after only a couple of fancy meals, she was now complaining about a plateful of more nutrition than most residents of the Tubes saw in a week—hell, even a month.

Mikka swallowed her mouthful of peas. She would have to watch herself. As much as she was beginning to believe in Aries' cause, she would begin to let him change her if she wasn't careful. She had to remember where she came from. She had to remind herself of the people they were trying to help when all this was said and done. People like her mother. People with nothing on their plates for dinner.

She decided to change the subject.

"Have you figured out if we've docked somewhere?" Mikka kept her voice low as she surveyed the guards at the entryway. Their captors were involved in their own conversation and ignoring Mikka and her navigator for the moment.

"I'm sure we have." Kiara poked mindlessly at her peas with her fork. "The ship's inertial compensation must be top class, but I don't believe we're moving. Even on a ship this size, we'd still feel the engines occasionally firing to keep us in Lunar's orbit."

"You don't think we're drifting somewhere?"

Kiara shrugged. "Anything is possible with that screwball, but I don't see her sitting around doing nothing. My guess is we're at a private space dock. I don't think the PA would authorize the ship to idle for days after it landed."

"Only if we landed somewhere within PA jurisdiction," Mikka replied. "There are a lot of settlements on Lunar's dark side that they ignore."

"For all we know, we could be on our way to Ganymede, Meeks. Except for that one mention of Lunar's dark side, this lot have been tight-lipped about where we are or what they're up to. I still don't understand why they're holding us like this."

"Any ideas how to figure it out without getting a glimpse of a viewport or the nav systems?"

"Get Abigail drunk and hope she lets it slip?"

"I'm pretty sure she's always drunk. I don't think there'd be enough alcohol on the entire ship to loosen her tongue."

Kiara let a smile slip through. The navigator had been cordial toward Mikka because of their shared plight, but the warmth of their friendship had faded since their argument over Aries. Mikka understood Kiara's hesitancy to trust the man, but surely if Mikka could get past her reservations about Aries, Kiara could as well. The navigator hadn't been a fan of taking on the Aries' delivery contract, despite the commander providing luxury apartments and care for both Mikka's mother and Kiara's children.

But at the heart of it, Kiara didn't trust Aries. Perhaps Mikka couldn't blame her. Maybe she'd just have to be patient, allowing Kiara to see she was wrong about the Syndicate commander's intentions. Once he revealed his true nature, Kiara would quickly realize where Aries stood and how he would change the entire system under his command.

But that was a battle for another day. For now, it was

comforting to know that, however standoffish, Kiara was still in her corner.

"If we're on the ground somewhere, we're going to have a hell of a time flying out of here. We'd be shot down before we even made it out of the gravitational pull. Ideally, if we're docked, we could punch the *Redemption* through the cargo hold door and be on our way."

"Or we could be stranded out in open space." Kiara's eyes narrowed. "Do you remember how well the *Redemption* outran this ship the last time? If we're on our way to Mars, we've got a hell of a journey to get back. Even with a day's head start, the *Chimera* would be on top of us in no time."

"Something tells me Abigail's sticking close to Earth's orbit."

"What makes you say that?"

"She's teamed up with Marvin and the Resurgence. They're going to want to hit the Syndicate where it hurts. There's no reason to fly further out into the system."

"Unless her little prophet told her to."

Mikka paused. There was always that possibility. The pirate was putting an inordinate amount of faith in what that modded kid was telling her, and people put their faith in the most unusual things if it meant they didn't have to be held accountable for their own decisions.

"Well, I'd rather not sit around, waiting to find out," Mikka said. "If we're on the surface, we look for a chance to hop out and escape on foot. If we're in space, we figure out a way to get the *Redemption* off this ship. I just wish there was a way to tell before we make our next move."

Kiara thought for a moment, scratching at a spot above

her ear. "If we could determine whether the gravity plating is active, then we'd know for sure. No gravity, we're in space; natural gravity, we're on Lunar."

The navigator's logic made sense, though it wouldn't be an easy hypothesis to prove. If they could access the controls to turn off the gravity, they could probably look at the ship's navigation systems, too. Which meant there was almost as much chance of them accessing the gravity metrics as there was of them commandeering the entire ship.

"Do you think we could shut it down? Even for a moment?"

"If I had enough time with a console."

"If we're asking for miracles, why don't we ask to look out a viewport?" Mikka shoved a forkful of gray beans into her mouth.

"You asked me a question, that's your answer." Kiara's fork slipped, sending a pea off her plate and onto the floor beside her.

Absentmindedly, Mikka glanced under the table to where the kernel had landed, a green orb in the center of a three-foot square tile. Standard gravity plating made up the ship's flooring, comprised of a grid of squares, with each individual piece constructed as a cube that descended into the floor. Each unit worked in sync, making up a network of gravitational cells that channeled powerful quantum forces regulated by the plate itself. It was a refined process that only the physicists and engineers on Earth and possibly the science stations on Ganymede understood. Mikka, with the education she'd received in the Tubes—or more accurately, the lack of it—couldn't begin to explain exactly how they functioned, but she knew one thing.

"We don't have to shut it off. We just have to disable one cell."

"Meeks, you know the adjacent cells will compensate. That's why the plating is built in blocks: if one fails, the others bridge the gap until it can be fixed."

Mikka leaned in closer to Kiara. The guards were still engaged in their own conversations, but she didn't want to risk them overhearing. "If you place something small on the cell, like a button"—she smiled as she picked one of the legumes from her plate and held it between her thumb and forefinger—"or a pea, and a plate malfunctions, there will be enough gravitational loss to momentarily lift it off the grid. It doesn't need to be much—or for long. All we're looking for is a glitch. One millimeter, and we'll know the only thing holding us down is the plating."

"That's not what I'd call a master plan . . ."

"It will let us know if we're docked somewhere with gravity. If not, we can fly the *Redemption* out of here. If we're landed or parked on a space dock with its own gravity, we can crawl out of the ship and try to contact Aries. I know he's not your favorite person, but we might need the big guns to get Monroe to back off. Either way, we get off this ship."

"Maybe," Kiara said. "But killing a gravity cell isn't easy. They're built to be durable. We have no tools and no weapons. You won't be able to jam a butter knife into it and expect it to blow. Plus, if we aren't on the surface, we still need to make it out of here, and that means squaring off against the *Chimera plus* three other ships that can easily outrun and out-gun us—again."

"If we're at a spaceport, they'll be attached to the dock. They'll need time to disengage. If we're not at a port, there's nothing to say the other vessels stuck around. If either of those scenarios is the case, then we might pull it off."

"We might also find ourselves dead."

Mikka gestured to the tables around them. "Would you rather stay here? Do you really think they're gonna let us fly out of here when the boy wizard says it's okay? Monroe's got us pegged here for something; I just haven't figured out what yet. Given the lengths they've gone to, there *has* to be a reason for Alejandro wanting us to join the Resurgence."

Kiara smirked. "Maybe he thinks you're cute."

Mikka scoffed. "*Please*. Best guess, my reputation makes me valuable—but my pirating days ended eight years ago. I can't see how he thinks I could be that integral to his plans for tearing the Empire down."

"He was a mercenary a decade ago," Kiara offered. "Maybe he understands age is just a number. That old habits die hard."

"And won't he be in for a surprise? I can't even deliver a damned package to a FLOW station."

"Maybe he's hoping to distract you from Aries and whatever game your dutiful commander is playing."

"There's more to it than that. And whatever it is, involves Zee too. Abigail has her hopes wrapped up in this kid and his parlor tricks."

"You think the kid's full of it?"

"You don't?"

Kiara looked at Mikka intently. "All I know is, there are

forces in this universe we don't understand. Who's to say an implant didn't fry the *right* part of his brain? Maybe he can see through space-time. Maybe he's able to glimpse into the fourth dimension and see what's coming."

Mikka scoffed. "I have no doubt the implant is showing him *something*, but do I believe he can see the future? Hell no. But belief is a powerful motivator, and if the Resurgence believe they have a psychic on their side, I can see how that would instill a crazy level of confidence."

"And *if* he is seeing likely outcomes?"

Mikka smiled. "Our chance of success might be slim, but the odds are never zero."

CHAPTER TWELVE

Mikka

The *Chimera*

"That's enough talking! Back to your rooms."

Victor, clearly tasked with keeping the *Chimera*'s captives in line, had a grizzled look about him, the veins that popped out of his balding temple gave him the appearance of being fifteen years older than the forty years of age Mikka had guessed him to be. A modified implant installed on his face covered one eye, harboring a mechanical lens that protruded in and out of his eye socket.

Victor waved for Mikka and Kiara to stand and gestured for them to exit into the passageway. He escorted them along with a second pirate whose name Mikka hadn't caught—a younger man, clean-shaven, with a baby face that was amplified by his reddened cheeks.

This second man steered Kiara down a separate corridor with a bored-sounding "This way Miss Ryson," as though he'd been assigned the task but wished for nothing more than to be elsewhere.

For some reason Abigail—perhaps for no reason other than Abi being Abi—had embraced theatrics in their confinement. Although there was much fanfare in their separation, Kiara wasn't kept far away. Even with the crew's best efforts to mislead them, Mikka often realized she had been led on a deliberately meandering path to her quarters. During their brief lunch encounters, the two women had determined they were sleeping only a few bends in the hall apart.

At first, Mikka believed Victor was guiding her to her quarters. She could already recognize the numbered units that lined the route, but partway through, he steered her into a lift and arrived at a deck Mikka had yet to visit.

The floor was noticeably more staffed than where Mikka's quarters resided. Though the pirates seemed to be engaged in more casual activities than working on anything official. Most of them were relaxing on chaise loungers, playing games and laughing with each other, rather than performing anything technical.

Put pirates on the most advanced ship in the system, but they're still pirates.

That didn't mean that there wasn't anything of importance happening on this level, though. As there were several crew members who appeared to be hard at work.

Computer systems dazzled with analysis that Mikka strained to read, hoping to make out something that would provide a clue as to where they were that she could later use to their advantage.

Those attending the stations appeared to be making more out of the data than Mikka could glean from her quick glances. And Abigail was no fool. Mikka was intentionally being led past readouts that would either be of no benefit to any escape attempt or had security screens mounted in front of them. The data streams she was able to interpret consisting of internal air pressure readouts and systems diagnostics. As useful as the information was from an operational perspective, for Mikka's purposes, the consoles might as well have been stationed at the center of the sun.

Concealing the *Chimera*'s location was a well-calculated play. Without knowing where they were, escape became more of a gamble. If Mikka and Kiara tried to escape aboard the *Redemption,* they could find themselves flying into an unsuspecting dock filled with workers and civilians. Equally, they could try to climb out a maintenance shaft—safety protocols would ensure they couldn't fling open a hatch into the void of space—but they risked sounding the alarm before they even made it that far. If it failed, such a move would likely cost them what little freedom they had.

Had Abigail decided to keep them in the dark? Or had Zee calculated the odds of best keeping them in line?

If Monroe was erring on the side of another of Zee's predictions, he had done a good job, but like she had told Kiara, unless Mikka was dead, the odds were never zero. There was no denying she was a little rusty, but Mikka hadn't been known as the best pirate in the system for no reason.

The pirates led her through a narrow series of passageways. After a while, Mikka was certain she had to be getting closer to the bridge. Though, like everywhere else on board, any navigational holo-screens or infographics relating to critical ship components had been conveniently deactivated.

Whatever game she was playing, Abigail knew she wasn't messing with an amateur.

The pirates steered Mikka into a mid-sized cabin. Model ships decorated the shelving embedded in the bulkheads, miniature wooden hulls, masts, and sails reflective of an age of piracy from centuries gone by.

A little cliché, Mikka thought, but then again, Abigail seemed to thrive on age-old pirating stereotypes. It was little wonder she didn't have a parrot for a pet, or that she hadn't coveted Victor's eye modification for her own.

A wall to the side appeared to be made entirely of a single viewport, which would have provided spectacular views of the stars had it not been tinted over with a privacy shield. Again, Monroe was not letting even the smallest detail slip in her concealment of their location.

Abigail Monroe sat in the center of the room behind a wide table. Behind her, two pirates stood. One of them was Penelope, her bionic hand clenched and emitting a pattern of orange lighting. The second was a man that Mikka recognized from the loading bay where she'd first landed the *Redemption* but had never been introduced to. Neither looked impressed to be there, likely only called to be present to deter Mikka from doing something stupid, like attacking Monroe.

Abigail's fingers pressed together and her lips pursed until she made eye contact with Mikka.

"Thank you for joining me, love."

Abigail's lips curled into a grin as she pushed herself up from her seat. She had ditched the formal wear she typically wore around the ship in favor of something much more casual—a red and black form-fitting bodysuit. It was a choice that seemed wildly out of character for someone Mikka had only ever seen wear long coats, cloaks, and capes.

"That's quite the outfit," Mikka observed. "What's the occasion?"

"Do you like it?" Abigail thrust her hips out as she ran her hands along the smooth black material. "I have a very important meeting, and I wanted to dress to impress."

"Who are you meeting with? Alejandro?"

Abigail straightened and smiled a toothy grin. "Listen, love, if you want to be invited to the party, you've got to join the inner circle. Until then, I can't let you know what's going on in case you go running off to tell that Prince Charming of yours."

"You realize he's a wanted mercenary? He's killed dozens of men and women."

"Yes, well . . ." Abigail paused, as though considering. "Our pasts are rather hard to escape, aren't they?"

"He's an interesting partner for someone who claims never to kill."

Abigail furrowed her brow. It was the closest Mikka had ever seen her to looking serious. "You're one to talk about questionable bedfellows. You don't think blood covers the hands of Aries?"

"Whatever else he may be, Aries has noble intentions—and at least his army doesn't consist of a half-strung group of misfits and terrorists."

That earned a few annoyed looks from Mikka's pirate

escorts. Victor even reached toward his blaster, but he kept the weapon holstered.

Abigail didn't flinch. "You of all people should know what it means to do whatever it takes to survive—or has wine and fine dining made you forget all of that?"

Mikka swallowed. That was the second time today she'd been accused of forgetting how hard life was in the Loop.

"At least Aries is giving me the choice to decide where I fit in."

Abigail snorted. "And that makes him some sort of saint? You're nothing more than his pawn. Surely you haven't lost your wits to the point you can't see that for yourself?"

"And what am I to *you?*" Mikka growled.

"With me? Well, you could be anything you like," Abigail said. Then lowered her voice, the seriousness returning. "If you are aligning yourself with Aries simply because you want someone to keep you warm at night." She raised her eyebrows. "I can help you there too, love. But I'm begging you—don't sell your soul to this man. Whatever he's promised you, I assure you he'll break your heart."

Mikka swallowed. Was *that* why Abigail was so hell-bent on keeping her away from Aries? Jealousy?

As flattering as that though might have been, she needed to change the subject. "How long do you intend to keep us here? Wherever 'here' is?"

"Until Zee believes there's more benefit in letting you go than holding you. He says that there are so many moving pieces, it's hard to keep straight where things will land."

"And then what? You let us go? Or are you waiting until we beg you on hands and knees?"

"I think I've made it clear that if you ever want to get on your knees for me, I won't stop you." Monroe eyed Mikka up and down with a smirk and took two steps closer, until she was within arm's reach. "But that's not what this is about. Zee believes you will see reason in our cause sooner or later, but right now, this is the *only* way to limit the shit-storm that's coming."

"He's a *kid*, Abi! What the hell does he know? He doesn't even fully comprehend what he's seeing!"

"Numbers never lie."

"That's not how war works, and you know it! That's not how *people* work. There have been hundreds of battles across history that haven't gone the way they were statistically supposed to because humans fuck up. You're looking at statistics, but a 99.9% chance will still fail once every thousand times."

"I understand we can't control the future, love." Abigail ran a finger down Mikka's cheek. Her long white nail was square at the end and gently scraped over Mikka's skin, sending an electrifying chill down her spine. "But we *can* stack the deck in our favor. Don't you see? That's how wars are won. That's how heroes are made and empires crumble. An ancient Earth general once said, '*If you know the enemy and know yourself, you needn't fear the result of a hundred battles.*'"

"I'm pretty sure Sun Tzu was talking about *studying* the enemy, not rolling the dice based on the speculations of a supposedly psychic child."

"I think you'd be surprised how many influential

leaders used unordinary means to one-up their opponent. Zee is just another example of that. And for once, the people who have been held under the thumb of the privileged and wealthy will have the advantage. We were never meant to play among the stars for so long."

"You can't honestly believe the Earth is ready for an onslaught of humanity, do you? The Syndicate may hold a few ancient cities, but I've seen the feeds: most of Earth is still a wasteland. Our ancestors didn't climb onto starships because it seemed like a fun idea. The FLOW stations are the legacy of a time driven by desperation and survival."

But even as she'd said the words, Mikka wasn't sure if she truly believed them. Aries had hinted that there was more happening down on the surface than the Syndicate was prepared to reveal. Who knew what state the planet was really in?

"But who got to choose their fate, love? I sure as hell didn't."

"And you think Syndicate citizens are going to choose to follow a group of pirates and mercenaries? You think killing the Prefect is going to stop whoever's next in line from launching an attack? The void will be immediately filled by some other ambitious fool, likely hand-selected by the Council. The Empire's probably got more firepower than you could ever dream of. At least with Aries at the helm, we know what we're getting."

"Hoodwinked is the only thing you're getting with Aries." Abigail took a step back, and Mikka could feel the weight of the air between them lighten.

"You haven't seen the man he really is," Mikka argued. "You only see the man he appears to be; the man the Syndicate make him out to be. He knows what it's like to be pushed down by those in power."

Abigail let out a sigh. "He's really worked a number on you, hasn't he? Those with a troubled past are often the most ruthless when it comes to taking what they want. Out of anybody, you should know that."

"I also know it's easiest to use a broad stroke to paint the enemy as a devil; to forget that individuals form their own opinions, or can deviate from what's expected of them. I *was* once a pirate, you know."

"Captain Monroe," a hidden comms device chirped. "We're going to need you to come to the bridge. Alejandro is waiting."

Abigail's eyes flashed with a look of irritation, almost too quick for Mikka to catch. *Almost.*

"I'm on my way," she replied.

"Tell me," Mikka said, stepping in front of Abigail before she could scurry out. "What is about this Marvin Alejandro that makes him fit to lead a revolution? He's been stuck on a FLOW station for the past eight years. Surely there are better people to bring the Empire down?"

"Like Aries?"

"Yes, like Aries. He already has authority. He has an army at his disposal."

"And he's still a *Syndicate* commander," Abigail countered. "And as much as a wolf claims to have the best interest of the sheep in mind, he's still gotta eat."

If only Monroe could understand that Aries wasn't like the rest of them; how he had worked his way up into his position to avenge his father's murder. He *was* different.

"What if people could see how Aries wants to help

them, the choices he's made . . . *why* he made them? You call David a wolf, but that's just the part he's had to play to secure the resources he needs."

"The sheep don't need someone pretending to be a wolf; they need a shepherd. Someone they trust. Someone who has proven they have their best interests in mind—and I'm sorry, love, but you can't do that while looking down on the people you're supposedly fighting for from a Syndicate penthouse. That is why Marvin has to be the leader of this movement. Aries will be a distraction for the Syndicate that will benefit us, but my goal in keeping you here is to ensure that he inflicts as little damage on innocent lives as possible."

Mikka scoffed. "Well, I look forward to seeing the look on your face when he proves you wrong, pirate."

Abigail took a quick step toward Mikka, coming uncomfortably close. The smell of vanilla rum wafted from her, giving her a sweet but potent aroma. Mikka wanted to step backward, but she couldn't. She had to stand her ground, even though she didn't know whether she was going to get a knife in her chest or a hand on her ass.

Abigail's hot breath danced on her neck before whispering in Mikka's ear, "You'll always be a pirate at heart, love, but somehow, Aries has convinced you to trust him too easily. Maybe it's because you want to believe you can make up for the poor decisions of your past, but you've already made one mistake that cost innocent lives. Don't let another poor choice add to that tally."

Mikka bristled at the accusation. *So, Abi knows the truth.*

"The poor decision I made," Mikka said, catching her

breath as her pulse quickened, "was choosing to become a pirate in the first place."

Abigail pulled herself in closer, her warmth flowing over Mikka like the rum she had so obviously consumed prior to their meeting. She turned her head slightly so that Mikka's nose brushed up against her forehead and pressed her body against her own.

"I'm not sure you believe that. Something keeps pulling you back."

The hair on Mikka's skin unexpectedly stood on end. Maybe she *did* have something this pirate wanted, after all. She leaned into the few inches between her face and Abigail's, letting her lips release a warm breath against the pirate's skin. "Maybe you could convince me to stick around."

Mikka pulled her head back far enough to establish eye contact with Abigail, playfully biting her own lip. Skepticism and confusion melted away from Abigail's face, replaced with an intrigued, satisfied grin.

Without missing a beat, Mikka used her right hand to grab Abigail's waist and pull her fully into her own body in a fluid movement. She pressed her lips to Abi's, wrapping her tongue around hers, tasting the intoxicating flavors of vanilla, rum, and caramel. Mikka lost herself in the moment, surprised by the intensity of the kiss, before the pirate gracefully withdrew, giving Mikka's bottom lip a playful bite as she did so.

Abigail let out a satisfied breath as she pulled away, running a playful finger down Mikka's chest.

"We'll have to finish this conversation later." Abigail winked. "Perhaps over dinner, in my quarters?"

Mikka batted her eyes and smiled seductively. "I wouldn't dream of being anywhere else."

"I'll send my detail for you at nine."

As Monroe's escort led their captain out of the room, Penelope couldn't restrain herself and gave Mikka a snarl of disdain. The second guard looked more amused than anything.

Victor pushed Mikka out the door and down the hall in the opposite direction. He led Mikka back to her quarters, told her to her to wait until someone came for her, and then left.

Leaving Mikka alone with a handful of peas in her left pocket—and Abigail's stun baton pressed against her right hip.

CHAPTER THIRTEEN

Eventide

The *Inanna*

Eventide could barely think straight as she staggered out of the MedLab.

Morales had needed to show the Caregivers *some* sort of reaction to prove Eventide's implants were working—the pain receptors, at least—without having to resort to more "extreme measures."

The doctor hadn't been keen on explaining what she had meant by that, and Eventide was pretty sure she didn't want to know. The "non-extreme" measures alone had caused her entire body to writhe in pain, to the point of vomiting all over the MedLab floor. It sickened her that the Caregivers had a level of torture that was beyond that.

Perhaps the doctor had meant the Caregivers would toss her out the airlock and be done with her. That seemed to be the standard Syndicate threat, no matter where Eventide had found herself within their empire.

Again, she cursed her bad luck that her pain receptors

were working fine while her pleasure centers regulated how much dopamine her brain created. Why couldn't they at least block the lingering sting of her torture session?

The pain had subsided the moment Doctor Morales had terminated the signal to Eventide's implants, but that didn't mean there weren't lingering effects. Her muscles twitched, causing her to shake as she walked. The trauma had left her entire body weak and drenched in sweat, tears streaming down her face as it took all Eventide's concentration to stay upright.

And Morales says she's on my *side?*

Other than revealing some of the secret history of the Caregivers, Morales hadn't given Eventide much to go on. She hadn't shared an escape plan with her, nor a way to shut down the *Inanna* or to expose the truth to the unwitting Domani on board. All Morales had told her was that she was different, and that was reason enough for the doctor to risk defying her superiors.

Great.

Eventide believed in luck, but she also believed in being well prepared. Generally, that meant knowing *what* she was supposed to be preparing for, but Eventide was as much in the dark as the stars that surrounded the *Inanna*.

More secrets. History repeating itself, with another vessel trying to hide the truth from its inhabitants. And I'm trapped on board—again.

Of course, being on the *Inanna* was different from her life aboard the *Eclipse*. And by different, Eventide meant infinitely worse. The Domani knew what existed in the system beyond the ship's metal hull, but they were oblivious to the reality within their own minds.

If Eventide could choose between being trapped on a station and being a prisoner inside her own head, it would be no contest which she would choose. She couldn't imagine a much worse fate than not being able to control her own thoughts. Even being demoted to farming aboard the *Eclipse* somehow didn't seem as bad in comparison.

This Syndicate Empire seemed to have an appetite for exploitation.

There had been so many more questions Eventide had wanted to ask Morales, but their time had run out long before she was satisfied with what she had learned. How many of these trafficking ships were there? How was the Syndicate structured? How could she make her move and chance escape if she could still be reduced to a ball of screaming pain whenever she stepped out of line?

Play along.

It was such bullshit advice. It reminded Eventide something Django would have said He was always trying to steer her toward levelheadedness, always so willing to go with the flow.

It was partly this that reinforced in Eventide's mind why the two of them would never work romantically. Django was willing to settle for mediocrity, for homeostasis, and she never could. They were like fire and ice. He was cool and composed, while Eventide burned with a desire to better herself.

They would never work.

Would they?

She absently ran her hand across her cheek, moist with tears. She wanted to blame the torture she had endured for opening the floodgates, but Eventide knew it was more than that.

Her entire life had been spent trying to break out of the mold she had been cast in. Everything she had done had been to get into, and excel at, the technicians program. How many long hours had she spent studying? How much blood, sweat, and tears had gone into her training? And her reward had been to run from her life, to cast everything she had worked for to follow Django off the station. She had given up so much to build a better future for herself, only to lose it all.

It wasn't so much having to leave the *Eclipse* that bothered her. It was better to know the unpleasant truth behind the station's purpose. The comfortable ignorance the *Eclipse* relied upon now turned her stomach. Being separated from Django was worse, but only because she feared for his safety. There was no way the dope would be doing okay without her.

What bothered her the most, though, was that even after she had learned the truth behind the lies she had been living under, she was still cast into a prison—this one even worse than the first.

At least there, the only part of her body the powers-that-be wanted was her mind.

There was an entire universe out there, filled with technology and systems that Eventide would have loved to be learning about, but instead, she was forbidden to even *look* at it, never mind study it. An expanse of forbidden knowledge, just out of her reach.

Her body quivered as the realization took hold. Now, Eventide was not only limited by the place she was born, but she also had a physical gatekeeper embedded into her skull that would forever hold her back—one that had been biologically bonded to her, and if Morales could be believed, could never be removed.

The best that she could hope for was that her kidnappers would refrain from using its functionality, or that she could destroy whatever device caused the torturous sensations—if that were even possible.

That was her best-case scenario.

Eventide clenched her fists and took several deep breaths in an attempt to keep her fury at bay.

Destroying the ship would be a start. Of course, not while she was *on* it—but perhaps that was the only way to ensure the Caregivers' technology wouldn't be used again. If she could disrupt the source of the data transmissions, maybe the enslavement of future Domani would die with her.

That was a big ask, though. First of all, she didn't even know where she would begin with destroying a ship, especially one as large and advanced as the *Inanna*. While she was intimately familiar with the systems aboard the *Eclipse*, she had yet to see any schematics of the *Inanna*. Never mind that the systems appeared to be decades, if not centuries, more advanced than the tech she was used to dealing with.

Plus, a station was meant to stay in place. There were no engines, no propulsion systems, or navigations systems. Hell, the station didn't even communicate with the outside world. She wasn't afraid to admit that as much as she could probably assess and understand her new environment, if given the opportunity, that she was well outside of her element.

Regardless, explosives would do it, or a bigger, more powerful ship that could blast this one out of the sky. But she was fresh out of those at the moment.

Also, before she would even attempt such an act, all the Domani would have to be off the ship. Destroying a ship was one thing, but destroying a ship *with people on it* was unimaginable. No matter how much the Caregivers deserved it, the Domani certainly didn't.

Was that it, though? Was the source of their pain and misery confined to the ship? Or would the Caregivers have the means to broadcast the transmissions elsewhere?

The ship hummed around her as Eventide stumbled down its passageways, cursing at both the doctor and her own circumstances every step of the way. She ran her hands along the cold, textured wall panels as she tried to maintain her balance. The hum of the ship warbling beneath her, taunting her. The *Inanna*, of course, was free to travel through the system, while her own fate was bound in its belly, unaware of its destination and unable to alter its course.

Her quarters beckoned to her, encouraging her to lay down and drift into a dreamworld. The call was tempting; she could drift away into sleep and all of her troubles would disappear with it. No more worries of Caregivers, Domani —or a best friend who wanted to be something more.

Eventide let out a tired chuckle. Of course, he had never been that, had he? As much as she'd convinced herself otherwise, that damned boy had been crushing on her since they were twelve years old.

She could even pinpoint the exact moment when it had happened.

They had spent the day running down the space station halls together, like they often had, laughing and drawing the ire of the people around them. It hadn't mattered to them, though; they were kids. The station was theirs. Their world. Their universe. There was nothing else that mattered.

That was the last day they had experienced that level of innocence.

Eventide clearly remembered the look on her mother's face when she had broken the news that her father wasn't coming home.

There had been a mechanical failure in one of the *Eclipse's* electrical substations. Her dad, a systems laborer, had been called upon to ensure the D-Ring didn't completely lose power and life support systems. The power converters had been malfunctioning for weeks. During that time, her father, came home complaining about them every night.

"But what can I *do about it?"* he would say. He was a grunt worker, doing whatever he could to keep the station's systems operational with what little the Admin provided them.

And if only a damned technician had come down to sort out the computer glitches, they wouldn't have had to try bypassing safety mechanisms—keeping the station running on quick fixes and hushed prayers.

If only a damned technician had done their job, they could have fixed the problem—and her father wouldn't have died when the converter exploded.

And with those fated words from her father, Eventide's path had been set.

She pledged to be more than a D-Ring grunt worker, more than a wrench monkey like her dad or a farmer on the fields like Django's parents. She had decided to become the person her father had needed; the chance he had never had.

She'd vowed to become a technician.

Her father's death had destined her for more than the typical D-Ring life—or so Eventide had thought.

But that had also been the day Django began to see her as more than a friend. He'd wrapped his arms around her in a consoling hug, as any friend would have done, but as the embrace ended, he'd reached for her hand. She'd thought it was nice at first. Comforting. She had just lost her father and having her best friend by her side had helped to numb some of her grief.

But when he'd tried to grab her hand again the next day, Eventide realized he was hoping for their friendship to be more than it was.

They were still kids, not even teenagers, and they hadn't learned enough about intimacy to know what those silly gestures could mean in the long run. At least, Django hadn't.

If her world hadn't just been rocked, if she hadn't been forced to grow up overnight, maybe things would have been different. Maybe they would have continued to hold hands. Maybe their teenage years would have been punctuated by romance.

But Eventide had known they couldn't last. She'd known that if she allowed Django's advances to continue, she'd hurt—and probably lose—her best friend. He would never move off the D-Ring, and she couldn't choose between him and the role she knew she needed to pursue. Her father's fate had already made that choice, and she couldn't lose her friend. Not ever.

And so, on that second day, the day after her father had died, she'd pulled her hand away. Allowing him to touch her would only lead to heartache. He had seemed to understand and hadn't pushed the idea further after that.

Except he had still looked at her the same way, hiding behind the slight waiver of fear and passion.

What was I supposed *to have said?* Django had never broached the subject, either. It was the unspoken agreement between them. He'd been afraid he would ruin their friendship, too.

In a world where she was fire, he was ice, even when it came to his feelings. He'd kept his cool, knowing the chasm between them was too wide to cross.

Until he'd pulled her in for a kiss aboard the *Redemption.*

She laughed, thankful there was nobody else in the passageway to hear her. Eventide had spent her entire life wishing for change, but she had foolishly believed it would be on her terms; that she could control how the cards were dealt and what they meant. But change had found Eventide—more change than she could ever have possibly imagined. That was the thing about change, she supposed; sometimes, it happens because of you, but more often than not, it happens *to* you.

She needed to flip the script.

Just because this was the hand she'd been dealt, didn't

mean she was resigned to hold onto it. She'd paved her own path forward once before. She'd do it again.

Her fingers twitched. Damn, she missed her deck of cards! Shuffling the deck had always been her way of steadying her mind and focusing her thoughts. But the Domani were not permitted any personal effects, so she was left with jittery fingers and a mind that seemed to spin in all directions.

Against the flashes of trembling that coursed through her, Eventide centred her thoughts. First, she had to learn more about her situation. Her interaction with Morales had been a start, but their discussion hadn't contained nearly enough to form a plan. All the Domani had proven to be unwilling or unable to share information with her.

But there was one person who might be capable of giving her some straight answers.

During Orientation, there had been a woman who had gasped when Caregiver Lin had mentioned that Domani who fell out of line might be terminated. This one small act was the only sliver of authentic emotion Eventide had seen aboard this ship—and it offered her hope. Perhaps Eventide wasn't the only one who could resist the transmission waves.

She'd have to be careful. Even after the painful procedure she had endured, Morales' words stuck with her, a subconscious alarm continually reminding her that defiance would come at a price.

Play the part. Bide your time.

Like hell that was going to happen!

CHAPTER FOURTEEN

Eventide
The *Inanna*

An empty floor greeted Eventide.

She had already returned to her quarters and showered off the sweat and vomit from Morales' torturous experiments. She'd also allowed herself to sleep and give her body a chance to recover from the lingering pain.

Mostly.

Her limbs still ached, and her nerves prickled as though waves of electricity were scraping against them.

When she awoke, Eventide had been surprised to discover she had slept through the night and most of the following day. She hated that she had wasted an entire day sleeping instead of working on her plan to flee, but Yunni had said her body would need to rest after the trauma of the surgery she had undergone when she'd first arrived on board, and the ongoing torture was likely only adding to that need.

Eventide still had no idea how long it would be until

the *Inanna* headed for port, and she didn't want to waste a single moment before they arrived. She surmised that her best chance at escape would have to be while the ship was docked. Her only other option would be to commandeer an escape pod, but Eventide didn't have the first clue about piloting one.

The first step in her plan was to find the gasping woman. Perhaps she would be willing to help, either with the escape or, at the very least, in providing information.

But as Eventide ventured into the corridors beyond her quarters, she found them empty, as was the rec room. There should have been dozens of Domani wandering aimlessly through the halls in the early evening, but instead, Eventide was alone.

Strange, she thought.

A pleasant smell hit Eventide's nostrils and caused her mouth to water, prompting a ferocious growl from her stomach.

She had been in so much agony after Morales' tests that she'd forgotten she hadn't eaten in days. With the smell of food wafting through the corridors of the *Inanna*, her knees grew weak, and Eventide realized where everyone had disappeared to.

The ship's dining hall was a stark departure from what Eventide was accustomed to aboard the *Eclipse*. Unlike the functional spaces she knew, this dining area seemed to embrace opulence and a bygone elegance. Candlelight cast gentle, flickering shadows across the room, revealing tables adorned with intricate settings. Rich, velvety tablecloths draped the tables, shimmering slightly as the flames danced.

The tableware was no less impressive. Polished silverware gleamed next to porcelain dishes, accented with gold trims. Elevated platters, designed to showcase the evening's dishes, awaited the fare they were to carry. Crystal wine glasses reflected the simulated candlelight that flickered around the room.

Paintings, possibly portraying past Caregivers or other important figures, adorned the walls. Thick draperies hung gracefully beside the room's tall viewports.

It all seemed wildly out of place, and didn't fit alongside the technological marvels of the rest of the *Inanna*. It was as though she'd been teleported to a medieval banquet instead of the dining hall of a spaceship.

The Domani sat with an air of expectancy, either engaging in hushed conversations or simply enjoying the ambient music—a soft orchestral piece reminiscent of Earth's classical era. This wasn't the *Eclipse*, where individuals queued to serve themselves. Here, in another display of Domani serving Domani, attendants who had ditched their usual pajama-like outfits were now impeccably dressed in white button-down shirts and black dress pants, darting gracefully among the tables.

Eventide wondered about the criteria dictating which Domani were chosen to serve, and which had the privilege of being waited upon. She couldn't help but cast envious glances at the servers' full-suited uniforms.

"I trust everything is all right?"

Eventide turned to find Caregiver Lin peering down her nose at her. However, at barely five feet tall, the woman still had to look up to meet Eventide's gaze. Lin's smooth face belied her actual age; she'd obviously undergone some sort of procedure to attempt to hide her years. While it might have worked better than Eventide cared to admit, Lin's dark brown eyes were hard, and her permanent scowl added years to her appearance. Her hair, too, was dyed to conceal its silver strands. Eventide, looking down at the top of Lin's head, couldn't help but notice the silver roots peeking through—a detail that would be hard for the Caregiver to hide for more than a week.

"You've missed every meal since Orientation," the Caregiver continued. "I was beginning to worry the doctor had been too hard on you."

Like hell you were.

Play the part. Bide your time.

For now, at least.

Eventide's muscles ached as though she had been tossed down a flight of stairs and then beaten with a metal pipe, but in order to play the part, she had to respond like everyone else in the room. She had to put up a front to convince Lin not to dig any deeper.

She caught a glimpse of the smiling faces plastered on each of the Domani—the transmission-induced, far-off looks of people being manipulated into thinking that nothing was wrong, that they were on the pleasure cruise of a lifetime until they were called upon to reside with a client.

The Earth sat outside the dining hall's floor-to-ceiling windows, a green and blue marble floating in the distance. The sight of it was enough to distract her from her current conversation, and she nearly lost her emotional restraint. No matter how many times she saw the planet this way, vibrant and full of life, she didn't believe she'd get used to its beauty. How many years had she only known the planet to be brown and lifeless? Now it hung outside of the viewport for anyone to see. There was so much more in this system that she'd never dreamt possible to explore—but she was still locked away in the prison of a space vessel.

More stuck now than she'd ever been before.

Stuck.

She couldn't remain locked away. Not in the D-Ring. Not on the *Inanna*. Not ever.

Biding her time was the last thing Eventide wanted to do. Every fiber of her being wanted nothing more than to grab Lin's face and jam it into her silk-adorned kneecap.

But she forced a sickeningly sweet grin, fought back the hate burning within, and ignored the shaking in her limbs.

"Everything is wonderful." Eventide performed the best impression of Yunni she could muster. She didn't believe in her own performance, however, and she didn't imagine for one second Lin was going to, either, but she would play the part anyhow.

If she could just be patient, she *would* leave this prison —and then she would burn it and the society that had built it to the ground.

However, Lin didn't question Eventide's newfound shift in attitude. But why would she? Correcting her mindset had been the whole point of sending Eventide back in to see Doctor Morales, hadn't it?

"Well, you must be starving, child." Lin's look melted from uneasy apprehension into concern. "Your regeneration requires nutrition. Your meals have been specifically catered for you based on the macronutrients, enzymes, and vitamins your body needs to restore itself. You don't want to go starving yourself if you're chosen to be showcased at our next stop."

The entire sentence made Eventide's head spin. *Regeneration.* She had almost managed to forget about the enhancements made to her body while she slept. The nodes stimulated her cells to build and tone her muscle. It was no wonder her limbs were so weak: they were trying to cope with the growth they'd been forced to undergo without fuel.

It was the closest thing to an explanation of anything she had received from Lin so far.

But Lin's last sentence hit Eventide like a ton of bricks. *Showcased.*

Her pulse quickened, but she dipped her head, hoping her face wouldn't reveal the panic in her chest. Who exactly would she be showcased to, and what purpose would they have for her?

She could take a quick guess.

Would this showcase be an opportunity to escape? Or would it make it harder to do so?

Instead of punching Lin in the throat, Eventide gave her another shallow nod and moved toward the tables.

There were several empty seats scattered throughout the hall, but she wasn't looking for a place to sit as much as she was looking for a person—the dark-haired, copper-skinned woman from Orientation.

Dozens of men and women with blank, empty stares conversed without a care in the world. If Eventide's hunch was right, the woman she sought wouldn't have the same hollow look in her eyes.

It didn't take Eventide long to find who she was

searching for. Seated several tables away from everyone else, the woman's attire almost seamlessly matched her skin tone and gracefully hung over her frame. This elegance was in stark contrast to the rugged expression on her face. Her dark hair had been pulled back, revealing high cheekbones and a defined jawline, and the Domani necklace that rested flat against the curve of her collarbone. A contrived grin touched her lips, but her dark eyes held weight to them, as though they were deep in thought until they met Eventide's gaze. She nodded subtly, gesturing toward the seat beside her in an obvious invitation.

"Okimi," she said, before Eventide had even sat down.

"Excuse me?" Eventide asked, not sure if she had heard correctly.

The Domani's eyes narrowed, annoyed. "My name is Okimi. Sit. I need some real company." Her smile faded with the comment, but as though realizing her error, she summoned another with a glance toward Lin to ensure the Caregiver hadn't caught the slip in her composure.

"I'm Eventide," she said sheepishly, taking the seat. "Sorry, it's just everything is so bizarre here. I'm having a hard time keeping up."

Okimi sniffed derisively. "You can say that again."

Eventide frowned, letting her own guard down as she shot daggers at Lin from across the room.

"Unless you want to be seen by the doctor again, I'd recommend planting a big smile on that face of yours."

Eventide winced, but nodded and forced herself to smile.

Okimi laughed obnoxiously. "Where are you from?"

Eventide paused, wondering how much she could trust

Okimi. What if she was a plant, told to act out by Lin to make sure Eventide's receptors were working properly? What if Okimi's job was to weed out defective Domani who still knew how to think for themselves?

Doctor Morales had told her she'd never met anyone else who was resistant to the Caregivers' transmissions, which now raised a red flag. If that were true, how likely was it for someone else on the ship to be unaffected?

But regardless of her cautiousness, Eventide couldn't pull off an escape on her own. She needed a friend, someone else on her side, and this was the best chance she had. Perhaps Okimi could give her some answers. If she wasn't willing to take a chance here, she might as well give up all hope of trusting anyone, on or off the *Inanna*.

Okimi threw her hands up defensively. "If you don't want to tell me, that's no skin off my nose. We all have a past."

"No," Eventide said. "Sorry, it's not that. It's . . . complicated."

"No judgment here. Before I came aboard, I lived in the hydrocarbon mines on Titan. About as far down the Syndicate ladder as it gets."

Morales had warned Eventide about sharing the detail she had come from a station, but she didn't see how that mattered now. Okimi could tell the Caregivers, but then what? She either had to risk being thrown out the airlock or be stuck on the *Inanna* by herself. And she'd likely already revealed enough for Okimi to blow her cover, anyway.

"I used to live on what the people here call a FLOW station." The words sounded strange coming from her own mouth. "We called it *Eclipse*."

Eventide had never felt as self-conscious as she did aboard this damned ship, and she hated it. Even among the B-Ring technicians and Admin staff, she had always held her own. But here, she was so far out of her element; it was like being a little kid at the adults' table. Even reaching out to the one person who might understand her situation caused her breath to catch in her chest.

Eventide could almost see the wheels turning in Okimi's mind as she processed the information. "That's not necessarily a bad thing. Some might say it's impossible—but unlike the rest of the zombies around here, I like to keep an open mind."

Eventide unconsciously scanned the empty faces around them. "Have you talked to anyone about why you're not acting the same way?"

Okimi looked over to where Lin stood, her arms crossed and giving the appearance of scanning the entire dining hall. Eventide could have sworn Lin had her sights solely locked on *her*.

Eventide's food arrived and she indulged eagerly. She was so hungry, she fought herself to eat with even a modicum of grace.

"We can't talk about that here," Okimi replied. "So far, all I know is, I've worked to stay under the radar. In fact . . ." She stood up abruptly, grabbing the remnants of her meal. "We shouldn't make a habit of being seen together in public. Meet me in the atrium in six hours. We'll talk more then."

Okimi put on her best placid smile as she stood and then she scuttled away.

Eventide didn't risk another glance toward Lin. The

Caregiver's eyes were burning through her. She was going to have to put on a more convincing show.

She put on her best smile, still not looking at anything in particular, and awkwardly continued with her meal. Despite meeting Okimi, she didn't want to smile; they were two rats trapped in the same maze. What she really wanted to do was cry, but those tears would have to wait until she was back in her quarters. As long as she was in the presence of the other Domani, she had to maintain the façade of being happy.

Play the part. Bide your time.

Anything else would cost Eventide her life.

CHAPTER FIFTEEN

Eventide

The *Inanna*

Eventide woke with a start. Relentless beeping invaded her senses, ripping her from the dream she'd been having of Django kissing her aboard the *Redemption*. In the dream, instead of telling him that it would never work between them, she invited him to join her on an adventure. To embrace a life they could share.

The reaction surprised her, and in her first few moments of grogginess, before she embraced the cruel reality she was in, Eventide realized how much she had meant it.

The incessant alarm penetrated her thoughts until she couldn't focus on anything else. Wiping the tiredness from her eyes, she lifted her head from the pillow and said, "All right! I'm up. Stop the alarm, please."

By chance last night, after she had returned from dinner, Eventide had discovered the ship's computer accepted voice commands in her quarters and she'd asked it to wake her in five hours.

"Open the blinds," she instructed, and the blinds responded with lightning fast speed.

Was the ship always listening?

Doctor Morales' shield of silence suddenly made so much more sense. The Caregivers weren't just spying on the MedLab; they were spying on *the entire ship*. Eventide reminded herself to be careful with what she said and how she acted, even when she believed nobody was watching.

How much had they heard of her conversation with Okimi?

She doubted what every Domani said was constantly being monitored by an actual person—that would take far more resources than she believed the Caregivers possessed —but the fact that they *could* sent a chill down her spine. She'd have to be more careful.

Rays of sunlight bounced vibrant red and gold hues off the carpeted floors as the blinds opened. The *Inanna* was getting closer to Earth, the sun seeming larger with every hour of travel. Compared to the distance the planet had appeared to be when she had first woken up aboard the craft, Eventide guessed they would arrive within a few days—if that was indeed their destination.

The ship must have traveled out further in the system, and, unconscious due to the unwanted surgeries the Caregivers had performed on her, Eventide had missed it. Yunni had told her she'd been unconscious for over a week. Part of her regretted having missed her first trip outside of Earth's orbit. However, it appeared now they were on their way back, which also meant they were likely heading further away from Django. Wherever these mines were he had been sent to, she was sure they were not on Earth.

She shrugged off all thoughts of Django and the mines, trying to spare herself the pain. She wouldn't be able to do anything for him while she was still stuck aboard the *Inanna*.

It was well after midnight as she slipped out of her quarters, and the ship was eerily quiet. Beeps echoed through the passageways, but it was nowhere near the level of background humming and creaking that she had grown accustomed to on the *Eclipse*. It should have provided her with a sense of comfort that the ship wasn't straining against the vacuum of space; that the propulsion systems weren't placing undo stress on the ship's hull; or that space debris couldn't be heard pinging against its side. She constrained her curiosity about how it all worked, keeping her mind focused on two things: meeting with Okimi and Orin's murder.

Doctor Morales had seemed confident that the Caregivers hadn't murdered Orin, but if not them, then who else could it be? That would mean the killer was still wandering the halls, and who knew whether she would become their next victim if she wasn't careful?

Her steps slowed as the realization hit her. *Could Okimi have stabbed Orin?*

Now that she thought about it, anyone brought up in a mining colony wouldn't be afraid to get their hands dirty—but blood was quite different from dirt and grime.

Did Orin do something to anger Okimi? Worse, am I walking into a trap?

Eventide gripped the silky fabric of her outfit, wishing

she had some way of defending herself if things went bad. Unsurprisingly, Eventide knew of nothing within her access that could be used as a weapon—not a stray tool, pipe, or so much as a lamp that could be picked up and carried through the halls. Another reason for the lack of guards and the Domanis' relative freedom to roam the communal areas of the ship.

If it came down to it, she would have to rely on her hand-to-hand combat training, and Eventide didn't like to admit it was her weakest acumen.

But she couldn't turn back, no matter the threat. It was just as possible that someone else was the killer and Okimi would need Eventide's help—and it wasn't as if Eventide had a lot of options.

As the doors slid open to the expansive room, a wave of humidity spilled out. A dense rainforest of plants, many of which Eventide couldn't name, canopied over a walkway that circled the space. A stone path crisscrossed the floor, cutting through a surface coated with thick black soil deep enough to allow tropical trees and other vegetation to flourish. Bright artificial lighting beamed down from above, making the room not only brighter than any place she'd ever been, but also warmer. Sweat formed on her skin and trickled down her back.

"Pretty impressive, isn't it?" Okimi stood a little further down the walkway.

There was a hum in this room that was absent across the rest of the ship. Presumably a consequence of the humidifiers and temperature controls needed to regulate the atrium to keep the place as green as it was. She could barely make out Okimi's voice from ten meters away—which explained why she had chosen this spot to meet.

The background noise would muffle the sounds of their exchange. If the ship's systems were listening, it would be hard to pick up their voices in this place.

"This is *incredible*," Eventide said, awestruck. "I've never seen anything like it!"

"Found this place my first day here," Okimi replied. "I come here after everyone's gone to bed and reflect on the stupid choices I've made in my life."

"The Caregivers don't mind that we're here after hours?" Eventide asked.

Okimi shrugged. "They never check. Everyone else is subdued enough to stick to their rooms. I've never seen anyone else out at night."

"How long have you been here? I assumed everyone at Orientation had just arrived, like me."

"Three months," Okimi answered. "They run orientation sessions once a month. I missed the first couple because the implants made me sick. Not constantly, but it seemed every time they held the bloody Orientation, I was in my room, blowing chunks."

"Three months?" Eventide echoed. "But you seemed shocked when Lin mentioned Domani would be terminated if they . . ." She paused and then relented. "If *we* fall out of line."

Okimi snorted. "Yeah. Would ya look at this place? Does it seem like the kinda place where they'd throw you out the airlock for looking at someone the wrong way? It's a freakin' *paradise*! The Caregivers have given us everything we could ever want."

"At the cost of our freedom."

Okimi shrugged. "How free are any of us?"

"How much do you know about the implants? You've figured out that you need to remain happy to stay under the Caregiver's radar."

"Where I come from, you blend in. Don't meet your quotas, you get flogged. Go over and, if you're lucky, you get a warning from the older miners. Don't heed that warning, and you'll find a knife in your back while you sleep. If the Syndicate found out we could produce more than the quota, they'd raise them the next quarter and make everyone work even harder. So, I learned that those who blend in, those who don't make waves, last the longest. I did the same when I got here. Everyone's happy, so I pretend I am too, until I get a feel for what's going on here. Along the way, I figured out those drones actually believe they're happy. Knew it had something to do with these damn nodes in the back of our necks, but I had no way of confirming that until you showed up. Too bad you don't know enough to keep your damn trap shut."

"Well, *excuse me* for trying to understand what's going on!"

"*Pfft!*" Okimi scoffed. "Trying to get yourself killed, is more like it. You rock the boat, you get tossed. If you want my advice, don't make waves."

Eventide was growing tired of that advice. "I worked hard to get where I was. I didn't sign up to be bought and sold like a piece of property."

"Well, we don't all come from a fairy-tale land, I guess. This is the Syndicate Empire—we're *all* their property. They own our mind, body, and soul, no matter what you think you're doing. Only ones who skirt the rules are pirates and mercenaries—and they're watching over their shoulders just the same. So what choice is there? When I got hauled out here, it was the best thing that could've happened to me. Better than sitting in a mining bubble on Titan, wondering if there would be enough food for us, or if the bolts would hold fast enough to keep our air supply in. Wondering if the crop yields on our little alien moon would be enough to sustain us another year. It's only a matter of time before Titan collapses altogether, but those morons will probably keep shipping kids over to work, even after it does."

Eventide wanted to argue that their freedom was worth fighting for, but her curiosity overcame her. There was too much she needed to know about existing outside *Eclipse.*

"Why did the Syndicate set up these bases if they weren't going to maintain them?"

Okimi's eyes narrowed, focusing in on Eventide as though she'd grown a second head. "Don't you know anything about the Empire?"

Despite wanting to sink back into herself, to clam up and retreat, Eventide held her ground. Conceding wasn't like her; she'd stood in front of a dozen senior technicians on the *Eclipse* and had successfully convinced them that she should be the first D-Ring citizen to enrol in the technicians program, and now, here on the *Inanna,* she felt like an intruder, an imposter, and her emotions were running wild, perpetually pushing the edges of control.

Eventide reined them in, tugging on them gently, guiding them rather than shutting them down. As long as she could keep her emotions in check, the Caregivers couldn't break her.

Eventide took a deep breath, unsure of how much she should share with someone she barely knew. But she longed for a friend and Okimi seemed to have her wits about her, at least. Yielding, she gave Okimi an overview of everything from her perspective: how the station administration had kept everything from them; how they had believed the residents on the *Eclipse* were the sole survivors of Earth's Climate Wars; how they had believed they were preparing the planet for humanity's return.

Okimi listened intently. Eventide expected her to laugh, to make fun of believing something so ridiculous, but she simply nodded along with keen interest, no judgment ever reaching her face.

"*Damn!*" Okimi exclaimed when Eventide had finished. "That's messed up!"

"The worst part is, I don't actually know *why* the station Admin hid any of it from us. They kept us in the dark. But I got out, and I want to make sure every last person there learns the truth. They deserve to know they're being exploited. And I will not be held here in yet another prison."

"Station Admin?" Okimi arched an eyebrow. "You think the commander of your station is responsible?"

Eventide blinked, not sure she understood what Okimi was getting at. "Him and his staff. They all knew there are others out here."

"I hate to break this to you, but your Admins are pawns in a much bigger game."

"What do you mean?"

"The Syndicate control *everything* in this system, including your station admin. Your commander is one man within the Syndicate machine, and he's probably being given as little choice about what goes on as you are. You think anybody *wants* to be in the position they're in?"

"The Admin were in a position to change things. I was there when they told us how the viewports worked!"

"Nobody is going to change anything, sweetheart. Those who are on the planet make the rules. The rest of us just fall in line. We make smart choices when and if they're offered to us.

"This is the one place within the Empire that allows people to escape the fate they were born into; to live among the elite. When we're delivered to the clients, we'll receive everything a Syndicate elite does: a house, good food, a warm bed. No more having to slave away in the mines, sleeping on a rock floor. No more worrying if the cage you're in will still have air in the morning."

"But you'll still be in a cage."

"Outside this, or maybe piracy, we're stuck with the lot we're born into. There's no way around that. We don't need to be brainwashed in order to know this is a good place to be. It's more of a chance than most people get."

Eventide forced a deep inhale as a tidal wave of emotion overcame her. She shouldn't have been surprised, not after everything that had happened to her over the course of the last few weeks. Of course, there were bigger forces at play, but the connection between her brain and reality was hard to align. For such a long time, the station commander had dictated the boundaries of Eventide's existence. To find out there was an entire apparatus overseeing *him* . . .

She couldn't think about that now.

"You didn't answer my question," Eventide had to learn more. "Why did the Syndicate set up bases on the planets, on the moons of Saturn and Jupiter, way into the recesses of the system where our tech can barely reach them, if they weren't going to support them?"

A glimmer of something flashed in Okimi's eye. Ridicule? Suspicion? Uncertainty? Eventide was having trouble reading emotions, but whatever it was, it disappeared as quickly as it came.

"Because the Syndicate *didn't* set them up. They took them over after Earth had been evacuated."

Okimi lifted an eyebrow, as though she couldn't believe she needed to explain something even a child probably knew, but Eventide wasn't one to shy away from questions that might make her look stupid. It was the only way to learn.

"But if Earth was uninhabitable, why did anyone stay behind at all?"

"*Almost* uninhabitable," Okimi corrected. "People could live in some places on the surface, but between irradiated farmland and nearly obliterated supply chains, there was no way of feeding them all. The wealthy had gotten used to a certain way of life. You see how well this ship is decked out, yeah? This is standard on Earth—or at least, that's what I've been told."

"You don't know for sure?" Eventide asked curiously. "Surely you must have learned about Earth cities somewhere? Seen photos?"

Okimi shook her head. "Only the holo-feed propaganda. The Syndicate like their secrets. The FLOW stations, the Domani—they're all held close to the Syndicate's chest. But they're even more secretive about what's on the planet. There are only two ways someone from the Loop gets through the planet's defenses: on this ship, or via the cargo elevators on the space docks."

Eventide had so many questions, but Okimi was taking so long to answer her original one that she thought it best to put them aside until later.

"So, why bother with the colonies? If the Syndicate didn't build them, how did they get there?"

Okimi pursed her lips in annoyance. "I told you, the colonies were *already* there. Old nations of Earth had set them up for research and exploration. During the Climate Wars, they were cut off from Earth and its resources. At first, the Syndicate's funding was welcome. The new Earth-based regime provided the funds for the colonies to mine nearby asteroids, extract ice within craters to provide water, and solidify life support systems that were barely holding together after years of neglect. They helped to stabilize the colonies that had already been spread too thin across the system."

Eventide quickly joined the dots. "They helped in order to extract the resources for themselves . . ."

Okimi nodded. "Exactly. The elite hoard the wealth and pat each other on the backs for becoming the first and only off-world empire Earth has ever known. They're happy to work their subjects to death while they reap the rewards."

"So, you've caught me up on the history," Eventide

said. "Catch me up on the present. Why is this ship so special?"

Okimi opened her mouth to answer but was interrupted by a sharp snap in the nearby foliage.

Both women whipped their heads around as a Domani man cursed under his breath and ducked behind a bush. The sound of footsteps signaled his retreat.

"*Damn!*" Okimi said. "Come on! We've got to stop him."

Eventide grabbed her arm. "There's something I haven't told you yet . . ."

"Can't it wait?"

Eventide shook her head with urgency. "Last night, I found the body of another Domani—Orin. Dead in the ship's study. I'm pretty sure he was murdered."

"*Shit,*" Okimi cursed as she surveyed the darker recesses of the atrium. "We'll talk about that later. How good are you in a fight?"

CHAPTER SIXTEEN

Django
Shackleton City Tubes

Django's arm ached from the impact with the transit car's floor, which had plateaued as a throbbing discomfort he hadn't been able to stop rubbing since Rowyn had thrown him on board.

The noise in the cavern had finally died down, leaving only the clacking of the tracks beneath them and the low rumble of the walls echoing the sound of the train's passing.

His mind hurriedly tried to piece together the wild theatrics they had overcome to board a simple transport line. The transit car rumbled down an uneven track, the jarring vibrations making Django's already unsettled stomach sway.

The car's interior was tired. Blue trim ran around the edges of the floor panels and the old plastic chairs that looked to have once been upholstered with cushioning that had worn away long ago. Rust skirted the edges of bolts that desperately tried to hold pieces in place.

Silver screws glistened in spots that had been refurbished, which meant that there had at least been some maintenance to the car in the last century or so. Whatever work had been done had been on an as-needed basis; nothing about the ride screamed that the train was used out of anything more than absolute necessity.

"Sorry," Rowyn said, noticing Django's discomfort and straightening her burgundy cuffs. "I should have given you more of a warning. This transit's part of the Resurgence's line into Asteria."

His curiosity overrode his discomfort. "What's Asteria?"

"Home base. Marvin and Wilder are there. They'll be happy to see you."

"Finally." It felt like ages since Django had been in the tunnels with them, fleeing from the assault on the transition house. To ensure their escape, Django had brought the tunnel ceiling down on the soldiers' heads. He was lucky to still be alive after that.

He was ready to see his uncle.

The Resurgence will disappoint you.

Django thought back to the deal he had made with Commander Aries. He had been tasked with finding the location of the Resurgence's hideout, learning what he could about their plans, and then reporting back to him with the details.

He still wasn't sure whether he would complete the mission. But he hadn't ruled it out yet, either.

I have to rescue Eventide. Nothing else matters more than that. If Marvin can't help me find her, Aries said he will.

"Several of these rail lines were set up when Lunar was first colonized," Rowyn continued. "After the wealthier colonists successfully terraformed their cities and moved above ground, they established transportation networks on the surface. These subsurface systems fell into disrepair over the years and were forgotten. Most of the entrances were even covered up. The Resurgence has spent the last decade restoring them; the lines we wanted to use, at least."

"But all that back there? The chairs, the rumbling, the urgency? What the hell was that all about?"

"We can't let anyone stumble across one of these trains and find us, least of all the LPF or the Front. That would undermine everything we've been working on for the past ten years.

"The squealing is the signal to get your butt in the chair. If someone sits down before it starts or after it ends, the platform won't descend. The retina scan ensures you have the right credentials to travel. Since you're unchipped, I had to override the system to grant you access. If I hadn't, it wouldn't have let us descend. If my retina didn't correspond with my chip, it wouldn't have let us descend."

Django smirked. "So, someone would have to steal both your arm and your eye to rig the system?"

"Hasn't happened so far—but if a person's desperate enough, they'll do a lot of things you'd never believe possible."

Django scratched his forearm. He wondered if he really wanted an implant that would make him a target for dismemberment.

"Don't worry." Rowyn chuckled. "If anyone cuts your arm off, the chip won't work. It's more likely they'd drug you or knock you unconscious and then drag you to the scanner."

Django swallowed. "Is *that* supposed to make me feel better?"

"Unless you prefer losing an arm."

He leaned against the side of the transit car. The train ride was smooth compared to the earlier rumblings, the once jarring vibrations now slight and strangely calming.

"So, someone would have to knock you out, use your chip and eye to unlock the platform, and then they're in?"

"Not quite. These chips hold all your vitals. We program our systems to rely on that data. The chair interfaces with my chip to know how much I weigh. If someone was holding me down, the system would recognize an error with the weight distribution. Each person on the platform has to be seated in their own chair."

"And the rumbling?"

"The rumbling disguises the noise of the train. It's more than it needs to be, but it's an effective distraction."

"Seems like a very complex system . . ."

"It has to be. We have a lot riding on Asteria. That said, the chances of someone being in that room for the exact five minutes needed to gain access are slim. The train doesn't run on a regular schedule and, as you saw, there's only a small window before those doors close and the train leaves. There's no time to mess around."

"So, we were just lucky to be there at the right time?"

"I don't believe in luck."

Unlike Eventide, Django thought. *Almost everything she does is based on luck.*

"And in case you get any stupid ideas, the system won't let you in without an escort."

Find out what you can of their plans and report back to me.

Django snorted. "Like what? Betraying my uncle?"

Rowyn folded her arms. "For starters."

The comment stopped him cold. *How close* am *I to doing just that?*

The transit car slowed. At this point, Django was so confused, he wouldn't even have been able to point Aries toward the hideout, even if he'd wanted to.

Rowyn's implied accusation stung. It didn't help that it was accurate.

"Why would I betray the one person who's stuck his neck out for me? The one person who might be willing to help me?"

Because he's not really my uncle. Because he lied to me. Because I'll do anything to get Eventide back.

Anything.

That thought made him pause. Eventide had rejected him, and still he'd do anything to save her. Why?

Rowyn stood before him now. Django wasn't blind. She'd shown more interest in him during the past few hours than Eventide ever had. Even now, she was studying him with her beautiful green eyes—more with curiosity than suspicion.

But regardless of how Eventide felt about him, she was the closest friend he'd ever had, and whether or not anything would happen between them, he'd still give his life to save hers.

"But that's just it, isn't it, Django? You know why.

You'd do anything to save that little princess of yours—even betray those close to you."

"You know nothing about me," he growled. "Don't pretend that you do."

The train door slid open, and she turned to face him. "Don't I, though? Isn't *she* the reason you keep pushing me away?"

Rowyn didn't wait for the answer. She stepped onto the train's platform.

Pushing you away?

Where had that come from?

With everything he'd dealt with the past few weeks, Django didn't think he had it in him to play whatever complicated game Rowyn was after. Still, he searched his memory for what could have gotten to her. He'd flinched when she'd physically shocked him in the transition house, a reaction she had mistaken for disdain. Then he had kicked her out of the bathroom while he was trying to change—a perfectly reasonable reaction for anyone he barely knew trying to invade his personal space. Otherwise, he wasn't sure if he'd pushed back enough. He didn't want to lead her on.

Maybe he'd said more than he realized and Rowyn had picked up on his cues.

Was he being ridiculous? Maybe Rowyn was right. But the truth was, *he* was the reason Eventide was on that ship, and he couldn't bear the thought of what that meant for her.

The sun hit his eye as he stepped off the train, and it took him a moment to orient himself.

The transit car had brought them to the surface again.

Django guessed Asteria was far from Shackleton City, but his knowledge of Lunar geography was nonexistent. How many cities dotted the Moon's surface? Past the vegetation growing upward and the squat buildings that were visible underneath, rock walls rose from the perimeter of what he could see. They had returned to the surface, but in fact, Asteria was still dozens of meters below ground, in what appeared to be the bottom of a shallow crater. At first glance, he couldn't tell what was preserving the settlement's oxygen supply or protecting it from the radiation of space above them.

It was yet another mystery about the tech of this new normal he was just going to have to get used to. Eventide would be curious about how it all worked, but as long as it did its job and kept him alive, that was good enough for him.

Django stepped out, and the city of Asteria unfolded before him in a blend of technological wonder and rugged lunar terrain. Neon signs, tinged in blues and purples, flickered above narrow alleyways where merchants peddled what he could only assume was black-market tech and food synthesized from lunar crops. Tall, slender spires pierced the lunar skyline, adorned with holographic banners, each with the same double-circle emblem as the pendant he wore.

Contrasted with the neon glows were dark metal structures that pulsated with dim, rhythmic lights. Django could see figures moving on suspended catwalks, their shadows tied to the structures they walked along and cast shadows onto the street below them.

Soldiers marched in formation up and down the streets,

executing maneuvers that Django assumed were military training exercises. His only reference for such activities came from history feeds, so while he couldn't be certain, their disciplined movement through the city bore all the hallmarks of a well-trained military platoon.

People from various walks of life seemed to traverse the street. Multi-colored fabrics adorned those who passed, their unique styles blended cybernetic enhancements that whirred and pulsed with soft lights. Animated tattoos shifted and changed on some, while holographic accessories floated around others. Unlike Shackleton, where everyone seemed to be either suspicious or desperate, each person here moved with a purpose and intent.

He took a deep breath, letting the artificially generated air fill his lungs. Breathing on the Moon's surface shouldn't have seemed as strange as it did; it wasn't as though there was any more reason to trust the oxygen levels on a space station. Still, the open space above made him queasy. What would happen if that protective barrier failed? What if the oxygen stopped pumping?

Even though the crater was vast, the surrounding cliff walls provided Django with a sense of protection, subduing the sensation of being pulled into the ether he'd experienced on the Upper Rim of Shackleton City.

"Come on, station boy!" Rowyn called out. The ire in her voice had faded and her playful smirk had returned. "You can sightsee later. We need to let Marvin know you're here, so he can call off the search."

Django hadn't known what to expect from Asteria—maybe a small cluster of regolith homes or caves carved out of Lunar's rocky terrain. He certainly hadn't expected a small city.

Albeit a fraction of the size of Shackleton, Asteria was no less impressive. There had to be hundreds, if not thousands, of people filling the well-maintained streets that crisscrossed between the buildings. Skyscrapers reached over a dozen floors tall, but, not surprisingly, didn't stretch as high as those in Shackleton City. Neon lighting, hovering vehicles, and holo-screens appeared no less advanced than even the wealthier district of Shackleton offered.

Announcements echoed on street corners from unseen speakers. Django couldn't hear much of what was being said, but he caught the words "Resurgence," "Prefect," and "Alejandro" repeatedly at several intersections.

Rowyn didn't slow down enough for him to listen to a full message, but he could still parse some of the news they relayed.

Many holo-screens displayed the image of the new Prefect, just as they had in Shackleton. But now the overwhelm had subsided, and he could focus on the screens and their projections. The Prefect was younger than Django would have expected—perhaps only five years older than himself—and handsome, almost artificially so, wearing a grey high-collared jacket with black cuffs.

He wasn't sure what the fuss was all about. This man didn't look like the intimidating warmonger that everyone had pegged him out to be. If Django had to use one word to describe the man based on his appearance alone, it would have been 'charming'. But perhaps it was his charm that made the man dangerous.

But unlike Shackleton, the tone of the broadcasts here was less optimistic. Django caught shreds of tightening spending for the colonies, missing leaders, and increased tensions. None of it resembled the celebratory anecdotes of the Prefect's achievements as presented by the Syndicate.

The news of Marvin's return, however, was a cause for celebration here. It was strange seeing Uncle Marvin's face plastered everywhere. Django had never known the man as anything but his eccentric—and often drunk—uncle, who was supposedly a retired pilot.

In Asteria, he was a hero.

No wonder Aries was so worried about Marvin. Somehow, in this hidden city, Marvin had developed a cultlike following that appeared to have only grown in number over the years he had been hiding out on the *Eclipse*.

"I was only expecting a modest hideout," Django admitted as they crossed yet another street. "How many people live here?"

"It depends on the day, but usually a hundred thousand or so."

A hundred thousand!

It was a fraction of the people who lived aboard the *Eclipse,* and Django didn't believe it would be anything but a fraction of those who called Shackleton City home, but it was a hell of a lot of people to keep quiet. It also sounded like a much bigger opposing force than Aries was expecting.

Despite the size of Asteria's population, the city didn't seem to cover a large area, and Rowyn navigated the streets efficiently. Django and Rowyn reached what appeared to be the city limits within a matter of minutes. Holo-screens buzzed above them, but Django was no longer interested in their content.

As awe-inspiring as Asteria was, he had wasted too much time already. Eventide could be anywhere in the system by now. Hell, he didn't even know how big the system *was*. How far did the Syndicate Empire stretch? On the slave ship, Wilder had mentioned Europa, one of Jupiter's moons. Had humanity really ventured out so far? And how much could the Resurgence hope to influence an empire with such a sphere of influence?

The Resurgence wants anarchy.

Asteria seemed to suggest the resistance movement was considerably more orderly than Aries cared to believe.

Rowyn stopped in front of a short building, constructed, like many of those that surrounded it, from glass and metal. The building lacked the holo-screens and colored LED lights that adorned so much of the rest of the city; the perfect hiding place for the Resurgence HQ. Nothing distinguishing, and yet hardly humble. If Rowyn hadn't stopped, Django wouldn't have looked twice at the place.

A short cement staircase rose from the sidewalk into the building. Behind the glass doors Django could make out several of the purple banners that carried the double-circle emblem he was growing more familiar with.

Toward the rear of the complex, short shrubbery and greenery grew along the building's edge before disappearing into the cliff face of the crater that surrounded the entire city. It rose several dozen feet above the building before disappearing into the black sky above. Such a cliff-side made the perfect protectorate. And Django would bet that the building extended far into the rock wall, and perhaps even provided an alternative means of escape from the city.

"What's *he* doing here?"

The commanding voice of Taku Kondo echoed from the steps above them, causing both Rowyn and Django to stop in their tracks.

CHAPTER SEVENTEEN

Django
 Asteria

Django winced as Taku's broad frame descended the stairs, his full-length leather jacket nearly dragging on each step as he descended.

Rowyn stood firm, the sunlight catching her red hair and lending her a heavenly shine. "You know Alejandro has been looking for him since the raid."

Taku's short, raven black hair, tipped with blonde, stood in spikes, his narrowed eyes and taut muscles mirroring a predator readying itself for a strike. "Looking for him and bringing him into Asteria are two different things."

"And what was I *supposed* to do? Leave him at the Velvet Underground until the Founders vote him in? Marvin's word is practically law."

"That's not how things are going to operate here." Two other men stepped up behind Taku, both with black cloth covering their faces up to their noses. Only their eyes were exposed. The double circle symbol matching the pendant around Django's neck was daubed in reflective silver on each of the masks. "Alejandro has been gone a long time. We don't throw out a decade's worth of protocol just because the man's returned from the dead."

"Are you saying we shouldn't do what he asks?"

"I'm saying we need to be more careful than he was a decade ago. We're on the Syndicate's radar now, and we're in the final stages of preparation. The Founders are in place for a reason."

"Do you think I'm stupid, Taku? Do you think I'd bring someone here without taking precautions?"

"Where has he been the past few days?" Taku stepped toward Rowyn, towering over her with a gloved finger pointed at her nose. "Last time you saw him, the SF were hauling him out of the tunnels while you and Wilder escaped. Then he shows up at the Velvet Underground a few days later? Why? Anybody else found with us would still be in a cell, if not hung with the pirates."

Django shivered as he tried to shake off images of the skeletons swinging above the Shackleton City port where the *Redemption* had docked when they first arrived on Lunar.

Regardless of the truth of the sentiment, he didn't appreciate Taku talking about him as if he wasn't there.

"If you want to ask me something." Django tilted his head to meet the man's gaze, "then ask me."

"Well?" Taku said, stepping over to Django. The man's jacket carried the sharp scent of leather and cold air, as if he had stepped out from a refrigeration unit. "Where were you?"

Django weighed his options. He knew Taku wasn't going to like the truth, but he had a feeling the Resurgence would have ways of finding out where he had been, anyway. If he was caught in a lie at this stage, he would never gain their trust. And besides, Rowyn knew he'd been taken in by the Syndicate; there was no point in denying his interaction with them.

"You're right, I *was* arrested. I was thrown in a cell somewhere in the middle of Shackleton City. The woman who piloted the ship that brought me in with Marvin—I believe her name's Mikka—she appealed to have me released."

So far, he had shared nothing but the truth.

"And why would she do that?" Taku demanded.

Django shrugged. "Maybe she felt responsible for bringing me off the station. Maybe she felt guilty that the first thing that happened to me was getting arrested."

Taku crossed his arms. "And they just let you go? No questions asked?"

Django's mouth ran dry. Taku was a hand-width taller than even Uncle Marvin, with a few less years and the sort of presence nobody could ignore. It was easy to see why he had become a leader in Marvin's absence.

But Taku was also a man whose bad side Django did not want to be on. If he started out his time here being suspected of espionage, there would be no chance of the group helping to find Eventide. At best, he'd have botched helping both Marvin and Aries. At worst, the Resurgence would send him out an airlock.

Django shrugged. "What reason do they have to keep me? I'm a nobody."

Taku didn't even blink, continuing to stare Django down, as though expecting he might reveal something more through sheer will alone. "That means dick all to the SF."

Django gritted his teeth. "What do you want me to say? That I paid off the guard? I haven't got a credit to my name. And even if I wanted to tell them something, what could I say? I know absolutely nothing!"

Taku turned his attention back to Rowyn with a huff. "You're sure you took the necessary precautions?"

"Are you questioning me?" Rowyn spat the words. "Listen, Taku . . ."

"I have no doubt in your abilities," Taku snapped back. "Just your judgment. Aries has been after the location of Asteria for years, and it just so happens that in the same week Marvin Alejandro triumphantly returns to the fold, his supposed nephew also shows up, having had a miraculous encounter with the SF. Aries doesn't exactly have a reputation for being forgiving, and he's sure as hell not known for granting favors without getting something in return.

"So that begs the question, Django—what *did* you offer Aries in return for your release?"

Django resisted the urge to swallow at the insinuation. The incredibly accurate insinuation.

"I promised nothing." It wasn't exactly a lie.

"How can you be sure you weren't followed?" Taku asked. "That you weren't tracked?"

"Rowyn made very sure I left anything Aries provided for me behind."

Taku huffed. "They could have put a tracker anywhere. In your shoe, in your underwear—"

"I watched him strip myself!" Rowyn's playful smile returned, which made Django's cheeks redden.

Rowyn's comment drew Taku's gaze, and his consternated stare softened into momentary confusion.

Rowyn took a step toward him, lifting her own finger to his chest. The man dwarfed the petite redhead, but a fire had been lit inside Rowyn, and there was no doubt who now held the upper hand. "I know you're feeling threatened by Alejandro's return, but don't you dare question my ability to do my job."

Taku pursed his lips as he calculated what to say next. "Rowyn, I would never . . ."

"You just did, dumbass! Django may be green, but if it weren't for this kid, I'd be dead! That should count for something, at least."

Taku's chest swelled as he took a deep breath, his jaw clenching tightly. He held a silence that buzzed with tension before he spoke again. "We've kept this city secret for nearly a decade. We can't get sloppy now."

"And you would know a thing or two about being sloppy, wouldn't you?"

A sharp gasp escaped Taku's lips. His teeth gritted together and his face contorted, his eyes narrowing with fury.

"You better hope he checks out. If he doesn't, the end of the Resurgence will be on your head—and I swear to the stars, I'll see it removed if that happens."

Taku spun, his jacket flowing behind him as he stormed back into the building, his two men following close behind.

His shoulders slumping, Django made eye contact with Rowyn.

"Don't worry about him," she said. "Taku's always been cautious, but he's been a total dick ever since Marvin showed up."

It's not Taku I'm worried about.

If Django betrayed Marvin, Rowyn would suffer the fallout for letting him into the compound in the first place.

"Would he really behead you?"

Rowyn's hand fluttered to her jacket, straightening the fabric with slightly trembling fingers. A grin tugged at the corners of her mouth, but it lacked the confidence of her usual wry smile. "Why? Are you planning on double-crossing us?"

She lifted an arm as though she was about to rub Django's shoulder in consolation, but pulled it back as if second-guessing the decision. Her gaze refocused over Django's shoulder before she added, "But to answer your question: beheaded, no. Executed? There's no doubt. It'd be a short walk outside Asteria's boundary. If *anyone* were to compromise the secrecy of the city, we couldn't tolerate that."

"What about Taku? What was that about him being 'sloppy?'"

Rowyn's gaze now rested fully over Django's shoulder, and he had to turn to see what she was looking at.

"That was Rowyn speaking out of turn." Marvin stood not five feet behind Django. Bags had formed under his uncle's eyes, but a faint smile appeared as Django met his eye. "I'm glad to see you're unharmed."

"My apologies, Commander Alejandro. Taku was questioning the validity of your orders."

Commander Alejandro?

"Taku is cautious, but as you know, he has his reasons.

Don't take it as a commentary on your skill. We're grateful for your talents."

Rowyn's eyes lit up momentarily, but she quickly deflated. "All the talent in the world didn't stop my team from getting caught during the Callisto raids. If you hadn't come to our rescue . . ."

"Enough, Connor, we've been through this. We're family here. We help one another out. Taku has told me you've gotten our people out of tough spots more times than he can count. You can't let one bad decision cripple you. Besides, your efforts weren't in vain. We still managed to secure a number of the Syndicate's stealth ships. And this is just the start of what's to come. Nothing we're going to do will come without risk."

Marvin turned to look at Django, though he seemed to continue talking to Rowyn. "We all make mistakes, but it's the sum of our actions that define who we are. And hopefully, that outweighs a few poor decisions along the way."

Upon entering the Resurgence headquarters, Django was struck by the stark contrast between its unassuming exterior and the buzzing hive of activity inside.

Multiple levels of stairs zigzagged above the high ceiling of the lobby, leading to vantage points that overlooked the bustling promenade below. Everywhere Django looked, Resurgence members engaged in animated discussions, their faces a mix of determination and camaraderie. The pervasive hum of activity occasionally punctuated by laughter.

The technological marvels of the base reminded Django of the Syndicate headquarters in Shackleton: holo-screens flickered with details of Syndicate strongholds, immersive projections showcased views of space docks and ports—more than Django could have imagined possible—and transparent glass walls were illuminated with schematics, codes, and real-time communication streams.

Marvin led Django and Rowyn through a warren of elevators and corridors and past a large atrium, filled with trees, grasses, and flowered bushes. Django's gaze lingered on the lush greenery. He hadn't realized until then how much he missed his work on the farms of *Eclipse*. A hollow pang coursed through his chest. Despite the occasional plant life integrated into the city infrastructure in both Shackleton and Asteria, this was the first place where the vegetation seemed to be the intention of the place rather than just an afterthought. He longed for home.

A large shaft stretched upward, opening to Lunar's surface above them, allowing natural light to descend into the depths of the base.

They passed the space far too quickly for Django's liking. The rest of the halls had the same clean and clinical feel of the Syndicate HQ; the same scent of bleach as the B-Ring.

He sighed as they walked. The familiar scent of detergent, once an annoying hallmark of the B-Ring, now carried a haunting echo of Eventide.

I don't think this could ever work.

Resolve hardened his heart.

As they ventured deeper, the tone shifted swiftly.

Vast training arenas sprawled out, revealing dedicated

rebels engaged in grueling physical training, their sweat-laden faces showcasing the sheer intensity of their routines. Adjacent rooms burst with strategy: clusters of personnel gathered, poring over vast digital walls displaying intricate maps, troop movements, and supply chain details.

They passed more men and women engaged in combat training, both hand-to-hand and with weaponry. The sound of a gunshot was one that Django would now never be able to get out of his head. Instead of fighting against an enemy, men and women lined up along one side of a long range, firing at targets set at varying distances.

Every corner of the facility reverberated with one unified message: The Resurgence was preparing for war.

"Why do they train with bullets?" Django asked as they passed. "Why doesn't the Resurgence use energy weapons?"

"Blaster charges are expensive," Marvin replied. "And rare outside of the Syndicate ranks. We have a supply, but we can forge ballistic ammunition ourselves. We have to steal energy cells, and it's never a guarantee we'll have access to them. It's best if we can save them for when we need them most."

"The station guards didn't use bullets," Django thought aloud. "Because those guards were backed by the Syndicate."

"You're catching on," Marvin said. "Speaking of which, I have something to show you later. Don't let me forget."

Django nodded. "Later? Where are you taking me now?"

"Right now, I'm taking you to your quarters. You'll have

a lot of training scheduled over the coming days, but we need to get you settled in first."

Django stopped in his tracks. "I'm not settling in anywhere until we find Eventide."

A flicker of movement caught his eye. Was Rowyn rolling her eyes? A surge of irritation welled, but he pushed it down. He had more important things to worry about.

Marvin turned, the LED lights casting cold shadows across his face. "We know where she is."

CHAPTER EIGHTEEN

Django
  Asteria

"You know where she is?" Django repeated the statement, hardly able to believe it. "Well? Where is she? What are we waiting for?"

Marvin raised a hand. "Take a breath. We *think* we know where Eventide is, and we believe she's safe, but we need to clarify a few details before we can form a plan. I have a couple of our recon specialists working on the details now."

"Well, what's taking them so long?" Django demanded.

"You have to realize, kid, the men and women here are doing us a tremendous favor putting *any* resources into finding her. Unfortunately, a single woman being sold to the Domani isn't exactly a rare occurrence and it's a distraction from our primary mission, which is reaching a crucial stage. Just remember, I care about Eventide, too; I practically watched both of you grow up. But the Loop is a lot bigger than a FLOW station. The only leverage I have is your willingness to help us. We also don't have the manpower to waste chasing after false leads. And since she's not chipped—or at least, she wasn't—it makes it that much harder for us to find her.

"The best thing you can do right now is let Rowyn show you to your quarters and get settled in. Let us handle the intel and devise a strategy. We'll know more soon, and once we do, we'll fill you in on everything."

Django's heart pounded. *We know where she is. We believe she's safe.*

For weeks, he had wondered if he'd ever see her again. Even if it wasn't confirmed, a possible lead was enough for him to cling onto with both hands. He knew he shouldn't get his hopes up, but he also knew that this could be his only chance to make right the events he had set in motion.

No, he reminded himself. *The events Benson set in motion.*

He pushed his rage for the station commander aside for the moment, but Django couldn't pretend that it had no part to play in the actions he would take. He couldn't settle the score for Benson's sins yet, but he could at least make up for his own.

"How can I help?"

A smile crossed Marvin's face. "Don't worry, there's plenty for you to do. You're key to everything, and I'll make sure recovering Eventide is a part of that. But right now, you need to rest. We'll brief you on the plan and your role in it as soon as we can."

Beside him, Rowyn laughed. "Come on, station boy. You haven't had a proper sleep in over a week."

Django opened his mouth to protest but let out a yawn

instead. Rowyn was right; he'd been on the move since Celeste's wedding, and he hadn't had a restful sleep since.

Begrudgingly, Django followed Rowyn through the Resurgence facility, trailing another endless series of halls. They entered what was clearly a dormitory for rebels on active duty, comprised of a dozen rooms filled with six beds each, all made with identical dark gray sheets.

Django continued to mull over his uncle's words. The Resurgence had found Eventide. *Finally, a breakthrough.*

Rowyn was quiet, just as she had been since their earlier encounter with Taku. No, come to think of it, since *their* argument earlier.

Django was still puzzled by what she had meant. He hadn't been pushing Rowyn away; if anything, he felt guilty by how close he'd let her get. He had so much to process. How could she expect him to let her in?

Regardless, Taku shouldn't have treated her the way he had. Rowyn had stuck her neck out for him the entire day. How long had she hung out in that dive bar, waiting for him? And instead of being commended, she'd been questioned and accused of negligence. Even Uncle Marvin had been abrupt with her.

Taku hadn't exactly been wrong, but it hadn't been Rowyn's fault. What was she going to do? Ignore Marvin's orders? Rowyn had shown him nothing but kindness since they'd met and she'd saved his butt more than once.

"Thank you for your help, Rowyn," Django said, forcing a smile. "I appreciate everything you've done. And seriously, I don't know what Taku's problem is."

Rowyn nodded. "Don't mention it. I meant what I said

—you saved my life. What was I going to do? Besides, we've all got our demons to battle. Taku's no different."

Django nodded. "Still, it's no excuse to act like an asshole."

"Sometimes it is. Trauma looks for ways to prevent the past from repeating itself. You seem to be a grade A example of that."

"What are you talking about?" Django crossed his arms defensively. "I haven't been an asshole!"

"Easy, station boy. I was talking about earlier. This Eventide—she's obviously your girlfriend. I heard you talking to Marvin about her before. You lost your whole family, and now you're petrified you'll lose her, too."

"She's not my girlfriend," he muttered, sitting on the nearest bed and not caring whether it was actually his or not. "She's just a friend."

Rowyn's demeanor softened as she sat on the bed beside him. "I don't believe you. You've been so worked up about her ever since we met. You act like you're responsible for her well-being."

Django shook his head. "I *am* responsible. Eventide followed me off the station. Not Marvin, not the idea of someplace better . . . *Me*. She trusted me, and I let her down. We had no idea where we were going. We thought we were headed for Earth."

Rowyn smirked, but the pain didn't leave her eyes. "Yeah, I seem to remember you thinking that when we first met."

"Not even five minutes of being on Lunar and Eventide and I were both arrested and sold. She had her whole life planned, and between Benson trying to control us and me pulling her off the station, I ruined everything. It was never supposed to be like this. It wasn't ever going to be what I wanted, but it was never supposed to be . . . this!"

"It doesn't sound like she's someone you see as just a friend . . ."

"Evie's been my best friend for as long as I can remember—and yeah, I've had feelings for her ever since we were kids. I don't even know why I'm fighting so hard to find her. I made a move, and she rejected me."

"It's not really the rejection that getting to you, though, is it? It's because she was the one last thread of normalcy you had left."

Django studied Rowyn's green eyes. There was a wisdom behind them that betrayed her age.

"And you're definitely *not* an asshole!" she said reassuringly. "Don't make the mistake of thinking I can't read people. You might be naïve, so you're prone to making mistakes along the way, but you want to do the right thing. You think that just because she doesn't want to get in your pants, you're not important to her? That she isn't worth rescuing? Damn it, Django, pull your head out of your ass."

Django blinked, the words hanging in the air like an unexpected chill. Silence filled the space around him as he struggled to form a response.

Rowyn placed a hand on Django's shoulder, her fingers digging into his flesh. "You think a girl wants someone moping around feeling sorry for themselves? Dude, *nobody* wants that!"

Her words struck home, resonating in the caverns of his mind. He let them swirl, brushing against his own self-doubt and guilt. It was a bitter pill to swallow, to think he had been wallowing in self-pity while his friend was out there somewhere, potentially in danger.

Django knew Eventide wouldn't give up easily; she was the strongest person he knew. But he couldn't leave her to fend for herself, either. Dwelling on his past, on his failures, was doing her a disservice. The guilt, the fear, the uncertainty—it was all-consuming, leaving no room for action. But he had to act. To move forward and grab this new universe he found himself in by the horns.

Rowyn was right: he *had* to stop blaming himself. His friend was out there, and she needed him.

Taking a deep breath, Django nodded; the weight of his guilt lifting, replaced by a renewed sense of determination. "I've never been good at waiting."

"Well, unless you have the means to scan the system for her, I suggest you wait for Alejandro to pull through. He's put a lot of resources into this—more than most are happy with. We need to be committed to monitoring the Syndicate, not searching for one person, but he's convinced the rest of the leadership that bringing you on board will be worth the payoff."

Django knew Rowyn was right: he had to trust in Marvin. He just hoped they would find Eventide before it was too late.

"That must have taken some convincing. I'm a farmer from a backwards station that didn't even know the Syndicate existed a month ago. I still don't understand how I can be this valuable."

Rowyn smirked. "You'll understand soon enough, but for now, I agree with Marvin. If you want to be of any use, you need to get some rest."

"What's *he* doing here?" Taku growled.

Django jumped. He hadn't even seen the Resurgence soldier walk into the room.

"We've been through this, Taku," Rowyn responded, jumping to Django's defense. "Alejandro assigned him to these quarters. This is the only room with a spare bed."

"There isn't a spare bed in this room." Taku's eyes darkened, their intensity burning. "Marvin might be back in charge, but there are a couple things he's going to have to get up to speed on."

"Taku, be reasonable. It's been two years. We're short on room, and having an empty bunk just doesn't . . ."

"I wasn't asking for your opinion. The bed stays empty. And when it does get filled, it will be by someone more deserving than this half-wit." Taku nodded toward Django. "He's already got our recon unit trying to find his stupid girlfriend. He might be from a FLOW station, but he's got to realize this isn't a playground."

Django's blood boiled. He clenched his fists and took a step forward, but Rowyn's hand landed on his chest, holding him back. The attempt earned a chuckle from Taku, which did nothing to lessen Django's anger.

"At least the person he's after is still out there," Rowyn stated. "At least the resources he's using are on someone who can still be helped. An empty bed isn't helping anyone, Taku."

Fire burned behind Taku's eyes and Django braced himself, unsure of what the man might do. What did he do to tick this guy off? Taku had been distant at the transition house, but he hadn't been this hostile. Django had stayed behind to save Rowyn. He'd joined their movement. Wasn't that enough?

Django tried to steady his heart rate, but the adrenaline still pumped through his veins. Whatever Taku's issue was, he'd rather not wake to find a dagger in his side.

"It's all right." Django tried to keep the quiver from his voice. He was overtired, but that didn't mean he was ready to break down. "I'll find somewhere else to sleep."

He pushed past Rowyn's arm and past Taku. Django was half-expecting the rebel to take a swing at him as he passed, but Taku simply followed Django with his icy glare.

Rowyn was by his side before Django realized she had followed him. They walked in silence for a few moments, as he tried to calm his thoughts.

It was hard to keep the quaking from his limbs. He wasn't sure why Taku intimidated him so much. Perhaps it was because of the hatred in the man's eyes; the determination that nestled there to make sure Django knew he wasn't welcome.

Taku's expression reminded him of Commander Benson, as though he were a fly waiting to be swatted. The stare carried such disdain that it left a sickly feeling on his skin.

"There are no other beds, Django," Rowyn said softly, placing a hand on his shoulder. "We're filled to capacity."

"I'll manage. I'll sleep in the hall if I have to, though I don't doubt Marvin will have a trick or two up his sleeve. He always did on the station, at least."

He'd sleep on the floor if he had to.

Rowyn was quiet for a few moments, but then nodded,

her playful smile returning. "You might end up sleeping in the cafeteria, though."

Django allowed himself a grin. "Well, why didn't you say so? Easy access to midnight snacks."

Rowyn let a smile touch her lips, but her face was still marred with concern.

"Listen," Django continued, "I'll take that over getting shanked in the middle of the night by your friend there. But if I'm going to leave it empty, I would at least like to know what Taku's deal is with that bed. It didn't sound like it was just because he doesn't like me—though that did come through loud and clear."

"It's complicated," Rowyn replied. "Like I said earlier, Taku has his reasons for not trusting you."

"Care to fill me in?"

"Some other time, maybe. Though, it's not really my story to tell."

Django shook his head. "Fair enough. But he could at least work on being less of an asshole."

"Taku's right about one thing: Alejandro has been gone a long time. The Resurgence has grown beyond anything he could ever have expected in eight years. When he formed this group, they were just a dozen rebels hiding out in Asteria's abandoned buildings. Taku had a lot to do with growing the Resurgence's operations when Alejandro left. You have to remember, everyone thought he was dead."

"In the *Infinity* explosion."

"You know about that?" Rowyn asked, evidently surprised.

Django nodded. "Marvin told me enough."

"Everything after that got even harder. I don't know whether Alejandro's clued into that yet."

"Harder? How so?"

"With one-twelfth of the Earth's resources knocked out, the Syndicate cut *our* resources and began syphoning off our food to fill their pantries. On top of that, *Infinity* was the one place that grew a specific strain of Corielus seed that combatted Lunar sickness. Once that supply was knocked out, the disease ran rampant through the Tubes. Things were bad before, but the people who didn't have the luxury of living on the surface no longer stood a chance.

"The Resurgence could have died out after your uncle went missing. Taku was just a young soldier back then, conscripted by the Syndicate and witness to some of the worst atrocities the regime committed. Alejandro had given him hope things could be different; that the Loop could be run without terror and without the widespread inequality between Earth and elsewhere. He used your uncle's death to inspire others. The great Marvin Alejandro had given his life trying to make the Loop a better place. Taku made him a martyr. You saw the statues out there? The plaques? The holograph feeds? That was all Taku's doing. It took a few years, but eventually, the followers came in droves. It was almost too much for him to handle."

Django nodded, catching on. "And now Marvin's returned, not knowing anything about the hero he's become. The world passed him by for eight years, and he's trying to pick up where he left off. Trying to take over a movement built on the backs of Taku and the other surviving members."

"Exactly," Rowyn said. "And instead of working together, him and Taku are butting heads."

"Do you agree with Taku?" Django asked. "About finding Eventide, I mean. Do you think it's a waste of resources?"

"Honestly? Yes. There are a lot worse places to be than on a courtesan ship."

"But isn't she going to be sold for sex? Evie would never agree to that."

"You think she wouldn't be raped in a prison cell? Or in the mines? Nasty shit happens out on the Loop, station boy."

"That doesn't mean we should just let it continue."

"Of course not. Look around you. Everyone here is ready to lay down their life for that cause. But in order to stop it, we need to fix the system. Change the entire paradigm. Until that happens, going after one person doesn't make sense. Finding her isn't going to make a difference."

"It will make a difference to her—and to me. But that doesn't mean we can't do both. You were right about one thing. It's time I step up and pull my head out of my ass."

CHAPTER NINETEEN

Mikka

The *Chimera*

Mikka had done worse things to get a date, though it hadn't exactly been a date she'd been after.

She rolled Abigail's baton between her hands for what seemed like hours, deliberating what to do when the guard came to retrieve her. Mikka expected that her dinner plans were the least of her worries; Monroe, though aggravating, wouldn't attempt anything as bold as poisoning her during dinner, though she would probably reconsider after learning Mikka had pulled the wool over her eyes.

She had led the pirate on, and Mikka was sure Abigail was expecting something more than a bite to eat.

Mikka paced her room, twisting her fingers through her hair in. 2100 hours was an obscenely late hour to make someone wait for dinner, and by the time the hour was upon her, Mikka's stomach was protesting audibly while she quietly considered what lengths she would go to in order to get a satisfactory meal.

Her room on board the *Chimera* was incredibly plain. A single digital display projected the time above the door to her room, but otherwise, there was nothing interesting about it. The bed was comfortable enough, and the walls were made of glossy white institutional paneling with spaces void of holo-screens.

At 2100 hours precisely, the door slid open and two female pirates shouldered their way into her quarters. There was no act of rigidity, as Mikka would have expected from Syndicate guards; these weren't military personnel. The *Chimera*'s crew were merely men and women who had thrown their lot in with Abigail on her crazed quest for revolution.

"The captain has requested your presence on the bridge," one of the guards with rich taupe skin barked in a thick accent. Her speech pattern suggested the pirate was from Europa, Saturn's moon composed mainly of ice and water. Europa's vast oceanic composition meant it housed most of the water supply for much of the outer system.

Most of Europa's residents never left the moon's surface, so it was rare to come across someone who called it home. The moon's isolation left its residents with accents consisting of a mismatch of the remnants of humanity that had first settled there. Centuries of time had allowed it to evolve into its own speech pattern. Mikka sometimes wondered if most Europans even realized they were under the domain of the system-wide Syndicate Empire; that, despite the harsh conditions they lived under each and every day, their natural resources were providing wealth for a world other than their own.

"The bridge? I thought I was joining her for dinner?"

"There's been a change of plans." The second guard's voice held a gruffness to it, textured by an accent Mikka found much harder to place. This woman was built like a miner, strong and sturdy, with broad shoulders that strained against the fabric of her fatigues. Her hair and skin bore the same copper hue, both equally rough as if weathered by the Sun on a moon where the UV protection wasn't as strong as it should have been. The shirt she wore stopped high above her belly button, revealing a taut stomach sculpted by hard work and dedication. A stark scar cut across her abs: a harsh, straight line reminiscent of the work of a cold blade.

Was it from surgery? Or a fight?

"Best not to keep her waiting." The guard gestured to the door and stepped out, while the second woman held back to follow.

The guards' watchful eyes weighed on her, boring into Mikka's back. Oddly, it bothered her more that she was being stood up at the last minute—mainly because she was starving. Her stomach rumbled insistently, a distracting underscore to her thoughts.

"What's your name, pirate?" Mikka asked the Europan leading the way. The pirate's hair was long and silver, nearly reaching to her waist, and it flowed like the oceans of her homeworld.

"My name is Bri'mnay," the Europan replied absently. "But everyone calls me Bree."

"Have you served Monroe for long?"

Bree shook her head. "We were all recruited by the Resurgence. Some of us are pirates—or *were*, at least. Most of us were looking to channel our dissatisfaction at how the Syndicate's running things."

It was the most any of the *Chimera's* crew had been willing to speak to Mikka since she boarded, and she didn't want to waste the opportunity, but how much could she learn before she started pushing too far?

Only one way to find out.

Mikka glanced at the guard with a casual tilt of her head. "Are there many Syndicate dissenters on Europa?"

Bree looked to her companion over her shoulder before answering, lowering her voice as if the very walls might be listening. "The numbers . . . They're growing," she revealed. Her gaze held a hint of caution. "But it's a slow, careful process." She paused, a shadow passing over her face. "We can't risk causing too much of a fuss. The Syndicate will only respond with violence."

"They attacked your colony? On Europa?" There were so many raids over the years that Mikka struggled to keep track of them all.

Bree scoffed. "Those who raise waves go missing. Their families go missing—either shipped to the mines or killed and their fisheries taken and sold, usually to a bastard who has never even seen Europa's shores. The money from the sale goes back into Syndicate coffers, and then workers are hired under vulturous contracts so the rich can profit."

Mikka nodded. Sadly, it was an all too familiar story.

"So, now you're working to replace that system? One where the Resurgence calls the shots?"

"We fight to govern ourselves." Bree's eyes grew distant. "Or at least, we will, once the fear of retribution diminishes."

Was that what the Resurgence was working toward? Not replacing the Empire with a new, cohesive centralized government, but with each planet governing itself?

"How will that work?" Mikka couldn't help but ask. "The system's resources are so integrated, if you pull out one cog, the entire machine will implode."

The Resurgence seeks lawlessness. Anarchy. That's what Aries had told her. Was this what he meant?

"The Resurgence . . ."

"Bree! *Enough!*" the guard behind Mikka barked. "You've told her too much already. Monroe instructed us not to discuss any Resurgence operations with her."

Bree's eyes popped out at the rebuke, but she quickly composed herself, muttering something that sounded like a half-curse, half-apology.

"If you have questions," the gruff pirate continued, "you ask Monroe."

"And what's your name, pirate?" The term didn't seem to fit anymore, but it was a hard one to shake for anyone serving under Monroe's command.

"My name doesn't matter," the guard rebutted. "No more talking."

Mikka bristled, the heat of indignation flaring in her cheeks. Her muscles tensed and a retort form on the tip of her tongue, but after a moment, she repressed the response.

The door to the bridge slid open. Mikka's heart slammed into her ribcage as she took in the sight of Marvin Alejandro standing in the center of the room. For a split second, hope surged within her. *We must be docked on Lunar!* Her breath hitched as she stepped closer, scrutinizing his figure. But then, like a deflating balloon, her enthusiasm waned. Marvin was noticeably shorter than his real height and partially transparent—an illusion, a hologram.

Mikka recalled the tired man who had boarded her ship; the man who had narrowly escaped death. A man who had spent eight years out of the Loop.

She studied the hologram, squinting to catch every detail. The man she remembered was sallow, pallid; a ghost of a man haunted by the past. But this figure was different. As her eyes traced the contours of his face, she noticed the change in color: the once pallid skin had a richer, warmer tone now and the cheeks that had hollowed out from years of malnutrition had gradually begun to fill.

His voice had an assuredness to it, a commanding presence that echoed around the room. His stance was unwavering, meeting each person's gaze without flinching. He held an air of authority that was new, a stark contrast to the hesitant man she had seen weeks ago. This man was a leader; someone who knew there were people looking to him for direction. It was as if he had found a renewed sense of purpose.

Mikka quickly scanned the bridge, hoping to find a clue as to the *Chimera's* present position, but all viewports had been clamped shut and any panels offering useful information had been set to standby. Abigail stood central to the bridge, facing away from Mikka and toward the very high-definition holo-projection of Alejandro.

"He'll be undergoing the procedure once he's settled in and the Founders have given their final approval," Marvin said as Mikka stepped onto the bridge. "Once they give the green light, we'll launch the Alpha mission against the dock."

Dock.

The word was enough to send Mikka's thoughts into a spiral. Her heart raced as comprehension flooded through her. She knew what was coming; why she had been brought here against her wishes.

"He's too fresh off the FLOW to be pushed into this," Abigail said. "I've told you, force this play too fast and he'll do something stupid. Give this plan of yours more time to breathe. Everything Zee has foreseen relies on him."

The FLOW? Was Abigail talking about Django? What sort of mess had Marvin roped the kid into?

"If we wait too long, the Prefect will have time to gain support. We need to start the destabilization process now."

The nameless guard cleared her throat and Abigail whipped around to see their party enter.

"Ah, wonderful! Marvin, I believe you've been acquainted with my dish of a guest."

Marvin's hologram turned to face Mikka with a smile. "Yes, of course. I apologize. I had to run before properly thanking you for delivering me off the *Eclipse.*"

"No apologies needed," Mikka said hesitantly. "But I wasn't aware of your history then."

Marvin's face saddened for a moment. "Ah, I see. Well, Ms. Jenax, I'm sure you can appreciate when a person does what is necessary in order to survive. I hope you, of all people, can understand that our past doesn't define our present; that we hope our past mistakes won't define our future legacy."

It wasn't an accusation toward her; it was a plea for

himself—a seemingly genuine desire to cast himself in a better light—but his words still cut her deeply.

How many of Earth's past atrocities had been committed with a genuine desire to do good? How many times have the mistakes of the powerful hurt the most vulnerable?

"It takes more than goodwill to right our past wrongs," Mikka replied. "And I'm afraid only the histories can determine how we are remembered."

"Well stated," Marvin acknowledged with a nod. He turned his gaze back to Monroe. "Have you let your guest know of my inquiry?"

Abigail smirked. "I thought I'd let you have the honor."

Marvin inhaled apprehensively. "Very well." He clasped his hands behind his back, pacing within the confines of wherever he was located. On the holo, however, it appeared as though he was walking in place, the camera following his stride. "I realize this might be a sensitive topic, Mikka, but I need your help."

Mikka braced herself for what she knew in her heart was coming.

"We are planning a mission that could determine whether a challenge to the Syndicate's authority will succeed or fail. We want to cut off the supply chain to Earth. If the Empire can't get resources to the surface, it will slow their efforts and afford us a fighting chance."

She didn't wait to hear his request. Mikka crossed her arms and steeled her voice. "You want me to help you infiltrate a space dock."

"You're the only person who's ever got close to taking one on."

"And I failed."

"Yes, but you can tell us where you went wrong. You can ensure we don't make the same mistakes."

The heist at Space Dock Nineteen was part of a past Mikka so desperately wanted to leave behind, but lately didn't seem able to avoid. There was no way in hell she was going to be involved whatsoever in any plan involving the docks. She'd made that mistake once—never again.

"You've got the wrong woman."

CHAPTER TWENTY

Jax Luana

Kraken's Fury — Space Dock Nineteen

Eight years ago

Guards. There are way *too many guards.*

Space Dock Nineteen had far more of a protective detail than Jax Luana had expected. Far more than should have been needed for a small, unassuming station tethered to Earth in the middle of the Pacific Ocean.

Jax monitored the guards uneasily, but the patrols were far from her most pressing concern. They urgently needed to override the encrypted security metrics safeguarding the dock's hold. Lex Martinez had been working on gaining access ever since they'd docked and, infuriatingly, had been hitting one firewall after another.

Lex cursed from behind his workstation, slapping the side of his datapad in frustration. "I can't do this from here."

"What do you mean?" Jax snapped back. Their entire plan centred around Lex staying on board the ship with her. Jax's role was to guide the crew, while Lex would be the key to unlock whatever doors and access panels were needed to get them safely there and back. It was bad enough that Jax was going to have to deal with guards boarding their ship; if Lex was on the dock with the others, it left a vital sector of their plan exposed.

"I mean, their systems have integrated protocols to prevent this exact scenario from happening. It's deeply coded. I don't even know if most hackers would have caught this if they were already this deep. It's meant to catch us off guard and sound the alarm if it's breached from anywhere but an internal connection. I can unlock Level One and Level Two areas, but if you don't want all hell to rain down on our team, I've got to get off the ship. Their security is displaying a false wall, tempting hackers to penetrate its defense, but it's a decoy routed through the circuits. If I'm not directly connected to the dock's internal system, this whole thing goes boom."

"Literally or figuratively?"

"Does it matter?" Lex tugged at his earlobe, a nervous habit he'd developed. "Boom means boom. We're thousands of kilometers from help—if there was anyone to help us. You know I've always got your back, Captain, but we've only got one shot at this—and it's not a good one. If you want any of us to get out of here alive, you either have to trust me or call the whole thing off."

Jax nodded. She looked around at each of her crew, their faces a testament to the trials they had overcome together. Lex, with his unwavering focus on his screens. Julia, her eyes scanning the room, missing nothing. Each member of her crew was the best at what they did, and Jax knew it. She had assembled this team, devised their plan, and she had faith that they would execute it flawlessly.

Most importantly, Jax believed this was going to be the payoff that would set their lives in a different direction. No more shit jobs, raiding transport ships flying between planets. They could distribute the credits from the haul and improve life for thousands in the Tubes.

A lot of people saw pirates as selfish. In a lot of cases, many were, but many more were just trying to make ends meet any way they could. But Jax? Every mission she embarked upon had one goal in mind: to make a difference.

The potential bounty of their haul was tantalizing. Better gear for Kenzo, advanced tech for Lex to work with, and improved living conditions for the residents of the Tubes. Maybe even enough to transfer to the outer colonies. With each image that flickered through her mind, the importance of this one single haul was evident. And she was set on making sure it happened.

"Fine," she said. "I assume you've already found a port to make it happen?"

Lex's lip quivered, but he bit back whatever it was he wanted to say. "I have."

Jax didn't question him about whatever protestation he was holding back. If she had, would she have changed the plan? Would she have changed course?

As the years went by, she would have liked to think that she would have heeded the advice of the smartest man on her team, but deep down, in the recesses of her mind that she never allowed herself to explore, no matter what Lex would have told her in that moment, she knew she wouldn't have changed a damned thing.

"Good," she replied instead. "Prep what you need. We'll be docking within the hour."

The docking bay access port unlocked as four guards entered the ship, each grasping a military grade blaster that was years ahead of the standard issue 117s. Jax started and mentally checked herself before she reached for her own weapons. It was a reflex that had kept her alive during so many past encounters. The crew's fingers twitched with the same anticipation.

Her heart tripped as the dock crew marched aboard, faces hidden behind graphite gray helmets. The information triggered a jolt of surprise. Prior to their arrival, she hadn't considered being boarded as a possibility. Jax ran through the standard protocols at each port she had ever docked at in her mind. Not one had a boarding protocol unless there was an issue found upon entry. This was a new game entirely.

"Is there a problem?" she asked instinctively.

Unlike Syndicate guards in other jurisdictions, the uniforms here were a cold graphite gray, complete with helmets and darkened visors that covered their faces, masking their genders, ethnicities, and identities.

"*Plan C.*" Julia's voice broke through the silence of her headset, her words piercing the tense silence. The entire team was on standby, waiting for the signal that it was safe to disembark onto the dock.

Jax breathed a sigh of relief that they hadn't jumped straight to Plan E. That involved Kenzo's plan to attack the guards and take them down. She wasn't even sure if they would even be able to take these four guards out with their advanced tech suits, never mind doing so undetected.

"Please hand over the item in question." The lead guard ordered, hand outstretched as though Jax might reach out and drop it into his palm.

"*No, wait,*" Lex chimed over the channel. "*I've got a plan.*"

"*Lex, this is no time to improvise.*" The grit in Julia's voice came through in her transmission. "*Stick to the plan.*"

"*Captain, if you can stall them for thirty seconds, I promise it'll be worth it. If it isn't, they'll be none the wiser and we'll carry on with Plan C as agreed.*"

Jax smiled at the guards. "Give me thirty seconds."

It was as close as she could get to signaling the crew without alerting the helmets that there was another plot unfolding.

Jax moved back through the ship, with the group of four guards following closely behind, weapons in hand. Their blasters were the same graphite gray as their uniforms; red LED lighting along the edges of the weapon was the only flash of color on them. They were nothing like any small arms Jax had ever come across.

"*Are there more waiting outside?*" Kenzo asked.

Jax could tell he was getting impatient, but she knew the man would hold back until the okay was given to move.

"*Four more at the ready, right outside the cargo hold.*" Butterfly's normally collected demeanor cracked in a quiver of uncertainty. "*Guys, I think we should drop the package and take off. We're in over our heads.*"

"I knew this was something we should hand over to the

authorities," Jax said to the guards as she continued through the ship, doing her best to ignore the chatter in her ear. "Dark matter wasn't something we wanted to mess with."

"Just get the item, ma'am." The guard's arm extended, their graphite-gloved hand outstretched toward Jax. The movement was mechanical, devoid of warmth or sympathy, as cold and unyielding as their voice through their helmet's synthesizer. "Once we have it, we'll ask you to scrub your ship's navigation history of your arrival here, including all routes and time stamps. After that, we'll let you be on your way."

Jax stopped, thrown by a second snag that went against what she had expected. "You're not going to let us know if it's really dark matter? I'd love to know whether our source was reliable."

"That won't be necessary, ma'am. You can patch through details of the merchant on your way. We'll take care of the rest."

Jax couldn't even tell which of the boarding party was speaking. The instructions were being amplified between them, dissociating any one person from the others.

I'd love to get my hands on one of those suits . . .

"Right this way." Jax led the guards to the recesses of the cargo hold. The bay was empty, in anticipation of being filled with stolen xenon.

Embedded in the far bulkhead was a hidden containment module that could be used as a safe for small, valuable cargo. Jax waved her arm in front of the panel and several clicks signaled the locking mechanism releasing. On their way to the dock, she had removed the item from beneath her captain's chair and stashed it in the safe. Even though the capsule was harmless, Jax still went to the trouble of making it appear as though she believed it was deadly. Of course, if it *had* contained dark matter, its gravitational effects on ordinary matter would be profound. A case the size of her palm held the capsule suspended in an anti-gravity chamber, hovering in the center of the space that was barely thirty square centimeters.

Jax reached in and removed the case. "Here it is," she said. "This is what we came here for. We should be about ready to go?"

The question was for Lex. If the crew didn't do some-thing now, the mission was over, and they had likely blown their one chance at a heist on Space Dock Nineteen. They would never get another chance to dock here, especially once the Syndicate realized the *Fury* had delivered a capsule of low-grade uranium. Not worthless, but hardly valuable. Radioactive, but not the prize that dark matter would be—and not worth the time of the black ops base.

The nearest guard reached out, his armored hand clamping down on the case Jax held and causing her to jump in surprise.

"Kill them," the guard said.

Jax nearly choked. "I'm sorry, what?"

The guards remained silent as their grips tightened on the weapons they were now aiming at the present crew. Their graphite weapons beeped and flashed three red bars.

Blaster fire erupted in the *Fury*'s cargo bay. Jax dropped to her knees, snatching her own SC-117 pistol from its holster on her hip as she rolled behind an empty crate that had been stacked beside the nearest bulkhead.

Kenzo and Butterfly came charging in, weapons in hand, ready to fire . . .

But they stopped in their tracks.

Something was wrong.

The four guards stood frozen in place, their own weapons still pulsing red, suspended in midair as though time had stopped. The guard closest to Kenzo had a few scorch marks on their body armor from where Jax's bolts had found their mark, but otherwise, the guard seemed unharmed.

It was like Jax had been caught in a dream. If Butterfly and Kenzo hadn't had the same confused looks on their faces, Jax would have questioned whether she was actually dead.

"What the hell is going on?" Kenzo swore. "We just about got our asses kicked!"

"*I've hacked their suits,*" Lex said over comms. "*I don't know how long I can hold them in place, so it'd be best if we get moving.*"

"Are they aware of what's happening?" Butterfly asked, waving a gloved hand in front of one of their visors.

"*To be honest, haven't got a clue.*"

"Can we take the suits?" Jax asked. Donning them would help the crew blend in a little longer. "I'd really love to add these to our haul."

"*Negative,*" Lex replied. "*They are locked to their user through both their chips and bio-signatures. Even if we kill the wearer, I don't know what the result would be if you put one on. Best case, it would alert the rest of the dock. Worst case, it'll kill you.*"

"All right then," Jax said. "Everyone leave the suits alone. What about the four stationed outside the airlock?"

"Immobilized as well, but I wasn't able to stop any others. Once the team is past the docking bay, we'll have to avoid any other guards we come across."

"Understood. Lex, find an access panel inside the dock and patch the surveillance footage to the *Fury*. I'll steer the rest of you through the facility."

It took no time for Lex to plug his workstation into a panel in the space dock entrance. Once he gave the all clear, the crew rushed through the airlock to the loading bay with almost no effort. The lack of security after squaring off against the initial escort was surprising.

No one was expecting this. Those guards were the dock's only line of defense.

Ironically, the conspicuous lack of personnel and the high-level security measures that surrounded the classified cargo could be attributed to the dock's covert status. Space Dock Nineteen was an impenetrable fortress. From a security perspective, the fewer number of people that worked there, the fewer leaks there would be. All protocols had been focused on stopping anyone from getting this far.

Jax watched via holo-screen as the team reached the main cargo doors.

"This is the moment of truth," Lex said over comms. *"Entering the credentials now."*

The bay doors opened and Jax caught her breath, mesmerized by the dozens of crates of xenon sat unguarded inside. Just as she'd imagined, but hadn't dared to hope.

"The room is clear, Captain." The awe in Lex's voice suggested he was just as surprised as she was.

Each crew member unfurled their foldable wheel sets. Artificially guided, the crew would need to slide each crate onto the device and program it to roll back to the ship—which could only be accomplished with an empty hallway.

"Lex, can you keep the path to the *Fury* sealed until the package is secure?" Jax asked.

"*Confirmed. Doors are sealed.*"

As long as the crew hurried, they would have the xenon loaded and be on their way before anyone was the wiser. There was the unfortunate problem of what to do with the debilitated guards, but Jax would deal with that once everyone returned to the ship.

"*Captain.*" The trepidation in Kenzo's voice was palatable through Jax's headset. "*We've got a problem.*"

Over the surveillance feed, the lights dimmed, followed by a flashing red warning that erupted across the panels throughout the entire dock.

Through the screen, Jax watched as guards who had been standing idle at their posts jumped into action.

"Shit!" Jax cursed. "Lex, how long can you keep those doors closed?"

"*I don't know, Captain. They know we're in the system now and they're working real hard to shut me out. I'd say five minutes—if we're lucky.*"

That wasn't nearly enough time.

Jax issued the command. "Abort! *Abort!*"

They might lose the xenon, but hopefully, the crew could still get out.

"*Captain,*" Lex said, his voice shaking, trying to control his panic. "*If they kick me off the system before the team gets back, you're not going to be able to disengage the locking clamps. You've got to leave. Now."*

"There's no way in hell I'm leaving without the rest of the crew, Lex."

"There's no way they're making it back in time. The least I can do is save your life."

"Don't be stupid! Keep working at it," Jax implored, but she could feel Lex shaking his head. *Stubborn ass!*

"Lex, I am not giving up on my crew!"

"They're not going to make it!" Lex's voice was somehow both urgent and calm. The hacker had an annoying habit of being able to separate logistics from his emotions. *"There's no need for you to die, too, Captain."*

"A captain always goes down with her ship, damn it! If there's anyone that *should* die, it's me!"

The click of the *Fury's* doors alerted Jax to their closing. The ship shook subtly as it detached from the dock.

"*No!*" Jax shouted through the comms.

Over the camera feed, the doors to the docking bay slid open. Lex had lost control of the system. He'd used his last seconds of access to release the *Fury* from the dock.

"Damn it, Lex!"

Shouts from the others surged through her headset. Shouts and the cacophony of blaster fire.

The holo-screens cut out as the dock security teams regained control and locked down their systems.

"Lex!" Jax shouted, pounding on the *Fury's* docking bay door as if it would make any difference. "Lex! Don't do this!"

"Tell Penelope I love her." Emotion now seeped into his

voice and he was barely keeping the tears at bay. *"Tell her I died fighting to make a better life for her. Please, Jax."*

Tears uncharacteristically streamed down Jax's face as she pounded on the interior frame of the *Fury*. It should have been her on that dock. She wasn't supposed to be standing on her ship like a useless ass.

Screams streamed through the comms.

Her crew. Her friends. Dying.

And there was nothing she could do but listen.

CHAPTER TWENTY-ONE

Mikka
The *Chimera*

Mikka's footsteps echoed in the confined space of her quarters as she paced restlessly back and forth—as best she could, at least. The cabin was barely longer than the length of the bed. It wasn't a prison cell by any stretch of the imagination, but neither was it a luxury suite. It was smaller than a standard crewmember's quarters, equipped with a bed, a small chair, and a washroom the size of a closet with a sink, a toilet, and an automatic sliding door.

The room must have been designed for an ensign or assistant. It was nicer than the room Mikka had grown up in back in the Tubes, though not much larger. If she reached out her arm from the bed, she could almost touch the other side of the room. But the space had a bed, and it beat just a mattress on the floor. Even the chill from the bare floor was a comfort compared to the dank, dark cells she had seen that week.

Earlier, Mikka had departed the bridge without

providing a shred of information to Alejandro. She couldn't bring herself to, knowing that the Resurgence would use the information to create obstacles preventing David from turning the Syndicate Empire around.

Attacking a space dock for no other reason than to disrupt the supply chain was nothing short of an act of terrorism. Whether Abigail called herself a pirate or she had thrown her lot in with the Resurgence, it didn't matter; it was two sides of the same coin.

She had gotten off the bridge by providing vague answers and promises that she would think about what information she could provide. Her noncommittal responses seemed to appease Marvin, at least for the time being, but that wouldn't hold for long.

How long could she stall before Marvin and Abigail decided they needed to resort to something more drastic to pry the information out of her? Would they dispose of her if they didn't believe she was going to give them anything useful?

And when Abigail discovered Mikka had manipulated her, how would the woman react?

It didn't help that whatever information she possessed was nearly a decade out of date. Any systems or obstacles Mikka could reference were probably obsolete. And attempting a heist on Space Dock Nineteen was far and away a different operation than on any of the other space docks. Only Nineteen was a top secret facility; the rest were merely shipping yards for the planet. Though, over the past decade, it was possible the systems had been outfitted to the same level of intensity.

And there was always the possibility that no matter

how much information Mikka provided—or how useful—she would still be sent out the airlock.

Unlike Abigail, Mikka hated gambling, and targeting a Syndicate space dock was one hell of a wager. And unlike the pirate and her child charlatan, Mikka preferred to make her own luck rather than trying to guess what the outcome might be.

She needed to escape, and she needed to do so now.

Which meant that first, she had to confirm whether the *Chimera* was outside of an external gravitational field.

There were eight accessible artificial gravity panels that lined the floor of her quarters, two across and four deep. One was all she needed. Mikka pulled the baton from the elastic in her pants. It was only a matter of time before Abi discovered her baton was missing and pieced together what had happened, so Mikka had to act fast.

She positioned herself on the bed, praying that whoever had furnished the cabin had ensured the bed wasn't conductive to the floor cells. It was rare for floor units to short, but it wasn't as though it never happened.

She flicked the switch on the baton and it hummed to life. It was a modest weapon, intended to subdue rather than kill. Its highest setting would be painful, even excruciatingly so, but not lethal. But Mikka had no way of knowing what would happen once she planted an electrical charge on top of one of the panels. She hoped the baton would short the cell long enough to test if the plating was working. Even if it was, Mikka would only have seconds before the surrounding panels would compensate and fix the gap in the gravitational field.

A strip on the side of the device allowed her to slide the

power up to its highest setting. Blue sparks emitted from the weapon's tip. One wrong move and she'd be writhing on the floor with one massive headache.

She jammed the baton at the floor. Sparks flew as it connected with the panel; first from the device, and then from the panel itself. Mikka dropped the baton as smoke turned to heat and burned her hand.

"Damn it!" Mikka waved her hand, instinctively blowing on it while inspecting it for a welt or burn. Her hand was red, but it would heal. "Like wrapping my hand around a curling iron," she thought out loud.

There was no time to nurse the wound now. If her plan had worked, she only had a few precious seconds to test it. She reached into her pocket and grabbed the handful of peas she had snagged from lunch.

"Here goes nothing . . ."

The peas fell from her hand toward the plate and stopped a few centimeters short, suspended in midair. They hovered for several seconds until the surrounding plates compensated, taking hold and pulling the green orbs to the floor, where they smoked as the overheated panel burned the legumes.

"Well, I guess we're in space."

Mikka darted from her room, intent on reaching Kiara. It took only seconds for her to realize two important details: they weren't on Lunar or any other moon or planet, and Abigail was distracted. The time to act was now.

Despite Alejandro's holo-presence keeping Abigail

occupied, Mikka didn't want to risk drawing attention from the rest of the crew. She suspected other crewmembers might be monitoring her from the shadows. How closely would determine what happened next.

She walked briskly toward Kiara's quarters.

Abigail had assigned the two of them quarters far enough apart that it would be obvious they were in the wrong corridor when they snuck off to one another's room, but the cabins were still close enough that a single pair of guards could easily watch over both of them. Smart on Abigail's part.

But it also meant if that single pair of guards became distracted, there would be nothing standing between them. So far, though, that opportunity hadn't arisen.

Every day they had been aboard the *Chimera*, Mikka had tried to get to her navigator. Each time, she'd failed. During every other attempt, there had been at least one guard positioned on the corner central to the two rooms.

Mikka slowed her pace as she turned the corner. Her first response was relief. It seemed providential that, for the first time since they'd been taken aboard, she both knew the method of their escape—the *Redemption*—and she was able to reach her navigator.

But that also gave her pause. *Why are there no guards here?*

Creaks in the ship's paneling highlighted the emptiness of the hall.

Something's wrong.

Mikka's gut had been instrumental in keeping her alive as a pirate, and it hadn't failed her yet. It was now on high alert, sending tingles to every one of her nerves. She regretted shorting out Monroe's baton. Any sort of weapon would have come in handy against a would-be attacker.

Am I in danger? Nothing on the *Chimera* had made her believe so until now.

As she turned, a flicker of movement caught her eye. Someone was in the corridor with her.

Mikka carefully stepped around the corner, her heart racing as adrenaline coursed through her veins. Her heartbeat thumped loudly in her skull.

"You need to leave."

Mikka jumped a foot in the air and readied herself for a fistfight as she spun around, caught off guard by the youthful voice over her shoulder.

It was only when she saw that the voice belonged to Zee that Mikka relaxed her defenses, though her heart still surged frantically.

"Zee, you scared the shit out of me!" If he hadn't been a kid, she would have slugged him for taking a few good years off her life. She took a moment to catch her breath. "Why the hell are you sneaking up on me like that?"

"It's not safe for you here. You've got to go."

"Yeah, I'm working on it, kid."

The teenager stood with his hood pulled over his head, his one yellow eye pulsing as though it were a probe, scanning her for something. The black one spun as though an empty void, unsuccessfully searching to pull light into its depths.

"I'm only here because you've been giving Monroe wild ideas." Mikka didn't have time to deal with the kid now; she had a narrow window of opportunity for escape.

"I only tell people what I see. I can't control what they

do with what I say." Zee sighed, his expression down turned. In that moment, he seemed more like a kid than a wannabe prophet. "People don't understand. The future isn't so black and white. There are millions of outcomes that could arise from any choice. It hurts sometimes to try and understand what I'm seeing. Numbers constantly changing. When I try to explain the patterns, people only hear what they want to hear. They want to bend the future to their will, but you can't control all the variables. No one can."

"Why are you helping Monroe if you're not sure of the outcome?"

"I'm sure enough." The pulsing in his eye stopped, fading to an iris that, though still a fluorescent yellow, no longer glowed. Zee's focus drifted, as though suddenly unhappy. "And it's not like I had much of a choice."

Mikka sighed. She need to get moving, but her curiosity was overwhelming. "How did you end up with her, anyway?"

"My last owner nearly left me in a Martian tavern after I called the wrong winner of an Exo-horse death race. The animal was statistically favored to win nine hundred and ninety-nine times out of a thousand, but the animal tripped on a stone after three hundred meters and broke an ankle. My owner lost his life savings on a fluke accident that couldn't have been foreseen. He couldn't bear the thought of trying to explain what had happened to his wife, so he blamed it on me. Abigail recognized my ability and offered the man a way to be rid of me and make a fraction of his credits back."

"Monroe . . . bought you?" Mikka choked on the words,

the harsh reality of life in the Loop crashing down on her once again. It was common knowledge that people sold others out of desperation, resorting to such cruelty when they'd run out of ways to make a living. She had also half-expected Monroe to have acquired Zee through less-than-savoury means, but it was a reality Mikka could never grow accustomed to.

Even during her pirating days, human trafficking was something Mikka had refused to have a hand in.

Zee nodded, his expression somber. "That doesn't matter now," he said quietly, urgency creeping into his tone. "What matters is you. Every minute you stay here, your odds of survival dwindle. In fact . . ." Zee's voice trailed off as his eye pulsed once again. "If you don't get off the *Chimera*, we all die."

Mikka started at the revelation, but she pushed the prophecy aside for the moment. "I thought you were telling Monroe to hold me here?"

Zee nodded. "For a time. Keeping you here has prevented much death and suffering. I can't always explain what I see. But your role is related to the Lunar comman-der. You being here has already prevented many deaths, but now the odds invert. If you stay here, you'll be killed. Many more will suffer."

Probably something to do with Alejandro's plan to disrupt the space dock . . .

Then she nearly slapped herself. What was she think-ing? The kid was no fortune teller. He was relying on vague suggestions and allowing a person's own mind to fill in the blanks.

Mikka rolled her eyes. "And my life is somehow tied to

the fall of the Syndicate? Please, kid. I'll gladly leave. But I make my own luck. Just let me know if someone's coming."

Mikka pushed past Zee, strode down the hall, and hit the buzzer on Kiara's wall. "Open sesame, my friend."

There was no answer.

"Come on, Ki, it's not that late." Mikka hit the buzzer again and counted to ten. There was no noise from within, but she had a hard time believing her navigator was already asleep. Kiara wasn't a heavy sleeper, either; the buzzer would have roused her.

Mikka fumbled around the access panel. The doors weren't locked; the crew had been able to come and go as they pleased.

Mikka peered into the darkened room, unable to make out anything except for the floor tile as light crept in from the hallway.

Perhaps she's turned in for the night after all.

Mikka flipped on the lights. A gasp escaped her lips, and she nearly fell as she stumbled into the room.

Kiara lay face down on the bed, the fringes of her purple hair dipped in the blood that had spread from her chest into a pool around her.

"*Shit!* Kiara!"

Mikka ran to her navigator's side and turned her over. Kiara's body was limp.

Lifeless.

Dead.

Jagged cuts marred the fabric of her jacket, the frays wet. Her blue tank top had turned purple and black, soaked through with blood.

Bile rose in Mikka's throat as she examined the torn

flesh beneath. This wasn't a simple murder, it was an act of savagery, and her mind raced to comprehend who could have done this, or why.

Mikka stood frozen, Kiara's lifeless torso cradled in her arms. Blood still flowed from the dead navigator's chest, warm to the touch. She must have been attacked within the hour.

"Who did this?" Mikka asked the empty room as emotion roiled through her. Tears streamed down her face as she rested her friend back down onto the bed.

How many words had she said the past few days that she now wished she could take back? Kiara hadn't even wanted to go on the mission that had brought them here.

Now, she was dead because of it.

Mikka stood. Rage burned deep in the pit of her stomach.

This was supposed to be a simple contract.

Mikka had left piracy behind because of actions like this. Because she was tired of her friends dying; tired of being the reason they died.

Air struggled to find its way into Mikka's lungs. She removed her own jacket as it constricted around her and laid it over Kiara to cover the worst of her wounds. She quickly scanned the apartment for some sign of who might have done this, but there was nothing other than an unmade bed and the pool of blood that now spread across the sheets and dripped onto the floor.

Before she could register her actions, a hooded sweatshirt filled her grasp, and her triceps strained as Mikka lifted Zee off the ground to meet her at eye level. The boy stared blankly at her.

"Who did this?" Mikka spat the words, anger seeping through each syllable.

"Someone who wanted to hurt you," Zee replied, his tone emotionless and his gaze searching her, confident in his response.

They weren't looking for Kiara. They were looking for me.

There was only one person who had made her motives known.

Penelope.

CHAPTER TWENTY-TWO

Mikka

The *Chimera*

There were moments when Mikka wasn't sure if the gravity panels were working as she flew toward the bridge. The metallic air hummed with energy, while the sterile blue light overhead cast long shadows along the corridor ahead of her, paving the way to the bridge with a haunting energy she hadn't felt since she'd arrived on board. Penelope would be there with Abigail, with her bloodied hands and blackened heart.

The bitch would answer for Kiara's death.

Kiara had been a family woman. She had grown up on the streets of Shackleton City; not in the tall towers of the Upper Rim among Syndicate suck-ups and corporate leeches, but in their shadow. Her family had worked hard to secure a relatively modest but comfortable life for themselves.

Kiara wouldn't have made it as a pirate; she hadn't been prepared for combat, or the undertow of treachery that continually threatened to drag a person down and suffocate them. In the moments just before her death, half asleep and inattentive, she wouldn't have noticed a well-trained assassin sneaking into her room until it was too late—if she'd noticed them at all.

If the killer had entered Mikka's room as they'd intended, Penelope's dead body would have been the one bleeding out on the floor instead of Kiara.

It still would be.

Rage boiled in Mikka's veins, her blood pounding in her ears. She held her clenched fists at her sides, the muscles in her jaw straining with barely controlled anger.

There would be hell to pay.

It was a quick sprint to the bridge, and Mikka made it to within a few steps of the automatic door before Zee rushed in front of her, blocking her path so suddenly that she collided roughly with him, lost her footing, and slammed into the white-tiled floor.

Zee was on his feet before Mikka could comprehend that she had tripped over him.

"Do not go in there!" Zee hissed, his yellow eye ablaze in the shadows. "You need to *leave!*"

"Out of my way, kid. Do *not* get involved in this."

"*Think* about why Kiara was killed and not you! If you continue, you will be trapped on the ship, and the events that lead to your redemption will be disrupted."

Redemption. Was there anything left to redeem? The fire that coursed through her told Mikka no, but deep down, there was a flicker that reaffirmed it wasn't true—something else buried, whispering to her to hold off.

Even now, it hinted at something more important, something inescapable . . .

The boy was gone; the sage having returned in his place. If she wasn't so infuriated, Mikka would have allowed herself to study why the Wayfinder's bio-mods made him such an enigma. Instead, her gaze wandered to the pulsating control panel at the hallway's end, a constellation of softly glowing touchpoints embedded in the ship's seamless architecture. The only thing standing between her and revenge was that access panel.

Thoughts of wrapping her hands around Penelope Martínez's thick neck and choking the life out of her consumed her mind.

"Please, stop!" His determination supplemented with an urgency in his eyes. "You *need* to get out of here."

"I don't care what your damn algorithms say, kid." Mikka pushed past him. "Kiara was my best friend. Maybe my only one."

"But you *do* know that by setting foot on that bridge, you'll be giving the killer what they want."

Cognizance took hold as soon as Zee uttered the words, causing Mikka to stop in her tracks.

Perhaps the kid was on to something—it *would* be a classic play. Penelope knew damn well which room to find her in. Mikka had never been the target of the assault; Penelope wanted to anger her. She wanted her to react.

She wanted to hurt her. Not physically, but emotionally. She wanted Mikka to feel the same way she had when Lex had died all those years ago.

I'm being set up, but why?

And the whole time, the kid had seen through Penelope's plan while Mikka had taken the bait.

How does someone so young see so much?

As Mikka spun around, Zee's wide-eyed surprise was palpable. His pale complexion turned ashen, and he instinctively recoiled, clutching the fabric of his shirt at his chest, afraid she might decide to pick him up again.

"What are you seeing? What's going to happen if I storm the bridge?"

Mikka's chest heaved, her sweat-soaked shirt clinging to her back. Her nostrils flared, but she could feel her blood vessels relaxing slightly, even though her mind still thirsted for revenge.

Zee's face saddened. "It doesn't work like that. Nobody ever understands! It doesn't work like that."

Mikka was losing her patience. "Then how *does* it work?"

"I see trajectories; the larger the event, the stronger the trajectory that must be followed. The bigger the impact, the brighter the stats are, but also the more frequently the numbers shift. Every small decision affects the outcome.

"I can only see numbers based on the path you're on. The more likely your choice, the brighter the outcome. The bigger the influence, the brighter the path. Some people are more likely to affect the future of our solar system. You, Captain Monroe, Alejandro, the two you helped to escape the station, you all possess the brightest lines I've ever seen.

"If you storm the bridge, your path fades and then ends. It's tied to the bigger picture of what Monroe and Alejandro are planning. But even more so, your fate is tied to the man from the *Eclipse*. The combination of you following this path and his actions leads to your end."

"You can still leave. You can save yourself, and in doing so, the lives of many."

"So, if the new Prefect is allowed to live, things will get worse?" Mikka asked.

"The Prefect has a role to play. His death would be a pivotal play for humanity's future—but not necessarily a good one."

"And Aries?"

"His path is one of much destruction, but some of that destruction will be necessary to prevent even further deaths."

"The lesser of two evils." Mikka shook her head, cutting Zee off before he could continue. "I don't understand why I'm so important."

"Your life is integral to humanity's future."

Mikka cursed as her lungs filled with the *Chimera's* stale air. She wasn't sure why she was entertaining Zee and his nonsense; his musings were nothing more than a party trick. Vague statements that could be construed to fit any potential outcome, if needed. There was no way he could account for all the variables at play. If he could, then he could have prevented Kiara from being murdered.

Whether anything else Zee was saying had any credence to it, her gut was warning her she had been set up, that pursuing Penelope was the wrong move. And Mikka always trusted her gut. Zee's interruption to her rage had allowed her enough of a pause to hear its alarm.

How many times had the tingling in her fingertips or the flash of warning in her stomach prevented her from death? More than a dozen times she knew of. The one time she had ignored the warning, she had been approaching Space Dock Nineteen.

That day, she swore she'd never make the same mistake again—but today, she almost had.

Zee's gaze met her own, his eyes shadowed and weary, the light of youth extinguished by the weight of experiences no child should have to bear. Abigail had presented the kid to her as a prophet. And like Abigail, all Mikka had done was use Zee to confirm her own biases.

That wasn't right.

She wondered what kind of strain constantly analyzing every scenario that played out would place on the boy, constantly contrasting figures that couldn't possibly provide him with a complete picture.

"Why don't you come with me?" The question was impulsive, one Mikka hadn't even realized she was going to ask until it had come out of her mouth.

"You want to use me for my mod?" The boy's shoulders slumped. It wasn't an accusation, but the resolve of a timid teenager who had been used his entire life and could see no other reason someone would ask him to join them. "I belong to Captain Monroe."

"No." Mikka placed an arm on his shoulder. "Nobody should own a person, regardless of what an implant can do." Slavery was prevalent in the system, but that didn't make it right.

Zee wrinkled his forehead. In the ship's dimly lit hallway, the glow from the seer's eye pulsed rhythmically, casting eerie shadows that danced all around them. It dimmed and the boy simply nodded, his gaze returning to the distant look Mikka was accustomed to from him. She didn't know the boy well enough to know if he was reluctantly joining her because he still didn't believe her intentions or because of something he saw in his algorithm that he didn't want to deal with.

He can't see the future, she reminded herself. *Only paths forward. Only numbers. If anything meaningful at all.*

The hallway split in two directions ahead of her. If Mikka turned left, it would lead them to the bridge—to Penelope and Abigail. She'd have no problem overpowering Kiara's killer and probably the rest of Monroe's security, too. Abigail herself was still a wildcard, though, and Mikka didn't know if she could outmatch her while contending with however many other pirates would surround her.

The rage within her melted into sadness as she turned and cast her gaze back down the hallway, toward where Kiara's body lay. It felt wrong to leave her friend behind. Not only had they been through so much together, but Mikka didn't know whether Abigail would even grant her a proper burial.

Notifying Kiara's family would fall to Mikka. How could she explain why Kiara had died so senselessly?

Had Abigail even been aware of Penelope's actions? To what lengths would the pirate go to get under Mikka's skin?

"I'm sorry, my friend," she whispered. "She won't get away with this, I promise."

It wouldn't help Kiara if Mikka stayed, only to get herself killed. Neither would allowing thousands to die by the hand of the Syndicate because of a bullheaded decision. She had to keep the big picture in mind.

If this was her one chance to leave the ship, she had to take it.

Kiara would have been the first to warn Mikka not to jump into a situation on impulse. In fact, she had warned her not to jump into *this* situation.

That realization made this outcome even harder to swallow. Kiara had died because Mikka hadn't listened to her.

Mikka sighed, fighting against the weight of everything threatening to pull her to her knees, as though someone had cranked the gravity to 3 g.

Kiara had often been the voice of reason against Mikka's impulsiveness. Nearly eight years of being colleagues and friends, gone in an instant. Mikka wasn't one for tears, but her heart hung heavy as the magnitude of the evening's events finally broke through the wall her anger had erected. And now she had to leave. Once again, she was permitted to live, while her closest friend had died for her mistakes.

It wasn't fair. But as Mikka had learned long ago, life was rarely fair.

She mentally put a black mark against Penelope Martínez's life; a move that Mikka hadn't made since her pirate days. She had sworn she wouldn't ever be put in this position again, in a place where she was plotting murder—revenge for a fallen ally.

But Mikka wasn't done with Penelope yet. There was a debt to be paid for killing Kiara, and Mikka intended to collect. She thought of asking Zee what the odds were of the pirate dying by her hand, but she didn't want to use the kid as Abigail had.

Besides, she already knew the answer: 100%.

Her gaze drifted back to Kiara's room. The hallways were still suspiciously vacant. No doubt the entire thing had been planned. Had there been others involved, too?

Taking a deep, steadying breath, Mikka's hand instinctively rose to her face, fingers brushing away the wet trails left by her silent tears. This wasn't done. Not by a long shot.

Something about leaving Kiara's body in the ship's quarters didn't feel right. She should be returned to her family to receive a proper burial in the soil of Lunar, where her family had lived and worked for generations.

But Mikka couldn't risk carrying Kiara's corpse through the *Chimera* to the *Redemption*. The corridors were empty now, but that didn't mean they'd stay that way.

She let out a sigh, releasing with it the weight of the tragedy she knew she would never be fully free of. "Come on, Zee. Let's go."

Zee eyed her with an open mix of optimism and doubt.

The navigator's death didn't seem to faze him.

How much death has he seen in his short life?

How many people had lied to him, told him he'd be given status if he went along with one more prediction?

Mikka knew the type to take advantage of a kid. They would tell him whatever they thought would work to get him to comply.

People like Abigail.

Nobody deserves to be bought and sold like a scrap of metal.

She locked eyes with him, unable to ignore the fact he had yet to move. "This has to be your decision, Zee," she said. "If you'd rather stay on the *Chimera*, stay loyal to Monroe, I won't force you to join me. But I'm giving you the option."

Zee's eye pulsed again, but his brow furrowed as though he didn't trust her.

Voices buzzed from the other side of the door to the bridge. The longer they stood around in the halls of the *Chimera*, the more likely they were to be caught.

"Okay," Zee said, the intensity of his eyes subduing. "I'll come with you."

Mikka

The *Chimera*

Leaving the *Chimera* had been a long shot. Despite the empty halls and distracted captain, Mikka had still come up against a dead end.

In the form of a locked hatch.

On any other ship, hacking into the cargo bay's computer and unlocking the bay door wouldn't have been a hard task. But the *Chimera* wasn't any ship, and Abigail Monroe certainly wasn't just any captain. The key codes had been encrypted, and Mikka couldn't even begin to decipher how. It didn't seem to be a passcode, and the mods to the chip in her arm could easily unscramble almost any basic key code.

There had to be another piece missing.

Biometrics were too much of a hassle, as multiple crewmembers would have reason to access the bay. Not only was it overkill for such a mundane task, but pirates weren't the sort to allow biometrics data to flow through their chips easily. Too many wore their frequency blockers like a badge of honor. Wrist guards and armbands isolating their chips prevented the Syndicate from being able to track them.

But on a ship where every effort had been made to keep Mikka from knowing the *Chimera*'s location, maybe it wasn't such a stretch. Perhaps only certain personnel willing to have the data transferred to them would be on duty while Mikka was on board.

Mikka shook off the thought. *No sense in being paranoid.*

It was possible that a physical device or key card was needed as an override. An access card system was archaic when compared with the wealth of technology aboard the *Chimera*, but it would be an efficient way of passing control from one pirate to the next. That would make much more sense.

Either way, ACCESS DENIED flashed across the screen. Mikka cursed as she landed a fist on the side of the console.

"There has to be a manual override somewhere," she thought aloud as she scanned the cargo bay for signs of one. The ship was so unique that she wasn't even sure if that was true.

The holographic displays reminded her of those Aries and his staff were surrounded by in their Syndicate Front headquarters, but never had Mikka seen such systems on board a vessel that had clearly been built for combat. Each console and interface shone with a complexity she'd only glimpsed behind reinforced glass in military control rooms.

The integrated holo-displays, pulsing with information, were leagues ahead of the usual starship tech.

"Any insight, Zee?"

The kid shook his head as he scanned the systems, offering nothing further.

Kiara would have figured this out by now.

Memories of the navigator, her face lit with understanding as she cracked complex codes, flickered through Mikka's mind. A knot tightened in her chest as her hands trembled slightly on the console. With a deep, steadying breath, she turned back to the task at hand, a silent vow hanging in the air—Kiara's sacrifice wouldn't be for nothing. Mikka couldn't let her friend's death be in vain.

Movement behind her caused Mikka to jump. The door from the main access corridor had slid open.

Someone was coming.

Mikka ducked behind the cargo bay console before she could identify the arrival. She reached over and pulled Zee in beside her, lifting a finger to her lips.

"I know you're in here." Penelope's voice echoed through the vast cargo hold.

Mikka would get her chance at revenge after all.

She wished she had taken a few extra moments to arm herself, but there had been no time to go searching for weapons, and she'd been forced to leave all of hers on board the *Redemption.*

Her ship sat only a few dozen meters away. So close to freedom. So close to her SC-117 pistol.

"I'm not going to hurt you."

Penelope's boots ticked against the floor panels. It

would only be a matter of time before she would be on top of them.

The ship's holographic control panel stood on a pedestal in the opposite corner, the only thing separating Mikka and Zee from Penelope's grasp. She shifted on her haunches behind the console; the lights of the cargo bay reflected off the silver in Penelope's biometric hand.

There was nowhere to run where they wouldn't be seen. Mikka thought of putting Zee between herself and the pirate as she made a break for it, only in the hope that the youth would force Penelope to hold her fire, but she quickly dismissed the idea, embarrassed that she'd had it in the first place. It was a low move, and that wasn't who she was. Not anymore, at least. Besides, if Penelope was willing to stab someone in their sleep, she likely wouldn't hesitate to open fire on a child.

It was possible, though, that the thought of retribution from Abigail might be enough to dissuade her. After all, as far as Penelope knew, Zee was still assisting her captain with her plans. But Mikka couldn't risk it. It might have been something she would have done in her old life, but not now. She had to protect Zee. She couldn't fail two innocents in one day.

"We won't be alone in here for much longer," Penelope called out. "You need to get on your ship."

Get on my ship?

Suspicion clouded Mikka's mind. Was this a trick? If so, it was a pitifully weak one.

As the pirate drew steadily closer, Mikka saw a chance to overtake her. She still needed to figure out what to do after, but it would be one obstacle out of the way.

"Wait here," she whispered to Zee. "Don't make a sound."

Without waiting for a response, Mikka crept out from behind the console while Penelope's gaze was fixed on the center of the hold. As quietly as she could, she crept along the back wall, hoping to avoid detection.

The hum of the ship masked her soft footsteps. Penelope scanned the cargo bay while stepping toward the *Redemption*, clearly assuming that was where Mikka would be hiding.

Mikka would be upon her in a few moments, and she still needed a plan. Exposed beneath her black jacket, Penelope's belt held several weapons: two ballistic firearms, an energy weapon, and a six-inch serrated knife.

The blaster would likely need to be activated and, depending on the model, would need Penelope's biometric reading to fire. The guns would be too loud, especially within the cargo hold, presenting too much of a risk of raising the ship's alarm.

That left the knife. Mikka's gut turned. There was a good chance it was the exact weapon that had killed Kiara. It would be a fitting choice for justice.

Mikka took a moment to ground herself, pushing down the rage that brewed inside her, and allowing herself to focus on the task at hand. She'd have to hurry, or she'd risk Penelope spotting her.

Her eye on the knife, Mikka sprung into action.

There was only twenty meters between herself and Penelope, a distance she could cover easily, but she only took two steps before her target spun around, blaster in hand.

A scream of caution echoed in the back of Mikka's mind, but it was too late. Her muscles were already coiled, her legs propelling her forward in a charge she couldn't halt. Her shoulder connected with Penelope, sending the two women over into a sprawl on the floor.

The impact knocked the weapon out of Penelope's hand, but Mikka was unable to grab the knife in the tumble. She wound up a fist for a punch, finding only air as Penelope dodged the assault. The momentum knocked Mikka off-kilter and Penelope used the gaffe to her advantage, taking Mikka's shoulders in each hand, turning her over, and pinning her to the ground beneath the strength of her bionic arm resting on her chest.

"Idiot!" Penelope cursed. "What the hell are you doing?"

Mikka struggled under the mechanical grasp, but in an instant, Penelope had the serrated knife to Mikka's throat.

Mikka swore. Without the enhancement, she would have been able to overpower Penelope without question, but against the bionic arm, she might as well have been wrestling a runabout.

"Stop struggling!" Penelope hissed.

"Fine!" Mikka spat. "Kill me like you killed Kiara! It won't bring your father back. And I hope that sits heavy on your soul for the rest of your days."

Penelope raised an eyebrow and lifted the blade away from Mikka's neck. The cool, regulated air had never felt so good against Mikka's skin.

"What are you talking about? I didn't kill anyone! I came to help you escape."

In what universe would this woman want me to escape?

"Why would I believe that?" she challenged. "The first thing you said to me was a threat to watch my back."

Penelope scanned the cargo bay, as though assessing for another threat. "Your purple-haired friend? She's . . ."

Mikka didn't let her finish the thought. "Murdered."

Penelope's eyes widened in horror. "You've got to believe I had nothing to do with it! My words to you when you arrived were a *warning*, not a threat. Like I told you, I've already made my peace."

It didn't make sense. Penelope had the means and the motive, but something in the woman's eyes told Mikka she was telling the truth. "If it wasn't you, then who? I don't believe Abigail would . . ."

"Captain Monroe is the biggest ally you have, but she made a mistake leading you into a pit of vipers. I saw enough to know your life was in danger here. Just because I've moved on doesn't mean others have. I'm sure I don't need to remind you how many enemies you've made."

Anger roiled through her. Mikka wouldn't put it past Penelope to be lying, but she had the opportunity right now to finish her off, and she wasn't taking it. If somebody else attacked Kiara, who would it have been? There were dozens of crewmembers with access to their quarters. So few of them had made a memorable impression, and Mikka certainly hadn't recognized any of the other pirates. She typically had an eye for faces, and an even sharper one for enemies.

Penelope sheathed her knife and stood, pulling Mikka to her feet in one smooth swoop.

Mikka staggered back, her muscles tense, still on edge that Penelope's actions might be a ruse.

"Go on, get on your ship. I'll open the cargo bay doors. Monroe should be with Alejandro for another hour, and then we'll be aiding a mission that should distract us for a while. More than enough for you to get a head start. But there will be crewmembers arriving any moment, so you've got to leave now."

Alejandro. Does his call have something to do with Kiara's death? It couldn't have been a coincidence that the two events coincided.

A wave of dizziness washed over her as her mind scrambled for answers. She now had no leads on who had murdered her friend.

"Who's in charge of the guards who were supposed to be watching over us?" she asked. "Why were the corridors empty?"

Penelope's eyes widened. "There were no guards?"

"How the hell do you think Kiara ended up dead? No, there were no guards. Is it possible *they* were the ones behind this?"

Penelope shook her head, but she was clearly hesitant. She answered slowly, her accent thick, as she seemed to mull over the possibility. "I don't think so, but I wouldn't rule anything out."

It wasn't fair that Kiara had got caught in the middle of her mistake. It wasn't right.

"You can mourn your friend later," Penelope continued. "I'll see that Abigail contacts her family, and I'll ensure we do a thorough investigation. Monroe will be furious that this happened on her ship."

"Why are you doing this?" Mikka could tentatively accept that the woman might not want to kill her, but helping her escape against the captain's orders bordered on treasonous.

"I hated you for a long time, Jax Luana. Many years passed where I would have given anything to throw you out the airlock. But the older I got, the more I realized my father trusted you for a reason, and his trust wasn't easily earned. That was confirmed when I saw the look on your face when you learned who I was. There was sadness and regret in your eyes that I've never seen from any other pirate. You cared about my father, and I feel like he would have wanted me to do this."

Mikka nodded. "I meant what I said. Lex was a good man."

"I also meant what I said: watch your back. There's still plenty of people who'd like to see you dead. Monroe hasn't done you any favors in digging up your past."

So, that was how it went down. "Abi let it slip that I'm still alive?"

Penelope flexed her cybernetic hand. "I wouldn't say that exactly. At least, not intentionally. But you know how it goes. Pirates can't keep a secret. One person gets a scent of juicy gossip and the entire ship knows. Soon every pirate from here to Neptune knows Jax Luana is dead in name only."

For nearly a decade, Mikka had kept her secret. She should have known her luck would run out eventually. Somehow she had grown complacent, thinking the past was behind her.

Penelope continued. "On top of that, the augmented kid is saying your life is key to the outcome of the Resurgence's rebellion. There will be plenty of friends of the

Empire who will want to ensure you don't get that chance."

"*Pfft*. He's just a kid."

"I wouldn't be so sure . . ." Penelope trailed off. "Belief, whether grounded in reality or not, is a powerful enough motivator for people to take action."

"I believe we make our own luck."

"That might be, but people *want* to see signs. They want to see patterns. They want this cold reality to make sense when it so rarely does. And they want someone to blame for their hard times. Give them a couple clues that seem to link, and they lose their minds. At least Monroe had the decency to lock you away until the odds changed in her favor. There are many who would simply have done away with you."

"Well, hopefully, I've taken some of that pressure off. Come on out, Zee."

The Wayfinder poked his head out from behind the console, his hood pulled up over his face, his yellow eye and the stripe along his cheek aglow.

"Get in the ship," Mikka said, gesturing toward the *Redemption*. "We're leaving."

"You're stealing the kid?" Penelope arched an eyebrow as Zee hurried over to the ship and eyed him as he ascended the access ramp. "You really want to piss Monroe off, don't you?"

"She had no right to him in the first place," Mikka said. "He's a person, not a pet. And I'm not 'stealing' him. I gave him the option to join me, and he accepted."

"I doubt the captain will see it that way. Be careful with

that one, though. You might end up with more than you bargained for."

"What's that supposed to mean?"

"Zee may seem innocent, but there's more to that kid than he lets on."

"He's seen more than anyone ever should. He's been forced to perform his entire life, all because of a side effect from a faulty implant. I'm taking a chance on him, just like someone took a chance on me."

Penelope grunted, then shot out a robotic palm for a handshake. "Good luck to you, Jax. I hope when our paths cross again, it's under better circumstances."

"It's Mikka now," she said, grabbing the cool metallic hand. Its grip was more lifelike than she was expecting. "And thanks for your help. Your dad would have been proud."

"For what it's worth, he spoke highly of you. It's what saved you from gaining me as an enemy. Maybe we'll cross paths again. Who knows, maybe we'll even work together?"

"I'd like that," Mikka said, hoping that burying the hatchet, in some way, honored the hacker to whom she owed her life. "But not for the Resurgence, and not as a pirate. I've left that life behind."

Penelope gripped Mikka's hand tighter. "Sometimes, fate pulls us in directions we didn't choose."

Mikka smiled. "Well, it's a good thing I don't believe in fate."

Eventide

The *Inanna*

The floor of the atrium was littered with coarse pebbles, a fact Eventide had failed to notice until her fabric slippers began to slip on the loose, bumpy stones underfoot. Eventide was no stranger to running, and she could feel the strength in her newly enhanced muscles, eager to show what they were capable of. Yet her limbs still shook as though their untapped strength wasn't ready to be utilized. Not yet. On top of that, it was almost as though the Domani-issued footwear had been purposely designed to be as impractical as possible.

The Caregivers want us to be docile, heads down.

If she hadn't been concentrating so hard on staying upright, she would have vomited.

Eventide pushed the nausea aside. Right now, she had to focus on catching the man currently running from them.

The man who had killed Orin.

The assassin, whoever he was, certainly seemed more

adept at running on the slick stones than she was. Loose rocks spun as Eventide tried to push herself harder. The more she tried to find her footing, the more her legs flailed in every direction.

She moved between hedges and bushes and jumped over a small babbling brook. The atrium was surprisingly sprawling, considering it was on board a spacefaring vessel.

Her foot slipped and the ground gave way beneath her, causing her to tumble forward. A mass of lush green leaves broke her fall, but a mass of branches slid across her skin, leaving an array of scratches along her arms.

"Damn it!" she cursed, louder than she intended.

"Quit goofing around!" Okimi hissed, but her voice somehow still carried above the hum of the atrium. "Get over here!"

Okimi sat on her haunches, eyes wide, alert and focused on the path before them, ready to spring into action.

Eventide felt like a hot mess. She had trained for worse situations than this, so why was she feeling so off her game? Patches of dirt clung to her outfit, as well as the exposed skin of her stomach and chest, not that stains to the silk would have mattered at all; she had a dozen more of the exact same outfit hanging in her closet.

She rolled her eyes.

Eventide allowed her fingers to sink into the moist dirt beneath her as she inhaled deeply, grounding herself. Her hamstrings and calves shook beneath her, as though struggling against her own weight.

Just breathe. It's just a side effect of whatever damned procedures Morales did to me.

She steadied herself. She wouldn't catch the assassin by flailing around like a mad bull. Somehow, Okimi had adjusted to whatever enhancements had been done to her. Eventide had to trust that she would grow into hers as well.

It's like my first day of training all over again.

Broad green leaves brushed against her skin, and Eventide had to stop herself from wasting time by brushing them out of her hair and just hoped they weren't poisonous. All she needed was a rash—that would help her blend in. She already wondered how she would be able to mask the scratches.

"Did you see where he went?" Eventide whispered, scanning the darkened atrium. The emergency lighting overhead provided some visibility, but the greenery was so thick, the man could have been hiding anywhere. The hum of the atrium was constant. They would need to be on top of the man before they'd hear him.

Her eyes darted from leafy bush to thick grass. The assassin had to be here somewhere, and she couldn't dismiss the image of Orin's bleeding and broken body on the rec room floor.

Okimi shook her head, her eyes still vividly scanning their surroundings. "Let's move to the exit and try to prevent him from leaving. We need to split up. Follow the path around to the left; I'll take the right. Keep your eyes peeled."

She moved before Eventide had a chance to agree.

Okimi disappeared into the darkness with the stealth of a cat. Eventide paused. *Who is this woman? And where did she learn to sneak around like that?*

For a moment, doubts infiltrated her thoughts, but

Eventide shook them off. Carefully, she made her way toward the atrium's exit, still berating herself for being a clumsy fool as she consciously considered each step. She'd trained hard to be at her physical peak; she wasn't about to allow slippery stones stop her.

A flicker of movement was all she'd needed to pounce.

With the realization that he'd been seen, the man bolted, but not before Eventide got in front of him and sent an elbow into his stomach. Cartilage grazed ribs, and the wind was knocked out of him with a huff.

The blow wasn't enough to stop his shift in momentum, though, and they both went hurtling to the ground. Muscle and silk tangled together as Eventide struggled to grapple with the man. His skin was slick with the sheen of the atrium's humidity, and her hand grazed silk that wasn't her own.

He's Domani. Eventide pushed a knee deeper into his groin.

The man grunted with the sound of a strangled cat, but the force wasn't enough to cease his struggle.

Sweat and dirt coated her body as the man pushed her to the atrium floor. He was stronger than her, but the muscles the Domani pajamas proudly displayed were mostly for show. Still, Eventide narrowly dodged a hand wrapping around her neck.

The hand grabbed for her throat a second time, finding it this time, and shoved her against the base of a tree, knocking the wind out of her. Eventide grabbed a handful of her assailant's jet black hair and pulled the man down to the edge of the nearby artificial stream.

Eventide shoved the man's face into the icy water and

counted to twelve before pulling him back out. He broke the water, gasping, and she tossed him to the ground.

Seizing her opportunity, Eventide pressed her knee into the Domani's back.

"Who are you?" Okimi demanded, breaking through the bushes to Eventide's left.

"And why did you murder Orin?" Eventide spat.

"Agh! Stop! Stop!" the man cried. "My name is Matthias. I wasn't going to hurt you, I swear!"

"Then why were you spying on us?" Eventide pressed.

"I've never seen anyone else in here this late before. I didn't know who you were. Then you started chasing me. What was I supposed to do?"

Lines of dirt streaked his cheeks. Stepping aside so his face was free of the shadows, Eventide could get a better look at the man. He was tall, with dark brown eyes that seemed to absorb the harsh light of the room. The look on his face marked annoyance, but also worry, because of the knee Eventide hovered over his crotch.

She stood up, rolling her eyes as she released her death grip.

Okimi wasn't on the same page, and she took over from where Eventide had left off, pressing the full weight of her bony knee down onto the man's chest.

"What about Orin?" Okimi demanded. "Why did you kill him?"

"Agh!" Matthias cried. "I don't know what you're talking about! I didn't *kill* anyone!"

Okimi pulled Matthias roughly to his feet and held him at arm's length. "*Why* are you here?"

"I come to the atrium at night." Matthias' gaze shifted

between the two women, as though he wasn't sure which he should make his case to. "It's peaceful. I can be alone with my thoughts without the others telling me how wonderful everything is."

Eventide studied the man for any signs of deceit. His eyes continued to dart around unfocused, but they weren't glazed over.

"You aren't affected by the neurotransmitters." Matthias would be the third to elude the Caregivers' transmissions, and Morales had claimed she had never seen anyone not be affected before. So, what was going on?

"The what now?" Matthias said. "Is that why everyone's walking around here like a zombie? Some kind of freaky mind control?"

"You didn't know?" Eventide asked.

"Hell no, I didn't know! I just thought this place attracted the weirdos, but that sure explains a lot."

Two others who could think for themselves. Yet neither of these two seemed to know why they were special.

"Am I the only one of us who's gotten a talking to?" Eventide asked. "They knew my implants weren't working practically right away. I got a lecture from Doctor Morales to keep my mouth shut. Why haven't they done the same with you?"

"Because we haven't been running our mouths off like an idiot," Okimi snapped. "You've been poking the bear since you got here. It's like you've never been in a situation where asking too many questions could land you in trouble."

Matthias' eyes were still wide, looking at the two

women as though he was struggling to keep up with the conversation.

"And who are you two, exactly?" Matthias asked. "I've never seen either of you around here before."

"I've only just got here. I'm Eventide, this is Okimi. She's been here three months."

"I'm surprised we haven't run into each other before," Okimi said, her tone making it sound more like an accusation than a statement.

"I keep a low profile."

"How long have you been here?" Eventide asked.

Matthias cleared his throat, still trying to dust off the dirt from his silk outfit. "Almost a year. I didn't know exactly what was happening, but I knew something like mind-control must have been going on. So, I kept my mouth shut and tried to stay out of the way. I half-expected whatever it was would come for me eventually, but it never did. Thought maybe they forgot to run the program on me, but I wasn't going to argue."

"Great," Eventide said. "I guess I was the only one dumb enough to open my mouth."

"Looks like it," Okimi winked.

It was something Django would have said. He had always got a kick out of being able to outsmart her if he could. If it *had* been Django, she would have given him a swift punch to the arm, but she didn't know Okimi well enough for that yet.

"We still have a problem." Eventide straightened her outfit. "There's still a murderer running around the ship. And if it's not one of us, then we've got to watch our backs."

"Bah!" Okimi waved a dismissive hand. "Orin probably pissed off one of the Caregivers."

"That doesn't make it any better."

"Maybe, but it does mean that if we keep our heads down, we'll stay out of trouble."

Eventide was growing tired of that advice.

It *would* make more sense for the killer to be a Caregiver, but Morales had denied it. Eventide would have believed she was lying, but why defend them in one breath only to criticize them in the next? Something about it didn't feel right, but until they discovered an alternative, they would have to watch their step.

Eventide assessed her two new friends—if she could call them that. Matthias was still breathing heavy from their tussle, his mop of black hair sticking to his medium brown skin. Okimi had relaxed her stance, her fists at her side, not clenched but still tense.

They were islands in a sea of uncertainty. And she didn't even know if she could trust them, but for right now, they were all she had.

"Well, it's the three of us then," she said. "Since we're the only ones thinking clearly on this ship, I say we need to work together. It'll be easier than going it alone."

"Work together to what end, exactly?" Matthias raised an eyebrow.

"We need to come up with a plan. How do we get off this ship without raising the suspicions of the crew? Since we're traveling toward Earth, I'm guessing we're either heading there or to the Moon?"

"Earth," Matthias confirmed. "Which is rare."

"Whoa, whoa, whoa!" Okimi protested. "Hold up!

What do you mean, 'get off the ship?' You mean, leave the *Inanna*? Escape?"

Eventide placed her hands on her hips. "That's exactly what I mean. I don't plan on being held prisoner forever. I've got friends out there." She paused, her shoulders hunched as a heavy wave of sadness hit her in the gut. "Well, one friend, at least. I don't know if he can take care of himself. I need to find him."

"Look, friend." Okimi clasped a hand on Eventide's shoulder. Despite her petite frame, her grip was firm. "I hate to break it to you, but I don't wanna go anywhere. This is as good as it gets, especially if we have a chance of being chosen by some rich Earther." She whistled approvingly. "That's as sweet as any of us could ever dream."

"I don't understand." Eventide checked over her shoulder, suddenly self-conscious about their conversation. It was a topic she was uncomfortable breaching, but it had to be asked. "We're being sold for . . . *sex*, right? I don't know about you, but I didn't sign up for that—it doesn't matter how nice a room they give me. I'm an engineer, a scientist—not some rich person's plaything."

Okimi shrugged. "Sounds like fun to me. And I sure as shit'll take that over the mines any day."

Matthias was still overly concerned with dusting himself off. "I'm with Eventide. I'd rather smuggle goods for some lowlife pirate and sleep on a cot than put up with this." He grabbed his silk outfit in disgust.

Eventide grinned. She knew the feeling.

"But what do you propose?" Matthias continued. "We're stuck here until we're brought to a client. And we only get to leave the *Inanna* if a client chooses us. I've heard some stories about Domani trying to escape their clients before, and it never ends well. We're disposable and replaceable."

Eventide raised an eyebrow. "Other Domani have tried to escape the *Inanna*? Maybe this neurotransmitter isn't that good after all."

"Not the *Inanna*." Matthias clarified. "It only happens once they arrive with their client. I guess the client they ended up with wasn't as accommodating as this vessel. Though I guess it would be more difficult to leave the ship before it docks."

"No." Realization struck Eventide. "It's not that. The clients don't realize the Caregivers control the Domani through pleasure."

Eventide quickly explained what Morales had told her about their implants and how the Caregivers used them to keep the rest of the Domani in line. "If the clients don't realize the Caregivers feed the Domani with constant pleasure . . ."

Matthias cut her off. ". . . Then the Domani try to go off in search of it. They're addicted."

Eventide nodded. "Constant levels of dopamine are habit forming, so that's a real possibility. But even more likely, the buyers try to control the Domani through pain instead. Morales said the Caregivers tried that at first, but it didn't work as well as constantly delivering a low level of pleasure stimuli. If they don't share that information with the clients, then they probably turn to using pain out of frustration when the Domani don't do as they're told."

Matthias grinned. "But we don't respond to the wavelengths, which means we can escape without fear of being punished."

"Actually, I'm not sure about you, but I *do* respond to pain stimuli. All too well." Eventide's hand subconsciously went to the back of her neck, her fingers tracing the connection her necklace made to the two nodes. She wasn't sure she'd be able to forget the debilitating pain she'd endured. If Domani underwent that every time a client was dissatisfied, no wonder they'd try to escape. "Since we don't know the reason our nodes haven't established complete control over us, I think it'd be best to assume the two of you could experience pain, too—unless you've had an encounter that would suggest otherwise."

Both Okimi and Matthias shook their heads.

"Okay. How do the Caregivers choose which Domani to bring before a client, Matthias?"

The man shrugged. "I haven't paid that much attention. I would assume the buyer submits preferences to the Caregivers and they select Domani to match."

Eventide lifted a finger to her mouth. If they were headed for Earth, that would be the best chance she had of getting off the ship. She could find a way to track down Django from there.

Eventide studied her newfound companions. Okimi was short, with copper skin and a toned but petite build. Matthias, on the other hand, was tall, muscular, and dark. Eventide was fit, lean, shorter than Matthias, but a good twelve centimeters taller than Okimi, and her skin was about as pale as she'd seen. Physically, the three of them had nothing in common.

"Unless the client wants someone who doesn't respond

to the neurotransmitters, I don't see a way the three of us would be chosen for the same buyer."

"It's likely there'll be multiple buyers," Matthias suggested. "Especially on Earth. But we would be split up at some point, so we'd have to plan accordingly. We've made six stops since I've landed and I've not been called down once. There's no guarantee any of us, never mind all of us, will set foot on the surface."

Eventide nodded. "So, our only chance of getting out is sneaking off between landing and drop-off. Making a break for it once we're at a docking port."

"That's a crazy plan!" Okimi protested. "Have you forgotten about these nodes in our heads? If what you say is true, the Caregivers can flip a switch and send us into insurmountable pain. And that's only if they don't realize what we're up to until we're missing. They are able to track us, remember?"

Eventide was trying not to think about that part yet. If they could set up a jammer field, it should be possible to negate that reality. Or maybe they could cause a distraction . . .

"Besides, like I said, I want to stay, or to be purchased by some wealthy Syndicate official. Are you kidding? Even as a Domani, we'll have guaranteed breathable air and no shortage of food. There's nothing else I could do in the Loop that would come close to that, especially if my choices are between that and having the chip in my head explode on me."

Eventide shook her head. "You can do whatever you want. Join us, help us, or get out of the way. As far as the implants go, I'd assume their range isn't infinite. It's likely we'll need to be close enough to the ship, or someone with a transmitter."

"Maybe," Okimi said, grimacing. "But even if that's true, you don't know how big of a range that is—and you definitely don't know how much damage they could inflict before you're out of it."

Eventide winced at the memory of that morning's experience. How much further could the doctor have turned that dial? Morales had hinted at a lot more.

But how much was Eventide willing to risk in order to gain her freedom?

Everything.

There was no question in her mind, she had to try. She couldn't resign herself to the life of a Domani, not after everything she'd worked to achieve.

"I'm in," Matthias said. "My guess is we have just over a week until we land on Earth."

"Perfect," Eventide said. "Okimi, you'll have until then to change your mind."

"Won't need it." Okimi crossed her arms defiantly. "Don't crawl back to me when the Caregivers explode your brain."

Eventide hoped it wouldn't come to that.

CHAPTER TWENTY-FIVE

Eventide

The *Inanna*

The next day, Eventide found herself in the Recreation Room with Matthias. They situated themselves on a couple of beanbag lounge chairs in the corner, far enough away from prying ears, but still in a position where they could watch the Domani who passed by. A small table sat between them, with a gaming datapad laid flat upon its surface. Eventide had been intent on brainstorming ways they could find data on the ship's operations, but without being able to access outside of the Domanis' sheltered section of the ship, it was all speculation—which also annoyed Eventide to no end.

The rec room hummed with muted conversations and gentle laughter. Like most areas of the ship the Domani could access, it was a stark white space, complete with immaculate paneling and innovative tech lining its walls. Every detail had been meticulously planned, from the sleek interactive touchscreens to the avant-garde artwork projected onto the holo-screens. It was a tantalizing cocoon of distraction, effectively shielding the Domani from their fates. But dress it up anyway you like, the *Inanna* was still a prison.

Despite being out in the open, Eventide wanted to use every spare moment to plan their eventual escape, but there wasn't much information for her to access and it was hard to concentrate knowing that there had been a murder committed on board. So, instead, she contemplated what had happened to Orin, and if there was anything that could be done to prevent the deaths of others on board.

"Try not to think about it," Matthias offered. "It's not going to bring him back. I'm sorry if this guy meant something to you." There was a certain comfort in his voice that Eventide hadn't expected; a quiet strength that drew her attention.

Still, Eventide bristled at the suggestion. "Another Domani was killed by somebody on board this ship and you think the only reason I could possibly be concerned about that is because I might have feelings for him?"

"It's possible," Matthias lifted his arms and leaned back, resting his head on clasped hands.

"How can you be so heartless?" Eventide fumed. "*Your* emotions are supposed to be working, remember?"

"Hey!" Matthias raised his hands defensively. "I didn't say I didn't care. But sitting here worrying about it isn't going to solve anything."

"If we figure out who did it, then we can prevent it from happening again! In case you haven't realized, not being susceptible to the stimuli makes us prime targets to be done away with."

Matthias gave a noncommittal shrug. "I've gone without detection for this long. As far as I'm concerned, the weak link here is you."

Eventide grunted in frustration, prompting several wide-eyed Domani to turn and look at her with concern. Realizing she'd attracted unwanted attention, she slackened her jaw and forced a smile as she insincerely waved to the men and women.

Maybe he has a point.

"I don't know what life was like where you're from," Matthias continued, leaning toward her and lowering his voice, "but people here, in the real world, they die. They're murdered. If not, their souls are slowly sucked from them until they wish they were. There's always a chance someone is going to do you in. If you want to escape, then focus on that. Chances are it was the Caregivers, anyway, and you always need to look out for them."

Eventide sighed. "So, you think it was Lin?"

"Her, or one of the others."

Matthias picked at some crust underneath his nails; dirt that must have been embedded from their tumble in the atrium the night before. His hands were rough, calloused.

"'Others?' How many Caregivers are there?"

"On board? It changes depending on our destination. Usually half a dozen. There are also dignitaries and executives that will pay top dollar for transport from one colony to another. This is the most luxurious ship in the system."

She didn't know why, but the idea of passengers being

on board the vessel struck Eventide as odd. She glanced around the room, her gaze falling on the other Domani who lounged on plush, modern couches, lost in their stimulated bliss. Their eyes were glazed, smiles vacant, as they enjoyed the titillations being fed to their brains. Despite their physical presence, they were light-years away, oblivious to the desperate scheming occurring in their midst.

The thought of other passengers walking around elsewhere onboard made her skin crawl. Were they aware of the circus that surrounded them? Were they okay with the people on other decks of the ship being manipulated and forced into servitude?

Eventide shook her head. From what she'd heard so far, people in the system would likely not bat an eye.

If that were the case, then there was no reason other areas of the ship couldn't be used for paid transport. But to think that there were passengers in quarters above or below them who were free to come and go as they pleased—who'd had the opportunity to better themselves and maintain agency over their own lives—gnawed at her insides.

But that information also presented other opportunities.

"So, if we could find our way into another part of the ship, we could pretend to be passengers and take off with them?"

Matthias pursed his lips, curling his thumb and forefinger around his smooth jawline. Eventide couldn't help but follow the tracing of his beautifully defined features. Had the Caregivers performed surgeries on their faces, too?

"Even if we could find our way out of this section," he replied, "we wouldn't be able to walk off the main gangplank without being scanned. The comings and goings of all citizens are tracked. And once you wave your Domani chip in front of that scanner, you'll be discovered. Plus, if our destination is Earth, nobody else will be allowed off the ship, either. We're stuck either way."

"What do you mean? They're prisoners on board, too?"

Matthias lifted a scrutinizing eyebrow. "Where'd you say you grew up? No off-worlders are allowed to set foot on the planet, except those being showcased. Everyone else will be on lockdown until the ship leaves."

Okimi's petite frame appeared in the doorway, her eyes immediately falling on them and narrowing.

"What are the two of you doing?" she hissed as she approached. "You can't be seen together like this!"

"Why not?" Matthias asked, gesturing to the other Domani in the room. "It's not like we're the only ones talking."

Eventide studied the others in the room. While it was true the other Domani were lounging together, none of them seemed to be as engrossed in conversation as they had been.

"She's right," Eventide agreed. "We can't give the Care-givers any more reason to be suspicious. Plus," she scanned the room cautiously, "isn't it possible they're listening to everything we say? Shouldn't we save this chat for the atrium?"

"You're overthinking it," Matthias said, waving a hand dismissively. "We'll be fine."

Okimi bit her lip and hugged herself as though chilled, but she didn't argue. "Have you come up with anything?"

"Nothing useful," Eventide replied. "If only I could get

access to the ship's systems, I'd be able to figure something out. Even if I had a bloody map, I'd at least know which direction we had to go."

"You know your way around computers?" Matthias lifted an eyebrow skeptically. He pushed himself up off the elbow that had been supporting him, suddenly interested in the conversation.

"Haven't you been paying attention, thickhead?" Okimi snipped. "She says she was an engineer on one of the FLOW stations."

Matthias gave her an unconvinced look, as though he couldn't quite believe someone like her could be skilled with tech.

She rolled her eyes. "What? Am I too pretty to know my way around a ship's systems? Trust me, that surgery they performed when I arrived did wonders for my figure."

She kicked out a leg and spread her arms, showcasing her newly acquired muscle definition.

At the gesture, she noticed a flicker of surprise in Matthias' eyes. It was gone in an instant, but the warmth it sparked within her lingered.

"What I mean," he said, gathering his composure, "is that few Domani come from a background with much technical knowledge. Most sold to the ships are from farms and mines further out in the sector. Not exactly a pool of people used to working on computers and starships."

"Well, if you stick around long enough, I'm bound to surprise you." Eventide had meant the words to be light, but they came out as annoyed.

"Anyway," Matthias blushed, "you could try to access

the network through one of the rec room datapads. A while back, I came across a back door into the ship's system. I can help you gain access, if you'd like."

He stood, as though about to leave.

"Wait, what?" Eventide moved to stop him. "You know how to access a back door to the system?"

Matthias shrugged, his features unreadable. "When you're stuck here with nothing to do but play games on datapads, you get bored. One time, I stumbled upon a system error that displayed some of the ship's data. It wasn't much—a network error—but it was enough to know that the pads are connected to the ship's systems. Through that, we could probably access some of the data in the main computer systems."

"But . . . that doesn't make any sense." Eventide struggled to process this new information. "Why would *recreational* datapads have any connection to critical ship's systems? Especially if anyone can stumble across them?"

Matthias smirked, his eyes briefly glancing toward a group of Domani clustered near a holo-screen. They were engaged in a simple game that flashed vivid colors every time one of them got a point, their eyes vacant and their smiles plastered. "Do you really think if they happened across any logistical data, they'd do anything with it? Would they even know what they're looking at?"

He casually brushed a hand over a datapad sitting on the table before them. "Just don't get too excited about it. Best-case scenario, we access some metrics. It's not like we'll be able to send out commands from a rec room datapad. But who knows, it might give us a lead."

Eventide frowned, her mind racing.

"Their brain chemistry is being manipulated," Okimi pressed cautiously. "It's not like they're idiots."

Matthias shrugged. "Either way, I don't think the Caregivers are too worried about Domani getting somewhere they don't belong."

Eventide blinked, studying him as if he would provide more answers. If there was even a sliver of a chance they could access details about the ship—blueprints, controls, operations,—they had to take it.

When Matthias didn't offer anything else, she hesitantly grabbed the pad. "Okay," she said. "Let's give it a shot."

Okimi bit her lip. "What sort of information are you looking for, exactly?"

"Anything we can use to find a way out of here. A floor plan of the rest of the ship would be a good start. Information on security systems, access codes . . . whatever we can find."

Matthias raised an eyebrow. "You seem to know your way around this sort of thing."

Eventide snorted, her thoughts briefly flickering back to the panic-ridden corridors of the *Eclipse* and her escape with Django. Her past success, however, felt miles away on this alien vessel. "Let's just say, I've had some practice in getting out of places I don't want to be."

"Leave that one here." Matthias pointed to the device in her hand. "I'll track down some more datapads that won't be missed. I don't think we should do this out in the open. We can get started in the atrium tonight."

"What can I do to help?" Okimi volunteered.

Eventide grinned. Information was power, but she could use a little luck on her side.

"I've been dying to get my hands on some playing cards," she said. "Any chance you could track some down for me?"

CHAPTER TWENTY-SIX

Django
    Asteria

Despite Marvin's insistence that the bed in Taku's room was sufficient, Django convinced his uncle that he didn't want to make waves during his first week in Asteria.

"You can't keep your head down like you did on the *Eclipse*," Marvin said when Django approached him later that day. "You need to show Taku and the rest of the Resurgence that you belong here."

"I'll pick my battles," Django said. "If that means sleeping elsewhere to avoid being stabbed in my sleep, I'll do it."

Going without a bed was a small sacrifice he'd been willing to make, and while he didn't really believe Taku would kill him—Django was *unchipped,* after all—he didn't want to take that chance.

"I know you better than that," Marvin said. "You're avoiding conflict. You always do."

"Just fights among my supposed allies. Don't worry, I'm

willing to plunge headfirst into whatever battle you've planned for me."

Django spent the next few days exploring the compound. The white-tiled floors and paneled walls reminded him of the upper rings of the *Eclipse*. Glass windows provided views out onto the Rim and beyond, to the blue and green Earth above.

Other than Taku, everyone Django encountered on the base treated him with kindness, even those who had no clue about his affiliation with Marvin. It made his decision to fight with the rebels easy to swallow. All of them had chosen to be here and seemed genuinely happy about that fact. Whatever Commander Aries had imagined this place to be, it was a far cry from the hub of anarchy and desperation he had depicted.

Everywhere he went, the seeds of hopes and dreams seemed to be taking root. Soldiers trained together, their camaraderie echoing in synchronized laughter. Scientists huddled around tables, passionately discussing their latest theories. Families hugged their children tight after a long day of work.

Here, bonds formed and thrived, friendships nurtured on shared struggles and common dreams. It was clear in the shared smiles between Rowyn and Wilder, a warmth that didn't belong solely to them, but reflected Asteria's spirit. The compound was a bastion of hopes and dreams; of found family and friendships.

Rowyn and Wilder weren't the exception to the rule here. They were the norm.

Ironically, in all those but the rebel leaders.

Django was in the midst of these thoughts when

Marvin found him in the training area, watching the recruits learning hand-to-hand combat techniques. Despite having punched two people now, Django had received no formal combat training himself. The back-and-forth dance of the sparring members mesmerized him, but when asked whether he wanted a turn, he politely declined.

It wasn't because he didn't want to, but because he didn't know where to start. The trainer laughed and said they could hook him up with a beginner program if he came back in a couple days.

"We've got a meeting with the Founders," Marvin said as he pulled Django out of the combat rooms.

"Founders?" Django asked. "Rowyn said *you* were the founder?"

"Maybe once."

Marvin led Django through a series of halls and unknown sections of the base he hadn't traversed, passing levels of security clearance that prompted Marvin to vouch for Django's presence.

They entered an open space with an enormous set of windows along one wall, overlooking Asteria and the bustle of people on the streets several storeys below. A formidable oval table sat in the room's center, with a dozen men and women seated around it.

"I have a lot of clout," Marvin whispered as they entered, "but the Founders' Table organizes our strategy against the Syndicate. In my absence, the organization has grown too large for one person's leadership. A frustrating change," he said with a sigh, "but a necessary one."

Other than Taku, who sat staring daggers, Django

hadn't been introduced to any of them. Not one had gone out of their way to greet him since his arrival in Asteria.

The epiphany made Django feel smaller and much more of a cog in their machine than he'd been led to believe.

He stood before the dozen Founders, thinking back to what he had learned about them over the past few days. In keeping with their title, half of the council were founding members of the Resurgence, while the other half were replacements for those who had fallen over the course of the last decade. They were an even split of both sexes, with a diverse mix of backgrounds from their ancestral home-lands on Earth. An empty chair sat at the front of the table for Marvin.

Django wondered if the chair had always been there, symbolically left empty until the day Marvin had surprised them all and returned to fill it.

And these were supposed to be his allies?

The faces reminded him of Taku: skeptical and suspi-cious. Each of them eyed him up as though he was their prized pig, headed for slaughter for their holiday dinner. It was an odd mix of fascination and disdain.

"He has no military training," one of the women, with skin a similar shade of brown to his own and a bright yellow outfit, was saying as they walked in. "No espionage back-ground. And we're going to pin the fate of the movement on him? Do you think we'll get more than one chance at this?"

"Nobody thinks that, Myr'na." The man who chal-lenged her was younger, with a pale complexion and lucid blue eyes. "But even you have to see that the timing of this couldn't be better."

The room was cold and sterile compared to the rest of the compound. The oval table the Founders sat around was formed from a blueish-gray metal. Their chairs were made of the same material and almost egg-shaped, cushioned with bright blue padding that was form-fitted to the shells' interiors. At least the room didn't smell of bleach.

There was no question the men and women in this room held authority. They had an air of privilege about them; an air of superiority that reflected the stance of Taku.

Whatever their motivations *had* been for joining this movement, Django could almost guarantee those had been shuffled aside long ago for personal ambitions and prestige.

Asteria's people had seemed to be the antithesis of what this council portrayed. *How can there be two such opposing dynamics within one movement? Why are those pulling the strings so cold while the rest of its members are warm and inviting?*

"He doesn't need training." Marvin's voice boomed across the chamber, silencing My'rna. Even Marvin seemed surprised at the intensity of his own voice. He softened and followed with, "Not yet."

"Marvin." Myr'na looked up and carried on as though he had been part of their conversation the entire time. "I know you have fond feelings for the boy, but if anything goes wrong, we blow our window of opportunity, and who knows if we'll ever face the same vulnerabilities ever again."

The light shifted, revealing the bags under Myr'na's eyes. Her striking silver hair flowed around her ears, shining as though it had once been taken care of, but its ends had frayed and the strands were unkept.

Marvin stood firm. "And how often does the Prefect change? Ptolemy reigned for twenty years. His son is only twenty-five. We already know the Syndicate council doesn't trust him. Are we going to wait another fifty years until we reach the same level of instability? I hope to live to be an old man, Myr'na, but I have yet to meet a Lunarian that has reached the age of eighty-five."

There was implication behind Marvin's words, and Django didn't believe it had anything to do with his own age.

On the *Eclipse*, Django had known only a handful of A-Ringers over fifty, Benson being the prime example, but My'rna, for all her vitality and formidable presence, could easily have been Benson's senior by a decade.

She frowned. "Do you really think this lad is capable of what is required?"

The rest of the room leaned forward in anticipation. All except Taku, who leaned back and crossed his arms.

"For stage one? He just needs to show up. Under the guidance of Taku and myself, our team will handle the rest." Marvin now appealed to the Founders' Table as a whole. "Look, there will be time for training after we drop the payload at Space Dock Seven, but there will be no better opportunity to destabilize the Empire than there is right now. Not in our lifetime. The only remaining thread left to pull is to implant the chip. Once the upload has been made, then we prepare him for the next stage."

All eyes in the room remained on Django. Holo-screens

sat dormant behind the Founders, their hum filling the spaces between words.

"Marvin, you know I trust you more than anyone else." The man who spoke was a similar age to Marvin. His skin was a pale gray, and his voice had a deep rasp to it that suggested he'd had his fill of whiskey, cigars, or perhaps exhaust fumes from some piece of equipment in the mines. A scar ran down the left side of his face, accompanying a series of black cybernetic chips that had been implanted into his temple. "But you must understand why we're skeptical about implanting this chip in just anyone. If the boy fails, for whatever reason, we don't have another one. And it's not like we can rip it out of him and plant it in someone else."

Django cringed. Ripping out the chip likely meant he'd be dead.

"Or worse," Myr'na interjected, "what if some pirate wins him over? Or the Prefect? This chip isn't only a means to ending the Syndicate; it's granting the user unlimited access to all their systems."

"Find me any other adult who's compatible with it and we can discuss options. I have watched this young man grow up for the past decade. I can assure you, there is nobody with more honor and dedication than Django Alexander. He'll do what's right, even to his own detriment."

Django had to force himself not to swallow as the Founders' icy glares pierced through him.

The deal he had struck with Aries hung over him.

The Resurgence seeks lawlessness. They will *disappoint you.*

He'd thrown his lot in with the Resurgence for now, but the Syndicate Commander was still a card he held in his pocket.

Heat burned in Django's chest. For now, at least, he'd decided to help his uncle. If he could rescue Eventide without the help of Commander Aries, it was the road he'd prefer to follow. But regardless of who was willing to help him, he was done sitting on the sidelines.

A few of the Founders nodded to indicate that Marvin's word was good enough. Others, like Taku, looked as though they would rather murder Django where he stood to rid the rest of the Resurgence leaders of their choice.

"Listen." Django's voice earned a glare from Marvin. His uncle wanted to be the one to lead this fight, but Django was done sitting back. He was sick of relying on others—on Marvin, on Aries—to get him through. This had become about more than Eventide; more than Benson. "I'm capable of doing whatever needs to be done."

This had become about the people dying in the Tubes beneath Shackleton. This had become about the people who would be sent to the mines for trying to make a decent living, and being sent off to die, not for any great purpose, but to make an already rich empire richer, for the promise of a scrap for the family they had left behind. This had become about the thousands ripped from their homes, living on the streets with air that was barely breathable, desperate for any ounce of food they could find.

Django's family had died because of the Syndicate, but at least they had *lived*. They had been ignorant to their slavery.

Does that make it better or worse?

It was about the people who had died on the *Infinity*. The haunting image of *Eclipse*'s doppelgänger, not exploding in an instant, but powering down. Its rings stopped spinning, its air supply system shut off, leaving its residents to suffocate.

He'd had enough.

"Like all of you, I've seen firsthand what the Syndicate can do to those just trying to get by. It's time for change."

"That's all well and good when you're standing here," Myr'na said. "But what happens when you need to make a hard decision? What happens if you have to choose between someone you hold dear or the benefit of the Loop? What if you're faced with a choice to save Marvin or complete your mission? You haven't had the training to psychologically endure what you might face."

"How prepared are any of us?" Django snapped. "How prepared is a child to lose his father to the mines? Or a parent to have their daughter kidnapped by a courtesan slave trader?" Django cringed, but he tried not to let the thought of Eventide steer him off course. He *needed* to be trusted with this mission. He needed that chip.

But he also needed to help bring change to the system. To put an end to the lies.

"You keep saying you have one chance to take this new Prefect down. I'm that chance! And you're going to let that slip past you because you're uncertain? Because I assure you, if you're looking for certainty in this life, you will not find it."

Life can change fast, and in ways you don't expect.

"You all thought Marvin was dead; a martyr for your

cause. But here he is! I bet you were certain the Syndicate wouldn't destroy one of their own space stations, but *Infinity* proved that wrong as well! Are you just going to hide here, in your safe little compound, waiting for the right moment, while your fellow citizens are out there dying? Rioting in the street because they're so desperate for change, only for the Syndicate to gleefully slap them down? Or are you happy to let those still outside Asteria's walls take the ire of those in power so you can sit at the Table for another day?"

"That's quite enough." Myr'na didn't raise her voice, but if Django's speech hadn't silenced the room, her words certainly did. "You know little of what you speak, boy. I suggest you hold your tongue. If Mr. Alexander could step out and allow the Table to conclude our discussion and take a vote on this matter . . ."

Marvin nodded to Django, and reluctantly, with his heart pounding a mile a minute in his chest, Django retreated to the next room.

CHAPTER TWENTY-SEVEN

Django
    Asteria

The committee deliberated for hours as Django paced the lobby. Out the window, Earth hovered above, while Lunar fought to stay afloat in orbit, circling around it until one day it, too, would inevitably escape the planet's gravitational pull and be flung into the reaches of space on a suicide mission, a crash course to either the Sun or Jupiter. That fate wouldn't happen for millions of years, but Django wondered how much sooner he would crash and burn.

He itched his forearm. Somehow, he, a space station boy with no aspirations to do anything but farm, had ended up a key component in this madness. And what made it worse was knowing he had just encouraged it.

All I ever wanted was for things to stay the same.

But if Django had known the truth about the Syndicate, would he have put his hand up sooner? Of course, in his world, the D-Ring was habitually oppressed by the A-

Ring, and he had been happy enough to sit back and farm the soil that filled their bellies.

At that time, though, he had believed he had been helping. He had believed that he was working toward a purpose. And now? The veil had been pulled back, and he had come to realize it wasn't so much a life of comfort he wanted, as a life of purpose.

The Founders ended up voting in favor of Django receiving the implant, eleven to one. Marvin wouldn't tell Django who the dissenter was, and Django had to admit he was surprised the vote had gone in his favor, never mind being so overwhelmingly one-sided.

That meant that either Myr'na or Taku had voted *for* him. Django truly didn't know who the more likely candidate was. Myr'na had petitioned hard against him while he was in the room, but Taku had held a grudge against him since the moment he had arrived on Lunar's surface.

In the end, it didn't matter much—except he'd be trusting his life with one of those members. The other would wait in Asteria to hear the results.

If Taku had voted against Django's involvement, would the man go out of his way to ensure Django would fail? Rowyn still seemed to trust Taku, but Django knew little about him. How far would he go to prove that his dissenting voice had been correct?

Rowyn and Wilder were beside themselves when they heard the news.

"Finally!" Wilder said, the large man rubbing his knuckles. His green tattoos shimmered as though they were also eagerly anticipating what was to come. "We're going to smash the skulls of those Syndicate bastards!"

Django couldn't help but smile. The man talked a tough game, but as he remembered from their teamwork at the transition house, Wilder would do anything to help his friends.

"We won't be doing anything of the sort." Marvin was more eavesdropping than engaged until that point. "At least, not yet. This is a strategic mission. We need to weaken the cities of Earth. If we can compromise the space docks, then we control the flow of traffic and goods to and from the surface."

Marvin explained the plan to them. It seemed simple enough in theory, though Django imagined it would be much more complicated in execution. Django would board a pirate-controlled ship that would convey him to one of the space docks that orbited the Earth. These docks acted as both waypoints for anyone who needed to enter or leave the Earth's atmosphere by way of space elevator and thus, they were also the arterial access points for the Syndicate's distribution network. The pirates would cause a distraction, and Django would use his newly acquired chip to upload a program into their systems.

Not just any program. A virus.

Their computers would fail, one by one, as the malignant code penetrated the Syndicate systems. As per protocol, the failing vessel would establish a network connection with a neighboring dock—maybe more than one—to assess the problem. That connection would spread the virus to the aiding station and, once again, the virus would duplicate. Once the infection spread, all of the docks would be rendered useless. Haulers weren't authorized to enter

Earth's atmosphere and wouldn't dare try. Without resources, the Syndicate would be backed into a corner.

It was a game of chess, and Django was being signed up to make the first move. After everything the Empire had done to make humanity suffer, he was more than willing to give them a taste of a life of scarcity.

Marvin wasted no time in hauling Django down to the MedLab, sending Wilder and Rowyn away to prepare for departure. The team was to leave as soon as the doctors cleared Django, though nobody would give him a straight answer as to when that was likely to be.

Marvin eyed Django as he led them through the corridors. "I've never seen you stand up for yourself like that," he commented. "You proved to everyone in that room you have some fire in you, after all."

Django smirked. "You should have seen me bark at Wilder back at the transition house. I'm tired of sitting and waiting. Of being jerked around by everyone around me. It's time to take a stand."

"Your father would be proud, you know. Though he'd probably kill me for bringing you into this."

Except Dad knew the secrets you kept and held some of his own.

"I'm starting to think I knew my father just about as well as I knew you."

"You knew your father just fine. He was forward-thinking, but he was a farmer, same as you."

"And the weapon I found under his bed?"

"The Renegade blaster? *Hah!*" Marvin let out a belly laugh. "Lad, your father was many things, but a fighter wasn't one of them. That weapon was mine. He agreed to hang on to it for me for safekeeping in case the Station Guard came snooping through my things."

Django's heart jumped at the implication. "What if they'd searched *our* quarters?"

"Do you think it's easy to just appear and adopt a persona on a space station? Bunks aren't exactly plentiful. I had to live in shared quarters, and even then, if it wasn't for Avery, things would have been a hell of a lot more difficult than they were."

"What did Avery have to do with all this?" The space station guard had helped Django and Eventide off the *Eclipse*, but she had seemed to have a soft spot for his uncle.

"Err . . ." Marvin stuttered, his face turning red, and suddenly, Django connected the pieces.

"She doesn't know you're alive." Django remembered the look on Avery's face when she had given him the news. There had been a deep sadness in her eyes. She'd no doubt given similar reports to countless families over the years, but *that* report had affected her. At the time, Django had mistaken it for her feeling sorry for *him*, but it had nothing to do with him at all. "You let her think you're dead."

"What was I supposed to do? Bring her with me? She's better off where she is. A FLOW station guard? She's in the safest place she can be." He cleared his throat. "But enough of that. Let me worry about the consequences of my decisions."

"Don't forget, I'm one of those consequences as well." Django said coldly. "And you're more than happy to shove me into the fire."

Dozens of beds lined the rooms down the corridor along the way to the MedLab.

Django thought the rooms were odd for a community the size of Asteria. He had also heard Rowyn talking about other MedLabs in the city. *Why did they have so many beds if they were just going to remain empty?*

At first, Django was offended. He'd been sleeping on a cot in a closet next to the cafeteria when he could have been stationed here for the past few days. His eyes darted around the room, resting on each empty bed, and a sudden chill crawled up his spine.

These weren't for recovery; they were for casualties.

"Stage two is war," he said, thinking out loud more than anything, then he directed his thoughts toward his uncle. "You're preparing for the Syndicate to retaliate."

"It's not quite that straightforward, but do you expect them to sit back and let us waltz in?" Marvin asked. "War is inevitable."

Images of ancient wars Django had studied filled his thoughts: the destruction, the loss, the aftermath. But Django had only read about them. War wasn't something he'd ever believed he would have to experience in his lifetime.

"This was what the Table worried I wasn't ready for. It had nothing to do with the chip. They didn't think I was ready for the fight."

Marvin gave a slight nod. "I wouldn't say 'nothing'. You were right, though. None of us are ready. The Syndicate forces are far greater than ours. That's why we need to hit them while they're in transition. We need to slow them down."

"But what happens when they discover we uploaded the virus?"

"They'll have no way of knowing. This isn't about declaring our names in an act of terror; this is about slowly bleeding their resources. It's about reshuffling the deck they've stacked in their favor for two centuries and giving us a leg to stand on. By the time they'll be able to pinpoint the virus, it will be too late. By the time they realize it was us, we'll hopefully already have overpowered them."

Somehow, Django hadn't really thought that far ahead. Perhaps the committee was right; what *did* he know about taking down an empire? He envisioned the domino effect of his actions: cities in ruin, lives lost, families torn apart. Was this the future he was to set in motion?

"You can't start a revolution without being willing to sacrifice," Marvin continued, as if reading his thoughts. "People will die by the Syndicate hand, whether we fight or not. The problems in the Tubes have grown worse in the time I've been gone. Reports say that Mars and the outer colonies are the same if not in worse shape. Taku has managed to build up Resurgence arms on Mars, Ceres, and Callisto, and those outfits have obtained both fighters and ships. Out there, they need to be heartier. They're built for the farms and the mines."

They stopped walking as they reached a surgical station—a chair with a rest for an arm and straps running up and down each side in order to hold a patient down and prevent them from struggling.

"I'm going to be awake for the procedure?" Django asked, a lump forming in his throat.

"We've got to ration our anesthesia for the upcoming battles. We're going to be facing far worse than a slice to the arm in the coming days."

Marvin reached into his jacket and pulled out a flask. He shook it slightly as though testing the weight, perhaps gauging if he'd finished it himself or not. He took a swig and passed it toward Django.

The odor of the dank booze wafted from the vessel, overpowering the stale recycled air of the MedLab. Django was reminded of the drink he had tried at the Velvet Underground when he'd first ventured into the Tubes.

He raised a hand. "I think I'm good."

"Trust me," Marvin said, "you're not."

Django sighed. He would have felt better if he didn't have to be awake for the surgery, but he had nothing to lose by accepting Marvin's drink. He turned his nose up before the elixir even touched his mouth; it was vile, dank with the smell of bog water and paint thinner. Django couldn't believe people actually drank this stuff for fun.

He grimaced. "This smells worse than the piss on the station."

"Bah!" Marvin feigned offence. "Station liquor tasted like dirt. This might not be Earth whiskey, but our own distilleries made this right here in Asteria, with real grains. You won't find a better one made anywhere on the Moon's surface."

Django held his nose as he sucked back the potion. If this was the only buffer between him and the surgeon's knife, he would deal with it.

"Easy there, lad," Marvin said, swiping the flask from Django's hand. "If you throw it all back up, it defeats the purpose. You can't be chugging whiskey like that."

Django let out an unexpected belch. His throat burned, and he coughed from the intensity of the liquid.

The door slid open to reveal a light-skinned woman of average height, dressed in scrubs that identified her as the one performing the operation. Two men, who were noticeably less sterile appearing, accompanied her, with sizable energy weapons holstered to their sides. The woman approached as the two men took positions on either side of the entryway.

Are they here to ensure nobody else enters? Or to make sure I don't run at the last minute?

As she entered the room, the corners of the woman's mouth lifted into a warm, reassuring smile.

"I'm Doctor Ballard. You're later than I expected."

"I heard you were out of anesthesia, so we had to stop to take matters into our own hands," Django said, making light of his concern.

The doctor rolled her eyes with a chuckle that would have put even the most nervous patient at ease. "I bet you did." She turned to Marvin. "It's bad enough I have to constantly be on his ass about his drinking. Don't be passing on your bad habits to this one, Commander. You might not be after a long life, but the kid's got a right to one."

"She prattles on as if *anyone* in the Loop has a long life. We aren't on the Rim, Diane. I've already lived a longer life than most." Marvin tipped the flask to his lips as though proving a point, then he offered the flask to Django. "Why shouldn't we be allowed to enjoy it? Or at least, numb its suffering. Here, boy, drink up."

Django grimaced as he reached for another hesitant swig.

"Enough of that! Just because we won't put him to sleep, doesn't mean we haven't got anything for the pain. Alcohol will only dehydrate him, and water is one thing we need to be cautious about wasting."

Holo-screens lit up with Django's medical file. Unsurprisingly, there wasn't much data there. The screen listed his weight, height, and blood type, but most of the other rows that listed headings were blank. Place of origin. Genetic dispositions. History of illness. All blank.

Other fields were listed beneath a heading titled "BIO-METRICS." Heart rate. Blood pressure. White blood cell count. These, too, were blank.

The listings represented readings that every person with a chip would constantly be tracking. Everyone outside of the FLOW stations.

Everyone except him.

Django pulled up his sleeve and held out his arm.

"Oh dear child," Doctor Ballard said with a smirk. "This isn't a tetanus shot. I wish it was going to be that simple. On second thought, you might want to take another sip of your uncle's drink."

CHAPTER TWENTY-EIGHT

Django
Asteria

Django awoke from a deep sleep in more agony than he'd ever experienced.

Each muscle in his body ached with an intensity that rivaled the worst days working the fields, while a dull, relentless pain pounded in his skull, echoing the aftermath of downing a dozen of Martin's bog water drinks.

It wasn't until the second time he vomited that Django remembered what Doctor Ballard had told him before going under the knife: until the integration was complete, the adult immune system had a harder time accepting the chip as part of the body.

Django lifted an arm to his pounding forehead—or at least, he *tried* to. His forearm seized with pain and sent the rest of his body into waves of convulsion.

"Easy there, station boy." Rowyn's voice was a blend of concern and sass. "You're dehydrated. Ballard says I need to make sure you're getting your fluids."

The MedLab bay beeped and hummed around him. The bright lights of the surgical room were now replaced by dimmer, more soothing hues. This room wasn't one of the dorms designed for the mass casualties of war; instead, he had been given a private room. Monitors recording and charting his vitals beeped all around him, and he could make out charts and graphs that displayed readouts and biometrics.

My biometrics.

It was done, then. The chip had been implanted, and it was providing the Resurgence with all the information they could ever want about him.

A cold uneasiness crept in, prickling his skin. The reality of the procedure, the chip now embedded within him, felt overwhelmingly invasive. *Should* the Resurgence be able to collect all this data on him? What did they need it for? And if they could receive this much data from the chip, could they also send data *to* it?

A little late now.

His eyes strained, attempting to decipher the cascade of numbers that occupied the screen, but they swam and smeared in front of him, blurred as if being viewed through a dense fog. In truth, it was a challenge to even keep his eyes open.

"Why can't I see?"

"Your body is trying to adapt to the chip," Rowyn explained. "Don't worry; it's normal. Doctor Ballard said that once you woke up, it would take at least another week before you were back to your charming self." She smiled—that much, he could see—and laid a hand on his good arm. "Drink this."

She offered a jar of liquid to him, and he gulped it down greedily.

"Once I woke up?" Django wiped his mouth off with his sleeve, searching his memory for any recollection of the implant being installed.

He remembered being strapped into the surgical chair and the doctor giving him some kind of root that she said would help with the pain. It had seemed more like witchcraft than science, and when he'd said as much, he got a laugh from Ballard and an explanation that the root had been genetically enhanced with painkilling properties.

"I don't understand . . . I wasn't given a general anesthetic. Why was I asleep?"

Rowyn raised her eyebrows in confusion, as though Django should have been able to piece together the answer for himself. "The valerian root didn't work. You passed out from the pain in the first ten minutes of the operation."

Django didn't remember any of that. Fragments of the surgery flashed through his mind: the cold, biting steel of the scalpel, slicing into his flesh, followed by a horrifying rush of warmth as blood surged forth, pooling on the surgical table.

And then nothing.

"How long have I been here?" Django's belly rumbled. "I'm starving. Did I sleep through the night?"

The amusement drifted from Rowyn's face. "You've been asleep for four days, Django. If that chip wasn't already welded to your arm, the committee would have already sent us out."

Four days!

With a grunt, Django heaved his legs over the side of

the bed, pushing against the mattress with shaky arms to prop himself up—only to immediately fall back on his side in a flash of all-consuming agony. Rowyn was quick to catch him and readjust his position on the bed.

"Easy now! You've got to rest!"

"There's no time to rest," Django said. "You said it yourself. The Founders want to move."

"It doesn't matter what they want; what matters is what you need—and that's rest. You're not going to be any help to anyone if you pass out. Everything rides on you being prime. The space dock will still be there in a week."

Django didn't wait a week. He couldn't.

Having Rowyn and Wilder cater to his every whim was a pleasant change, though. Rowyn barely left his side, and when she did, it was only to bring him food. She even convinced the nurses to bring a cot into the room so that she could sleep at his bedside.

The first night, she had tried to climb into his bed, but had accidentally rolled into his sore arm more than once, sending rivers of pain lancing through him every time.

Which was a shame. Django had to admit he enjoyed having her warmth lying next to him.

But guilt overrode any enjoyment he felt at her closeness. It felt wrong, which frustrated him to no end. He had spent so much time pining after Eventide that cozying up to Rowyn felt like he was betraying her. But, of course, he also knew he was being ridiculous. Eventide had had her chance, and she'd said no.

But guilty or not, he was too sore to cuddle, and after the first night, Rowyn moved to the portable cot the med staff had wheeled in.

By day three, though, he'd had enough of lying in bed, and even the banter between friends wasn't enough to keep him content.

"How quickly can we move?" he prompted, his patience wearing thin. "I'm ready to be out of this bed."

"Once Doctor Ballard has cleared you," Rowyn chided.

"Forget what the doctor says!" Django objected. "If I'm forced to stay in this bed any longer, I'm going to go crazy. My arm's a little sore, but otherwise I'm fine."

Doctor Ballard pursed her lips when Django requested to be discharged, but she didn't put up much of a fight.

She urged him to rest when he could, and then watched in uncomfortable silence as Django, Rowyn, and Wilder left the MedLab to begin preparations for the mission.

Django wasn't much more than a passenger on the *R-332X*. He paced the narrow passageways and constricted communal areas, searching for his purpose. The ship was small compared to some of the other ships the Resurgence docked in Asteria—about the same size as the *Redemption*. Wilder had called it a runabout-class ship.

The ships in the Resurgence fleet weren't named like other ships seemed to be. Wilder had explained that, as combat vessels, the Founders preferred for Resurgence crew not to become attached to their ships, in case they should ever need to abandon it or, worse, sacrifice it, and the absence of a name helped to reinforce that. Plus, it was just annoyingly time consuming. So, Resurgence ships were each given a designation: an initial for the class type, and a number.

The *R-332X* could hold up to a crew of ten. For its current mission, there were eight on board. Django was more than familiar with Rowyn, Wilder, and Taku, but others he recognized—Louis, Marshall, Amy, and Vlad— were also on board. Django hadn't seen them since they had parted ways at the transition house.

He was surprised he recognized anyone at all. There were hundreds of Syndicate soldiers, though it made sense that the men and women Marvin had trusted to retrieve his people from a slave ship would also be called up for this mission.

Django had just gotten used to the artificial gravity on the Moon's surface, even if he was still unsure of the science behind amplifying the forces required to hold them at nearly 1 g. Eventide would have had a better under-standing; at least she would have cared enough to ask. But Django knew enough to understand that the Moon had some of its own gravity, at least, which could have explained why the artificial plating didn't tug at his stomach the same way it did on board the runabout. The *R-332X*'s artificial gravity interacted differently with his body, pulling on him in waves of discomfort.

"You going to be okay there?" Rowyn asked him. "You're turning green."

Django nodded as he tried to quash his queasiness. "I'll be okay. Just takes some getting used to."

He had no way of knowing if that were true, but he decided that a little gravity sickness wasn't going to stand in the way of him completing his first task for the Resurgence —or of him finding Eventide. He'd have to deal with it.

"How long until we reach the space dock?"

Django had directed the question at Rowyn, but it was Amy who answered. "It's a quick trip from here," she said. "Twenty minutes."

Amy stood beside a navigational panel, preparing to steer the ship into dock when they arrived at the mission site. To be honest, Django wasn't sure why so many personnel were needed for the mission, but he supposed the more people who could pull him out of trouble, the better.

"Taku?" Vlad piped up. Django hadn't heard him say more than a few words since they'd departed Asteria. He was a short man, and though he couldn't have been much older than Django, his dull orange hair formed a crescent over his scalp. His face was clean-shaven, creating a strange contrast of baby face and old-man hairline. "There's a woman on Frequency Seven. Says she wants to talk to the captain."

Taku stood from his chair in the center of the bridge and looked at Vlad questioningly. "Did she give you a name? Nobody but Marvin and the Founders should know we're here. They'd know better than to connect with us."

"Says her name is Abigail."

"Damn it." Taku's face darkened. "Put her through."

Vlad tapped something on his holo-screen and then nodded back to Taku.

The main holo activated and a pale angry woman stood

staring at the crew of the R-$332X$ with both a fierce intensity and a childish smirk. Her hair was white, shaven on all but one side, and around her neck hung a collection of bones threaded into a macabre pendant.

Django shuddered. He'd heard the name Abigail Monroe before. The woman before him didn't match the image he had in his head. He'd heard discussions about her being a notorious pirate; a force to be reckoned with. This person was no older than he was. Her frame was petite, and she couldn't have stood over five feet. Maybe he had to put his preconceived notions of who held influence in this system aside.

"Monroe," Taku snapped, locking eyes with the holo-projection. "You shouldn't be here. And you absolutely shouldn't be calling us on an open frequency. This is supposed to be a *covert* operation."

The pirate pouted and flipped a wrist dramatically. "I'm disappointed, love. The last time we met, we had such a good time." She finished with a smirk, and Django couldn't tell if she was being sarcastic or flirtatious.

"Would you cut it out with the 'love' bullshit?" Taku growled. "You know no sane person talks like that? It's beyond irritating!"

Abigail's smirk widened into a dazzling smile, her eyes alight with deviousness.

"Well, *love*. Nobody has ever accused me of being sane." She paused briefly as though expecting a response but then carried on regardless, flourishing a hand as if too impatient to wait for one. "Besides, everyone needs something that distinguishes them. Something a person will remember them by."

Django caught Wilder's eye. The big man wore the same baffled look as he did.

Taku let out an exasperated sigh as he sat back in the captain's chair and lifted a hand to his forehead. "What you'll be remembered for is being infuriating. What is it that you want, exactly? I hope you didn't risk our operation just to hear yourself talk."

"Alejandro keyed me in on your plan. I'm simply calling to let you know it's a *bad* idea."

Taku was growing visibly irritated. "I know I'm going to regret asking, but do you care to elaborate?"

"You think you're going to hop onto a space dock, waltz into Engineering, and upload a virus? I know you've got guts, but that's suicide."

Taku's lips tightened. "Again, may I remind you we're speaking on an open frequency."

"My point is, that it's a good way to end up in a Syndicate prison cell, or, more likely, dead."

Taku buried his face in his palms and rubbed his eyes impatiently. "Did you show up just to criticize me? Or do you have something else in mind?"

"Well, that's why I'm here, darling. What you need is for someone to create a diversion. And I've got a lovely team of pirates here up to task."

"A diversion?" Taku reiterated. "I thought getting killed would be something you'd want to avoid."

"Oh, we'll avoid it. You don't need to worry about us. Just stay out of our way and try not to get shot."

CHAPTER TWENTY-NINE

Django
Space Dock Seven

Try not to get shot.

The pirate's words echoed in Django's head. His pulse quickened, his hands clammy against the cold metal of the ship, and a knot formed in his stomach, growing tighter with each passing second.

He'd been in danger before, of course—on the station and in the Tubes. But in those situations, he'd been on the run—the victim.

He was now heading into a situation where he would be the aggressor.

The role reversal gave him pause. But only briefly. Monroe's words reinforced how unfit he was to complete the mission; a supposed hero of the Resurgence, but only because he happened to be born in a place where they didn't worry if their subjects were chipped or not. The residents of the FLOW stations were so well controlled and contained, they didn't need to be tracked.

But as a station farmer, Django wrestled with early mornings and late nights, working his heart out in order to restore the Earth. Misguided as his actions were, Django had craved purpose.

Now he had one.

Though in his wildest dreams, he couldn't have imagined finding it in teaming up with a band of insurgents to infiltrate a space dock.

Django refrained from scratching his forearm. He wished he hadn't developed the habit over the past week, as the surgery site was now sore from the implant that had fused itself to his being. Doctor Ballard had given him medication to ease the inflammation, which Django guessed was nothing more than another herbal supplement, but the incision point only bothered him when he actively scratched at it, but it was a hard pull to ignore.

The space dock loomed on the R-$332X$'s primary holo-screen as they approached. It was almost as much of a space station as the *Eclipse*, though far smaller in diameter and stretching out to allow for ships to come and go. Several long gray terminals fanned out in either direction, lined with docking bays on either side of each module. A large cylindrical hub sat at the dock's center, connecting the pinwheel of activity. Dozens of vessels were berthed on the outer edge of its hulking frame, while several others were coming and going.

The efficiency of the operation was impressive, leaving Django to wonder whether the ships arriving at *Eclipse* were so well timed.

Most prominent were the gigantic cables that stretched out from the bottom of the dock toward the Earth below.

The restriction of ships accessing the surface had been established after the last sections of the FLOW Stations had been assembled. The only vessels that now flew between the surface and orbit were the Syndicate's own patrols—Syndicate Front combat ships that guarded the planet from threats from above—and the occasional Domani ship. Potential threats had been few in the last hundred years; the odd terrorist, pirate, or rogue attacker sometimes attempted entry, but the ODS—the Orbital Defense System—was merciless in its guard of the planet. Anyone foolish enough to test the Earth's defense network would meet an untimely end. The space elevators allowed for cargo to be sent to and from the surface without the threat of an armed spacecraft descending on the planet. Cargo was loaded under heavy guard and would deposit its payload on the surface below.

The anticipation of the R-$332X$ crew was tangible as they grew nearer to the dock. Taku excitedly tapped his gloved fingers on a standing console—pumping himself up for the task they were about to embark on.

"It's nearly game time," he said, to nobody in particular, with a slight shake of his head. "Abigail better not screw this up,"

Django swallowed. He was less worried about Monroe's competency, and more about the role he was to play. But this was his chance to pull through. The space station farmer finally making a real difference, and not just digging in the dirt, a puppet for a lie.

Abigail Monroe's ship, the *Chimera*, followed the R-$332X$ as it approached Space Dock Seven. Abigail had volunteered her crew to distract the dock's security while the Resurgence strike team, under the guise of making a fake delivery, made their way into the dock's central core. From there, they would upload the Resurgence-created virus into the dock's networked systems.

Simple. In theory, at least, but Django couldn't help but wonder how the execution would play out. At least his part didn't involve shooting anyone.

His hand went to the weapon at his side: the Renegade blaster he had previously believed had belonged to his father but had really been Marvin's. Now it was his, he supposed. He would use it if he had to, but he hoped it wouldn't come to that.

"Are we ready?" Taku asked as the R-332X banked on its approach.

A few nods, accompanied by *"Aye, sir,"* circled the bridge.

Taku's eyes rested on Django. "Don't screw this up. I'll be watching you."

Django suppressed an eye roll.

"Amy, take us in."

Everything on the space dock was automated. Django had expected their crew would need to wheel the dummy crates manually onto the station, but unmanned drones pulled up to the ship's loading ramp, etched a stamp into the side of the crates with some sort of laser, and then hauled them into the receiving bay.

Only the rear of the R-332X was clamped onto the dock. Unlike the *Eclipse,* where a docking ship would need to enter the structure, here the ship only connected at the entry point. The rest of the craft was suspended in space.

"Please stay on your ship."

A male guard with a crisscross pattern tattooed under his ear issued the curt instruction. He wore the same white uniform as the guards aboard the *Eclipse*. He raised a hand and stepped forward as Taku, Django, Rowyn, and Wilder had taken several steps onto the dock. The arm of the dock stretching out before them, with a string of doors on either side of the passageway, presumably leading to other docked ships.

Each piece of this strange new environment was so alien and yet held bits of the familiar. The double hexagon pattern on the guard's uniform contained a spindly pattern, which he supposed was a rough approximation of the dock they were on.

"No can do. We were specifically instructed to get visual confirmation of the delivery," Taku said.

The guard raised a hand. "I'm afraid that doesn't happen. You saw the item reach the dock. It will be inspected and then delivered to the surface, and, as always, you will receive a shipping receipt. Return to your ship —*now*."

Taku lifted his hands as if in surrender and gave a slight nod of his head. "I'm sorry, sir. This is a new route for us." He made a show of directing his attention to the rest of his crew and waving toward the *R-332X* while taking a couple of steps in the same direction.

The sound of gunfire echoed down the corridor, immediately snapping the guard's attention away from Django and his crew.

The guard lifted a hand to his ear. "What's going on down there?"

The voice on the other end of the communication was muted, but the shouting that followed further down the passageway said everything.

Abigail had arrived.

The dock's paneling shifted from its standard blue to a flashing red, and a harrowing alarm overwhelmed the shouts and gunshots. Security officers whipped past with their helmets pulled up and guns drawn as they darted toward the sound of the noise.

"I'm on my way!" the guard in front of them shouted over the cacophony before turning back to Taku. "Bloody pirates!" he added, just loud enough to make himself heard between the screeches of the alarm. "Return to your ship and stay there. We've got an incident here, and we can't accept any civilian casualties."

Taku's eyes widened as he put on a good show of being frightened by the commotion.

The guard snapped the visor on his helmet into place as he charged deeper into the arm, but not before hitting the command panel on his way out. The large bay door immediately closed, separating the docking bay from the rest of the station.

"They locked us out!" Django exclaimed.

Rowyn let out a cackle. Wilder looked as confused as Django, but Taku studied at him as though he had grown a second head.

"Why do you think we brought you?"

Django lifted the chip that dangled from the string around his neck. Given to him by Marvin just before their departure from Asteria, the chip held the virus that would contaminate the dock's systems. Django had fastened it to a separate chain from the one his double-looped Resurgence pendant hung from, left for him by Marvin after his supposed death.

"You really are dense, aren't you?"

Taku grabbed Django's arm and lifted it into the air with enough force that Django worried he might rip it out of its socket.

"Even Wilder could throw a chip into a console. This is the *only* reason you're here." Taku shook his arm again to emphasize the point before releasing his grasp. "Any computer, any override."

Django resisted the urge to elbow the Resurgence leader in the gut.

As much as Django hated to admit it, Taku was right: he had forgotten the purpose of his implant aside from the final stage of their mission. He rolled his shoulder, attempting to shake off the discomfort of Taku's assault, and with a grimace, he moved to the console embedded beside the door.

Rowyn already had her ear pressed to the cool metal of the bay door, listening for an opening in the chaos.

A distraction.

"Rowyn!" Taku hissed. "Get away from the door!"

Rowyn gave Taku a dirty look and a hand gesture that Django could only guess was derogatory.

"Dumbass, we're more prepared than that," Taku said, his tone suggesting the comment was more in jest than critical. He reached into a mid-size tech bag that rested on a tabletop in one corner of the hold. He handed a small wire to the redhead, then tossed one to each of the others.

Django snatched his wire out of the air. At the same time, Vlad fumbled with his, cursing as it nearly hit the ground before Marshall caught it with his free hand and handed it to him.

"Careful!" Marshall said, giving Taku a disapproving look. "These aren't easy to replace!"

Taku ignored the rebuke and gestured for Django and Rowyn to wrap the wire around their ears.

As soon as Django equipped the device, a small, augmented display popped up in front of him. It took him a moment to orient himself to what he was seeing.

A hallway. Guards moving.

It was a projection of the hallway on the other side of the bay door.

"You didn't think we were just going to fumble our way to Engineering blind, did you? Amy's hacked into the surveillance feed. She'll be guiding us through from the ship."

"If the dock is being monitored, how are we going to get in without being noticed?" Django asked. "Dock security will be on us before we get anywhere."

"Amy's got that taken care of, too," Taku replied. "She'll mask our presence as we move through. Nobody will know we ever left this room."

Django was in no position to question Amy's capabilities, so he simply nodded. "All right. Let's do this!"

"Now, the objective is Django inserting that chip, scanning his credentials, and uploading the virus. That's our number two priority."

Wilder gave their leader another confused look.

Number two? Django wondered. "What's number one?"

"Keeping *you* alive!" The words should have rung triumphantly, like music to Django's ears, but the venom with which Taku spat them was unnerving. "Frankly, I don't give a rat's ass about you, but the Founders voted to put that chip in *your* arm. It's not like we have a storage room full of those things. If you go down, the Resurgence goes down with you."

Django resisted the urge to look at his arm. He knew the stakes, but he wasn't used to everyone resting their hopes and dreams on his shoulders. He had said yes to the mission, so now he had to deal with the consequences.

But Taku's comment made it clear who had voted *against* him. Django could only hope that Taku's loyalty to the Resurgence would supersede his disdain for him should the moment to rescue him ever arise.

"All right," Django said. "Let's move."

The hallway outside of the loading bay was clear.

Django pushed a button at the side of the exit. Unsurprisingly, it displayed a message that the door had been secured.

Taking a deep breath, he slowly waved his wrist in front of the panel. Despite everything that had just been discussed, he was still a little surprised when the panel beeped and the display flashed from red to green.

There was no turning back now.

Django
Space Dock Seven

Django did his best to reconcile the view of the hallway through his new eyepiece with what was actually in front of him. His brain had to perform mental gymnastics to piece together the visual inputs of two different hallways at the same time.

Taku led the charge, cautiously slinking around corners as Amy fed updates from the surveillance feed of what awaited them. Each time they approached a new junction, they paused briefly to ensure the way was clear.

Taku held his blaster at the ready, his breathing steady. Django followed closely behind as Wilder, Rowyn, Marshall, and Vlad tightly took up the rear. Louis had stayed behind to stand watch for Amy.

Shouts and gunfire, both bullets and energy weapons, hung in the air. Though the sounds were distant, Django was acutely aware of their presence, barely audible beneath his own pulse pounding in his ears.

Two guards appeared around the next bend, and Django's heart lurched.

"It's just the feed," Taku hissed, noticing his reaction. "They're up ahead."

Django swore. He still hadn't fully adjusted to the eyepiece.

Taku lifted a hand, motioning the others to the inside wall of the curve. The two approaching guards wouldn't notice them until it was too late.

Taku didn't hesitate to pull the trigger. The first guard tumbled in a heap of searing flesh. The second guard hit the deck as his companion fell, drawing his own weapon, and returned fire.

Wilder went down.

Django screamed.

Guards like these had killed his family.

He wouldn't let them take his friends, too.

All at once, his muscles tensed, his grip tightening around the Renegade's handle as every slight, every injustice, every memory of loss from the past weeks roared in his mind, transforming into a blinding, all-consuming rage.

Django jerked the trigger and sent the guard to the ground. He didn't stop screaming—and he didn't stop firing.

By the time Taku reached him and pulled him back, both hands locked around his shoulders, Django's weapon had lost a full charge. Without thinking, Django ejected the spent energy cartridge and tried to shake Taku off so that he could immediately load another.

"That's enough!" Taku yelled, but his voice was lost in the ocean of Django's rage.

Slowly, Django's vision cleared to reveal the guard's uniform, now charred from taking the brunt of the assault. Overwhelmed with emotion, Django would have fallen to his knees if Taku's arms hadn't still been wrapped around him.

Rowyn and Vlad had pulled Wilder against the wall and sat him up. His barreled chest shaking as he drew uncertain breaths, but he was awake.

"I can take him back to the ship," Vlad said to Taku.

"Can you walk?" Taku asked Wilder.

The bulky man's eyes were wide, darting frantically around the hallway, the whites stark against his dark irises.

"I'm . . ." Wilder swallowed back tears as the realization of his narrow escape sunk in. He nodded. "I'm okay."

He put a hand to his knee and lifted himself in a reverse squat, using the wall for support. His face contorted as he put his full body weight on his left leg. Blood oozed from a black, charred mass of burned flesh on his hip. A second shot had struck Wilder's shoulder; a few centimeters to the right, and it might have hit something vital. He would live, but he was far from "okay."

Taku motioned to Vlad. "Take him back, then wait there for us. Get the ship ready to depart."

Vlad nodded and wrapped a steadying arm around Wilder, placing himself squarely beneath the man's massive shoulders.

"And *you* . . ." Taku prodded a finger into Django's chest. "Control yourself. You're lucky you didn't bring a dozen other guards down on us, firing like that."

The dead guard lay sprawled on the floor, his flesh as blackened as his uniform. In the attack, the man's helmet had come off. His face had escaped most of the barrage but was left locked in a frozen scream.

"Sorry," he replied, though Django hated admitting fault to Taku. "I saw my friend go down. I lost control."

Taku sighed, and for the first time since Django had met him, his face softened.

"Listen." Taku lowered his voice and pulled in closer. "I get it. I know what it's like to lose someone to these Syndicate bastards. But you've got to look out for those of us who are still alive. Losing your head like that puts us all at risk." The fleeting softness in Taku's eyes was replaced by the more familiar icy glare as he stepped away. "Remember, this whole thing is riding on you."

It was the closest thing to compassion Django had seen from Taku since they met, and it was the only sign of warmth he'd shown toward Django.

Taku circled a finger in the air to signal they were done standing still. With Vlad's help, Wilder hobbled back toward the ship, and Django prayed to the stars they didn't encounter any interference along the way, but that was up to Amy now.

With Vlad and Wilder on their way back to the R-3, completing the mission was down to Django, Taku, Rowyn, and Marshall.

Django took a deep breath as Taku lifted the body of the guard by the shoulders and dragged him into a small engineering duct he found by dislodging a panel in one of the bulkheads. The smell of burnt plastic and flesh was overwhelming and a wave of nausea swept over Django, bile rising in his throat as the full weight of his actions crashed into him. He hadn't just killed a man; he had *obliterated* him.

Is this the kind of person I want to be?

Was his fate to kill men in cold blood, as his uncle had? Was he doomed to follow in Marvin's footsteps?

The guard's eyes remained open, staring blankly as Taku repositioned the panel to conceal the corpse.

Did the man have a family? Friends?

Django fought with himself to stay on course. If he hadn't killed him, the guard would likely have killed someone else. Wilder, maybe, or Django himself. But as much as he tried to convince himself otherwise, he knew ending the man's life hadn't merely been a defensive act.

It had been one of rage.

The strike team continued pushing forward, Amy in constant contact through their headsets, warning them if there was a guard coming. It was difficult to avoid them, but the team ducked into an empty bay or obscured corner anytime reinforcements headed their way.

It wasn't long before they reached the center of the facility, where the long arms of the dock joined into one central hub. This would be where all the amenities were: food halls, quarters, offices, and engineering.

The Resurgence team had studied the layout of the space, but Amy still whispered directions in their ears. There was a greater chance of running into guards in this section, as well as civilians who worked on the station.

"How's Monroe doing?" Taku asked. They had decided not to link their own comms directly to the pirates' feed; there couldn't be any trace that the parties had been working together. Amy maintained one encrypted frequency for emergencies that ran directly to Monroe so they could still coordinate if needed. But for the most part, she was monitoring the dock's communication line to follow the siege.

"They're holding up," Amy replied. "But this entire wing is now in lockdown. You're lucky you made it to the hub. If you want to make it back to the ship, you're going to have to keep Station Boy alive."

Django grunted. "I have a name."

"Understood." Taku ignored Django's banter. "That was always the plan. Just keep those damn cameras off us."

"I'm swapping out feeds as you go. I can't initiate a system-wide ruse with the pirates still going at it. That showdown is being watched intently. Any glitch will be noticed."

A relentless throb of adrenaline coursed through Django's veins, each pulse point in his body hammering against his suit as it sought escape. This all rested on him now.

"You're into the hub," Amy said. "Most of the crew have been put into lockdown because of the attack, so you shouldn't come across too many people from here on in. But be careful if you do: you're in civilian territory, so watch your fire."

Django subconsciously nodded to the request; he imagined the comment was specifically directed at him.

With Amy's guidance, the team navigated through a few more doors and hallways before the space opened. An elevator off to one side traveled up and down at least twelve floors. Each floor was open to the one below, with walkways connecting usable space. The team's present position was four levels from the bottom floor, and there were at least twice as many floors above them. It was as almost as if they were in a giant open-space office tower that orbited the Earth.

Potted ferns and spider plants decorated the balconies. On some of the levels below, elm trees sprouted from artificial dirt nestled in the center of their floors, spreading their branches two and three floors above their roots. The entire space was walled with giant viewports on either side, allowing the sun's natural light to pour through. Artificial illumination shone from the ceilings of each level, providing the walkways with light when the dock faced the dark side of the Earth. To the team's right, tinted panels filtered out the harshest of the sun's glare, while to their left, the Earth dominated in all its blue and green glory, and meter-thick suspension cables guided cargo containers to and from the surface.

On the team's current floor, desks sat abandoned. Holo-screens still danced above them, displaying cargo manifests and marking the scheduled back and forth of deliveries.

Django's knuckles whitened as he clutched his weapon, eyes darting around the vacant space for any hint of movement or threat. But the floor remained eerily quiet, empty.

"You're going to want to go up two more levels," Amy said, "cross the promenade, and then head to the rear. You'll know the doorway once you see it. And hurry—Abigail's doing her best, but I don't think dock security will tolerate this stalemate for much longer."

Taku nodded and flicked two fingers in the direction they were meant to go, toward a set of stairs that wound between the levels of the fortress.

As the team neared the sixth level, gunshots and blaster

fire caused Django to flinch, his pulse rising once again, but the sounds were distant, faint, and hollow.

Django's breathing eased as he and Rowyn exchanged an uneasy look. At least he wasn't the only one unnerved by the outburst. But they both pushed forward to keep up with the others, not wanting to fall behind.

Taku lifted a hand as he reached the top of the stairs, signaling for the other three to halt. He poked his head cautiously above the rail and then quickly ducked.

"Amy, why didn't you tell us there were civilians on this floor?" he whispered, just loud enough for the team to hear.

"They're distracted, watching the attack on the holofeed. You're clear if you hurry and remain quiet."

"Are you one hundred percent certain about that?" Taku challenged. "If we're spotted, this entire operation is blown. All it takes is one person looking toward us at the wrong time. We can't take out a floor of civilians."

Amy sighed over the feed.

That's where the sound of weapons fire is coming from. The people are watching the siege remotely.

"There is one other option . . ." Amy said. There was a different tone to her voice, but Django didn't know her well enough to place it.

"All right," Taku said. "Let's hear it."

"Keep climbing to the seventh floor, cross over to the back of the dock, then rappel back down to the entrance."

Marshall snorted and Rowyn rolled her eyes, but Taku looked up to the next level as though considering it.

"She's joking." Marshall's eyes widened slightly,

darting between her and their leader, a crease forming on his forehead. "We haven't got the gear for that."

"How much access do you have to their systems?" Taku asked. "Could you disrupt the gravity on that level so we could jump down?"

"If I had that level of access, you wouldn't need to be dancing through the entire dock to get to Engineering. Of course I was joking! Get on with it before they get bored with the feed."

Sweat clung to Django's skin. The docking facility wasn't particularly warm, but between the pressure of the situation and the gear he was carrying, he couldn't help the beads that dripped down the back of his neck.

"You doing okay?" Rowyn asked as Django wiped off his forehead with his arm. His shirt was already soaked, so it did little to help.

"Yeah." His heart was racing and his knees were shaky, but Django didn't want to admit he was terrified. "Just not used to this."

He did his best to push his fears down into some recess of his psyche he wouldn't have to deal with until later. Other than when he was being chased through the maintenance halls on *Eclipse*, trying to escape with Eventide, he couldn't think of another time when he had been so stressed about anything. He wasn't a space station farmer anymore, and he had to deal with that. The thought of Wilder lying in the hall with blaster wounds burning his flesh still shook him to his core. Django wanted to make a difference, but he didn't want any more lives to be lost on his behalf.

It's not about me. They're willing to sacrifice themselves for the people. You're doing this for the people.

And for Eventide.

Once he completed the mission, they could recover her, head back to Lunar, and then figure out what the Resurgence had in store for them both.

Rowyn ran a hand over his shoulder. He cringed at his sweat-soaked clothing, but if she thought anything of it, she hid it well. Her mouth opened slightly, a hesitant word teetering on the brink of being spoken. Her eyes softened, flickering with the glow of unspoken encouragement. But before the words could form, Taku moved, cutting the moment short. She looked at their leader, nodded to Django, and motioned with her weapon that they should follow.

CHAPTER THIRTY-ONE

Eventide
The *Inanna*

The atrium on board the *Inanna* was kept both warmer and more humid than the rest of the ship, and as a result, a fine gleam of sweat lingered on Eventide's skin. Matthias held the same glow, but on him, it was rugged and masculine, clinging to the definition to his muscles that Eventide hated to admit was appealing. Her own skin felt sticky and inappropriate. It was such a damned double standard, and she hated it. The allure of her bed chamber called to her, and the cool shower within.

Regardless of what limitations her brain enacted on the transmissions, the call to her bed was strong, like a homing beacon that beckoned to her in the depths of a dark, misty night.

"Do you not feel any of the positive wavelengths?" she asked as she stifled a yawn. "Every fiber of my being wants to return to my quarters and turn in for the night."

Matthias laughed as he poked away at one of the datapads he'd brought with him. "I feel it, but I've learned to tune it out. It's strong because sleep is something you already want to do. Your brain isn't trying to fight the signals. It needs rest."

"There's no time for rest. If you're right, we only have another two days to figure out how to get out of here."

They had been trying to test Matthias' theory for nearly a week already, and so far, they'd been stonewalled at every turn. Either they hadn't been able to get the right datapads or they'd been under the watchful eye of Caregiver Lin. Finally, they'd had a stroke of luck and had been able to arrange a meeting tonight. But Eventide was starting to fear they were cutting things much too close for their plan to succeed.

"You realize that even if we're able to get into the system, there's no guarantee we'll find anything useful? This could all be a waste of time."

"Who knew that the smiles we have to plaster on here hid such a pessimist?"

She swiped one of the devices off the table in front of Matthias, where he had three datapads laid out—supposedly one for each of them, but Okimi had yet to show.

Probably called it a night after all. Eventide wouldn't blame her for deciding to answer the pull to her room. It was strong tonight. Her body must have been craving the rest.

She stifled another yawn and walked through the steps of unlocking the datapad's hidden connections. "I still don't understand how you figured out how to gain access through these." She scrolled through screens of files and system logs. There was so much information, she hardly knew where to look. She was used to the complex systems on the *Eclipse* and she was sure she would manage, but the sheer quantity of information was overwhelming.

"There's a lot you don't know about me." Mattias' concentration never left the datapad in front of him, his brow furrowed as though trying to focus on whatever was on the screen.

"That's the problem . . ." she said. "I don't know *anything* about you."

Matthias rolled his eyes. "What exactly would you like to know? It's not like I'm trying to hide anything here. You haven't exactly asked, either."

"Well, now I'm asking," she said. "Where did you learn how to do this?"

He sighed, his fingers idly spinning the datapad around. "My parents were law enforcement officers on Mars. When the *Infinity* went down, things got . . . difficult. The Syndicate started cutting our rations. There were a lot of hungry mouths to feed, and my parents were worried about riots."

"And so . . .?"

"And so, I started poking around, finding back doors into the supply systems. Adjusted our allotted numbers. Kept a lot of people from starving. So, you could say it was out of necessity. I learned a lot about finding cracks in Syndicate systems."

It sounded plausible, but Eventide had a feeling there was more to it than Matthias was sharing.

"But these aren't law enforcement systems, these are gaming datapads. I don't understand why Caregivers would sync them to the same network as the rest of the ship's processes."

"Do you think I'm making it up? It was your idea to study ship schematics. I'm telling you the only way I know how. I don't know why the Caregivers have linked these devices to their network, but they have."

Eventide grabbed the deck of cards she'd stashed on the inside of her outfit. Okimi had come through and provided her with a deck. She hadn't said where she had snatched it from, but Eventide didn't care. With her fingers flowing over the stiff paper cards, she felt like she could focus on the task at hand.

Or at least, she would have been able to focus if Matthias wasn't being so obnoxious. Faron had been the same way. Though not as toned as Matthias, her partner technician on board the *Eclipse* was easy on the eyes, but he was also a douchebag who was completely full of himself. She was getting the same vibe from Matthias.

As the cards riffled against her fingers, Eventide told herself she was being paranoid. The implants in her head were probably not helping with that. But trust was something she was having a hard time giving, especially after everyone who was supposed to be a figure of authority on the *Eclipse* had lied to her.

That wouldn't be an easy thing to overcome.

But Matthias wasn't supposed to be the focus of her attention; the details accessed by those datapads were, and if they couldn't figure out a way to escape, she would be stuck on the ship for who knew how long. And she might never get another chance if she couldn't bite her tongue.

Just as she thought she would be able to get to the task

at hand, Okimi appeared down the semi-lit path, a self-satisfied smirk on her face.

Eventide didn't like the position she found herself in. There were two people on the entire ship she could talk to—three, if she counted Doctor Morales—and she didn't trust a single one of them.

Despite Matthias' attitude, neither he nor Okimi had done anything overtly untrustworthy. However, Eventide was all too aware that she barely knew either one of them.

"We didn't think you were coming," Eventide said. "You said you didn't want to be a part of this. I thought you'd given up on us altogether."

"Yeah, well, I couldn't sleep. And like it or not, you're the only two idiots I'm actually able to talk to."

"Couldn't sleep, or didn't trust me alone with her?" Matthias nodded to Eventide.

Okimi leaned against a small tree that had rooted itself in the corner of the path. Her petite frame caused the trunk to bend, but only slightly. "There's no reason for me to trust you, is there? As far as I'm concerned, either one of you could have murdered Orin."

"Me?" Eventide lifted a hand to her chest. "I was the one who told you about him!"

"Which means you were the last one to see him alive," Okimi observed accusingly. "I have no more reason to believe you than him. Maybe you were looking for a way to convince us to leave the ship with you. Maybe you're a spy for the Caregivers and you're testing our loyalty."

Eventide grimaced, fighting to keep the venom from her voice. "I'm not a spy."

"I think I might have found something to help us

uncover who our murderer is," Matthias chimed, eyes still glued to his datapad.

"There's something in the system about it?" Eventide asked, the edge to her voice melting. "Did they actually document what they did to him?"

"Not exactly," Matthias said, flipping the datapad around. "But I think I may have found the next best thing."

The screen showed an image of the rec room, where Eventide had found Orin's body.

"Surveillance footage," she said. "If we can find the footage from the other night, we might be able to see who did it."

"Yep." Matthias nodded. "Give me a couple seconds to find the right time stamp. You said it was two nights ago?" he asked as he scrubbed through the recording.

Eventide could barely breathe while he searched. "It was the night before we met you here."

"You mean, the night before you attacked me?"

Okimi stuck out her tongue in a playful taunt until a puzzled look crossed Matthias' face.

"What's wrong?" Eventide asked.

He passed the datapad to the two women and started the playback.

The image was of lower quality than standard holos, but it was still clear enough to make out important details. Orin stood by a console that accessed the room where Eventide would later find him. He held a forearm to the panel, and the door slid open with a quiet hiss that was lost to the silent footage.

The feed followed him inside the room. Familiar plush carpet lay beneath his feet—carpet that Eventide remembered being soaked with blood. She forced the image from her mind, her breath hitching in her throat as she did so.

Orin moved to a second door, pausing to glance over his shoulder in a way that screamed of guilt. The time stamp at the bottom of the screen–00:37—the same time Eventide would have been meandering through the *Inanna's* corridors.

Why were you up, Orin? Was the call to your bed not pulling on you?

A shadow seeped across the wall behind him, indistinct and formless but unmistakably human. Orin's eyes widened in a display of raw terror and his hand came up, fingers splayed in protest or supplication. Then, without warning, static devoured the screen.

The abrupt interference caused Eventide to jump. The image of Orin's frightened face and the menacing shadow lingered even as static filled the datapad's display.

"What happened?" Okimi asked. "Why'd it cut out?"

"The feed disappears at that point," Matthias said, his expression stern. "It's just gone."

"What do you mean, 'gone?'" Okimi questioned, her brows furrowing in confusion. "How does a feed disappear?"

"The data's been corrupted," Matthias shook his head. "Or erased. I'm not sure which, there's a chunk of missing time on this feed. Hang on, I'll see if there's anything else I can pull up."

Eventide chewed on her lower lip, her mind racing with possibilities. "Could someone have . . . tampered with it?" she ventured, her words laced with uncertainty.

Before Matthias could answer, the screen came back to

life. On it, Eventide saw herself, standing over Orin's body, then turning to run away.

"Can you explain this, Eventide?" Matthias asked, his brow furrowed in a mix of suspicion and confusion.

Eventide was taken aback. "I don't know, Matthias." How was she supposed to respond to that? "I didn't even know this footage existed until now!"

"She's right," Okimi said, shifting so that her yellow Domani outfit reflected the atrium's cool light. "This isn't exactly a smoking gun, is it?"

"But as far as we know, she was the only one there when Orin died. Doesn't that seem suspicious to you?"

"It's not great," Okimi admitted, "but don't you think if she went to the trouble of erasing that footage she wouldn't have also removed her face at the end? If anything, I think someone's trying to set her up, to make it look like she was the one who killed him."

"But why?" Eventide asked. "Why bother? They already have a chip in my arm and an implant in my skull. What more could the Caregivers possibly want to do to me?"

Okimi rested a hand on her shoulder, her skin surprisingly cool. "I guess someone out there has a sick sense of humor. Imagine, you, a scapegoat. What are the odds?"

A hint of sarcasm tinged her words, and Eventide couldn't quite tell if Okimi was trying to comfort her or mock her.

"But if they wanted to frame me, why am I still free to roam the ship?" She frowned, shrugging off Okimi's hand. "Why haven't they called me in for questioning, or shot me out an airlock?"

"Probably because you've managed to keep your mouth shut so far," Matthias quipped, grabbing his pad back. "And nobody's created a stink about Orin being missing."

It was possible, but it still didn't sit right with her.

Eventide rewound the footage and watched it play out one more time, trying to analyze the shadow that appeared on the wall right before the feed cut out. It looked menacing in the frame, but only because of the person's positioning in front of the light source.

There were no distinguishable features to analyze. It was like they were looking at a ghost.

"Can we get back to finding a way out of here?" Matthias said. "Assuming you're not planning on killing the two of us as well?"

Eventide let the comment roll off her, though she was growing tired of Matthias' prickly attitude. "Fine. Let's see if we can figure out something useful. Maybe we can figure out where we are on the ship, at least."

She returned her attention back to her own datapad and began sifting through reams of information. Most of it was useless—systems reports that told her the ship was operating in normal parameters—interesting, but not particularly helpful. Maintenance logs were something she was familiar with, but they were boring as hell. Communications logs might be useful, if any of the names or location stamps were familiar to her. They seemed to be recorded in a numeric code. Eventide couldn't retrieve any specifics of the messages, just that they had occurred.

"Crew rotation schedule," she read out loud. "Maybe we could use that."

"How so?" Matthias asked, his interest piquing away from his own screen.

"Well, if we can figure out where the crew won't be, then we can come up with a plan to navigate outside of these halls."

"That's cool in theory," Matthias said, "but let's not forget our little problem here: we're still stuck in the blasted Domani section."

He was right, and Eventide knew it. But with all the details on screen, she had to be able to find some way for it to be helpful. It seemed like the answer was so close, but also frustratingly just out of reach.

"I'm not going to stop looking until I find something that can help us. If we all work together, I'm sure we'll think of something."

She hoped—prayed to the stars, or to any ancient deity who might be listening—that whatever it would take for her to be rid of her prison would present itself.

How free are any of us, really?

Okimi's biting remark from days before clung to the back of Eventide's psyche. What if this was it? Maybe freedom was an illusion.

Not a chance. The words imposed themselves over all her doubts. This wasn't going to be her life.

"Keep looking. We'll find something."

CHAPTER THIRTY-TWO

Eventide

The *Inanna*

Matthias shifted in his seat, his gaze darting to a large holographic clock projected onto the wall with an increasing frequency that made Eventide uncomfortable.

"I think we're wasting our time here," he said.

Eventide raised an eyebrow, her fingers still on the datapad.

"We've only been at this for a few measly hours," Okimi bit. "Here I was, thinking we were throwing an all-nighter for the fun of it. Let's all take a nap."

Eventide shook her head, choosing to ignore Okimi's sarcasm. "We don't have time for that. We can't be seen hacking our way into the network. That means we're not on these datapads outside of this room, or during daytime hours. We've got a few more hours before the makeup twins come around, and then only one more night before we're supposed to dock on Earth."

Okimi let out a deep-rooted sigh before pushing herself

off from the bench next to Eventide. "Well, I'm going for a walk. I need to clear my head, maybe take a piss. I'll be back. Try not to kill each other before then. I'd hate to miss all the fun."

Eventide tapped her blue-painted nails on her device, ignoring Okimi as she exited the atrium and instead turning her attention to Matthias. "So, what do you propose? That we give up? I'm not ready to do that."

"No," he scoffed, leaning back and running a hand through his hair. "But I don't think this is the way. None of this data is useful. I was hoping your big engineering brain would have worked out something by now."

She swallowed hard, trying to keep her temper in check. "I'm open to ideas."

"Look, I didn't mean . . ." He sighed, the hard edges of his voice softening. "I just don't want to waste our energy on dead ends."

"You've been on this boat awhile already," Eventide said, steadying her voice. "Why the rush to get off now?"

Matthias didn't answer immediately, instead letting out a heavy breath as he moved from his seat to the one next to her, where Okimi had sat a moment before. It was an odd gesture, but his demeanor had shifted.

"I guess . . . now I have a reason to worry."

"You're worried? About me?" The words resonated strangely within her. It hadn't been an accusation, but a confession. An unexpected swell of warmth coursed through her, and Eventide wasn't sure whether she should have been flattered or insulted. She set the datapad down and turned to face him fully. "I appreciate your concern, Matthias, but this is my choice to make.

You don't have to be involved anymore if you don't want to."

In the prolonged silence that followed, their eyes met. His usual stoic exterior had been replaced with an intensity that caught Eventide off guard. She found herself being unnaturally drawn toward him. She wanted to push away, yet all she felt was this unfamiliar, electrifying pull . . .

"Why do you care?" She threw the question up like a shield.

He tilted his head, taken aback, as though he hadn't expected the question, but he didn't look away. "I've been alone on this ship for a long time with nobody sane to talk to," he confessed. "I guess I . . . I don't want to see you get hurt."

A small laugh escaped her. "Is that a hint of humanity I detect, Matthias?"

Matthias' smirk softened the atmosphere between them, making the atrium feel less like a battlefield and more like an unexpected refuge. "Don't get used to it."

A smile surfaced on her lips. A lightness spread through her, and before she could suppress the thought, she heard herself say, "I think I might like you when you're not being a jerk."

The words hung in the air. Matthias held her gaze, and Eventide swore there was an unspoken energy in the silent exchange. She couldn't pull her eyes away, and her skin tingled with the odd sensation of pins and needles.

"When have I ever been a jerk?" A hint of playful sarcasm lingered in his tone.

A complex tapestry of emotions unfolded within her—surprise, uncertainty, anxiety. Eventide couldn't help but suspect there was a wave of disaster about to wash over her, but she was powerless to stop it. And she wasn't sure she even wanted to.

The moment hung between them, charged with electricity. Her heart pounded in her chest as his gaze dropped to her lips, his own parting slightly.

The subtle glance spoke volumes, and she caught her breath before he made his move. He was going to lean in, and the thought sent a jolt of electricity surging through her. Her heart kicked up a furious rhythm against her chest, its pounding so loud she was sure he could hear it. It was as though she stood at the edge of a cliff, not knowing whether she was going to fly or fall.

Before she even realized the gap between them had been filled, their lips met in a heavy, impulsive kiss that ignited a rush of sensations within her. It was soft and gentle, but it descended like a whirlwind that swept her off her feet. The world around them faded, leaving nothing but the overwhelming awareness of each other. A shock wave of sensation pulsed through her.

Was this what it was like to connect with someone on an intimate level? Was this what she had been afraid of? Getting too close? Of physical contact?

Eventide could feel the skin of Matthias' chest pressing up against her, and she was surprised to find she welcomed the touch.

Eternity passed before they pulled apart, their eyes meeting once more. This time, the tension between them was different, crackling with a new intensity.

Eventide cleared her throat, trying to regain her composure. "Well, that was . . . *unexpected.*"

Matthias chuckled, a low, deep sound that made her stomach flutter. He pulled back and studied her, his brown eyes moving from her lips and back to hold her gaze. His brown eyes reminded her of something . . .

Of someone else. Someone distant, like a person she was trying to remember through a fog.

Eventide pulled back, horror replacing bliss as reality crashed down in a startling cacophony of the senses. The atrium's gentle hum screamed at her as the physical bubble she'd fought so hard to maintain regained its fortitude around her.

Matthias' face twisted in confusion, and then in pain.

"What's wrong? What did I do?"

"I . . ." She didn't know. Everything she'd felt in the last minute—the pull, the draw. But it dissipated as quickly as it came on. "I don't know what that was."

"You're kidding, right?" He smirked, then opened his mouth as though about to say something, but thought better of it. He put his hands up. "I'm sorry. I wouldn't have done that if I didn't think you wanted me to."

"No, it's not that."

His eyebrow lifted. "I'm not following . . ."

"Me neither, actually." Eventide couldn't think over the pounding of her own pulse. "I know this is confusing. You're attractive, but . . . that's not me. I don't act that way."

"It's okay, Eventide." Matthias' voice was calming, trying his best to comfort her but unsure of what to say. "We all get caught up in the moment sometimes. Let's . . . We won't worry about it, if that's not something you're comfortable with."

Eventide could tell he was trying, but he wasn't getting

it. It wasn't his fault; it was hard to convey the war that raged inside her without him taking it that way.

"No, that's not what I'm saying. I mean . . . I'm not comfortable with it. I wanted to, I knew what I was doing, but it felt like I was watching someone else—like I was *feeling* what someone else was feeling. I can't describe it. You did nothing wrong, but I also don't understand what just happened."

Matthias stood, clearly uncomfortable. Eventide didn't blame him. An awkward moment of silence filled the air as she struggled for the words to explain the tumultuous battle inside her own head.

"Matthias, I . . ."

"Don't worry about it," he said defensively, grabbing his datapad. "If you're not interested, just tell me."

Light footsteps diverted Eventide's attention to the path behind her, where Okimi glided out of the darkness.

"Whoa, what did I miss? You guys seem tense."

"A nap might not be such a bad idea after all. I'm done for the night. You two keep looking if you want," Matthias said and then stormed off.

Eventide fought the urge to chase after him. She hadn't meant to hurt him; to lead him on into something he clearly wanted more than she did. And it wasn't as though she wasn't interested at all; it just . . . wasn't like that. It was too fast. Too physical. Too intense. They had only just met, for crying out loud, and for the past week, he'd been nothing but a pain in her ass.

But the pull had been strong and Eventide couldn't shake the feeling that she hadn't been in control of her own faculties. If the thought of Django hadn't come to mind, what else might have happened?

"What's with him?" Okimi asked, picking her datapad up from the table and getting right back into it.

Eventide sighed. "I don't even know how to begin to explain it to you. Let's just keep looking."

A shift in the atrium's ambient light signaled the transition from night to morning. Eventide and Okimi had continued to search the datapads all night, but with little success. She had somehow managed to push her encounter with Matthias to the back of her mind, but she knew it wouldn't stay there. She *had* wanted to kiss him, and she'd gotten caught in the moment. But there was more to it than that.

Could these transmissions being projected into my head be involved?

Her stomach churned at the thought. The idea that her emotions could be toyed with to that degree made Eventide want to vomit, but she couldn't shake the thought.

It was something that would have to be dealt with— later. Right now, finding their way off the damned ship had to be their priority. If they made it that far, she'd find a solution for the rest of it.

They needed to get to their rooms soon, before Phoenix and Solara arrived to do her hair and makeup. Even if nobody else noticed her absence, those two certainly would, and she didn't want to have to explain where she'd been. The bags under her eyes and drooping skin would be hard enough to explain, especially when everyone else on board was unable to resist the call of their beds.

"Well, there's no little sign saying, 'Exit Here,' but I suppose it's better than nothing," Okimi said. "We now know the layout of the ship."

After several hours of searching, they had found a map—a blueprint of some kind dating back to when the *Inanna* was built—and that was a starting point, but with no legend or labels, it was practically useless.

"It's more frustrating than finding nothing at all," Eventide replied huffily. "Essentially, we have a floor plan, but without knowing which rooms we'll be walking into, we're still completely blind. We have a crew rotation with room assignments and times, but we don't know which rooms are which. It's almost as if we've been given just enough information to think we're making progress, but not enough to actually do anything with it."

"I hate to say it," Okimi deflated, "but you're right. I think this lead is a dead end. There's a reason the Caregivers haven't blocked access to the network: there's nothing useful there."

"It makes no sense, though. It makes even less sense to give us partial access. Why not lock out the whole thing?"

Okimi didn't have an answer, and Eventide didn't expect her to. She wanted to pull her hair out in frustration, but instead her hands went to the deck of cards she had stowed in her outfit. She ran her hands against their edges, allowing the tactile sensations of the deck to draw in her focus.

"Maybe they're hiding the ship's schematics and Lin's favorite cookie recipe in another part of the network,"

Okimi continued. "The Caregivers probably don't view any of this information as any more sensitive than the Domani games."

That would explain things, but it still didn't feel right. What were the odds they could get this far, *only* to get this far?

Eventide pulled up the data streams one more time. There had to be something she'd missed.

"We need to head back to our quarters," Okimi urged. "Time to accept we've got zip."

"Just give me one second. I have to get this off my mind."

Okimi glanced over her shoulder. "The security footage? Again?"

They'd been poring over the images, hoping to find the feeds from the rest of the ship to at least provide them with visuals of what lay outside of their cocooned prison. But there only seemed to be footage covering areas the Domani had access to.

That aligned with Okimi's theory. Maybe Matthias had been wrong and the datapads didn't connect to the wider network after all.

"We went down that road hours ago! There was nothing there."

Eventide nodded, finding it hard to concentrate with Okimi talking, but she pulled up the footage Matthias had showed them of Orin.

"I know, but I want to watch this at least once more. There's still a murderer out there, and this is the only clue we have."

Earlier, she had tried to see if they could find any footage of the shadow coming or going. The only person they could find was of Eventide, lingering on the promenade, gazing at the stars. She pulled up that recording and played it side by side so she could watch herself as she moved toward Orin's body. The murderer had been in that room only moments before she'd arrived. So, where did they go?

Orin stood with his eyes wide in horror. The poor kid had seemed so innocent, so excited to be on board the *Inanna*—his life taken by a shadow.

She paused at the moment Orin stood at the second door, a glimmer of realization washing over her. How could she have missed it? That door . . . It was barely noticeable, almost merging with the wall. It was the kind of door she had seen countless times walking the maintenance corridors of the *Eclipse*.

"Okimi," Eventide beckoned. "Look at this. This door, the one Orin was about to walk into . . ."

"Yeah?" Okimi leaned over further to study the footage. "What about it?"

"This is a maintenance door. They're designed to blend into the wall. You remember I told you I was an engineer on a station? On the *Eclipse*, they're used by the technicians to navigate the station without the residents knowing. I can't believe I didn't realize it before . . ."

Understanding dawned on Okimi's face. "You think there's a chance there's a network of these hidden passages all over the ship?"

"More than that." Eventide nodded slowly, realization coming to her in waves. "There's no sign of the murderer coming or going because they traveled through *these* corridors. Someone came in from another part of the ship."

"To kill a random Domani?"

Eventide hesitated. "It's possible he was in the wrong place at the wrong time, though that in itself is strange. He should have been in his room. Maybe whoever killed him was surprised to see him there. Maybe he saw something he wasn't supposed to, and the murderer had to cover their tracks . . ." She trailed off as her thoughts continued.

"That would explain why there was no body," Okimi said. "If they'd hauled him out through the passages."

Eventide nodded, rewinding the footage. "Look at how he acts when he approaches the door; he didn't just stumble out of his room in the middle of the night. I think someone told him to meet them there."

"This gets weirder the more you look at it."

The edges of her card deck pressed against her fingers as Eventide fidgeted with them. "Well, either way, I think we've discovered our way out of here. If we can get into the maintenance corridor through that door, maybe we'll find a way to navigate off the ship. There's got to be a navigable map in the maintenance corridors. Those things are normally a maze."

The door to the atrium opened and Matthias walked in, his face clouded with sleep.

"Don't tell me you two have been at this all night?" he grumbled, rubbing his eyes.

"We might have found something," Eventide said, barely able to suppress the hopeful tone in her voice.

Matthias looked at the paused surveillance footage,

then at the two women. His eyes narrowed. "A door? That's your big lead?"

"It's a maintenance door. Leads to a network of corridors and passages," Okimi replied.

"And you think you can navigate those?"

"I know I can." Eventide's gaze was steady, her voice firm. "We used them all the time back on the station. They'll connect us with the rest of the ship."

Matthias chewed on the information, his brows furrowed. After a while, he sighed and ran a hand through his hair. "All right. But we obviously don't have the credentials. How do you expect to open it?"

"If we can track down some tools, that would help," Eventide replied. "But I bet I could find a way to get in without them."

Matthias nodded, sleep still clinging to his tired eyes. "And when do you want to embark on this suicide mission?"

"It has to be tonight," Eventide answered, a steely resolve in her voice. "We need to figure out where to be in order to escape when we land tomorrow."

Matthias nodded, his expression skeptical but focused. "Yeah, sure. Tonight it is, then."

A weight lifted from Eventide's shoulders, and for the first time since leaving the *Eclipse,* she felt as though something might actually be going her way.

CHAPTER THIRTY-THREE

Eventide

The *Inanna*

More than once, Eventide dozed off while Phoenix and Solara attended to her. Each time, they clicked their tongues in unison and muttered something that sounded like a curse in a language Eventide didn't recognize.

After she jolted awake for the second time, Phoenix made an exasperated sound. "What is with you this morning, child?"

"I had a tough time sleeping," she replied tersely. "I'm still getting used to my new chambers. It's a foreign place, and I keep hearing strange noises."

"What kind of strange noises?" Solara lifted a hand to her chest as her jaw fell open. "I hope it's not space rats! That would be the death of me! I can not stand those wretched beasts!"

"No, no," Eventide said, lifting a calming hand. "Nothing like that. Probably just shifting panels and the oxygen converters, that sort of thing."

"Solara!" Phoenix scolded. "You're going to give this poor woman nightmares. You think a prestigious vessel like the *Inanna* would have a rat problem? Don't be ridiculous."

"Where I come from, noises in the panels means space rats."

"It's not rats," Eventide assured her. There had been the occasional rat problem on the *Eclipse*, and it had always struck her as odd that they survived on the station long enough to *become* a problem. The residents of the station had always believed the ships that had been delivering goods to the surface were bringing them on board, and it had always been seen as something positive—at least *something* could survive on the surface, even if it was rats. "I just couldn't sleep."

"Well, I'll speak to Doctor Morales," Phoenix said, tugging at a strand of her hair with a comb. "She'll get you something that will help. The Selection is today, and if you're one of the Selected, you'll need to be at your best to see the Prefect tomorrow."

She squinted, her sleep-deprived mind barely comprehending what Phoenix was telling her. "Selected? Prefect?"

These words meant nothing to her.

"Yes, dear! Haven't you been paying attention during the morning huddles?"

She hadn't.

"Today, the Caregivers will let us know if we were selected to be brought before the newly elected Prefect and his Council. There's a special presentation planned for Earth's capital. It's the most prestigious position a Domani could hope for. Could you imagine? I could be selected to style hair in Reykjavík!"

"Iceland?" Eventide spoke the word before she could filter out the thought.

Phoenix raised an eyebrow, his face contorting in confusion.

She doubted it had been called Iceland since the Wars. She wondered how well people here knew their history, but it was definitely not something a Domani would have said when discussing the prospect of being brought before a client.

Play the part. Bide your time.

Ugh.

"Ice-what?" Solara asked.

"Oh, uh . . . nothing." Eventide brushed the comment off. "Hopefully, all three of us will be selected. It sounds like the most prestigious of placements!"

Her attempt at enthusiasm seemed to satisfy the two Domani, and they carried on as though Eventide had said nothing out of the ordinary.

The two finished their work, carrying on between themselves about how exciting the prospect of being selected might be, before finishing with a dramatic flourish and waving Eventide off the chair.

"Now, no need to dally," Phoenix said. "They'll be announcing the selected Domani in a matter of hours, and looking like that, there's no doubt who the Prefect will have his eye on. Don't forget to grab some breakfast; today is going to be fabulous!"

Eventide entered the grand hall, and it didn't take long for her to find Okimi. The yellow-clad Domani was stifling a yawn as she stood behind a group of others collected before one of the holo-screens.

"What's all this?" Eventide tried to avoid catching Okimi's yawn, which only made it worse, and she lifted a hand to cover the one that inevitably escaped.

"The Selection," Okimi replied as she strained to see over the head of the Domani in front of them. "They've released the names of those to be brought before the Prefect."

Eventide glanced at the screen, certain her name wouldn't be on that list. Not that she wanted it to be. Did she?

There was something inside her that yearned to be chosen—but it was a ridiculous thought. Other than being among the Selected, giving her a legitimate way off the *Inanna*, she refused to be a part of this sick system the Syndicate had arranged. Besides, even if she were to be paraded around Earth's capital city, Caregiver Lin still maintained a watchful eye over her whenever they were in the same room. If Lin had any say in her qualification to be among those brought before the Prefect, Eventide's name would be nowhere near that list.

"Phoenix and Solara mentioned something about that."

Matthias appeared on the other side of the room. His eyes glanced over the other Domani with only a passing interest, probably because he knew he was planning on leaving with Eventide, but the scowl he wore on his face would instantly have tipped off anyone still convinced he was under the Caregivers' control.

As it stood, laughs and high fives were being shared among the surrounding people. Others simply nodded as their eyes left the holo-screen. There were only two attitudes in the room: elation, or resigned acceptance. Some congratulated their peers, but most simply returned to their activities.

So much excitement building up to the shortlist, and not even a shred of disappointment if they didn't make the cut.

Eventide wasn't one to let her emotions get the better of her, but even she didn't know what to make of the subdued reaction. Despite not truly caring whether she was selected or not, she understood what it meant to be left off a list you'd been striving to achieve placement on.

Her mind drifted to when she had been working toward qualifying for the technicians program. Now, there was a competition she *had* cared about.

Her nerves had been on edge for days, anticipating the news. Seeing as nobody from the D-Ring had ever been accepted into the program before, her expectations had been low, and she *still* would have been devastated if she'd been denied entry. But the constant feeding of the Domanis' neocortices didn't allow them to feel that pang.

A gasp escaped Okimi's lips, her eyes still glued to the holo-screen and her mouth moved in disbelief. "I've been selected!"

Eventide scanned the list herself. It listed ten names she didn't recognize, but Okimi had made the list, as had Yunni and Phoenix.

She didn't know whether to congratulate Okimi or offer her condolences. To Eventide, it would have been a death sentence, but Okimi was beaming.

"Congratulations." Matthias' words fell flat, with no heart behind them.

"You're sure you want this?" Eventide asked. This wasn't a choice, this was a lack of options. "You can still come with us, you know. There has to be another way."

Okimi beamed and reached around Eventide in an embrace. Eventide recoiled before allowing her new friend the gesture. She'd allow it . . . just this once.

"I talk a big game," Okimi whispered in her ear, "but I've never been a rebel. I'll be happy with this life. A life on Earth!" She released Eventide, stepped back, and straightened her outfit. "But I'm getting ahead of myself. I still need to be brought before the Prefect. There's still a good chance I won't be chosen."

Eventide sighed. Her tiredness was weighing heavily on her, but if Okimi wasn't going to change her mind, then the least she could do was be supportive. "Not be chosen! They'd be stupid not to pick you!"

"Even if the Prefect doesn't choose you," said Matthias, a levity returning to his voice. "There are other diplomats on the surface that might. It's rare for a Domani showcased on Earth to be returned to the ship."

"I'm nervous," Okimi admitted, shaking her hands beside her. "I had hoped for this, but . . . I didn't think it would actually happen."

"The Caregivers know what they're doing." Matthias stuck out a hand in an oddly formal gesture. "May the most suitable Domani be chosen."

"Come here, you big oaf!" Okimi moved from Eventide to Matthias in a smooth shift. Matthias hesitated for a moment before returning the gesture, his movements stiff and forced. His eyes darted around, avoiding direct contact, and he shifted his weight from one foot to the other.

"If all goes well on the planet tomorrow," Okimi said, ignorant of Matthias' awkwardness, "this will be my last ride in a ship. Let's sit in the rec room for a while and watch the planet from orbit."

The three wound their way through the halls, an odd mix of emotions hanging in the air. Matthias refused to meet Eventide's gaze, no matter how often she tried to catch his. Awkwardness loomed heavily over them, but Okimi didn't seem to notice. She was elated, practically dancing down the halls.

"You need to tone it down," Matthias said stiffly. "The Caregivers are going to become suspicious."

Eventide cast a glance at Matthias, but he still refused to look at her. It was an odd comment. The entire floor buzzed with emotional fervor, and there was nothing about Okimi's behavior that was any more over the top than the rest of the Domani. If anything, it was Matthias' moodiness that stood out.

Earth hung beneath them through the rec room viewport as the *Inanna* descended into orbit. Dozens of other Domani were gathered there as well, most with the same blank looks of joy and wonder as they looked out upon the planet. Others, however, bounced around with the same giddiness as Okimi, and Eventide took them to be the chosen few that had been selected.

She couldn't help but laugh and turned to Matthias to give him a *"guess you were wrong"* grin, but the man's face had darkened.

"Are you all right?" Eventide asked quietly. "The Caregivers might not notice Okimi's excitement, but they *will* notice you brooding."

"I'm fine," he said sharply. "I'm going to head to my quarters, anyway, so you don't have to worry about me giving the game away."

He stormed out of the hall without another glance to the planet or those around him.

If it hadn't been for the passionate kiss they had shared the night before, Eventide would have guessed he was jealous that Okimi had been selected over him. If that were the case, she might not have blamed him; Matthias had been on board for nearly a year without being chosen by a client. She wondered at what point Domani were deemed to be disposable; when they became more of a liability than an asset.

But she couldn't help but think his mood had more to do with what had happened between them.

As if on cue with Matthias' exit, the ship's lights dimmed and Lin's voice chimed over the ship's speakers.

"All Domani are to report to the theatre for an important presentation."

CHAPTER THIRTY-FOUR

Django
Space Dock Seven

One of the space dock crew had turned up the volume of the projected attack. The holographic scenes extended out from the monitors and surrounded the spectators as if it were a sporting match, instead of their fellow crewmembers fighting for their lives.

It's worse than the A-Ring—or at least, Django assumed it was. Did Benson sit in the control room of the *Eclipse,* watching Syndicate forces crack down on planetary riots from the comfort of his desk chair? Did the bastards livestream the staged hull breaches and watch while unsuspecting men and women were pushed out the airlock? Did they cheer as each of them struggled for their last breath?

The hair on the back of his neck bristled at the thought of that arrogant ass of a man.

Despite the battle being waged on another part of the dock, the realism of the holo made it hard not to cringe at every bullet fired, at every energy blast discharged.

Each shot meant another person might have met their end.

He tried not to look over his shoulder to catch glimpses of the feed as they stealthily used the distraction to their advantage; but it was impossible not to hear the battle it was projecting.

"We're going to blow the unit!" a man's voice announced through the feed. It was calm and steady, unlike those yelling through the feed.

"Sir?" a woman replied. Though it wasn't clear in the feed who was speaking, it was clear she was in the thick of the battle. *"We've got men and women here. Blowing the unit will tear a hole in the hull if we haven't depressurized properly."*

"We can't let them breach the dock! Protect the Hub at all costs. If they get inside, the elevator's at risk."

The elevator, Django thought. *They're worried the pirates are looking for a way to the surface.*

"You catching this, Amy?" Taku transmitted through their own comms network.

"Loud and clear, Cap."

"Get a message to Monroe. Tell her crew to back off a bit. If the fight stops, there won't be anything to keep eyes off us."

The escalation in protocol was enough to distract the spectators as the team pressed on past the promenade. Django held his breath as they crept past, the holo-screen feed still screaming behind them.

"We're pushing them back," the woman's voice on the holo said. *"Hold off on detachment."*

"That was fast," Django whispered.

"A well-oiled machine," Taku replied, eyes forward.

"That's not your call, Lieutenant."

"It is as long as I'm leading the squad! We don't retreat until I say!"

"And as long as I'm commander of this dock, I will not allow pirates to hijack our elevator or disrupt our supplies. If your forces don't leave, your squad's deaths will be on your head."

"You want to explain to the new Prefect why he needs to fund a new wing? Because I sure as hell wouldn't."

There was a pause in the exchange as blaster fire raged on around the group in the hall. The security detail was pushing deeper into the area now, getting into position to subdue the pirates.

The commander's voice came through again. *"Better that than explaining how a group of pirates ended up on the elevator! Keep them at bay, or I will release the C-Arm. And I won't ask next time."*

The comment was met with pronounced silence, immediately followed by more energy weapons' fire. Abigail must have got the message to slow their attack.

Release the C-Arm?

"Are they going to detach an entire wing of the dock?"

"Don't worry about that, Station Boy," Rowyn chirped. "Let's drop the package and fly before it gets to that point."

The team was already on the move across the promenade, and it was only a matter of minutes before they stood in front of a door marked "AUTHORIZED PERSONNEL ONLY." The doorway was otherwise unassuming, but not hidden.

"You're up, Django," Taku prompted.

Django didn't hesitate in waving his arm over the access panel beside the door. The door slid open with a hiss, revealing the restricted area beyond. He lingered on the threshold, a sensation like static prickling his skin. This was power—a stark contrast to his efforts to escape the *Eclipse's* corridors. Back then, he was a fugitive, gliding through the shadows on Eventide's borrowed privileges. Now he held the keys. The power wasn't just in his forearm; it coursed through his veins, and it was a feeling as exhilarating as it was disorienting.

The four of them slipped through, leading into a chamber filled with holo readouts and displays. Virtual images of the space dock displayed different statistics relating to the facility's metrics. Life support, pressure readings, temperature controls—all pulsed in midair around the consoles. Six substations circled the room, each one representing an arm of the dock. One marked "C" flashed red warnings of security breaches and of being sealed off.

Projections of the ships connected along with the arm floated beside it. Django could make out both the R-$332X$ and Monroe's ship, the *Chimera*, but he didn't recognize any of the others. Some were no doubt pirates, while others had to be deliveries meant for the planet. Some might even have been carrying shipments from the *Eclipse*.

How many of those ships would the Syndicate be willing to sacrifice to prevent access to the planet?

Django knew the answer.

All of them.

Rowyn, Taku, and Marshall spread out at strategic points throughout the room. Django counted eight glass doors that led to other parts of Engineering. Eight images cycled via his eyepiece as Amy fed surveillance footage from each one. Three of the rooms contained civilian tech engineers, all of them glued to their holo-screens, watching the insurgency.

"Any chance you can lock them in until we're done?" Django whispered. It was probably not his place to ask, but he was risking his neck as much as any of them.

"*Your wish is my command.*" Django could almost hear Amy's self-assured smirk.

Green lights beside each of the doors flashed to red. Django swore he heard the clicking of the locks, but the crewmembers inside didn't look away from their screens.

"You can override the doors now?" Marshall asked. "What did we need to bring the kid for?"

"*Locking them is easy,*" Amy replied. "*Unlocking them's the hard part.*"

Rowyn rolled her eyes. "Each door will have its own clearance level, Marshall, and the upload needs *three* access codes to complete. Django's got them all."

And "Station Boy" is still my nickname.

"This is the access port to the ship's primary system." Rowyn had moved to the table in the center of the room. It was unassuming until she hit a few buttons on the controls, prompting a holographic rendering of the entire dock to appear above it: a three-dimensional replica, with six outstretched arms reaching out from the central hub. "This is where we need to drop the package."

Django approached the console, looking around for any sign that the dock guards were about to rush into the room, blasters firing.

It seemed too easy.

The Resurgence wants chaos.

From everything he'd seen, he still didn't know how the Resurgence's plans would play out after this moment. Chaos seemed like the inevitable outcome.

But did it matter? Bring down the Empire and stop more Bensons from killing innocents. Save Eventide. It was a win-win scenario.

For all their back-and-forth rhetoric, the missions of both Aries and the Resurgence seemed to be of the same vein. Fracture the empire. Start a new orbital order. One path led to anarchy, the other to chaos. How was one better than the other?

"Guys, pick up the pace," Amy buzzed over the headset. *"Things are getting dicey over here."*

So much for easy. "What's going on, Aimes?" Django asked.

Taku gave him a dirty look.

Marshall had already moved over to the center console, plugging in data entry to access the upload site they needed.

"Authorization needed for new data," the computer chirped.

"They've got Monroe pigeon-holed," Amy replied. *"If she can't turn this around, she's going to need to do something desperate."*

And then the dock commander is going to blow the arm.

"Never back a pirate into a corner," Taku mumbled.

"Is there anything you can do?" Django asked, becoming emboldened as each moment passed. He had the opportunity in front of him to help these people. "Assist her in some way?"

"*Not without exposing us.*"

"But if they blow the arm . . ." Django began.

"We'll worry about that then," Taku snapped, obviously irritated. "Start the upload so we can get the hell out of here."

"Where are we at, Marshall?" Django asked.

"We're at you getting the hell over here."

Django ground his teeth but moved to the command station, where the hologram of the dock hovered translucently above the console. Green and yellow lights reflected off his companions' combat suits onto the screen below.

Holographic letters appeared above the screen: AUTHORIZATION REQUIRED.

Django didn't hesitate. He reached his forearm up and allowed the device to scan.

READY FOR MANUAL UPDATE.

"There aren't going to be safeguards against this?" Django asked incredulously.

"Against what?" Marshall winked. "We're just updating a few system subroutines. It's a doctored routine maintenance package that would normally be pushed from the surface. Your override is only required because we're doing it manually."

Django grabbed the double circle pendant that hung around his neck and popped out the chip from the back of it. His fingers slowed as they ran across the coolness of the card.

Such a small thing to contain the downfall of an empire.

Insert a virus that will disrupt the transportation of goods to Earth and watch their society crumble.

He set the chip on top of a small green-lit panel that was relatively the same size and it flashed to yellow.

DOWNLOAD IN PROGRESS.

A progress bar appeared and a yellow bar ticked from left to right, signaling the data transfer.

10%.

20%.

30%.

The dock bucked beneath Django's feet like a startled horse, wrenching his balance away. His hand shot out, instinctively latching onto Marshall to stay upright, while Marshall grabbed onto the control panel to do the same.

"What's going on, Amy?" Taku barked.

"*Uh . . . Nothing good.* You wrapping things up soon?"

60%.

70%.

"Just about!" Django replied.

"*Care to elaborate, Aimes?*" Taku demanded.

"*No time for explanations!*" Amy snapped, desperation flooding her voice.

A cacophony of voices filtered through the control room door, their shouts bouncing off the walls in a chaotic symphony. Muffled by the control panel doors, it was hard to tell if they were cheers of celebration or cries of horror.

Perhaps they were both.

90%.

100%.

UPDATE COMPLETE.

Django retrieved the chip from the console and clicked it back into his pendant. "That's it! Let's move!"

Taku nodded, seemingly unfazed that Django was suddenly providing instructions. He hefted his weapon as he hit the panel to open the door back to the promenade while the others formed up around the door.

"Amy, once we're clear of the control room, open up the connecting doors," Taku said. "No need for the engineers to be any the wiser."

"*I can't, remember?*" she said. "*Locking, but no unlocking. It doesn't make a difference that I was the one who locked them.*"

Taku dipped his head as though trying to speak more directly into his mic. "Once they discover they're locked in, they're going to know something's up."

"*They'll assume it has to do with the lockdown.*" Amy replied. "*As long as you're not seen on the way out. Besides, they're still glued to their holos. None of them have so much as tried to piss since the attack began. Even that last jolt didn't faze them.*"

"Let's keep it that way," Rowyn said, her weapon ready as she pressed a shoulder into the wall beside the exit.

The door slid open, and Taku poked his rifle through the opening. The holographic display was still focused on the dock crew.

Amy wasn't joking. The situation had escalated.

A burst of intense light erupted from an unknown source, turning the promenade into a blinding, white inferno. Django squinted, the harsh light searing his eyes, unable to discern whether the perpetrator was pirate or guard. Despite it only being a holo-projected image, men and women in their high-collared shirts either ducked or lifted their arms against the blinding intensity that ignited the room.

The dock's commander's voice came through the feed amidst the chaos. *"You've got thirty seconds, Lieutenant."*

Thirty seconds to what?

"We're working on it!" the woman bellowed back.

Another flash, this one not as intense as the first. It was only then that it became clear that the holo was following the guards.

The pirates were further down the arm now, and Django recognized the hall they were in.

The guards are fleeing the C-Arm.

"Stars!" Django breathed, a note of dread creeping into his voice. "We've got to get back! Now!"

Without waiting for an answer, Django broke into a sprint.

"What's going on?" Taku asked, running to keep up with Django's breakneck pace back down the stairs. "Easy, soldier! We've still got to maintain our cover."

Django slowed only enough to answer. "They're going to detach the C-Arm! Amy, you've got to detach the runabout!"

"Working on it," she chirped back. *"Dock security have locked everything down. I won't be able to detach without clearance."*

"Damn it," Taku muttered under his breath.

A chill crept over Django as the commander's words echoed in his mind.

We're going to blow the unit.

CHAPTER THIRTY-FIVE

Django

Space Dock Seven

"They're not just detaching it," Django said, voicing his realization. "They're going to blow the whole damn thing."

"There are innocent people on those ships!" Rowyn protested.

"They blew an entire FLOW station to keep their secrets," Django growled. "You think they'll have an issue with a few extra delivery vessels?"

Rowyn's eyes went wide, and even Taku's mouth dropped as the realization struck him.

"Amy," Django said, "do you still have visual through the halls? We're coming your way."

"For now. The guards are using the maintenance corridors to retreat," she answered. *"But they've sealed the airlock. Detachment sequence has been initialized."*

They weren't going to make it. If they were caught on this side of the C-Arm, the guards would know the infiltration had gone deeper than a simple pirate skirmish, and everything they'd risked would be for nothing.

The dock shuddered beneath them as their feet pounded against the grated floors. It would take them at least ten minutes to get to the C-Arm.

"Two guards coming up the main corridor ahead of you," Amy crackled, her signal weakening.

How long until the arm blows?

Seamlessly, the team pulled their weapons. Django led the charge, turning the corner and firing on the guards before they even registered they were under attack.

Two male guards stood ahead, smiles on their faces, believing they had successfully kept the pirates at bay, even if that had meant sacrificing part of the dock itself. One was older, in his early forties, the second barely twenty. Shock registered on their faces as Django's shots went wild, giving the two a chance to draw their own weapons.

"We have a . . ." The guard never finished the sentence as two shots fired from Django's weapon found their mark as he tried to request backup. The smell of burnt flesh hit Django before the flare of blaster fire hit him in the shoulder, sending him stumbling into the wall.

"What's going on down there?" The voice of a panicked commander echoed through the downed guard's open helmet. *"Has the Hub been compromised?"*

A bolt from Rowyn's weapon brought the second guard down, just as Marshall reached the fallen body of the first and leaned over him. "All clear here, sir," Marshall said, altering the pitch of his voice. "The kid's a little trigger-happy after the attack."

"Keep it together. We've suffered enough damage today."

"Yes, sir!"

Taku scooped up the young guard's body with one arm. "We can't leave them here."

The additional weight was going to slow them down. The body they'd left earlier could have been explained away as part of the attack, but two corpses in the Hub would be a dead giveaway there had been an alternate plot at play.

Django bent to lift the second guard as pain ripped through his arm. Only then did he realize it hung uselessly at his side.

"Your arm all right?" Marshall asked as he took over, grabbing the second body himself.

Django tried to move his arm again, to no avail. It hung limp. The burning in his shoulder stung, but he didn't have time to think about the damage it might have caused. He had to help get the team back to the ship.

"Never mind. Let's get to the ship."

Rowyn gave him a concerned look, forcing Django to roll his eyes.

"What do you expect me to do about it now?" he snapped—and immediately regretted his tone. She was in this just as much as he was.

Rowyn pursed her lips and pushed forward, leading the charge now that Marshall and Taku were carrying extra weight.

It wasn't long before they reached a dead end. The team holstered their weapons as their hopes of escape sank. A small port window in the sealed doorway revealed a small depressurization chamber, but beyond that, the C-Arm floated weightlessly, making its slow descent toward the planet's surface.

They were too late.

"We're going to have to jump for it." Django spoke the words, but the thought had come from nowhere. *Is that even possible?*

Rowyn and Marshall shared a look that screamed: 'Station Boy is out of his damn mind.'

"He's right," Taku said, surprising Django. "We can't be left stranded here. We're getting off this base."

Dead or alive.

Django didn't have to be told this was up to him. He lifted his good arm—thanking the stars it was his chipped one—and waved it in front of the access panel to the depressurization chamber. A hiss signaled the air venting from the dock into the newly pressurized space.

"Helmet's up," Taku said, though he didn't need to. Only Django had yet to activate his.

Django clicked a button sewn into his combat suit's collar, which brought the protective shielding of a helmet up and around his head.

"You've thought of everything," Django murmured.

"Standard for off-ship missions," Marshall replied. "You can't take chances in space."

Only then did it truly dawn on Django what they were about to do.

"I've got to be crazy . . ." he thought out loud.

Taku smirked. "Then you're finally starting to fit in. Don't screw this up."

As far as compliments went, Django thought that might be the only one he'd ever hear from Taku.

And all it took was jumping off a space dock, likely to my death.

"How's this going to work, Taku?" Marshall asked skeptically. "It's not like we can jump over!"

Taku paused, his eyes going from the depressurization chamber door to the detached Arm, still drifting away from them.

Django waved his hand over a console on the bulkhead that separated them from the stars.

"What are you doing?" Taku snapped.

"I'm separating us from the rest of the dock."

Truthfully, Django didn't know if it was possible, but there had to be a way. He fumbled around on the system for only a few seconds before finding what he was looking for. An airtight divide came sliding down behind them, sealing them in a room between the dock proper and the vacuum of space outside.

"I hope you know what you're doing . . ." Rowyn warned.

"He's trapped us in here!" Taku snapped, grabbing a handful of Django's suit and lifting him so that the two of them were face-to-face. "What the hell do you think you're trying to pull?"

"Easy, Taku!" Rowyn yelped. "It's okay."

"Like hell it is!"

With Taku cutting off the airflow to his neck, Django struggled to get a word out, but he strained against the man's brute strength. "Pull out . . . your blaster," he rasped.

Confusion blanketed Taku's face.

"Everyone." Django pointed to the console on the edge of the bulkhead. A countdown sequence in large holographic numbers ticked down.

3 . . .

2 . . .

1 . . .

The team was jettisoned into space as the airlock seal opened and the force of the pressure leaving the chamber ejected them out. Taku lost his hold on Django's scruff as the decompression catapulted them from the dock.

Django grabbed the blaster from his hip and lifted it.

Taku's eyes went wide, and his arms scrambled to his belt to find his own.

"*Django!*" Rowyn's voice echoed through comms inside his helmet. "*Don't!*"

"*Point it at the dock!*" Django yelled.

He pulled the Renegade's trigger and was flung backward into the nothingness of space, as the explosion propelled him toward the dock that housed the *R*-3.

⁂

Django collided with the C-Arm with a thud. There was no need for pressurization here: the Syndicate wanted those on board dead, so they hadn't bothered to maintain any life support systems. Anyone still alive would be on board their docked ships, relying on their own systems. He only hoped it wouldn't be too late.

Rowyn, Taku, and Marshall stumbled in beside him.

"You could have told us what you were doing, you little shit!" Taku barked.

"Amy, we're in," Django muttered, ignoring Taku. "How much time do we have?"

"The arm will be clear of the dock in ten minutes. They'll wait until then to detonate the Arm."

Plenty of time.

It only took them three minutes to rush to the docking bay where the *R-3* was stationed. In the zero-gravity environment, the team clung to railings and doorways, struggling to propel themselves forward.

"You three, get into the *R-3*," Django said, scanning his arm over the panel to release the traction locks on the ship. "I'll catch up with you."

"Wait," Taku said. "Where do you think you're going?"

"Rowyn said there are six ships docked here. I'm not letting any innocents die because of our stupid plan."

"Um, the plan wasn't stupid." Marshall said, crossing his arms.

"That's *not* the takeaway here!" Django hissed. "Get on the ship. Amy, if I'm not back in five, detach and get as far away from this thing as you can."

"You are doing no such thing!" Taku countered.

"Those ships are locked in. If this thing blows, so do they."

"*Django, get on the damned ship!*" Marvin's voice shot through the comms.

"I'm not letting these people die because of this!"

"*If you die, this whole thing will be for nothing! The Chimera will be fine. Abigail's gotten herself out of tougher spots than this. Get out of there before the place blows.*"

Monroe might be okay, but what about those other ships?

The extended passageway stretched out before him.

Without artificial lighting or life support systems, it was haunting—a ghost of the Arm that had been attached to the dock mere minutes before. He accepted he would be cutting it close, but he couldn't just leave. *Isn't that what Benson would do? Stand by while innocents die?*

Marshall and Rowyn didn't hesitate to float onto the now accessible runabout vessel.

Taku stood looking at Django expectantly. "You're next."

"*Don't make me repeat myself, kid,*" Marvin crackled.

The Resurgence wants chaos.

Is this what that is? Chaos?

Django shook his head. He wasn't going to stand for it. "Back at the transition house, you told me that what makes the Resurgence different is that you look out for each other. What good is that if we let others needlessly die in our wake?"

With one swift move, Django planted a boot firmly into Taku's chest.

Taku groaned as the foot made contact, knocking the breath out of him, and the momentum was enough to push the man backward onto the *R-332X*. Django punched in another command and the ship's door shut, leaving Taku, Rowyn, and Marshall banging on the door from the inside.

He pulled himself down the corridor, away from the ship. With Marvin and Taku barking in his ear simultaneously, Django muted his comms.

Sometimes innocent people have to die in a revolution.

But that didn't mean they had to give up on saving the ones they could.

There was no time to activate the gravity, even if he

knew a way of doing so. He reached the first door and ran his forearm over the access panel. The door opened and Django ducked inside.

A second panel allowed him to run another scan of his forearm to disengage the traction clamps. There was no way for him to notify the occupants on board, so he had to hope their ships were actively monitoring their status.

Rapidly, Django disengaged the remaining locks and raced down the corridor.

There was one ship left before he would have to make his way back to his own. He unmuted his comms, expecting to be greeted with a sea of activity, but was instead met with silence.

"Aimes, I'm about done here. Get ready for me."

"*Django, there's no time!*" Amy hollered. "*If I don't disengage now, we won't clear enough distance to escape the blast!*"

CHAPTER THIRTY-SIX

Django

Arm C, Space Dock Seven

"Go then!" Django said.

"*Django, we cannot afford to lose you in the blast!*" Marvin bellowed. "*Get out of there!*"

"You heard Amy—I won't make it back in time. I'll find another way. Just get the ship to a safe distance and stand by to pick me up!"

If this had been a suicide mission, he hoped the other ships were grateful.

Django's words reverberated within his helmet, as though bouncing off the dark walls of the powerless space dock arm he now stood in. He wondered whether the crews of the other ships realized the price of their escape, or if they knew the mirror of their salvation held the reflection of his potential doom. Through the now-open bay doors, he could tell that the rest of the ships had taken advantage of their situation and disengaged. Sparks still sputtered around the sections where the *Chimera* and its sibling ships had blasted their way free.

The pirates saved themselves, and left the rest to burn.

There was nothing separating the empty cargo bay hold from himself and the emptiness of space.

All but one of the other ships had fled.

One last ship waited at the end of the arm. He repeated the same action he'd performed on the rest of the docking bay doors and the clamps clicked, signaling release.

Last one.

"I'm alone now," he thought out loud. For what it was worth, nobody else would die because he had failed to act.

"Django, you need to get the hell out of there!" Marvin's voice had turned from commanding to concerned.

"I've got nowhere to go." Even as he said the words, he was already on the move, pushing through the last hatch he'd released. If he could somehow get off the structure before the Syndicate initiated the self-destruct, he figured he might have the most minuscule shot at survival.

It was impossible to tell from where he stood, but Django knew the dock's arm was in free fall, hurtling toward the planet, desperate to escape the fate it was destined for. A sea of blue glowed below. It would have been a beautiful end.

But it would never make it to the blue planet below. Its end would be much more violent. Any moment, the arm would blow, and if he was lucky, he'd never know the difference.

He pushed his way into an open cargo bay hold, navigating through canisters and crates that floated freely through the bay. The vastness of space silently loomed ahead of him.

The distance was small, but with no gravity, it was nearly impossible to push his way through the mess of the hold—especially since his left arm still hung limply by his side.

This is taking too long . . . I'm not going to make it.

But Django refused to believe that this would be his end. Not like this. Eventide was still out there somewhere, likely depending on him to come find her, and there was still Commander Benson to deal with.

No, Django Alexander would not die today.

He used the floating equipment to push his way out of the cargo bay door, an infinite field of stars stretching out above him and the blue and green planet below. The thrust worked, but the momentum gained was far too slow to clear the path of destruction. The heat of the blast alone would be enough to incinerate him.

His blaster's charge had been depleted. He would get one more shot with it, and he wasn't convinced it would drive him out far or fast enough to separate him from the blast.

He was running out of time.

A canister marked "OXYGEN" that hadn't been tied down properly floated past him, giving him an idea. Compressed oxygen would certainly provide him with the force he needed.

Django launched himself at the canister, nearly doubling over backward as he struggled to maintain a grip on it with one arm. The unit was bigger than he'd expected, but for what he had planned, that was likely to be a good thing.

If he could hold on.

Django wrapped his legs around the composite container and, with his good arm, drew the Renegade from his belt.

One shot.

He pointed the canister so that he was facing toward the floating space dock arm, set the weapon to maximum as he aimed at the cannister's nozzle, and pulled the trigger.

In a rush, Django went flying backward, momentum propelling him deeper into the void of space and away from the compromised dock arm. He slammed into a hunk of metal that knocked the wind out of him and flung him off the canister, tossing the blaster from his hand.

He sucked in nothing as he struggled to catch his breath, gasping as though a hole had punctured his suit.

His arm frantically fumbled for his helmet readouts, fearing the worst, but everything lit green. The air had been knocked out of his lungs, but not his unit. His oxygen levels were a little low, but he would have enough as long as the team aboard the R-$332X$ didn't abandon him.

He steadied his breath. He was alive—for the moment. His suit was still pressurized, and he was still breathing.

The canister had catapulted him into a piece of space junk—a remnant metal hull from another spacecraft. Eventide would have been able to tell him which part it had belonged to, but to him it was merely a hunk of metal that had stopped him from escaping destruction.

Space Dock Seven still loomed far too close, one of its gargantuan arms casting an ominous shadow that seemed to reach out for him. The dread of imminent detonation pricked at his senses, each tick of the clock amplifying the heartbeat in his ears into a deafening roar. Mere slivers of time were all that separated him from the blast.

Isolation crept over him, a chill deeper than the cold of space, leaving him adrift in an uncanny, warped reality.

In the vacuum of space, an explosion unfolded differently than within an oxygen-rich environment; there was no grand pyrotechnics, no earth-shaking rumble, as oxygen was a scarcity it couldn't afford. Instead, silence was its messenger.

Without warning, the tranquil void erupted into a lethal downpour of shrapnel. Django, clutching his metallic sanctuary, found himself in the center of a deadly cosmic hailstorm.

Barely a heartbeat passed before he thrust his body around, using the metal barrier as a makeshift shield against the oncoming onslaught of debris.

He hung on as best he could as bits of metal whipped past his head, pushing him further away from the larger remnants of the dock's disconnected arm. The largest section hurtling toward Earth's atmosphere.

Django's muscles tightened at the strain of holding the metal against him. It shuddered as thousands of metallic shards peppered its side. One-handed, he wrestled to keep the plate between himself and the brunt of the onslaught. Even one inopportune shard would rip his suit open with no effort at all.

"I could use a little help here!"

The silence on the other end of the comms was deafening.

The force of the impacts pushed him back, away from the explosion, carrying him along with the shock wave. How far and how fast he was going, Django could only guess, but he was sure it was too fast for someone to jump down and rescue him.

The arsenal of debris was as likely to damage the R-332X as it was his suit.

His muscles trembled, a burning protest sizzling through his veins. Memories of wrestling stubborn farm machinery flashed through his mind, a silent testament to the reservoir of strength he knew he possessed. Yet, with every ticking second, that strength ebbed, slipping like sand through clenched fists.

Just as he thought he couldn't handle it any longer, the peppering of debris lessened, the impacts against his shield dying out as the hull fragment traveled further from the epicenter of the blast. Django breathed a sigh of relief, momentary solace coursing through his muscles—but it was short-lived.

The break in the storm was only because of the speed he'd picked up with the shock wave, propelling him at the same velocity as the dock arm's shrapnel.

He was accelerating toward the Earth's atmosphere, the beginning stages of atmospheric re-entry already making themselves known. A faint glow enveloped him, a precursor to the intense heat that he knew would follow.

If someone didn't rescue him soon, it would all be over.

"Rowyn? Marvin? Taku? Can anyone hear me?"

Sweat beaded on his face as the temperature inside his suit began to rise as the friction of himself hitting the atmosphere started to make itself known. It wasn't designed for this. He struggled to breathe as panic set in, suffocating him. He would have loved nothing more than to rip the damned thing off.

He couldn't die today. He wasn't done yet—not while Eventide still needed him. Not while Marvin still needed him. And there was still a commander named Benson that needed to pay for his crimes.

Eleven Commander Bensons.

There was still an array of things Django had sworn he would do to help anyone who'd had the wool pulled over their eyes by the Syndicate Empire.

"Is *anyone* out there? I'm entering the atmosphere. I don't know how much time I have left."

His fists mashed the buttons on his forearm, his heart racing in his chest as he hyperventilated and simultaneously wondered how long it would take before he ran out of air.

Maybe it didn't matter. He was hurtling so fast, he would probably cook before he suffocated.

Either way, he wouldn't survive.

The sound of his breathing was still the only noise he could hear, as smaller pieces of debris above him shimmered from the friction's heat. It was hard to tell how far he was from the flames. He shuddered as he wondered if he might burst into flames at any moment.

"Anyone?"

Seconds ticked by with only his pounding heart as a reply.

Tears welled in his eyes, a dam of emotion threatening to burst as his impending mortality clawed at his resolve. His fingers slackened their grip on the warming metal shield, his last tether to safety surrendering to the punishing heat.

The once-shielded hull fragment tumbled away into the vast abyss, a silent goodbye in the void. A light-headed sensation wrapped around his thoughts, a delirious mix of heat, heavy breathing, and depleting oxygen . . .

A cocktail of death.

Surrendering to the encroaching darkness at the edge of his vision, Django squeezed his eyes shut. He took a steadying breath, but the air tasted thinner, his lungs straining against the suffocating grip of the suit. The slick layer of sweat lining his back seemed to boil in its own skin-tight prison, the searing heat inescapable. He knew his suit could tell him the numbers, the exact degrees he was cooking in, but right now, numbers were meaningless. Survival wasn't quantifiable.

Stars greeted him as he opened his eyes again. An endless volley of stars lay above him, filled with lost hope and lost opportunity. He hoped that Eventide would find the means to escape. Maybe Marvin would still find her. Maybe she would get a chance to explore the untold number of worlds out there he never would. She'd like that.

It was too bad he wouldn't be able to join her.

Static filled his helmet as Django fought to keep his heavy eyes open. He wondered how much heat the circuits in his suit could take before they fried. The empty sounds of space pulsed in ways that mimicked speech as his consciousness faded, as though someone was talking to him through the void after all.

He could have sworn his dead mother was reaching out to him . . .

How long had it been since he'd last thought of her? The pain of her being tossed out of the airlock had been too much for him to digest. Django had filled his days since with a mission to save Eventide so that he didn't have to dwell on the dead that had amassed around him. Now, he regretted ignoring them, his family and friends whose ghosts he'd left behind on the *Eclipse*. This quest for adventure, one he'd never asked for, had stolen him away from their memory.

Now, he would be able to join them, to find peace for once.

How he longed for a moment of peace . . .

"Django . . ." The voice called to him. Faint. Distant.

"Mom?" he whispered, his voice trembling.

"'Mom?'" A voice that definitely wasn't his mother's broke through the static, ripping Django out of his trance. "Did you hit your bloody head when you flew out of that tin can, love? Hang on, I'm coming to get ya."

All thoughts of his mother and of home dissipated as the voice slammed him back into the present.

Not Mom. Monroe.

He was saved.

CHAPTER THIRTY-SEVEN

Mikka

The *Redemption*

"Where the hell have you been?"

It was the first time Mikka had heard Aries raise his voice; the first time she'd heard him get mad at *her*.

It had been hours since she had left the *Chimera*. There had been no assault on the *Redemption* once she'd left and nobody pursuing her. Penelope had been right; Monroe had been so wrapped up in whatever business she had with Marvin that nobody had noticed her departure.

But what could have been engrossing them for hours?

Mikka shrugged off that line of thinking. It was barely an itch in her brain compared to the furious Commander Aries whose holo-projection paced on the *Redemption*'s bridge.

"You should have delivered all those packages by now. We're way behind schedule!"

Heat rose in Mikka's cheeks, her eyes stinging with the unfamiliar sensation of shame entwined with her customary anger. But something within her was compelled to please David, and she'd let him down.

Or was it that she couldn't stand letting anyone else down?

She swallowed the feeling. Everything that had happened had been outside of her control.

"Pirates," she said, unsure whether she should tell Aries that Monroe and her crew were now claiming to be members of the Resurgence or not.

Why wouldn't *I tell him that?*

"'Pirates?' You must be joking. You could have bested any other pirate in the system when we first met! It took you *a week* to escape?"

"It was Monroe and her crew, sir." Mikka shook her head. "And these pirates had ships unlike any I've ever seen. I wasn't able to get away, and they would have torn the *Redemption* to shreds if I'd engaged them in combat."

"Monroe? I knew she was trouble as soon as I saw her on your ship's roster." Aries didn't look pleased with the news. "But I'm more surprised to hear that there are ships in the system that you're unfamiliar with. Can you tell me about them?"

Mikka described the vessels in as much detail as she could. Unfortunately, she hadn't been in a position to get the exact specifications, so she had to base her descriptions on their appearance and the few details she remembered Kiara saying about them.

As she spoke, Aries turned as white as Lunar's surface. "Are you certain?" he asked. "About their appearance? Their speed? Their ability to avoid detection?"

"The *Redemption* isn't equipped with top-of-the-line

scanners, but the third and fourth ships didn't appear at all until they were damn near right on top of us. They were flat, like they were trying to avoid detection, and Kiara . . ." Mikka cleared her throat. "Kiara believed their drives were powerful enough to reach Mars in a week."

Aries' face turned ashen. "Are you sure about their appearance and capabilities? The ships you're describing . . . They're not just any models."

Mikka narrowed her eyes, confused by his reaction. "What do you mean?"

Aries hesitated for a moment before replying. "They match the description of some classified prototypes in active development. I didn't think the Syndicate had put them into larger production yet. If these ships match those specifications, that's a troubling development, but even more so if they're now in the hands of pirates."

"They definitely fit the bill for prototypes. I've never seen tech like it."

"I'll need my men to investigate further," Aries said, his face returning to its resolute frown, as though that solved the matter. "Is the inventory intact? Did they tamper with it in any way?"

Mikka sighed. "I've inspected the shipments. I don't think they touched anything. Their sole purpose seemed to be stalling me, but for what reason, I'm not entirely sure."

"Well, if the only damage done was a delay in the delivery, then it's nothing more than an inconvenience. A frustrating one, but there's nothing that can be done about it now. I'd be interested to learn more about the tech incorporated on these ships once you return, though."

"There's something else, Commander." Mikka took a

deep breath. She still hadn't fully digested the reality of what had happened and each breath felt like a battle, the dull throb in her chest constricting tighter with every inhale, a constant reminder of her loss. "Kiara's dead."

Aries visibly softened, and Mikka imagined that if he didn't have a military background and wasn't accustomed to death, his jaw might have dropped.

"Mikka." It was a different man speaking than the angry military commander from moments before. This was a more compassionate man, one who had told her about his youth and had invited her into his quarters. "I . . . I didn't know. I'm so sorry."

He shook his head, his mouth forming a grimace, and inhaled deeply before meeting her gaze again. This was the man who had won over her heart, and not the military commander who had sent her on the mission that had cost her friend's life.

"I know Ms. Ryson and I didn't always see eye to eye . . ."

Mikka couldn't help but chuckle. She would have described Kiara's feelings toward the man as "loathsome."

"But she was an excellent navigator, and I know she was a good friend to you."

Tears welled in Mikka's eyes, the warm memories of her time with Kiara, now punctuated by their recent squabbles, growing distant, their last encounters a hollow echo of their once close bond.

"I apologize, Mikka. My comments about the inventory were insensitive. I should have asked about your well-being."

"You couldn't have known," Mikka said simply.

"What happened? Was this Monroe's doing?"

"I found Kiara dead in her bed." Mikka steeled herself against the memory of Kiara's lifeless body lying in a pool of her own blood. "I don't believe it was Monroe. I think someone on board meant to kill me. My past mistakes have led to many enemies. I imagine it was a shock to them to find out I'm still alive."

Aries nodded, pulling his hands behind his back. "You should come home. I can get someone else to deliver the packages to the FLOW stations."

Mikka bristled. She and Kiara had been close, but she had lost men and women before, many of whom had been her friends. It was part of the job. Part of being a pirate.

But I'm not a pirate anymore.

Mikka straightened. "I can complete the task, *sir*. I'm nearly to *Freedom* station now, ETA fifteen minutes. I'll have half of the run completed this afternoon."

"Given the circumstances," Aries' tone was soft, almost patronizing, "I wouldn't go back on my end of the deal, if that's what you're worried about. Your mother, Kiara's children, will still be taken care of."

"I said I was up to the job," Mikka bit back through gritted teeth.

"Mikka," he said, softer still. "You don't have to fight me. I'm not judging you. I'm trying to help."

"Well, don't. I'll return once the mission is complete."

Mikka cut the transmission. The holo-projector disconnected, and she nearly collapsed under the emotional weight of their conversation.

Just trying to help! He thinks I'm weak.

Mikka hadn't become the system's most notorious

pirate by taking a sick day every time one of her crewmembers died.

I'm not a pirate anymore.

Not a pirate—but her friends were still dying because of her.

What good would it do for Kiara to have died if it meant Mikka would crawl into bed and let someone else do the task at hand? She would be the one to make a difference; to bring the Syndicate under new reign. Making the deliveries played a small part in that, but it was one she had to complete.

Kiara did not die for nothing.

The guilt taunted her. David had been nothing but kind and, despite his disappointment, had treated her well. He had only tried to make sure she was okay. She shouldn't have hung up on him.

The one last friend I have, and I'm pushing him away.

Maybe it was for the best. Those close to her ended up dead.

"He's dangerous." Zee had been mostly quiet since they had left the *Chimera,* and Mikka had forgotten he was also on the bridge.

"Everyone I get too close to dies, Zee. He's not the dangerous one."

"Many will die because of him. There's no path that doesn't lead to that end."

"He's planning a war," Mikka reasoned. "Death can't be avoided. Spare me your prophecies, kid. I'm trying to make the system a better place."

Zee remained quiet, his expression empty.

Mikka shook her head. Badgering the poor kid wasn't

going to get her anywhere. It was time to change the subject. Instead of treating him like everyone else had, maybe she could learn more about him.

"What was your mod supposed to do, anyhow?" Mikka asked.

"It does what it was supposed to do: calculate odds. It just wasn't meant to see everything."

"What do you mean?"

"My previous owners hadn't thought that far ahead. They wanted someone who could win them money at the races. Help them beat games of poker and blackjack. It was Abigail who realized I could see much more."

That sounded plausible, at least. Slimy back-alley cutters were always looking for a way to make a quick credit. Mikka wouldn't have put it past any one of them to embed an untested chip into the kid's brain.

"But in the end, she was no better than any of them?"

"Abigail is kinder than most. She understands what I can do in a way that nobody else ever has, and she's always treated me like a person, not a novelty. She fed me well and has never beat me for being wrong."

"That's not exactly the benchmark for kindness, Zee. Are you often wrong?" Mikka asked, raising an eyebrow.

"With small things like card games? Rarely. But most of my owners have been greedy men."

Anyone who would use a child to predict the outcome of a card game would have to be.

"It's one hell of a leap to go from calculating the odds of a flush to seeing which choices will bring death and destruction." Mikka checked the status of their flight path as she spoke. She had a lot of space to cover.

"It's not as different as you would think. The mod has access to networks across the system. It can access information on everyone who's been chipped. The Syndicate keeps track of everyone's movements from the day they are born until the day they die. People like to think they're unpredictable, that it's free will that governs our actions. But we all follow patterns of behavior. Certain scenarios will elicit certain outcomes ninety-nine out of a hundred times. Nothing is certain, but most things that happen are likely. Monroe was trying to play the right card to elicit certain outcomes. Sometimes, you need that one in a million chance to pan out to get the outcome you desire, but that doesn't make it impossible."

Mikka nodded, only half-listening to Zee's explanations. Her mind was already elsewhere—on the deliveries, on Kiara's loss, on David Aries. She couldn't let him be next. She would help him, but from a distance. That was her lot in life.

Even now, she could feel the desire to be near him—to be wrapped in his arms. With him, she felt safe. It wasn't something she'd realized she needed, but ever since Space Dock Nineteen, she'd been looking over her shoulder.

And Aries had been the only one to ever offer Mikka the protection she needed.

But who's going to protect him from me?

CHAPTER THIRTY-EIGHT

Eventide
The *Inanna*

The exuberance had only turned down a notch with the announcement. The Domani, who could barely contain their fanatical levels of excitement, fought to contain their squeals of glee.

Steadily, the group filtered into the theatre. Since coming aboard, Eventide had yet to see inside this room. As she entered the space, she guessed it would have to be large enough to fit all the men and women held on board—or at least, those residing in the Domani quarters.

Row upon row of raised seating overlooked a stage in the center of the room. Golden pillars rose on either side of the stage, stretching upward to the ceiling, mounted with the images of winged seraphim from ancient Earth religions. Pewter carvings of Roman deities Eventide recognized from her studies were embedded into the walls, surrounding the stage as though guarding the room from whichever performer was set to display their talents—or perhaps, to worship them.

Theatrical laser lighting danced across the walls in a mesmerizing display that would be sure to dazzle anyone under the influence of mind-altering drugs, or perhaps, mind-altering transmissions.

What ran through the minds of the other Domani as they beheld such a technological performance? Eventide assumed many of them had seen such tech before, but perhaps that wasn't true. She had no concept of what life was like in the outer colonies, where most of humankind was caught in mining operations and extreme conditions. Perhaps this all seemed like magic to many of them, which would explain why they so quickly attached themselves to the idea that the Caregivers were their savior. To someone with no prior experience of spacecraft and holo-screens, coming from a place where food, water, and even breathable air was scarce, this must have seemed like a flying miracle.

The buzz in the air died down as people took their seats. The lights dimmed, and the Domani quieted.

Okimi sat beside Eventide, as wide-eyed as any of the Domani affected by the transmissions. There was a level of excitement in the air that was palatable, and it startled her to find a grin on her own face.

Eventide could feel the euphoria in the room. Actually feel it creeping into her bones and flowing through her veins like a drug invading her system.

The same sensations she had experienced kissing Matthias.

Reality hit her. The emotions she was feeling were

being manipulated by the Caregivers. By their transmissions. Doctor Morales had been wrong—Eventide wasn't completely immune to the pleasurable effects of her implants. She was just better at holding them at bay.

She pushed her epiphany aside as Lin walked onto the center stage, accompanied by someone who must have also been a Caregiver. The man's gray tailored suit matched Lin's, but he was younger. His dark eyes leant an intensity to his judgmental gaze as he scanned the room. He caught Eventide's eye and lingered there. In response, she did her best impression of Yunni, keeping a wide-eyed smile fixed on her face as she let the waves of excitement generated in the room flow through her. Her grin trembled when the man's stare didn't continue, leaving Eventide to question whether he'd actually bought her performance.

But overall, it wasn't the male Caregiver who garnered Eventide's attention: it was a Domani who had followed Lin on stage. The young man's happy-go-lucky presence reminded her of Orin, his reddish hair and ruby pajama outfit providing such a striking resemblance that it made Eventide do a double take. He was a touch shorter in height, but he could easily have passed himself off as the same person. If Orin's dead face didn't haunt her every waking moment, Eventide could have been convinced this *was* Orin, and his murder had all been a dream.

"Thank you for your promptness, Domani," Lin began. "We are privileged today to have in our presence a guest, though he is a dear friend to me. Caregiver Roberts has been traveling on board with us since we left Mars, getting acquainted with our ship and our technology, and how we run things. He is a Caregiver ambassador from Earth, and this is a historic day for him, as it is for all of you."

She gestured to the man, who was a good foot and a half taller than her, to step forward. Thankfully, Roberts' gaze was now looking out upon the audience, but seemingly at nobody in particular.

"As I am sure you have all heard by now," he said, "your next destination is Earth. Any visit to the home world is a special occasion, but tomorrow is particularly momentous. Some of you may have heard that a new Prefect has taken reign in Earth's capital. As per tradition, the Prefect will select three Domani as a symbol of Earth's allegiance with the Caregivers."

Not that the Domani will see any benefit of said arrangement.

"I know it must be a disappointment for those of you not among the Selected to be permitted to step upon the surface. But these are the regulations set out by our ancestors hundreds of years ago, to guarantee the Earth's protection. In accordance with our laws, twelve Domani, along with a selection of Caregivers, have been selected to attend a private audience with the Prefect and his Council.

"However, for the rest of you, as Earth's ambassador for this voyage, I have arranged a special message. I would like to introduce to you, for the very first time, the new leader of the Syndicate Empire, Prefect Eisner."

The theatre shook as the Domani erupted in a jubilant uproar. Eventide's abdomen vibrated along with the rest of the room, her core shaking with the sound of over a hundred Domani launching into a cacophony of adoration for a man who any of them had yet to see, let alone meet.

Does this Prefect Eisner relish the cheers of these men and women? Does he love the fact they throw themselves at his feet, mere mortals before their god? Does he care whether it is an action of free will or not?

That the *Inanna* was bound for Earth at all was the only answer Eventide needed.

Roberts stepped to the side of the stage, clasping his hands behind his back as a new figure flickered into existence. Lin motioned for the Domani to settle, and though it took a few seconds longer than an order would normally have taken to be followed, they did as they were asked.

The hologram of a man stood larger than life—a ten-foot-tall projection, towering over Lin and her newly appointed assistant, standing taller even than the first few raised rows of the auditorium.

A gasp flowed through the audience as they realized the height of the man who stood before them.

How many had never seen a holo-projection like this before? How many understood the figure before them was made of photons and air, rather than a flesh and blood Prefect? Even in their heightened emotional state, they should have been able to differentiate between reality and a hologram.

Couldn't they?

The man's attire was similar to the Caregivers—a black and gray suit with a white button-down shirt that framed his figure pleasingly. A black piece of fabric was tied around his neck, bearing a double-hexagon symbol emblazoned in holographic gold at its tips. The emblem phased in and out of the display as its frequency interfered with that of the holo-projected image, but the effect only added to the man's mystique. His eyes were a piercing green that Eventide would have bet wasn't natural, and he had a tattoo that ran down the side of his neck that glowed an alternating mix of colors: from blue to green to red, and a plethora of colors in between. The inkwork was both striking and mesmerizing.

What surprised Eventide the most was the man's age. Her only familiarity with leadership was Commander Benson and Lin, and both of them were well into their fifties. This man was practically a child by comparison—twenty-two, perhaps twenty-five, at most. It was hard to tell with the man's flawless skin and muscular build.

The man had obviously had work done to himself—similar to whatever nanobot enhancements the Caregivers had performed on her—but Eventide suspected it had been done to make himself seem more imposing. Even beneath the suit jacket, it was clear his shoulders sat wide and his arms were thick. He stood as though he had been commanding rooms like the theatre his entire life—and he likely had been. If he had inherited the Empire, he'd probably been conditioned to be in charge from a young age. The man held the bold confidence of a rightful leader.

In another situation, Eventide might even have called the man attractive.

But, in many ways, it was because of this man that Commander Benson had done his best to keep her on the D-Ring; the reason he tried to kill her when that had failed; why Eventide's body had been mutilated; why mind-bending tech had been drilled into her brain; why she had been separated from her one friend in the entire system;

why she now found herself trapped in a life where her captors intended to sell her like a plaything.

"For hundreds of years, the Empire has maintained an important partnership with the Caregivers and their work," Prefect Eisner began, his voice no less commanding than his appearance. "It is because of them that fine men and women have been lifted throughout our solar system and brought to Earth as a symbol of humanity's eventual return home.

"Generations of Prefects, Council leaders, and other heroes of the Empire have remained here on the planet's surface, much to our own peril. The Earth is still not ready for mass immigration, so we keep our fortress strong to three towers: Denver, Queenstown, and, of course, our Empire's capital city, Reykjavík.

"Some of you will come to the Courtroom tomorrow. It is there I will select three Domani for my personal escort. The rest of the Selected may be delivered to other members of the Council. But all of you who are brought before me will find a place in the Terminus. It is a great honor, one granted to only a small percentage of humanity. If you were not part of the Selected on this occasion, know that you still play a vital part in the hope of humanity. Our ancestors designed this exchange as a symbol of what the Empire represents. 'Domani' means 'tomorrow' in an old Earth tongue, and you were named as such because Domani represent a symbol of our path forward. A herald of hope for some future tomorrow, where all our citizens may one day return home."

The theatre erupted again. While Lin surveyed the

audience, Eventide put on her best smile, but inside, she seethed.

Whatever their ancestors had wanted, Eventide was sure it wasn't this. Humanity had slaved away from its home planet for far too long. This was bigger than her. She'd fought to be treated fairly on board the *Eclipse*, but now she fought for her own freedom—for both her body and her mind. Somehow, this Empire would meet its end, and Eventide knew that no matter what, she would be a part of ensuring it would happen.

She just had to figure out how to get off the damned ship.

CHAPTER THIRTY-NINE

Eventide

The *Inanna*

The rest of the day was spent in a haze. Lin gave Caregiver Roberts a tour around the ship. He took his time, inspecting each Domani at length, making careful assessments. Though he didn't touch any of them, his eyes were invasive enough.

"You've done a fantastic job here, Caregiver Lin," he said. "Some of the finest yet."

Eventide shuddered. *He acts as though he's inspecting this year's harvest.*

"We run an extensive intake program," Lin said as she led Roberts out of the rec room. "I should take you to see Doctor Morales' facility. You'll hopefully be impressed by the advancements she's made in the last few years . . ."

Lin's words followed them as they disappeared down a hallway.

"Meet me in the atrium," Matthias whispered as they left the theatre, his hot breath sending shivers down Eventide's spine. He took off in a direction that was decidedly not the way to the atrium.

What was his game?

Matthias had been noticeably absent from the presentation—or at least, Eventide had noticed, and she suspected his absence wouldn't have gone unnoticed by the Caregivers, either. She shook, as she feared his behavior was going to give them all away. They shouldn't be meeting in the atrium again. They'd already spent too much time with each other during waking hours.

"What's wrong?" Okimi asked, reading Eventide's expression as she approached.

"I don't know. Matthias wants to meet me in the atrium."

"There's something wrong with that?"

"I don't know. Do me a favor? Meet us there in ten minutes. We should probably all get together one last time before tomorrow, anyway."

Despite the need to remain under the radar, she at least wanted to give Okimi a proper goodbye.

Okimi shot Eventide a questioning look, but nodded. "I can't believe this is really happening! I'm going to be on Earth tomorrow."

"Just don't let your guard down now. Roberts seems to be scrutinizing us for some reason, and Matthias seems set on drawing attention to himself. If Roberts figures out your implants aren't working, there's a good chance you won't be going anywhere near the Prefect."

"I found this." Matthias dropped a metal box on the bench beside Eventide. There were other Domani milling around the atrium, but there was enough privacy provided by the trees and shrubbery to keep them out of sight.

Eventide stared at the familiar tin. There was no way it was what she thought it could be.

"Is that a toolkit?" she asked. It nearly mirrored the kit she'd been issued with back on the station. "Where did you find this?"

She rushed to open the box. Nearly everything inside looked like a slight deviation from what she was familiar with, but she understood each device's use: magnetic screwdriver, holo-multimeter, zero gravity wrench set, thermal imaging scanner, and what appeared to be a miniature-sized plasma cutter.

This was better than she could have hoped for.

Matthias ran a hand through his hair, looking at the floor. "I found it on my way out of the atrium last night. One of the maintenance staff must have left it behind—I just hope they don't notice it's missing. I've got to be honest, I don't know what most of that stuff is; my work has always been digital. But I thought as a station technician, you'd know what to do with it. Plus, I was kinda hoping it would make up for me being such a jerk last night."

Eventide's head tilted inquisitively, a playful spark flashing in her eyes despite the lingering hurt. "You *were* a jerk." She absently flicked a tool from its place in the kit and ran it through her fingers as she would a deck of cards, before setting it down again. "But I don't know if either of us were really ourselves."

Shock registered on his face, twisting in that familiar way it did whenever she posed a challenge.

"Say what you want, but I wanted to kiss you."

Matthias' confession hung in the air between them, a declaration fraught with longing, confusion, and a hint of desperation.

"And I wanted to kiss you, too," she admitted, her cheeks warming as the words left her mouth, each syllable dissipating in the quiet space between them, a truth laid bare. Her heart pounded in her chest, the rhythm as erratic as her thoughts. "But I never would have acted on impulse like that. And being swept away in the moment . . ." She had to catch her breath to keep her heart from racing at the wave of emotion even just the memory brought on. "The closest way I can describe it is the draw we feel to our quarters each night."

Matthias raised a suggestive eyebrow.

"Not like that!" She let out an exasperated groan. "Haven't you ever noticed that the call to your bed seems strong? That everything is pulling you to your quarters at night? You said it's because my body believes it needs sleep anyway, but I think there's something more going on. I felt it just now when we were in the theatre watching the Prefect. The wave of euphoria that swept the Domani in there wasn't natural. Like it was the most joyous occasion of my life, but I find everything that man represents to be abhorrent."

Matthias nodded stiffly, his eyebrow still raised. "You think there are only certain transmissions that are affect your pleasure centers?"

"There must be different wavelengths or something.

Anyway, the point is, we have to assume that our emotions are being toyed with, no matter how in control we think we are. Please don't hold any emotions I might have against me. I'm not sure I can trust them right now."

A visible softening came over him, his shoulders dropping and a sigh of relief escaping his lips. "I am sorry for how I acted. I . . . You're right, I haven't felt quite like myself, either."

A smile touched Eventide's lips. "Thank you. For now, let's focus on getting out of here, and we can worry about anything else that might happen after that?"

Something flashed in Matthias' eye. Was he worried? Something about what she had said had made him uncomfortable.

"What is it?"

He looked around nervously, as though unsure if anyone was close enough to overhear them. "You're still going ahead with the plan?"

"Of course. Isn't that why you brought me the toolkit?"

He nodded. "It is, but I couldn't sleep once I got back to my quarters last night. I couldn't stop thinking about Orin. He went poking around where he shouldn't have been, and look where that got him."

"We don't know that's the reason for his death," Eventide replied hesitantly. "The lives of Domani don't seem to hold much value."

Matthias smirked. "Didn't you hear the Prefect? Domani are the *future*."

Eventide rolled her eyes.

Before she could rattle off a retort, Okimi entered through the sliding glass door of the atrium, her silken

Domani outfit clinging to her figure as she strode down the atrium's path toward them.

"Speaking of which, I appreciate you pretending to be happy for Okimi. It might not be the life we'd choose, but she seems elated with the outcome."

"'Pretending?'" He lifted his hands in feigned horror. "No, no, I'm truly happy for her. It may not be what *I'm* cut out for, but it truly is an honor to be chosen for service to the Prefect."

The comment struck Eventide as odd. Matthias sounded sincere, but there was a tinge of something in his voice—jealousy, maybe?

Eventide was about to ask him if there was a limit to how long Domani could stay on board the *Inanna* when he turned slightly, his eyes flicking from Eventide to Okimi, an unspoken question hanging in the air between them. "Has she . . ." he started, his voice softer than before, almost as if to prevent his words from actually reaching Okimi. "Have you told her about . . . last night?"

His eyes held Eventide's, searching for an answer, his concern over their secret breaking their small, fleeting peace seemed to make him even more vulnerable.

"No, and I'd like to keep it that way."

There was no reason to share that information. It should never have happened.

Matthias let out a sigh, as though that was the answer he'd been hoping for.

Eventide barely caught a muffin Okimi tossed to her before it collied with her chest.

"I've gathered some food from the dining hall," she beamed, holding a burlap bag by her side. "Just a couple of snacks to keep you going until you find something with more sustenance."

"You've got to be careful," Eventide warned. "I know you're not going to be joining us in the end, but if you get caught, it could ruin the entire plan. Never mind what the Caregivers would do to *you*."

"Relax!" Okimi said, waving a hand. "On Titan, I'd pickpocket soldiers and never got caught once. I wouldn't do it otherwise. I don't want my fried brain, either, you know."

Eventide gave a shallow nod of thanks as she took the bag. Inside, Okimi had placed a half dozen dinner rolls, a few muffins, and several pieces of fruit.

"It's not much," Okimi admitted, "but it'll last you a week or so. You're on your own after that—hopefully you'll have figured something out by then."

She gave Eventide a bashful grin.

"Thank you." Eventide closed the bag and grinned. "Still, we can't afford to get sloppy now. We've already been hanging around each other too much today. We should probably split until we're ready to leave."

"Watch your back down there," Okimi said, ignoring Eventide's concern. "Don't go through all of this trouble just to get shot."

There was so much hope behind Okimi's eyes. It was strange that over such a short time period, someone could grow on you. Then it dawned on her that this was the last time she might ever see her new friend.

The silence between the three of them intensified as the realization set in, filled with uncertainty and apprehension. Okimi looked back and forth between Eventide and

Matthias, her normally bright eyes clouded with concern. "What's going on?" she asked. "Why are you two looking at me like that?"

Eventide cleared her throat; she had never been one for emotions. She stuck out a hand for Okimi to shake. "Good luck with the Prefect, Okimi. We'll miss you."

Okimi blew out a burst of air with her mouth. "Oh, *please!* You're not getting off that easily."

She wrapped herself around Eventide, pulling her in close for an embrace. Eventide tensed, closing her eyes against the unwelcome affection, to the point where Matthias chuckled.

"Oh, you think that's funny?" Eventide groaned. "I'm not a physical person, all right?"

Okimi grinned and gave Eventide a punch in the shoulder. "This isn't goodbye. We'll meet again, I can feel it."

"As much as I'd love to, I hope we don't. If we do, it means I've been captured, and I'm probably on my way to a prison cell."

"You'll be fine," Okimi said reassuringly. She reached out to grab Eventide's arm in a show of affection but stopped partway, thinking better of it. Instead, she grabbed the hand Eventide had outstretched and clung to it with a two-handed grip.

"But I mean it. Take care out there. The system is a whole lot more unpleasant than your station sounded."

Okimi released her hand and turned to Matthias.

"You better look after her!" Okimi scolded. "If anything happens to her, I'm blaming you!"

Matthias' eyes went wide as he grinned. "I'm pretty sure she's going to be the one pulling *my* ass out of trouble!"

That earned a laugh from Okimi. "Yeah, you're right. In that case, try not to make things harder on her than they already are. And that doesn't mean I won't still blame you!"

Matthias pressed his lips together but didn't respond.

"Anyway, chaps, I'm out of here! Wish me luck!"

Eventide fought back unexpected tears in her eyes, as Okimi exited the atrium, steeling herself against a surge of emotion. The resolve that had carried her this far seemed to falter, leaving only a hollow emptiness in its wake.

She turned to Matthias, and though her voice was steady, it did little to hide the disquiet behind her words. "We should get moving. We'll meet up at the entrance to the corridors at 0400. That will give us two hours to get into position."

Her voice had barely been above a whisper as Eventide allowed herself to reinstate the wall between herself and her emotions. There was work to be done—and for now, she needed to keep her head clear and focused on the task at hand.

CHAPTER FORTY

Eventide

The *Inanna*

Eventide had taken longer to return to her quarters than she'd hoped, bouncing from one game in the rec room to the next, mimicking the other Domani and pretending to mingle while under the watchful eye of Caregiver Roberts. She'd tried to excuse herself more than once, but Roberts' dark eyes had been trained on her like a hawk. There was something about her presence he'd seemed unsure of, as though intuitively he knew she wasn't behaving appropriately for a Domani. He never once approached her directly, thankfully—she didn't think her acting skills would have been good enough to fool him in a one-on-one interaction— but his unwavering stare had been more than unnerving.

Thankfully, she'd stored the technician's toolkit in one of the rec room lockers before he had arrived, otherwise that would have raised numerous red flags. Eventide once again silently cursed Matthias for being careless enough to hand it over in the middle of the day, especially with the new Caregiver milling about.

Roberts hadn't seemed to want to leave, and by the time Eventide retired for the night, it was nearly curfew. The rest of the Domani were also being called back to their rooms by the pied piper's song of shut-eye, yawning and stretching as they made their way down the halls to their quarters.

She had just enough time to grab the kit before sleep lulled her to her room—and it was more than the amplified transmissions being sent into her nervous system. It had been over thirty-six hours since she'd gotten a wink of sleep, and she didn't know if her legs would carry her to her bed, let alone through the maintenance tunnels in a few hours.

As she crossed the threshold into the hallway, it took all Eventide's willpower to maintain her composure and not stop in her tracks. Guards filled the hall, standing at attention in front of the Domani quarters. The hallway that divided the Domani quarters curved around the circular perimeter of the *Inanna*'s hull.

Disbelief momentarily paralyzed her.

From where the hall started, Eventide could see three guards. Around the corner, there was a fourth, standing right in front of her doorway. She recognized the man Lars, who had accompanied Lin the first day she had met the Caregiver and had been assigned as her supposed personal protector around the time of Eventide's Orientation.

In all of their plans, in all of their schemes, they hadn't anticipated that there would be an increase of guard duty. Halls that had once been all but empty, were now swimming with guards. Was it because of Caregiver Roberts that the detail had been enhanced? Because of their descent into Earth's orbit?

Or had she and Matthias been found out?

"Good evening, Domani." Lars stood a head taller than her. His face was rough, as though he hadn't shaved in a month, and short gray hairs bristled across the top of his head until they gave up and left a smooth, bulbous center that glowed purple as it reflected the hallway's ambient lighting.

"Lars," Eventide replied, trying to maintain an air of pleasantness about her while casually trying to divert attention away from the metal toolbox she was carrying. "To what do we owe the pleasure of such well-guarded rooms this evening? Should I be worried?"

She swallowed hard, saliva grating her dry throat.

"Caregiver Roberts' orders," he responded. "We'll be touching down on the planet overnight. Every precaution must be taken."

To her surprise, Eventide was able to maintain her cheery disposition despite the entirety of her insides curling into a ball and dying. Their entire plan had hinged on being able to move through the ship unencumbered, as they had done every other night.

Standing in front of her quarters, she peered to her left and right. There was one guard stationed on each corner, visible just before the hall curved out of sight. If she was silent—and extremely lucky—they might not notice her leaving if she was able to get past Lars, but for now, she certainly wouldn't be getting any further without attracting their attention.

"Thank you for watching out for us," she managed through a plastered grin.

She knew that his explanation wasn't the real reason for the increased security, but he simply nodded as she passed him to enter her quarters.

The door slid closed, and she immediately slumped against the wall. Sinking to the carpeted floor, she heaved a heavy sigh. Her plans just got extremely more complicated.

* * *

The wall alarm chimed at 0300, waking Eventide up from the corner of the floor where she'd curled up for the night. She hadn't wanted to risk sleeping on the bed in case the alarm didn't wake her, or in case the guard outside heard it before she did. She commanded the alarm to stop as she shot up to a crouch.

Despite the added level of complication the newly assigned guards presented, and as hopeless as her situation appeared, she wasn't ready to give up just yet.

There had been many an early morning during her technicians training where she'd been forced to engage in intense scenarios, hand-to-hand combat and endurance missions that had tested her limits to breaking point.

Despite her never having imagined being in a scenario like the one she found herself in now, tonight would be a culmination of all that training.

If she could make it out of her room.

She'd fallen asleep running through possible scenarios. There were plenty of tactics she could use to get Lars inside her quarters and possibly incapacitate him, but then there was the question of what to do next. She wouldn't be able to get back to the rec room without drawing the attention of the other guards.

Would she?

She opened the toolkit, pulling out the datapad she'd stashed in the slim space of the lid earlier.

"Please be there . . ."

She pulled up the blueprint files. As she'd surmised the previous day, without a legend, it was all but useless. But maybe there was something the Caregivers had missed . . .

She just had to find the right file.

Eventide sorted through the plans until she found the one floor plan that looked familiar. She hadn't paid much attention to it before because she already knew what she had access to on the Domani level. Except that, until after she caught the door that Orin had stopped at on the surveillance footage, she hadn't thought to look for maintenance tunnels behind the ship's bulkheads.

She traced her finger over the lines that ran parallel, adjacent to the main passageways and unnoticed by her before—yellow markings that could have meant anything with no identifiers attached to them. Then she scanned the floor plan, making note of the important rooms so she could orient herself. The theatre, the kitchen, the dining hall, the pool—those were the simple spaces to pinpoint, taking up large spaces on the floor plan. With those as guideposts, it was no problem figuring out the hall to the Domani quarters, winding in a semi-circular path along the edge of the ship's outer wall.

Marked passageways ran behind the walls she was

familiar with, crisscrossing to unmarked spaces with no other access points, as well as off the map entirely.

So, there *was* more to the floor she was on than just the Domani quarters.

Eventide wondered about the Caregivers' quarters, and perhaps something more. Matthias had mentioned there were other passengers on board, too, but she assumed the *Inanna* was large enough to house them on other decks.

None of that mattered, though—what mattered was the glowing yellow line that ran parallel to the hallway directly opposite her room. A yellow bulb intersecting with the hallway marked an entrance—right across the hall.

There was still a long road ahead on the path to escape, but this was one problem solved. If she could get past Lars and open the maintenance door across the hall without drawing attention to herself, she could follow the path to the doorway where Orin had died and rendezvous with Matthias.

When she thought about it like that, it seemed like such an unfathomable long shot.

And Matthias . . .

He'll have to find a way out, as well.

She paused, and her excitement waned. Matthias didn't have access to a toolkit like she did. She didn't even know if he'd held onto a datapad or would think to look for possible maintenance tunnels to escape.

What would she do if she got to the rendezvous point and he didn't arrive?

Would she leave without him?

Despite everything that had happened, her heart ached at the thought. She bit her lip and reminded herself that the nodes in the back of her neck were messing with her emotions again. No matter what, her mission was to get out and find Django. She could worry about the fate of Matthias and the other Domani later.

A worried sigh escaped her lips. *I'll have to.*

Her heart pounded like a steel drum as she considered her next steps. After a little searching, she pulled up the surveillance feed of the hall. Lars still stood outside her door, unmoved from their encounter hours ago. She needed a distraction—something big enough to keep him occupied.

She weighed the options in her open toolkit, her fingers brushing against the plasma cutter before settling on the magnetic screwdriver.

Nerves buzzing, Eventide crouched beside the control panel next to her door. The screwdriver came to life with a soft hum, its luminescent tip casting an otherworldly glow in the dim room. She took a deep breath, steadying her trembling hands, and set to work.

She had done this a thousand times during her training —meddling with control systems, usually solving malfunctions, rather than creating them—but never had the outcome meant life or death. If she failed here, the Caregivers would be alerted, and her hopes of escape would be lost.

She took a deep breath, her hands moving with trained precision, deftly manipulating the panel's wiring. All she needed was a short circuit.

A wisp of smoke curled upward from the panel, the acrid scent of burning circuits filling the room. Eventide stood, hanging onto the screwdriver as she backed away.

Now or never.

Eventide hit a button on the panel that allowed for communication into the hall. It was hot to the touch beneath the smoking console, and she cursed as it burned her fingers.

"Lars!" she called, feigned panic edging into her voice. "Something's wrong! The door panel is on fire!"

Through the datapad, she observed the burly guard looking up at her cries. He rolled his eyes as though annoyed he was being bothered by a stupid Domani girl who was probably just imagining things.

The door slid open silently as he stepped into the room, concern creasing his forehead as he studied the damage.

"Oh, *shit!*" He hesitated, his hand hovering above his communicator lapel, unsure if he should try to triage the problem himself or call for backup.

Unable to stand by with smoke billowing into the room, Lars opted for the former and rushed to the wall, grabbing a handkerchief from his pocket to try and smother whatever the source of the issue was.

Lars bent over the smoking control panel, providing the perfect opportunity. Eventide swiftly approached Lars from behind, the magnetic screwdriver still clenched in her grip. She delivered a swift, precise strike to the back of his neck with the tool's handle and the large guard crumpled to the floor, unconscious.

Eventide paused, adrenaline coursing through her veins. Her body shuddered along with her ragged breath, reflecting her shot nerves. Her training kicked in and she steadied her hands to correct the tampering she'd performed on the access control panel. There was no reason for an excess of smoke to be pouring out of her room to draw extra attention.

She glanced at the datapad to ensure the other guards hadn't noticed the prompt disappearance of their colleague. An elbow of each of them remained in view, both steadfast in their position and none the wiser that Lars had disappeared.

She didn't have much time. There was no telling how regularly the guards checked in on one another. There was also no guarantee Lars would remain unconscious until she—and hopefully, Matthias—escaped the ship's grasp.

She ran to the bed and yanked off the bedsheets. It wasn't much, but hopefully she could keep Lars detained for a couple hours.

With the bedsheet clutched tightly in her hands, Eventide rushed to Lars' unconscious form. There was no time to second-guess herself now. She knelt beside him, taking a moment to ensure he was still out cold, his deep, even breaths offering her the confirmation she needed.

Carefully, she maneuvered his large body onto his stomach and pulled his wrists together behind his back. She wound the sheet around his wrists several times, tying a tight, complex knot, and moved to his ankles next, repeating the process. The sheet pulled taut against his boots, straining under the weight, but it held. He was secure.

Once again, she glanced at the datapad. The guards outside were still oblivious, their attention elsewhere. Eventide let out a breath and finally opened the door to her quarters, her toolkit in hand.

She'd never been so grateful for the ship's hum as it

masked the faint noise of the door sliding open and the lightness of her sandaled footsteps as she crossed the hall over the plush carpet. The ship had been built for stealth, likely intending to mask the coming and going of the Caregivers, but tonight, she'd be able to use their deceptiveness to her advantage.

Eventide moved to the control panel on the outside of her door and held her breath. After a few quick adjustments, the door slid shut, a sharp whizzing noise indicating that the door was locked, sealing the unconscious guard inside. Eventide knew it wouldn't hold if anyone with credentials tried to get in, but it would buy her some time, at least. Right now, that was all she needed.

A quick glance confirmed the rest of the guards were still none the wiser. Swiftly, she moved across the hall to the hidden door. The hallways were a couple meters wide, and thankfully, this side obfuscated her position even further from the other two nearby guards. Unless they turned to look down the hallway, they would be none the wiser to her presence.

The control panel for this door would be in an access panel hidden within the bulkhead. If someone with the right credentials waved their biochip in front of it, the door would slide open. The only other reason to access it would be for maintenance.

The scan of the wall's surface, revealed no sign of a door existing at all. If it hadn't been for the map on the datapad, she would have feared she'd made a mistake. But the maintenance tunnels on the *Eclipse* had been designed the same way. They were meant to be discreet.

Eventide pulled out the thermal scanner from her kit

and held it up. The tool's screen clearly revealed the outline of the doorway, and Eventide couldn't help but let out the breath she'd been holding. A few inches to the right, she could make out the warm red and orange glow of the control panel.

Eventide made a mental note of where the panel could be found and set the scanner aside. The next tool in her arsenal was the plasma cutter. She picked it up just as a cough down the hallway nearly caused her to drop it.

She froze. Staring down the hallway toward the origin of the sound, her breath caught in her throat. She didn't dare to move—dare to breathe—for a solid three minutes.

When she determined that one of the guards must have been clearing his throat, Eventide inhaled again and continued. She pointed the cutter at the spot on the wall she'd mentally mapped a few moments before and hesitated. The cutter could be loud.

She cursed silently for not testing it before she'd left her room. There was also the possibility she'd slip and accidentally hit the circuits. There would be no masking that noise, as she could easily fry the panel altogether. But as she didn't have the dexterity to hold both the scanner and the cutter at once, this would have to do.

She winced as she switched on the device, fearing the dull roar of a heavy power tool. Instead, there was the spark of a flame and the hiss of plasma being emitted from the device's cartridge, but the noise level was minimal.

The plasma cutter made quick work of the wall, metal melting away under the device's powerful beam. The cut did smell of burning metal, but there was nothing she could do about that. A few quick cuts, and the console revealed itself.

A gaping hole in the wall would be an impossible renovation to conceal once it was made, but hopefully, it would go unnoticed for a couple hours.

With her task complete, she switched off the plasma cutter and stowed it back in the toolkit.

It continued to surprise her how similar the workings of this vessel were to the *Eclipse*, though the quality and luxury of the ship surpassed anything she'd ever seen on board the station. But one quick look at the console's components confirmed that, with a few simple adjustments, she'd be able to override it. The parts might have been newer and more refined, but the basic concepts behind them were similar, if not the same.

She made quick work and the door slid open, revealing a narrow maintenance tunnel ahead.

Eventide stepped inside, ensuring the door slid shut behind her. She was alone in the shadowy tunnel, armed with nothing but a toolkit and a datapad, and a whisper of hope that she might actually pull this off.

As she started down the unfamiliar service tunnel, she couldn't help but wonder about Matthias.

Had he escaped? Would he be waiting for her at the rendezvous point? Or would she be facing whatever awaited her alone?

CHAPTER FORTY-ONE

Django
The *Chimera*

Pirates.

Django lay on a bed in the *Chimera*'s MedLab; his body ached and his head spun, but he was still trying to wrap his head around the fact that a real-life pirate was the one who rescued him. Tales of sea-faring buccaneers and privateers had filled his childhood, but it was still hard to believe they existed out in the depths of space. He was sure this Monroe, eccentric as she was, had plenty of adventure stories of her own.

Adventure. Eventide would have been thrilled. He tried not to dwell on what she might be doing now—probably fighting off some Syndicate bastard's sick fantasies. He was sure she would rather be the one teaming up with pirates than trying to get out of whatever prison she'd found herself in.

And of course she would. Django couldn't ever imagine Eventide being content with going along with what was expected of her. She'd fight tooth and nail until her last breath.

Of course, he would never have believed half of what he'd done in the last few weeks, either. The existence of pirates seemed almost ordinary in comparison. Still, he struggled to reconcile the reality before him with the ordinary world he knew. In his half-groggy state, he had half-believed, perhaps hoped, it had all been a horrible dream.

If Lunar cities were real, pirates could be too. Why not?

Hell, he had a chip in his arm that could control any computer in a system of planets and moons filled with millions of people. So, who was he to question what was possible?

The *Chimera* made the R-332X look like a rowboat. Its MedLab was full of holographic imagery that rivaled the datafeeds on board Space Dock Seven. Semi-opaque charts and graphs danced around him, blue screens highlighting harsher white lamps designed for surgical procedures. There were nearly a dozen beds around him, all separated by glass partitions, with their own pieces of futuristic lab equipment hanging over each one.

It was a far cry from the antiquated scalpels and metal tools the medical staff used on the *Eclipse*.

"You gave us quite a scare."

A nurse stood over him, a man with a small scruff of a beard and a kind smile that reached his hazel eyes. His voice was soft and comforting. "Another few minutes, and you would have breached the atmospheric perimeter. We wouldn't have been able to retrieve you without setting off the proximity detectors."

Django nodded, though he didn't understand anything

through the fuzziness of his mind. "What happened to me? Am I going to be okay?"

"You're fine," the nurse said. "We've been monitoring your vitals to make sure. You were mostly suffering dehydration and fatigue, plus we've had to give you some cortisol and stimulants to heal that shoulder of yours. But our nanobots have stitched that right up."

Nanobots?

"You overexerted yourself," the nurse continued. "And your suit wasn't meant to endure that much heat and radiation. You've sustained some second-degree burns, but nothing we haven't been able to treat, and we've neutralized the radiation effects. A little more rest, and you'll be good to go."

"Did everyone get out okay? The other ships?"

"They all made it out, thanks to you," a familiar male voice replied.

Uncle Marvin stood at the edge of Django's partition. He hadn't even noticed his uncle's arrival.

"Rowyn? Wilder? Marshall?"

"The entire team made it back, and the mission was a success. It was a close one, but we don't believe the Syndicate has any idea that the virus was uploaded. By the time they realize what's happening, their network will be compromised. If we're lucky, they'll interface with Earth and infect the systems there, too. The Resurgence will be able to strike with minimal casualties, and it's all thanks to you. You're a hero, Django."

Heroic triumphs in his childhood tales had never involved waking up in a sterile medical lab, barely clinging to life. The hollow echo of victory rang in his ears, leaving Django feeling more like a casualty than a champion.

But it wasn't over yet.

"And what about Eventide? Did you find out where she is?"

A fleeting shadow crossed Marvin's face, the corners of his mouth tensing momentarily. The man knew something he didn't want to reveal.

"Why don't we wait until you rest up?"

The light in Django's eyes dimmed with disappointment. "Why? Is she okay? Is she . . . dead?"

Marvin held up a hand. "No, lad." His face relaxed, but there was still no eagerness in his voice. "Nothing like that. She's alive, and as far as our intel can tell, she's likely well enough."

"'Well enough?' What does that mean? Where is she?"

"Like I said, we should wait until you're up for it."

Django ripped off the covers that were draped over him, and the cold sterile air of the MedLab prickled against his bare skin. Tubes hooked into his arms were feeding him hydration fluid, connected to some sort of delivery system that fed into the panel above him. He swung his legs out over the bed.

"Be careful!" the nurse yelped, rushing over to Django's side to ensure nothing disconnected in the movement.

Django ignored him. "I'm up for it *now!*" His voice came out as nearly a growl. "I risked my damn life to get your precious chip planted inside my arm, hijacked a space dock, and nearly got myself killed trying to save the lives on half a dozen other ships. I *deserve* to know where she is!"

Marvin clasped his hands behind his back, his eyes

narrowing. "I never asked you to risk your life to unclamp those ships. In fact, I actually *ordered* you not to. You should have boarded the R-332X with the rest of the crew."

Django gritted his teeth. "*Not* the bloody point!"

Marvin paced, tension pulling at his forehead as he contemplated his next words. "All right. But please, think about what I'm about to tell you before you rush into anything rash."

Django smirked. "When have you ever known me to act irrationally?"

"Look around you."

"Enough people have died because of my actions," Django said, regulating his voice. He knew he would get nowhere with his uncle if he lost his temper. "I'd prefer there not to be any more."

Marvin sighed. "I will tell you where Eventide is. Just promise me you'll listen to reason."

"Fine. But just so you know, you're not doing a very good job of convincing me she's okay."

Marvin grabbed a chair from beyond the partition and sat down. Whatever revolution the Resurgence was planning had barely begun, yet the man's heavy-lidded eyes and slumped shoulders spoke volumes. Dark circles under his eyes hinted at countless sleepless nights, "Our people have found the Domani ship Eventide was sold to. It's about to land on Earth. If it hasn't already, it likely will within the next twenty-four hours."

Relief surged through him. "That's great news! Let's go get her then!" Django moved to stand, to the dismay of the nurse, who cursed as he was still wrangling the length of tubes descending from the distended ceiling panel above the bed.

Marvin held up a hand. "Not so fast, lad. That's not the whole of it. Even if we could infiltrate Earth's defenses—which we can't—our intelligence has informed us that the ship she's on is headed toward the Prefect himself."

Django arched an eyebrow in disbelief. "So, you know *exactly* where she is, and you haven't retrieved her yet?"

"Listen to what I'm saying, Django. Do you know how difficult it would be to stroll into the Prefect's chambers and retrieve one of his personal Domani? You might as well expect me to pull a filling from his back molar while he sleeps. It can't be done."

Django paused. "'Can't' be done?"

"Not at this stage. We need to take out Earth's defenses, and then maybe we can storm the Prefect's palace. But at best, we're talking about months from now."

Months.

That single word seared through Django's veins, igniting the blood within. He couldn't let Eventide stay for *months* with those self-serving assholes. His heart thrummed with a pulsating heat that swelled in his chest, but he forced the feeling down, quelling the tempest within him. His jaw set into a rigid line, the muscles in his cheeks quivering faintly as he bit back the hot words that threatened to spill from his lips.

"I'm sorry," Marvin continued, only partially aware of the war raging within Django's mind. "At this stage of the Resurgence's strategy, extracting someone from the surface isn't an option. I wish there was more I could do."

Django didn't respond. He inhaled deeply and pursed

his lips, attempting to calm the tempest within. Everything he had done on Space Dock Seven had been in the hope of rescuing Eventide. It had all been with the understanding that she would be found and rescued, not discovered and then ignored.

What unspeakable acts were being done to her on the surface by this 'Prefect'? Everyone spoke of him as though he were a beast, a monster, a demon. And now, Eventide was with him. As his prisoner? His *slave?*

A deep chill ran through Django's bones as he pictured his friend, scared and alone, under the looming shadow of such a man. He swallowed the lump that had built in his throat.

The Resurgence will disappoint you . . . They'll come up against a wall where they will be unable to deliver on something they've promised you . . .

When that happens, I know you will return to me.

There might not be anything else the Resurgence could do, but that didn't mean Django was going to sit and do nothing, either.

He composed himself before responding, his voice weak yet measured. "You did your best."

Marvin's gaze was firm, his acknowledgment a relieved but resolute nod. "I *am* sorry. And we will get her, I promise you that. But we can't compromise our strategy. Not even for this."

"I understand," Django replied robotically. "How soon before we return to Lunar?"

Mikka

The *Redemption*

Alarms sounded throughout the *Redemption* as Mikka did her best to throw every molecule of power she had at the ship's engines. Red lights illuminated every surface of the bridge. She had even gone so far as to turn down the main lighting systems, leaving the ship's bridge awash in an eerie red glow.

"Pull it up on the holo . . ." Mikka stopped herself.

Zee's eyes darted to the controls, his face paling as his hands fluttered uncertainly over the buttons, as if he were a musician asked to perform a symphony he'd never heard before.

"Sorry." Mikka swallowed. "Don't worry about that. I'm used to . . . Kiara handled the controls. It might take me a while."

She pulled up the holo herself, which showed the *Chimera* in pursuit behind them, steadily closing the gap between the two vessels.

Mikka cursed and then looked guiltily toward Zee. She nearly laughed at her own propriety; the youth had likely heard and seen far worse than her leftover pirate profanity.

They had evaded the *Chimera*'s detection for the better part of two days, but it seemed Mikka's good luck had finally run out.

"There's a light blinking on this console," Zee advised. "What does that mean?"

Mikka turned her gaze to the comms panel. There were too many systems for one person to monitor.

"Keep quiet," Mikka said to Zee. "Stay low. I'd rather Abi doesn't know you're here."

She hit a button to answer the hail. There was a small chance Monroe didn't know Zee had left with her, but admittedly, it was an infinitely slight chance—and it was in Mikka's best interests to keep the information to herself for as long as possible.

"Yes, my dear?" Mikka said. "Can I help you?"

The projection of an exhausted-looking Abigail hovered over the console in front of her. "Don't try to sweet talk me, love. You missed our date."

"If I recall correctly, it was you who pulled me onto the bridge instead of taking me to dinner. I wasn't sure if that was your idea of foreplay."

"Don't worry, love, when we're up to foreplay, you'll know it. Still, you led me on, and I don't appreciate it."

"I've gotta say, my best dates rarely start with a dose of Stockholm Syndrome and end with a villainous murder."

Abigail, for once, didn't seem amused. "To be fair, I'm questioning my own taste. I always knew you were a ruthless pirate, but I didn't think you'd kill your own navigator as a ruse to escape. That's a bridge too far in my books."

She thinks I killed Kiara?

"If you think for a second that *I* would do something that despicable . . ."

"As titillating as this banter is, you took something of mine and I'd like it back—assuming you've not resorted to killing children now."

"This coming from someone who kidnaps them and uses them for parlor tricks?" Mikka fumed. "Besides, maybe an act of retribution *would* be in order for one of your crew killing my navigator? I assure you, I know how to hold a grudge. Kiara's death was not the way to win me over to your cause."

"Listen, love, I've just been to hell and back for Alejandro. I dropped him and his precious Django off on Lunar, but I'm tired, and as much as I normally love our back and forth, I really am not in the mood for games today. You had every reason to stage a distraction. I find it extremely hard to believe you're not behind the girl's death."

Mikka clenched her fists, the claim as ridiculous as it was offensive. "You think I'd kill the one person capable of helping me escape, just to throw you off my trail for a couple days?"

"You're forgetting who I'm used to dealing with. There's no atrocious deed off the table when you deal with pirates."

"I'm starting to feel like a broken holo-recording. I'm *no* pirate!"

"So you say."

"I used to think you had good instincts, but the past week has had me questioning my own judge of character."

"Well, it seems like we're finally on the same page," Abigail said with a surge of sobriety. "Do you know how difficult it is to deal in the darkness of this god-forsaken Empire? Like many other pirates, this wasn't the hand I chose; it was the one dealt to me. You're not the only one with a painful past, you know? That's why I'm tying my horse to Alejandro. I thought *you,* of all people, would understand that, but you seem hell-bent on this alliance with one of the worst of the lot out there. Somehow, he's blinded you to reality."

Here we go again!

"Let's take a closer look, shall we?" Mikka's words came out taut as her voice quivered. "Aries has *saved* my life. Aries has provided *help* and a safe space for my mother. Aries will look after the children whose mother was murdered on *your* ship." Mikka didn't even try to keep the tears from her eyes. "And what have you done? Used my ship to rescue a wanted felon. Kidnapped me when I wouldn't join his terrorist group. *Murdered* my navigator and only friend and then gaslighted me about it, when we both know I'm not responsible. And I won't even get into the fact that you've been using a kid with a faulty implant as a modern-day Nostradamus!"

"I saved that boy's life . . ."

"You can't hide behind that one fake act of philanthropy! If you really cared about Zee, you wouldn't be using him for your own ends. You'd let him make his own choices."

Abigail snorted. "He's a child, Mikka. Zee barely

knows his head from his asshole. You can't ask a kid to decide their own life path. They need a little guidance."

"You're not exactly the person who should be molding young minds." Mikka crossed her arms.

"Anyway," Mikka continued, "we're done here. I have important work to do, so you'd be better off if you went about your business."

"You don't think I came after you just for a chat?" Abigail said. "After all we've been through."

"I thought you wanted dessert," Mikka said. "But I don't have time for that. I need to deliver the rest of these items."

"That's what I need to talk to you about," Abigail said. "You need to dump the deliveries."

"Well, the joke's on you. I've already delivered half of them. Why does the Resurgence have something against helping the people on those stations? It's food, for crying out loud!"

"Have you ever stopped to ask yourself why Aries is performing this act of goodwill, love?"

Why can't you believe he'd do something out of the goodness of his own heart?

"David had to work himself up from the bottom. He knows what it's like to be without."

"Are you sure that's the line you want to go with?"

"I don't know why we're still having this conversation." Mikka moved to end the call. "I'm done here."

"Wait, wait, wait," Abigail urged holding up her hands in protest.

Mikka paused, holding her hand above the comms panel, though she wasn't sure why she was giving this pirate any more airtime. Perhaps it was because the longer she could keep Abigail on the line, the more time Aries' forces would have to come to her assistance. Or perhaps she was just a sucker for a pirate trying to make a difference, no matter how misguided.

"You've got thirty seconds . . ."

Abigail audibly sighed. "I'll leave you with one question. Do you even know what kind of cargo you're delivering?"

Mikka nearly laughed. "Rice? Beans? A dozen other non-perishable foodstuffs stamped with the Lunar manufacturing location and information about the outside world. If that's all you wanted to know, you could have asked me before this whole mess started."

A moment of silence followed before Abigail replied, "Are you sure that's all there is?"

Mikka raised a brow. "What are you getting at?"

"Did you never think to ask why we didn't unload the cargo off your ship? All we needed to do was dump it out into space and we wouldn't be having this conversation. But we had to perform scans to be sure."

"Be sure of what?"

"You're right about one thing: Aries means to use the FLOW stations to disrupt the Syndicate. But the details are far more . . . *explosive* than he's led you to believe. Do me a favor? In lieu of the date you ducked out on, check what's left of your cargo. Do a thorough investigation. If you still believe Aries to be the philanthropist he's claiming to be, then be on your way to deliver the rest of the cargo. I'm not going to stop you. If not, call me back and we'll talk."

Mikka groaned as the feed clicked off. David Aries had

treated her better than anyone else ever had. There was nothing about the man that led her to believe he would do something stupid like use the cover of food deliveries to trick a station into taking on a destructive load of cargo—or to deceive her into delivering it.

But still . . .

The whispers in her gut told her she should check to make sure. The feeling that said she might have been wrong this whole time.

Mikka shook her head. It was just Abigail. The stupid pirate was getting into her head. She should never have kissed her; it had opened her up to being susceptible. Damn, that woman was good!

That was all it was . . . wasn't it?

It wouldn't hurt for me to check. It's probably nothing but Abi getting into my head.

She looked at Zee as if he might provide some answers, but the boy sat in his chair, staring blankly at the viewscreen that showed the *Chimera*. He shifted uncomfortably in his seat, his eyes never leaving the looming shadow of the ship before them, as though he were dreading something.

Like going back . . .

Shit.

Mikka marched to the cargo bay, allowing the *Redemption's* doors to slide open as she rushed through its passageways, past dozens of panels that flashed orange as they stood by for her command. The ship's shield plates hadn't been repaired since their last encounter, and all it would take would be one direct hit to blow the ship into a million pieces.

Yet Abigail was choosing to wait . . .

It had to be a ruse. Mikka told herself she should be on her way, leaving Abigail to whatever wild conspiracy theories she had dreamt up.

Except the pirate knew her better than that. Despite every protest in Mikka's being, she knew that her and Abigail were far too alike. Curiosity would eventually drive her mad if she didn't check.

Mikka grabbed a crowbar from a stack of tools and a folded stepladder that sat nearby. She didn't know what she expected to find—nothing but the bags of foodstuffs that Aries had showed her, she hoped.

But that wasn't what her gut was telling her. *Why did it stay silent until Abigail piped up?*

Her gut was all Mikka had going for her.

She approached the first crate in the hold. There were eight remaining. Twelve had already been distributed, plus the one they had delivered to the *Eclipse* weeks ago. A lifetime ago.

Her limbs shook. It had been some time since she'd eaten. She'd lost her appetite after she'd found Kiara's body. But the effects were influencing her performance.

She set the metal ladder on the ground next to the crate and erected it. She grabbed the metal tool, inserted it between the edges of the lid and crate, and lifted. Nails that had sealed the container shut wiggled loose, and Mikka had to repeat the action on each corner to loosen the lid enough to move it over.

She didn't have anyone to help her gently slide the lid to the metal floor, so she pushed it over, on top of the neighboring crate. Her legs shook as she stepped onto the stepladder.

Peering over the top of the crate, all Mikka could see were the same bags David had shown her in the Syndicate facility. Part of her wanted to feel a sense of relief, but the itch in her gut knew that appearances meant nothing.

She took the crowbar again, and this time, she used her height on the ladder as leverage as she inserted the crowbar into another seam and separated one side from the corner. The panel came loose where she'd wedged the bar, gradually separating from the rest of the box.

All the way down, large white sacks were stacked, one on top of another. Each bag stamped with the Syndicate Lunar logo. Each package filled with vegetables, grains, or lentils. With each inch of product she revealed, her heart pounded harder, her nerves vibrating. Her gut had all but sunk to her knees, but each crack of the wooden seam revealed nothing but food and dread.

It wasn't until Mikka reached the bottom of the stack that her nightmare became reality. The panel gave way to another piece of wood, standing a foot taller from the bottom of the crate than it should have.

There was something else packed inside these crates.

A wave of dizziness overcame her, and Mikka held onto the edge of the nearest wooden crate for support. She had to empty the crates, but she wasn't going to be able to do it alone—not in this state.

"Zee!" she called out to the bridge. The boy slowly wandered from the front of the ship, peering warily into the cargo bay, as though fearful of what Mikka might ask of him.

"These white bags contain food—flour, rice, and root vegetables, mostly. I need to access this container at the bottom. Can you help me pull the bags off? I can't do it myself."

Mikka had grown to know her body well enough at this point. She needed food—or sugar, at least—or she risked falling over, but she couldn't bring herself to stop what she was doing, as though whatever was in that box might sneak away if given the chance.

Zee furrowed his brow, the expression adding ten years to his face. "You're not doing well."

"I'll be okay. I just need some food."

He nodded, but his expression still bore concern. Without saying anything else, he fled the room.

Mikka sighed. "So much for help."

She unloaded the first few bags of food from the crate. If only some of the items had been cooked, she could have helped herself to a snack, but it was all beans, rice, and flour. Nothing immediately edible.

As it was, she grabbed one bag at a time and stacked them several feet away from the crate, methodically piling one bag on top of another.

She hadn't unloaded more than a few bags when Zee came rushing back to the cargo hold, his arms full of various sliced fruit and a pitcher of water.

"Here you are, Ms. Jenax. You should take a break before you hurt yourself."

Mikka laughed. How many times had she pushed herself too far and ended up needing bed rest for several days? How many times had Kiara been the one to slow her down?

And now, in her friend's absence, this youth had assumed the responsibility of coming to her aid.

"Thank you," she whispered.

Mikka gulped down the water greedily and inhaled the fruit so quickly that she wondered whether she had even chewed her food.

It took only moments for the sugar to flow through her veins and for Mikka's strength to return. She'd need a proper meal, but this would tide her over until then. Rejuvenated, she got back to work, grabbing bags and tossing them to Zee, who piled them on the floor beside the crates.

Mikka tried to suppress the thoughts of what might be in the hidden case. It could have been anything: weapons, more food, datapads filled with knowledge of the outside world . . .

Deep down, though, Mikka knew it would contain something far more sinister, but she wasn't ready to admit that yet.

Abigail couldn't be right.

Kiara couldn't be right.

She had to see it with her own eyes. She had to know; to prove them wrong.

Twenty minutes passed before all the bags were stacked neatly beside them, leaving a second wooden box staring up at them from the bottom of the crate, almost filling it from edge to edge. There was enough room for Mikka to walk around it and grab the lid from one corner.

"Grab the other side, Zee. Let's have a peek inside."

They heaved the bulk of the lid up and over.

Mikka cursed.

The flickering lights of the insidious contraption

nestled within the box. A cold shock snaked through her veins, siphoning away the little warmth left in her body. The bitter tang of betrayal filled her mouth and all she could do was stare, trapped in a moment of chilling realization.

Abigail hadn't lied. David had.

Every fiber of her being screamed it at her, the knowledge sinking into her like a serrated blade.

"Gods, he played me," Mikka whispered, the words falling into silence like the knell of a doomed ship. Her gaze didn't waver from the ominous glow, the harbinger of a truth she hadn't wanted to face.

Mikka had envisioned herself as a bringer of justice, but she was no savior. Nor was she a messenger of redemption.

She was an angel of ruin.

CHAPTER FORTY-THREE

Eventide

The *Inanna*

In the solitude of the maintenance corridors, it was a quick trip from the Domani quarters to the recreation room. After hurrying through the tight spaces, Eventide now stood in the doorway where Orin had been murdered only a few nights ago.

The clock on the holo-screens showed 0402. Matthias was two minutes late, which normally wouldn't have been a big deal, but under the present circumstances, was terrifying. Her pulse rampaged from her temple to her toes. Each second that ticked by was an eternity.

How long should she wait? Could she leave without him?

Come on, Matthias. Be okay.

It was entirely possible he'd remained in his room, considering the new arrangement with the guards. Maybe he had assumed she'd given up, but Eventide couldn't help feeling that by now, he should know better.

Giving up wasn't an option. This could be her only chance at escape.

She stepped into the room and shut the door behind her. If a guard did stroll by, there was no reason to be sitting there with an open door to the maintenance corridor. That would raise far more questions than she was prepared to answer.

She couldn't wait forever. There was an unconscious guard tied up in her quarters. Every second they wasted increased the likelihood that Lars would wake up and sound the alarm.

Another few minutes passed, and Eventide considered heading back through the maintenance corridors. Maybe she could access Matthias' room—but then again, she didn't have any idea *which* room was his. The best she could do was guess, and there was no way she would be able to do that undetected.

Time was ticking. She had to get moving if she was going to get into a position to get off the ship, and all she had was an incomplete map and her best guess of which direction to follow. Further into the corridors, there might be a chance to find a fully functional schematic, but she would need time to study it, and there was no telling how long it might take her to access and work out an escape route.

With any luck, the *Inanna* was already descending through the Earth's atmosphere. If what Matthias had discovered was correct, she would have less than an hour before it touched ground and less than two before Lin and Roberts would lead the Domani off the ship. They had to make their move during this time; there was no other window of opportunity. If there were access points already open to the outside, she would be able to take advantage of the situation—but she didn't want to do that without Matthias.

Damn these emotions being used against her! *Once I get off this blasted ship, they'd better loosen their grip!*

Eventually, she accepted Matthias wasn't coming. Whatever the reason, she had to go it alone, and she couldn't wait around feeling guilty about it. The man had made it on his own on the ship for nearly a year. He'd do okay for himself.

Steeling her resolve, she slid open the hidden doorway once again.

"You're not leaving without me, I hope?" Matthias' voice chimed behind her.

Eventide melted. "Where have you been?" she hissed. "You're nearly fifteen minutes late!"

"The halls are crawling with guards. I'm surprised you made it! I was worried that I'd have to figure out a way to break you out of your room."

He moved toward her as though moving in for an embrace.

"I wasn't joking before." Her hand went up, pressing against the cool skin of his chest. "I'm not good with physical affection."

She looked up at him—at his dark eyes studying her, at his lips parted slightly. Their kiss was still at the forefront of her mind, and she had to do her best to keep the overwhelming emotions at bay. She feared seeing hurt in his eyes, maybe anger, but instead, there was a softness, a wave of understanding as he nodded and took a step back.

"I apologize. I shouldn't have assumed."

"It's okay. Just something I've never been comfortable with."

"Then last night was . . .?" He lifted an uneasy eyebrow, not sure how to finish the sentence.

"Out of character," she replied. "I'm still trying to sort out my feelings and how this device is messing with them."

"I'm sorry I got bent out of shape about it," Matthias said sincerely. "You have every right to tell me no."

"Look, this isn't exactly the time to be unpacking our feelings. We can't stick around here any longer. There's an unconscious guard in my room, and a hole burned into the wall that's sure to raise a few eyebrows."

Matthias' eyes lit up with intrigue as he nodded toward the toolkit, still firm in her grip. "I'm glad to hear you've made good use of that. It sounds like you've been busy."

"Incredibly. Which raises a good question . . ." Eventide frowned. "How exactly did you get past the guards?"

"I'm craftier than you might think." He gestured toward the doorway. "But as you said, we don't have time to stick around here. We should move."

Eventide eyed the man suspiciously, but there was no use getting into it now. Somehow he'd found his way out, and that was all that mattered at the moment.

They entered the maintenance corridors and crept through the winding, narrow maze. Paths crisscrossed into near-darkness, with only the steady yellow glow of emergency lighting to illuminate the passages ahead of them. The eerie silence was punctuated by the occasional hum of the ship's systems and the pulsing echo of her own heartbeat in her ears.

With every corner a complete unknown, Eventide and Matthias had to treat each new intersection as a potential threat, every door a possible surprise. They moved in sync, one watching the front while the other watched their backs, stopping and moving as if connected by an invisible thread. There was a sense of cohesion that went beyond the immediate need for survival. Despite the uneasiness of their situation, Matthias' presence was reassuring, his calm demeanor an anchor in the raging storm.

"I don't get it," Eventide whispered after they were forced to press themselves against a panel to check for a patrol. "How do you know where you're going?"

Matthias shrugged. "Sometimes," he said quietly, "it's not about knowing. It's a feeling."

Eventide might have accepted "dumb luck", but *feelings?* That wasn't an answer. She raised an eyebrow but didn't press; for now, she would take any lifeline offered, no matter how cryptic.

Every corner put her nerves on edge, and she couldn't put Orin's murder aside. The fear of the unknown killer, the paranoia of not knowing their motive—it was a constant buzz in the back of her mind.

"Try to relax," Matthias whispered. "You're jumping at your own shadow."

"The last person I saw opening that door ended up dead."

"You think there's a murderer's running around now?" Matthias shook his head, darkened shadows dancing across his face. "Not a chance. With all the guards on high alert, they'll be laying low."

Unless it was *one of the guards.*

There was a host of problems with that theory, but Matthias was probably right. Nevertheless, the knowledge that additional guards were on duty didn't set her any less on edge.

"What were all these guards doing before this evening?" she asked. "Why haven't they been watching us until now?"

"Because Domani aren't a threat. But since we're going to be entering Earth's atmosphere, I'm guessing they aren't taking any chances."

It made sense, but it was an odd juxtaposition compared to the previous nights when they'd had free rein in their section of the ship.

"We've got to be getting close," she murmured, though close to *what*, she had no idea.

Just as she'd uttered the thought, an obstacle loomed ahead. A heavy blast door barred their path, its control panel dark and silent.

"Damn it!" Matthias muttered, staring at the imposing hatch with a frown. "There won't be a way around this, and I'm guessing wherever we need to go is going to be behind that door."

A lump of dread settled in Eventide's stomach, but she forced herself to ignore it. They didn't have the luxury of despair.

Matthias' shoulders slumped and he cast a sideways glance back to where they came. "I'm sorry, Eventide. This might be where our journey ends."

Eventide strengthened the grip on her toolkit and her resolve. *Not a chance in hell.*

"What if we don't go around?" Her gaze shifted

between Matthias and the locked door. "What if we go *through?*"

Matthias cocked his head to the side, his eyes narrowing. "Through the blast door? Eventide, that's solid steel. How—"

"Did you think I used my looks to get out of my quarters?"

Eventide set her toolkit on the ground, her fingers trembling as she opened it to reveal and sift through its contents.

She could feel the minutes slipping away, each passing second a reminder of the unconscious guard back in her room and of the need to find the exit before Caregivers Lin and Roberts opened the ship's hatch.

Eventide's mind whirred into motion as she stared at the formidable blast door, a fresh wave of determination coursing through her.

Reaching into her toolkit, she withdrew the miniature-sized plasma cutter. It had worked once before, but it was still risky, especially since, this time, she would be using it on the panel directly—a decision that could set off the alarms or otherwise fail spectacularly, destroying the very thing she sought to fix.

"Stand back," she warned Matthias, turning the device's setting to maximum before powering it up. A concentrated beam of fiery ionized gas emitted from the tool, casting an eerie, blue light against the stark corridor walls.

She cut a small, precise hole in the panel's outer casing, revealing the intricate network of wires and circuits within. She had to be quick; any extended usage of the cutter could heat the compartment too much, damaging the sensitive components within.

Smoke rose from the panel, the small carved hole in its surface glowing with a fiery intensity. Eventide held her breath as she waited for the waft of smoke to dissipate, hoping it wouldn't trip an alarm.

With the panel now exposed, she returned the plasma cutter to her toolkit and took out the magnetic screwdriver and the thermal imaging scanner. The scanner allowed her to visualize the heat signatures of the now exposed wires, giving Eventide an idea of which circuits supplied power and which controlled the biometric lock. The circuitry for the panel was much more complex than any she'd worked on before, but the concepts weren't foreign to her.

"It looks like there's a built-in redundancy here," she said, more to herself than to Matthias. "There are sets of extra chips here that are doing nothing but routing the circuits through a secondary unit."

"I have no idea what any of that means," Matthias said. "But it sounds like you know what you're talking about, at least. Does that mean you can open the door or . . ."

"If I can reroute the power away from the secondary system and directly into the main unit, it *should* open the blast door."

"Should?" Mattias questioned.

"There's an equally likely chance that I could fry the entire thing and trip the alarm. But I don't see that we have a better option."

Eventide put the screwdriver to work, using its magnetized tip to delicately manipulate the circuits. It was painstaking work, and time was a luxury they didn't have.

"Tick tock, Eventide," Matthias said softly, offering encouragement rather than pressure.

"Not helping!" she hissed. This was no time for games. "If you'd like to give it a shot, then be my guest. If not, let me focus."

Matthias backed off, allowing her to insert the last chip into place. Steadily, the panel flickered to life. A soft, reassuring hum filled the air, accompanying the restoration of power, but they weren't through yet. There was still the matter of the biometric lock.

Eventide also had to be careful not to trigger the device with her own forearm. If she did, she anticipated there would be safeguards that would lock the entire system down and trigger an alarm. All of her efforts would be for nothing.

Eventide paused, her eyes darting to her toolkit and an idea forming in her mind. It was risky and relied on a lot of luck, but it could work.

It *had* to work.

Using her screwdriver again, Eventide opened a small section of her holo-multimeter. If she could modify some of the tool's circuits, she could use it to send a series of rapid voltage changes to the panel. The targeted variance might be enough to confuse the readouts.

"Here goes," she whispered as she connected the modified multimeter to the biometric circuit.

The panel flickered, a sequence of colors and patterns dancing across it before it stabilized to a soothing green. The door groaned, shuddering before it slowly opened.

Matthias breathed a sigh of relief and Eventide's shoulders relaxed, the tight knots of tension unraveling.

But it wasn't time to celebrate just yet. They still weren't in the clear. Without more than a slight nod of acknowledgment of success, Eventide and Matthias moved through the now open door and slipped into an even narrower passage. It was dark, but at the far end, there was a faint glow of light.

"Is it just me or were you expecting that door to lead to something more impressive?" she asked.

"It's meant to be an air seal to contain a breach if the worst should happen," Matthias said, keeping his voice above a whisper. "That light belongs to the main part of the ship. We probably shouldn't say anything from this point on if we can help it. The next section of the ship will be heavily guarded."

"You seem to be awfully familiar with the ship's design. How do you know all of this?"

Before he could answer, the ship shuddered around them, a low rumble filling the small chamber.

"We're landing," Matthias announced. "We've got to find a way out of here before the Domani show up."

A wave of anxiety passed over Eventide. This was it. It was now or never.

They reached the end of the passage, stepping out into what appeared to be a loading bay. They stood on top of a catwalk that stretched out over a large hold, filled with crates and supplies.

"We need to find the passenger access ramp," Matthias whispered, his breath hot in her ear so that he could be heard over the groan of the ship. "Watch out for guards."

They navigated the catwalks, treading carefully. Shadows of guards stood behind doorways that led out of the cargo bay. The guards faced outward, expecting any intrusion to come from elsewhere. Eventide supposed they didn't expect someone to find their way in through the back halls of the ship. In theory, only authorized staff would have access to those passages.

They moved into a second bay. This one was more evidently meant for people. Red carpet surrounded off-white couches laden with plush pillows, potted plants, and aesthetically pleasing decor.

"This looks like a lounge," Eventide thought out loud.

"It is," Matthias replied, his eyes darting from one corner of the room to the other. Sunlight streamed through small viewports, dancing on floral arrangements and champagne flutes that had been stacked alongside silver bowls of water and ice. Bottles of sparkling wine rested in the bowls, some unopened, others with their golden liquid already emptied into glasses that lined the tops of drink carts. Through a small window embedded in a door to an adjacent room, Eventide could make out waitstaff preparing for service.

"What's happening?"

"No expense spared for today's ceremonies. It's a celebration of the Domanis' return. If you think the Domani on board are treated with lavishness, wait until you see what's being prepared at the Syndicate Headquarters."

Eventide huffed. "This celebration isn't for the captives."

"What do you mean? Why wouldn't it be?"

"There are twelve Domani and nearly *three times* as many glasses poured, plus bottles left unopened. Unless they're planning on getting the Domani completely intoxicated in addition to the signals they're sending, they're not meant to take part in whatever this is."

Matthias' eyes moved to the assortment of glasses, his eyes narrowing as though seeing it all for the first time.

"No, you're probably right. I'd guess it's for the Caregivers and the other passengers on board. A pat on the back for being in the right place at the right time. This is as close to Earth as anyone born off-world will ever get."

Close as anyone will ever get, and yet we've gotten this far.

Eventide had been so focused on getting off the *Inanna*, she'd hardly stopped to consider where it was they were running to.

Earth. Growing up, the planet had almost been spoken of as a fairy tale; a mystical place that they'd never be able to set foot on because of the mistakes of humanity's past. Yet here she was, meters from a door that would allow her to set foot on their ancestral homeworld.

Any dreams she'd had as a child could never have imagined this sort of scenario. Part of her had believed she would be stuck with the monsters on board the *Inanna* for the rest of her short life. Now, there was a door providing light at the end of a long and dark tunnel.

Matthias stood beside her, still studying the lounge below, his dark eyes revealing nothing of his thoughts. He'd been stuck on board the ship for the past year and now hope for him, too, lay outside a single doorway.

"Thank you, Matthias," she whispered, her voice barely audible over the hum of the ship.

The comment was so sudden, a look of confusion washed over him. "For what?"

"For getting us here." She met his gaze. His dark eyes were soft in the dim light, the lines of his face shaded with shadows.

"Hey, you figured out how to open the blast door." His features hardened in the shadows. "You were the one who discovered the holes in the *Inanna's* security operations."

"But you were the one who lifted the tools. I'd still be under Lars' guard if it hadn't been for these."

"You'd have figured something out. You're probably the smartest woman I know."

Eventide blushed.

"So, what do we do now?" she asked.

The exit had to be nearby. She wondered how far she could stretch the capabilities of the tools in her kit. At some point, she was aware she'd probably have to abandon them.

"We wait here," Matthias said, a note of finality in his voice that made her glance at him. His gaze was steady, resolute. "We blend in with the Domani when they arrive. It's our best chance of getting off unnoticed."

A knot of apprehension twisted in Eventide's stomach. That didn't seem like the best solution, but they were in uncharted territory now. She didn't think she'd be able to short-circuit her way off the ship, but with the amount of security that had been present outside the Domani quarters, she also didn't think they'd be able to sneak out along with the main procession. Surely someone would be counting heads or would recognize them.

Matthias found a shadowy corner of the catwalk to sink into and lifted a knee to rest his arm on. His face was wearied; still attractive, but hollower than when she'd first met him. They'd both been running on low sleep, and it was likely catching up with them, but Eventide still had enough adrenaline coursing through her veins to keep the fatigue at bay for a little while longer.

One thing was for certain: she wasn't going to sit around waiting for Domani to show up with their Caregivers and guards.

"I can't see that working," she confessed. "We should figure out a way out now, before they get here."

"We need to play this safe. If we get caught, we won't get another chance."

"And if we miss our chance, we won't get another one, either. You can wait here to get spotted by a guard, but I'm not."

"Come on, don't do anything stupid. Keep your head down. We'll get through this."

Play the part. Bide your time.

Fury raged within her. She was done with doing that.

CHAPTER FORTY-FOUR

Eventide
The *Inanna*

"Where are you going?"

Matthias' voice was no more than an urgent whisper, but it still echoed off the metal beams crisscrossing the bay's ceiling.

Eventide didn't bother responding. She was getting off this ship, with or without Matthias' help. Over the course of the last few days, she'd grown increasingly infatuated with his charms, but Eventide prided herself on being a woman driven by logic. Whatever future she thought might be possible with this man, it wasn't as important as escaping.

Logic, however, only took her so far, and to fill in the gaps, she had to rely a bit on dumb luck. Emotion wasn't part of the equation.

She ran her fingers along the cards that were still nestled in the inside pocket of her pajamas.

Damn, I wish I could find a more appropriate outfit.

She traced the cards with the tip of her forefinger, allowing her to focus, even as she moved over the catwalk that circled the perimeter of the waiting area.

The Caregivers and selected Domani would probably arrive any minute. If there was a way out, she had to find it now.

Even as she descended the metal access stairs into the bay, she could hear Matthias' hesitant footsteps keep stride and then slow behind her. Though he'd given up on trying to convince her to stop.

She scanned the bay for any sign of clues or systems she might use. The area was extensive. Even though only a dozen Domani had been chosen to descend to the surface, she imagined at least four times as many could fit into the lounge. Maybe more.

It didn't take Eventide long to discover what she was looking for: the way out.

Her heart pounded as she caught sight of the green-tinted panel tucked away in the lounge's corner. The green light signaled something even more incredible: it was unlocked.

Which also meant the Caregivers were on their way. They would never leave an access door unlocked and unattended otherwise. She had precious few minutes, maybe seconds, to get out before they arrived.

Despite this realization, Eventide exhaled a sigh of relief. They had done it. They'd found the way out.

A noise behind her stopped her in her tracks. She whipped around, her pulse screaming in both excitement and warning.

Matthias had followed her off the catwalk, but now sat

crouched below the walkway, staring, wide-eyed, at something across the room.

She followed his gaze to a uniformed figure at the far end of the lounge. A guard, his attention centered squarely on Matthias.

Matthias slowly straightened, his eyes never leaving the guard, his expression one of calm resignation. He signaled to her with a barely perceptible shake of his head, the message clear: he was discovered, but she was not.

Eventide's mind whirled. The taste of freedom lay mere feet away from her. She could leave; slip out the exit with the guard distracted. Matthias flicked a hand, gesturing for her to follow her train of thought. It was awkward, as he didn't take his eyes off the guard and was doing his best not to give her away, but the intention was clear.

Run. Go for the door.

There was no reason she shouldn't leave Matthias behind. He'd made it on the *Inanna* for nearly a year; he'd be okay staying a bit longer. It was the logical choice. The practical choice.

Every part of her wanted to run. Eventide knew that if she didn't escape the ship now, she might never get another chance. Django was still out there, and dying as a Domani in blue silk pajamas was not how she wanted her story to end.

And if she made a move toward Matthias, she was positive that would be the outcome.

Matthias stood his ground, providing her with a few precious moments to decide. If she didn't head for the door now, there wouldn't be a way for her to reach it and escape without being seen.

That was when she noticed the guard reaching for his communication device. If he sent out a call, Matthias' chances of escape would plummet to zero. If the ship was locked down, she would also be captured and likely subjected to more of Doctor Morales' testing.

Or worse.

Every instinct within her screamed to run, yet she knew with a certainty that surprised her that she couldn't abandon Matthias. She might have pushed him away during the most intense kiss she'd ever experienced, but that didn't mean she wanted to leave him.

It didn't mean she didn't have feelings for him.

The thought surprised even herself, but Eventide didn't have time to process her emotions right now. A tremble coursed through her. She didn't know what she was going to do, but she knew she had to do *something*.

She took two steps toward the exit, and the spread that had been set up for the arrival celebration. A few dozen poured champagne flutes lined the top of a decorated table. She lifted one of the flutes and threw back the golden sparkling wine it contained. Under any other circumstance, she would have remarked at how crisp and delicate the wine was, but as it was, she barely tasted the elixir—but perhaps it would calm her nerves.

She dropped her toolkit in favor of an unopened bottle she selected from a large bowl of ice and crept along the wall toward the guard.

From his position, Matthias caught her eye, his gaze flickering to the wine bottle in her hand. He blinked, surprised, but did not betray her intentions. Instead, he lifted his hands placatingly to the guard.

"I may have gotten a little lost . . ." he said.

The guard did not look convinced. "This is the last place you should be. How'd you even get here?"

"Listen . . ." Matthias said, casting a worried glance toward Eventide.

The fool's going to give me away. Quit looking at me!

She continued her path, slowly, steadily, one foot in front of the other, trying her best not to catch the guard's eye. Pillars and plants sufficiently blocked her from view, but she was still wearing a bright blue outfit in a sea of green and red.

"This is a big misunderstanding. It isn't what you think."

"Save it, Domani." The guard pressed a finger to his ear, ready to call for backup.

"If you will only let me explain, I'd rather not get Roberts involved."

"Yeah, I bet you wouldn't. Save it for the Caregivers."

Eventide closed the gap between herself and the guard, aimed the bottle square at his head, and took the best swing she had in her. The reverberations of glass shattering against bone tore through the bottle, and wine and foam exploded over both of them, sending shards of glass up her arm and across the guard's head.

Matthias' mouth fell open in horror. "What have you done?"

"Saved our asses," she said, wiping away wine from her arm and ensuring there were no cuts from wayward glass shards. That was two guards she'd knocked out tonight. "Quick! We've got to hide him before the others come."

"What? Leave him. We shouldn't be here!"

"If they find an unconscious guard lying in the middle of the lounge in a puddle of wine, it's safe to say they're going to sound the alarm! They can't find this guy until we're out of here!"

Matthias grunted but relented, picking the guard up by his armpits while Eventide grabbed his feet. They found a nearby janitor's closet that they shoved the man into. He was breathing, but he was going to have one hell of a headache when he woke up.

"What do you want to do about the wine?"

The puddle on the floor had spread, soaking into the carpet. "There's nothing we can do about that. If we're lucky, they'll assume a server was clumsy and dropped a bottle."

"We're relying a lot on luck today, it seems," Matthias quipped.

A rumble of voices approached the lounge.

"Luck is all we've got left. Come on, if we're going to get out of here, it has to be now."

Eventide turned to the green-paneled doors and drew a deep breath. Despite everything happening around them, part of her couldn't help but marvel that she was about to be the first person from the *Eclipse* to step onto the Earth's surface in generations.

A well of emotion—genuine, non-implant-transfused emotion—washed over her as she opened the access door with a hiss and stepped through to whatever lay outside.

Eventide

    Reykjavík, Earth

Blue sky.

Eventide stumbled into Matthias in front of her, not looking at where she was going. How could she? The sky was painted a color she'd only seen in old photos and recordings. A world that was supposedly destroyed. White puffs of cloud broke the otherwise unending brilliant hue that blanketed the silent sky above her head.

She inhaled sharply through her nose, the air cool and crisp, with smells she couldn't even begin to describe. Wind caressed her skin, cold enough to give her goosebumps, but there was something so refreshing about it that she never wanted it to stop.

Air. Breathable, natural air. Gone was the stuffiness of purification systems and artificial conversions.

Was this how the ancestors felt? Free?

There's so much open space.

There was nothing keeping them from going anywhere

they wanted—on this island, at least. *Iceland was an island,* Eventide reminded herself. But everything seemed so vast. She shuddered as she let the immensity of the space around her sink in. There was nothing tangible maintaining an atmosphere, only gravity and a combination of other invisible forces. There was nothing holding them in any direction. Past the vast space of the island, which was already far larger than Eventide's mind could comprehend, there was a massive body of water—the ocean, stretching around the globe, connecting to even more bodies of water and swaths of land.

Space was infinite, but it had always been outside of the station's hull. Here, there were no walls. The Earth felt as if it could stretch on in every direction forever, without end.

Below the blue canvas above them, mammoth statues stood high enough that they appeared to touch the sky itself. Marble, gold, bronze, platinum, and cobalt all intertwined into the forms of ancient Roman gods from centuries before the Earth had developed space travel.

Except these statues were new.

Built with the materials mined from asteroids and distant moons, the fruit of the system's labors had been erected into monuments of the Syndicate's dynasty. Instead of distributing the wealth of their empire to its people, the Prefect and Council had clearly let them suffer. They'd crafted idols in order to celebrate their exploitation.

They thought of themselves as gods, but acted like devils.

There were at least half a dozen of the mile-high figures scraping the skyline. A marbled statue of Apollo overlooked the landing pad the *Inanna* now rested on. The vessel didn't even reach the full height of the god's ankle. Neptune, with his trident, emerged from the sea less than a hundred kilometers away. To the north, the god Mars hovered above the landscape, holy terror carved into his face, and in the distance, a statue of Venus, built from black onyx marbled with strands of gold, raised a right hand to the sky with her left spread below, as though she were pouring blessings onto the city that had created her.

An exorbitant expense as an ode to their own conquests. This Empire was far more depraved than Eventide could ever have imagined.

"*Watch it!*" Matthias hissed.

How could she look at anything else? How could he be so focused when there was so much lavishness all around them?

With no other traffic in or out of space, they hadn't landed on a dock, like her and Django had on the Moon. Instead, they'd simply touched down on a modest pad several kilometers away from the Syndicate Palace.

They'd only been outside for a matter of minutes before the Caregivers paraded the Domani out. Each of their faces marveled at the spectacle of the planet they'd landed on, and Eventide thought it might have been the only time where her emotions must have aligned with theirs.

They didn't have far to travel: a large transport vehicle awaited them, which the Domani boarded one by one.

Matthias and Eventide ducked behind the *Inanna*'s landing gear and waited until they were alone.

It had been easy.

Far too easy.

But that was exactly why Eventide couldn't allow herself to be distracted now. One slip up, and there would be no other chance for either of them.

"Sorry," she whispered back as she forced herself to pry her eyes away from the surrounding marvels. They just had to wait out the return of the Caregivers somewhere they wouldn't be discovered. Once the *Inanna* departed, they would hopefully be in the clear.

Then the hard part began.

She was going to have to get a lot craftier if she was going to find Django, especially since she was on the planet's surface, and he obviously was not.

And as far as she knew, the *Inanna* was the only ship that came or left the Earth's surface, though everything else she'd encountered about the Syndicate had been built on lies, so who knew how true that was?

One disaster at a time.

Beyond the ship and among the statues, skyscrapers stretched high above the horizon, dozens of glass and metal structures that reflected the sunlight and blue sky on their surfaces.

Past the buildings, white-capped mountains poked between the artificial structures, reminding humanity that no matter what they did to its surface, the Earth had been around long before they had ever marred its surface, and it would still be present long after it left.

"You there!" an authoritative voice called out.

Eventide froze and cursed under her breath. Matthias looked as though he was going to make a break for it, but

Eventide laid a hand on his shoulder, prompting him to stop.

They had no means of protecting themselves. She had even left the toolkit on board the ship. And they were still clad in Domani pajamas. Surely the guards here wouldn't shoot two unarmed drones, whether they had escaped from their ship or not. Would they?

Eventide had no idea. She had no framework of what sort of rules existed here. How ruthless would they be with those who stepped out of line on the surface?

Matthias seemed to put the pieces together, too, but he gritted his teeth as he turned to face the voice's owner.

A guard appeared, jogging, weapon in hand. "Did you two get separated from the group? Come with me. I'll call back the transport."

For a moment, Eventide didn't move, and she avoided glancing at Matthias for direction. She had two options: play along and potentially be discovered later, or make a break for it and be discovered now, and likely shot.

It wasn't much of a choice. *Death now or death later.*

The guard wore a white uniform nearly identical to the guards aboard the *Eclipse*, and identical to the uniforms she'd seen during her brief stay at the port on Lunar. The only difference, once again, was the emblem on the chest. Here, the familiar double hexagon contained a glowing blue and green sphere.

"Come on." The guard waved a gloved hand in a beckoning motion. "You can't be here. Come with me."

His voice wasn't hostile, like the guard on board the *Inanna*. It was probably his job to ensure the Domani all made it to their proper destination. The guard's eyes reflected a hint of worry that suggested his ass would be on the line if they got away on his watch.

Eventide could feel Matthias' eyes falling on her. He was deferring to her to make a move.

She wondered how much this guard knew about their implants and their need to be compliant. She was guessing not a lot, or he would already have been suspicious.

"Don't say anything," she whispered to Matthias, hopefully too quiet for the guard to hear. "Play along."

"Do you have a plan?" he asked.

"The plan is to not get killed."

Matthias grimaced. "Anything more than that? We're going to throw this all away now?"

"No, I don't think so," she said evenly. "This might complicate things, but we're not dead yet."

Play the part. Bide your time.

She hated the mantra with every fiber of her being, but it was all she had to keep herself alive. Plus, it wouldn't be for long. Soon, she would be able to stand her ground, and the closer she got to freedom, the more she wanted to put a stop to the system that had done this to her. The pressure behind that feeling was building, and Eventide knew it was only a matter of time before the dam burst.

She moved toward the guard without saying another word. The cold air no longer seemed to touch her skin. Blood pumping on overdrive through her veins was causing her to sweat despite not being appropriately dressed for the cool breeze that struck her. That alone would have been a mesmerizing sensation under any other circumstances.

"Come on, I don't have all day." The guard lifted his

forearm to his mouth and kept speaking to someone out of sight. "Yeah, hold the bus. We've got two stragglers here."

The reply was either into an earpiece or was too quiet for Eventide to make out.

"I have no idea, but keep it quiet or Evan'll have both our asses. We're on our way now."

The guard hurried them down the tarmac to a large vehicle on wheels, not unlike the shuttle on the *Eclipse*, except the wheels weren't connected to anything except the ground beneath them.

Eventide and Matthias approached the vehicle with the guard at their backs. Eventide held her breath, the implications of her actions turning the air thick and heavy as she took each breath. On this vessel were the dozen Selected Domani, plus the Caregivers. Eventide's brain didn't connect the dots until she had already stepped on board.

"What is the meaning of this?" The all-to familiar lemon-puckered voice echoed through the vehicle before Eventide even had a chance to look around. Lin was in front of the bus' doorway before there was any time to contemplate a reaction.

"Found these two on the pad, ma'am," the guard stuttered with a half-wave, half-salute. "They got separated from the group."

The man looked as green as Eventide felt. Fear of reprisal washed over his face as he swallowed.

But Lin's gaze had no interest in the guard. Her eyes flitted from Eventide to Matthias.

"Matthias," the Caregiver said. "What is the meaning

of this? You weren't supposed to allow her to leave the ship."

Matthias straightened.

Eventide's mouth moved, unable to speak.

Not supposed . . . to allow her?

"Matthias? What does she mean?"

Matthias eyed Eventide briefly, something glinting in his eye. Whether it was guilt, shame, or malice, the look was too quick for Eventide to parse.

"I didn't expect her to get past the blast door. But you said it would be useful if the girl discovered whether the ship had developed any weaknesses, so I allowed her to carry through. I thought it was best to let her carry out her plan to see what those were. I tried to remain on board until you arrived, but she wouldn't listen."

Eventide's heart stopped beating.

Matthias had betrayed her.

This had all been a set up.

Her mouthed moved but no words came out. Why wouldn't Lin have stopped her? To see if she could recruit and influence others? To determine if she had a bigger plan?

How much had she revealed to him, thinking he was an ally?

Okimi's head peaked out from a middle row of the bus but Eventide wasn't about to give her away by seeking her out.

Did Okimi know? Did Lin know about Okimi?

Eventide's mind swirled in a panicked deluge. She had kissed Matthias. She'd fallen for him.

How could I have been so stupid?

A cold object pushed its way into her back; an energy weapon, held by Matthias.

"Should I shoot her now? Or bring her back to the ship?"

Lin sighed and rubbed her temples. "You can't kill a Domani on the planet's surface. Do you have any idea what kind of outrage that would cause? Bring her on the bus. We don't have clearance to be wandering around out there. You're lucky you found a guard as clueless as you are; this could have started an incident! We'll deal with her later. I can't afford to be late for our meeting with the Prefect."

Lin barked at the guard to leave them, and he obliged before the vehicle began its journey once again.

Matthias pushed the weapon deeper into Eventide's back, shoving her into the vehicle with a dozen smiling Domani men and women looking back at her with both content smiles and confusion.

"And *you.*" The short, unnaturally smooth-skinned woman grabbed Eventide's arm as she walked past, holding her datapad in the opposite hand and waving it so that there would be no misunderstanding as to her intent. Her voice lowered to a wretched growl. "We are about to showcase before the Prefect. I have no choice but to bring you along. But don't you *dare* get any ideas. If you so much as breathe out of place, I'll have you bleeding from your eyeballs."

CHAPTER FORTY-SIX

Django
Shackleton City

With the rest of the Resurgence team already in bed, Django lay on his cot, eyes fixed to the ceiling. They were in a transition house in Shackleton City, one last stop before they carried on to Asteria to proceed with the next phase of their plan.

Tonight, it had taken a while for the cankerous laughter to die down, for the last mug of ale to be put away, and for the crew to retire for the night. They would all be drunk, basking in the victory at Space Dock Seven, which was fine by Django. They would be less eager and, more importantly, less able to stop him.

As much as Marvin had assured him he wasn't a prisoner, there would have been no leaving the Resurgence safe house unescorted—not without questions. And these were questions Django couldn't afford to answer.

He was risking a lot, but then again, he'd already risked everything, and it had gotten him nowhere.

The current transition house was much nicer than the one they'd stayed in the night Django had been rescued from the cargo ship headed for the mines. Located on the Upper Rim and donated by a benevolent sympathizer, this house was well stocked and well equipped. The furniture was new, and the walls were freshly painted, and the suite was as luxurious as any Django had ever slept in. Its glass walls even allowed its inhabitants to look out over the neon lights and holo-projected advertisements of Shackleton.

Despite everything he had seen since leaving the *Eclipse*, Django still shook his head in disbelief. Who would have thought that a skyscraper on the Moon could be made of glass? But the artificial atmosphere contained within the surrounding force field kept the city's pressure to a similar pascal as Earth and kept stray debris from shattering its walls.

Django had even heard the Resurgence crewmembers discussing ways to engineer an atmosphere for all of Lunar once the Syndicate's funds were redistributed appropriately. A rumor among dreamers, most likely, but with all the marvels he had seen, he wasn't about to rule anything out. What else would humanity dream up if they were unencumbered by death, famine, and tyranny?

He absently scratched his forearm, feeling the scar from the incision. It had healed along with the gash in his shoulder, but there was still a faint scorch to the wound.

Sunlight streamed in through his room, as bright in the middle of the night as it would be mid-afternoon. It was one of the reasons why Lunar's early settlers had chosen this spot for the Upper Rim; its infinite solar energy, with a crater full of ice below. They likely had no idea that it would later produce a city full of sleep-deprived drones.

And it was during this bright and shining night that Django would make a move to leave; a desperate play to whisk Eventide safely out of the Prefect's arms. He had a card up his sleeve he hadn't thought he would have to play —until Marvin had told him Eventide was out of reach.

That left only one other person with enough influence to reach her.

Some sort of protective force field must have separated Django from Commander Aries and the two other men in his company, dressed in similar Syndicate uniforms. Their mouths moved, but there was no noise coming from any of them.

The man who had escorted Django through the Syndicate office tower stood at the ready beside the door, but he offered Django no instruction as to what to do while he waited for Aries to finish his meeting. Whatever it was about, it had been far too important for the guard to interrupt, so Django had crossed his arms and leaned against a wall panel to wait.

The circular room was a glass orb, bisected by vistas of the city below and the buzzing SF HQ within. On one side, was the lush wilderness of the Upper Rim, the containment field shimmering against the abyss of space. Turning around, he took in the inner workings of the headquarters, a hive of activity with personnel darting between workstations.

He couldn't decipher the data on their screens, but the prevalence of graphs suggested environmental monitoring and planetary reporting. In the deeper recesses of the HQ, boardrooms and think tanks housed more ominous activities. Django caught glimpses of what he believed to be star charts and strategic maps marking Syndicate ship locations, and holographic lines connecting dots on a projected map of Lunar—silent whispers of the Front's interconnected plans.

As he glanced at one of the larger office spaces, Django couldn't help but notice one particular map. One location was pinpointed with a large red star, and large letters spelling out the location's name, so there was no mistaking the identified landmark.

Asteria.

For all the Resurgence's secrecy and maneuvering, they hadn't been able to keep the city hidden from the Syndicate. How long had Aries known? Was his uncle aware that their city had been discovered? And would it mean Aries would no longer see any value in Django? Were his hopes of finding Eventide, even here, lost?

"Mr. Alexander." The commander's baritone voice jolted Django out of his thoughts. Had Aries noticed him staring at the map? And how much did it matter now, anyway? "Glad to see you've finally returned."

Whatever forcefield had separated them had been covertly removed when Django hadn't been paying attention. Aries stood in his office with a bemused look on his face.

"It seems you were right." Django uncrossed his arms as he pushed himself off the panel he'd been leaning against and moved to join the commander. "You're the only person who can give me what I need."

"Well, then." Aries' unsettling smile returned. "It seems our deal will prove fruitful after all. Your timing couldn't be better."

Django paused. "What do you need me for, exactly?"

Before Django could answer, the two men that Aries had been speaking with hurried out of the office, barely giving Django a second glance. Their faces were drawn tight, eyes flashing with concern as they glanced back at Aries before leaving.

"Commanders from other Lunar districts," Aries explained when he saw Django's scrutiny following the men out of the office. "It's been a task weeding out who will work with us when the revolution begins."

"And when will that be?" Django asked.

The hairs on the back of Django's neck stood on end as Aries smiled again.

"It can be today, if you'd like."

Django ran a hand over his neck, feeling the goosebumps that populated there. Aries was after something else. He didn't like it, but he couldn't figure out what it might be.

Just stick to the plan.

"What could I possibly offer you that anyone else couldn't?"

Django's forearm itched.

There's no way he knows. Aries might have found out about Asteria, but there's no way he could know about the chip.

Is there?

Aries pulled two glasses from beneath his desk and filled them with a yellowish liquid. "Believe it or not, we have similar goals." The commander picked up one glass in each hand and offered one to Django.

Django took it on reflex, though he wasn't sure whether he wanted to choke on another vile shot of liquor.

Aries slammed the drink back, the liquid disappearing down his throat with the reckless enthusiasm of a party-hardened youth.

Django took a more conservative approach and cautiously raised the glass to his lips. The liquid smelled unlike any alcohol Django had ever experienced: sweet-smelling vanilla with a hint of citrus. He took a sip and let the cool liquid run down his throat. It bore the heat of alcohol he'd become acquainted with, but this didn't have the vile acetone aftertaste of most concoctions he'd tried. This was actually pleasant.

"Let's step into the war room."

"I came here because I need help reaching Eventide," Django said. He wasn't interested in politics, or drinking, or whatever else Aries held up his sleeve. "She's on Earth."

Aries looked at him, expressionless.

"I'm only interested in helping her," Django continued. "The Resurgence aren't able to reach her. I need to know that you can."

"I have someone working on extracting her now," Aries said warmly. His stern features softened as a smile danced across his face, replacing the harsh cold of a military commander with the warmth of a friend. Django had seen the same transformation on Marvin dozens of times as he switched gears from leader to uncle.

Django's eyebrows arched high on his forehead. "You do?"

"I'm a man of my word," Aries said, "and I don't make bargains I don't intend to keep. I promised I'd extract your friend, and I plan on doing that. I also promised I'd allow you to take down this Commander Benson. I'll fulfill that request, too, but only if we act now."

Aries moved without waiting for an answer, tracking across the offices and passing through a sliding door toward the rear of the office.

Django hadn't noticed the lone panel in the room earlier, which was distinctively non-glass. The silver door, tucked beside the external windows, opened out onto a long, narrow hallway skirting the building's edge. The hall's opaque door contrasted with the glass wall surrounding it, offering an uninterrupted city view. Only at the hall's end, inside a solitary room, did the windows cease.

Aries and Django entered a dark room, similar in size and shape to Aries' office, illuminated only by the eerie glow of dozens of dormant holo-screens and the yellow and green panels embedded in the walls.

A dozen chairs surrounded a large circular table in the middle of the room, descended slightly into the floor, presumably so those at the table would have a less obstructed view of the screens littered around the room.

"What is this place?" Django thought out loud.

"This is where our solar system's future will be born."

Django gave Aries a side-eye, still unsure about what the man was getting at.

An active holo-screen hovered above the table, its spherical pattern depicting familiar-looking stations—

echoes of the *Eclipse*. There were twelve separate pieces to the image. Eleven of the videos showed a station in a slightly different orbital position above the Earth. One was empty.

Marvin had told him there were more stations like *Eclipse,* but this was the first time Django had seen each of the stations lined up beside each other like this.

How many farms and families lived on board each of those stations? How many Novas and Averys were living their lives, trying to escape the diplomacy of Commander Bensons shoving families out of airlocks to preserve a two-hundred-year-old lie?

So mesmerized by the display, Django had barely realized they'd walked right up to the table in front of the holosphere. Aries tapped his fingers on the black onyx table, summoning a virtual keyboard and control panel to rise before them.

Aries' fingers danced over the holographic keyboard, figures flickering and rearranging so rapidly on the screen that Django could hardly follow them.

"What is this?" he asked.

Reflections of the lights danced along Aries' bald scalp as the images danced before him.

"This is the answer to your wish," Aries said. "An end to Benson, and to those like him."

"You're going to take out Benson from here? How?"

"I'm not going to do anything of the sort," Aries replied, still typing furiously on the holographic keyboard. "*You are.*"

A lump formed in Django's throat, and he found it hard to swallow. An unsettling chill prickled his skin. How could they kill a man from a small room hundreds of thousands of kilometers away?

A persistent itch crawled up Django's forearm, like an invisible insect skittering across his skin.

The chips. The Syndicate had access to everyone via the chip in their arms.

Of course. No wonder the Syndicate was so eager to have everyone chipped.

Not only could the Empire control the lives of each of their citizens, but it could also control their deaths.

The thought sent a violent shudder through him. Django glanced at his trembling hands, still somewhat unfamiliar with the weight of taking a life. Django had barely gotten over the idea of killing someone at all, but killing from a distance? It was a macabre and unsettling thought.

He forced down the knot in his throat. He wanted Benson dead, but like this? It didn't feel right.

The screen Aries was typing on shifted and floated along the central panel, stopping where Django stood. Each of the eleven stations spread out before him on a second blue pulsing screen. Four were faded out, semi-transparent, while seven of them glowed.

"Pick one of these seven." Aries said. "The ones that are faded, unfortunately, are not ready yet, but I can't wait any longer."

Django raised an eyebrow. "What do you mean?"

"That chip within you can grant you your deepest desires. Scan your forearm against the sensor on the table and choose a station."

Scan your forearm. So, Aries *did* know about the chip.

But how? This must have been what the man meant, though, when he'd said he needed Django. Aries didn't have the power to take a man's life, not on his own.

But Django did.

So many questions swirled in his mind, he didn't know which to ask first.

"How do I know which one is *Eclipse*?"

Aries' creepy smile returned. "Let's make this interesting. Each one of these stations is run by a man equally, if not more, cruel than Benson. Each willing to toss unknowing citizens out into the abyss of space."

Django's jaw set firm, as his resolve hardened within him. Could one life save thousands? His finger hovered over the stations. If their leaders were all equally cruel, should he hit all seven stations at once?

He pushed the thought aside. First, he had to test the waters.

Each run by a man equally cruel.

Django studied the stations, each hovering on the console, lined up unnaturally next to the other, each torus ring rotating separately in order to maintain their own gravity levels. How was he to know which one was the *Eclipse*? He would rather be done with Benson and move on.

He had never bothered to look for distinguishing marks; the *Eclipse* was supposed to have been the only station; humanity's last hope. But the existence of the other ten had shattered that belief. His home, his reality—all a lie. When would the deceptions end?

Scan your forearm and one cruel leader will die.

This was why he was here.

Holding his breath, Django lifted his forearm, his eyes darting around the room. He knew he was stalling, but the weight of the choice transfixed him. He steadied himself, deciding to take it one station at a time.

Green text hovered above the images of the stations. AUTHORIZATION GRANTED.

Django wished he could see the man whose life he was taking. He didn't want to repeat the process eleven times, or even seven, but he also didn't want to ask too many questions for fear that Aries would change his mind.

The commander stood silently across the room, hands held behind his back, growing impatient at Django's indecision.

Without allowing himself to think on it any further, Django reached out and hit the fifth station. There was no rhyme or reason, but it felt as good a choice as any of them.

The station came to life above the console, floating above it in three-dimensional glory. It reminded him of the holo-feeds the staff on Space Dock Seven had observed while the dock security had fought off the pirate attack. It was detailed enough that Django could make out the viewports of different observation decks and a few larger rooms.

He wasn't sure what he was expecting to happen. A confirmation? An image of a dying commander, convulsing on the floor? It felt like minutes passed with nothing visible happening.

He was about to ask Aries what they were waiting for when a shift in the image caught his eye. It was small at first, merely a spark—then it all happened at once.

A fireball erupted from a section of the D-Ring that Django recognized as the cargo bay hold. The fireball spread, smoke and debris pushing out into the vacuum, then thinning out as it expanded.

An icy wave washed over Django as the fireball spread to the station's central hub. The entire hull depressurized and was ripped apart by conflicting forces traveling all the way up the shaft and into the A-Ring with unbelievable speed and precision. The detonation sent the remaining portion of the station into destabilized orbit, spinning wildly out of control toward the Earth's atmosphere.

All Django could do was watch, dumbfounded. His heart had stopped, along with his breathing, as had time. He'd wanted revenge. He'd wanted to avenge his family; to put an end to further Syndicate lies and death.

And instead, he'd killed everyone on board.

CHAPTER FORTY-SEVEN

Mikka

The *Redemption*

Mikka fell into the captain's chair, all strength escaping from her legs. She could barely sit upright as waves of nausea threatened to throw up the little food that Zee had brought her earlier.

She didn't have to check to see which space station had suffered the horrific blow; which one was now hurtling into orbit, breaking apart in fiery fury.

It didn't matter. It was one that she had delivered cargo to within the past forty-eight hours.

Hours ago, she had been on that station. If she hadn't left in time, she would have been blown to bits along with the lives of everyone on board.

Hundreds of thousands.

The loss of life was immobilizing. This was so much more than the handful of friends who had died because of Mikka's actions; more far-reaching than the dozens of family members who would never see their loved ones.

Hundreds of thousands.

The words Marvin had spoken ages ago rattled around inside her brain.

So many lives. Dead by my hand.

All because she'd been too stubborn to listen. Kiara had tried to warn her. Abigail had tried to stop her.

Hell, even Zee had told her she had teamed up with the villain.

Mikka gasped as she tried to catch her breath. Panic gripped her, squeezing her throat until it squeaked as she fought for air.

No, no, no! Her thoughts spiraled, digging themselves into her core and strangling each of her cells. Refusing to believe everything that had come to a head.

There will be much destruction.

The breath she was fighting so hard for filled her lungs with a wheeze.

"*You knew!*" she growled at Zee, fury replacing the shock. "You knew I'd be the cause of this!"

Over at the viewscreen, Zee's eyes were wide as he watched the pieces of the station fly into the void. The shock on his face matched Mikka's own.

No. His face reflects the innocence of a child.

A sliver of composure found its way into Mikka's conscious. Getting mad at Zee wasn't the answer here. He'd seen numbers. That was all he'd ever seen.

But the thread was thin. She wanted to scream. She wanted someone else to blame.

Have they all gone off? What was Aries planning?

Mikka quickly scanned the airwaves. There was so much noise; so much commotion surrounding what had happened. Newsfeeds filled the system, with talking heads reviewing current analysis of the explosion, their opinions filled with idle speculation. Some reports claimed it was an extension of the recent terrorist attacks that had plagued Lunar and Ceres. Others were saying it was a malfunction.

All of them were wrong.

Even if they would dare utter the words, not a single analyst could have known that the Commanding Officer of the Lunar Colonies was behind this. Not yet. How could they? Aries was their protector; the man who would come out declaring that the colonies needed to be shielded from this threat.

In time, it was possible the media would be able to piece it together if they were granted access to forensic analysis of the explosion—which they wouldn't be. But there was only one type of weapon that could have taken down a FLOW station that quickly: a plutonium bomb.

No journalist would openly dare to question the Syndicate. Not if they ever wanted their face to appear on the feeds again.

But nobody else was taking the credit for the attack . . . yet.

At any moment, Aries could push another button. How mad was this prince whom she'd made her bed with? Would he detonate the remaining devices all at once? Or watch those on the stations suffer, one by one?

One by one.

The realization hit her like a ton of bricks. Mikka had delivered thirteen bombs to seven of the FLOW stations—but that meant there were still eight in her cargo hold.

Eight *plutonium bombs.*

One was enough to take out a FLOW station. Eight would launch the *Redemption* halfway to Andromeda.

"Zee! Kiara's suit is in a storage locker on the edge of the cargo hold! It'll be a bit big, but it'll do. Put it on, and then wait for me here."

Mikka didn't wait for his response. Her hands flew over her control panels, opening up the comms channel once again and setting it to ship-wide speakers so she could move about the *Redemption* as she spoke.

"Abigail, are you still hanging around?"

"I'm here, love. I can't imagine you missed that little fireworks display?"

Mikka rushed into the cargo hold, transferring the comms to the ship's speakers. She stepped over sacks of food strewn beside the crate she had emptied with Zee's help. The crate that carried an explosive device with enough firepower to knock a space station out of the sky. She rushed to secure the ties on the carbon tethers that held the cargo in place. She couldn't risk the packages bouncing around the hold.

"This isn't the time for 'I told you so,'" Mikka said. "We've got bigger problems here."

Had Aries known which crates she'd delivered? Or had there been a thirty-six percent chance she'd nearly been obliterated? With the chain reaction of eight plutonium bombs in the close confines of her ship, nobody would be able to tell the *Redemption* had been a ship from the cloud of dust left orbiting the planet.

"So . . ." The sass was back in Abigail's voice, and Mikka wanted to reach through the console and slap it out of her. "You found the little present Aries left behind?"

How much time do I have? Seconds? Minutes?

Mikka's hands shook as she loosened the emergency hooks. She had to keep to together—at least long enough to get Zee to safety.

"Why the hell didn't you get rid of the cargo when you figured out what it was?"

"We would have, but you buggered off before our scans confirmed it. We had to be sure we knew what we were dealing with."

"It took you *a week* to figure out there was *weapons-grade plutonium* on board?" Mikka yelled as she continued to dislodge the cargo anchors. "You have one of the most advanced ships in space! You should have been able to detect that long before the ship even boarded!"

"Had we thought your boyfriend was willing to chance nuking you out of the sky, we would have. We thought it'd be something a little more . . . *subtle.* A virus, perhaps; poisoned peas; a holo of the Prefect standing in the buff. Guess Aries doesn't do anything by halves."

Mikka double-checked the magnetic restraints that held the crates to the deck. They would be deactivated once the power failed. The carbon ties would be the fail-safe, holding the crates against the cargo bay bulkhead until the hull ultimately failed.

Everything she had worked so hard for, all thrown away. And for what?

"I hadn't figured that out." She grunted as she pulled the manual release for the cargo. "Thanks for letting me know."

"Anyway, suffice to say, we didn't know until you'd already left. Trust me, I wouldn't have been comfortable with that payload on the *Chimera,* either. So, you did me a favor, really."

"Speaking of which, that's why I'm calling. We've got to do something about these ticking time bombs. I'm going to aim them at Point Nemo, but I can't do this alone."

"Happy to help, love."

"Just stay out of the way until I give you the signal, then come get us. We have no way of knowing when Aries will detonate the next one, so cruise with caution."

"All I heard was our date's back on. Call me when you're ready."

Mikka raced back to the bridge and entered the commands to seal the airlock between the cargo hold and the rest of the ship. Then she double-checked to ensure Zee had suited up.

"Why do I need to suit up if you're sealing the airlock?" The poor kid's eyes were still wide with terror as he finished donning the suit. Smart kid.

Mikka grabbed her own suit and pulled it over her body as quickly as she could. "We're not sticking around here, kid. Hang on!"

Mikka steered the *Redemption* toward the planet. Every second the ship bounced around in it put her on edge, and she gritted her teeth with each shudder.

How could David do this to me?

The ship's comms panel sprang to life.

Right on cue.

Mikka knew who it was before she even answered the transmission.

Looks like Zee's not the only psychic round here . . .

Her heart raced, causing her pulse to thump through

every part of her body as though her high school crush was on the other line.

Except David was no longer her crush. No longer her love.

In the span of a few moments, he'd gone from lover to something else—a monster. A destroyer of worlds. And he still held the trigger for more, including her own.

"Are those pirates still there?" No greeting and no acknowledgment of the lives that had been snuffed out of existence. He didn't even ask if she was okay. "Reinforcements are on their way. Hang tight."

As if it were pirates posing the greatest threat to her.

"Did you happen to check if that device was still on my ship before you pushed that button?" There was no hiding the grit in her voice; the rage that boiled beneath the surface of her skin.

"Listen, my darling. You don't understand . . ."

Mikka fired her engines, aiming for a lower orbital trajectory. She couldn't wait to make her move. This had to be done now.

"Did. You. Know?"

Mikka could hear Aries inhale deeply on the other side of the comm.

He had no idea.

"I didn't push the button."

In the process of sealing her helmet, she paused, closing her eyes. She refused to hang on to hope.

"You really can't expect me to believe that this wasn't your doing?" she asked, her eyes still closed. Her hands remained in mid-lock of her helmet.

"The people on board that FLOW station did not die by my hand."

He was lying—or at least twisting the truth. The Syndicate commander thought he was being crafty, which he usually was. But this? This was a poor effort at disguising what had really happened . . . It had to be.

"The Resurgence and that kid, Django—they're the ones responsible for this. He was hell-bent on killing his commander. The poor kid didn't even know which station was his."

Mikka scoffed. "Is that the official line? Because you've been having me deliver these death traps to each of the FLOW stations. Did you somehow think I was too stupid put the pieces together? That I wouldn't figure out you had me deliver weapons-grade plutonium to civilian targets?"

Aries paused uncharacteristically.

"When were you going to tell me?" Mikka continued. "Or were you? Were you just planning on blowing me out of the sky with the rest of them?"

Mikka imagined Aries in his office tower, fuming over being called out. *Does the little shit even have any remorse? Any compassion for the lives he's ended?*

"My feelings for you are genuine, Mikka. And I've told you before—there's no progress without sacrifice. The FLOW stations are the key to the Syndicate's strength on the surface. Without supplies, their forces will be devastated. They won't know how to survive without goods being sent down."

"Those are *human lives*, David!"

"It's for the greater good. I thought you'd understand."

Mikka clenched her fists to stop them from shaking. "How am I supposed to understand this?"

There was another pause. "I did nothing, Mikka. You were the one who delivered the plutonium to the station. With your prior history of being a pirate, surely, you're just another of Alejandro's followers, looking to take down the Syndicate at all costs. I bet you and the boy were in on this together."

Mikka froze, allowing reality to come crashing down on top of her.

He's never cared about me.

He hadn't seen something in her. There was no partnership in any of this. No path of redemption. Only ruin. All he'd wanted was a scapegoat; a willing participant to do his dirty work so he could keep his hands clean.

Oh, Kiara. You tried to warn me!

"And you've been channeling stolen Syndicate funds into your mother's account," Aries said as Mikka caught her breath. "And to Kiara Ryson."

"What exactly are you implying?"

"Think about it, Mikka. Nobody will believe a simple delivery contractor would have been able to afford two upscale apartments in an Upper Rim neighborhood, never mind three caretakers for the Ryson children."

He's got me by the balls. How could I have been so stupid?

Mikka couldn't respond; she was unable to force any words from her lips. The cold deck tiles pressed into her knees as she slumped. Zee was at her side, holding her arm.

"It doesn't have to be like this, Mikka. The life you always dreamed of can still be yours. We can rule the

Syndicate. We can lift the lives of those less fortunate." He paused again. "And your mother will be safe. Kiara's family, too."

She could cave to his threats; continue to work for him despite the evil acts he'd unleashed. She could convince herself she owed Kiara's kids that much.

Despite it all, there was still a small part of her that was tempted. Who knew what he would do to them if she didn't?

But Mikka Jenax wouldn't bow her head so easily. She might have been fooled by David Aries' cunning charm, by his sweet whispers and promises of a better Loop, but he had made a fatal error.

He'd crossed the wrong pirate.

You will kill David Aries.

"*You bastard!*" The growl left her lips as she ended the transmission.

There was nothing more she could do.

By the time you're convinced it's the right path, you'll wish you had done it sooner.

The cargo bay door complained as it separated the pressurized cabin from the vacuum of space. Crates shuddered as they fought between their straps and the vacuum outside. The crates and the plating of the plutonium bombs hidden within them wouldn't survive entry into Earth's atmosphere, not on their own.

But the *Redemption* could.

And with it, Mikka's own redemption would crash into an icy sea, on a world she'd never get to visit.

She couldn't allow the weapons to explode within the Earth's atmosphere. She couldn't allow the fallout to affect the rest of those in orbit, or to make landfall on the healing planet below. Point Nemo would offer the furthest point from any piece of land. If she could do her best to ensure their integrity until they hit the water, then the bombs could either rest or explode within the depths of the ocean.

Mikka adjusted the frequency on the comms unit inside her helmet. "Abi, get ready— we're coming your way. Stand by to pick up two drifters."

Her helmet hissed as it sealed to her suit, as did the door as Mikka opened the airlock. She grabbed onto Zee's hand and braced herself to be sucked out into the void, preparing for whatever her next chapter might be.

Mikka surveyed her beloved ship one last time, knowing full well that this was where her path of redemption ended. Only a path of ruin now lay before her. The stars only knew if she'd be able to pick up the pieces.

"Hang on, kid. We're in for one hell of a ride."

CHAPTER FORTY-EIGHT

Django
> Syndicate HQ, Shackleton City

Aries' men hauled Django down a shadowy corridor, pulling him inexorably toward a prison cell nestled deep within the Syndicate headquarters. His mind churned with the horror of what had transpired all those floors above.

How many souls had been on that station? How many lives were extinguished because of me?

It seemed irrelevant that Aries had duped him. If Django hadn't been so headstrong, if he'd heeded Marvin's warnings instead, if he'd just listened to his friends, none of this would have happened.

Now, his name was etched into the Syndicate's computer systems, in the minds of all who watched the holo-feeds, as a mass murderer. No other record of his existence would remain other than this one brutal fact. This was how Django Alexander would be immortalized—a terrorist born on the mysterious FLOW station *Eclipse*. A man who lost his sanity and annihilated his home at the first opportunity.

At least the histories would be accurate.

Aries *had* vowed to bring about Benson's death.

I'm a man of my word.

If he had been capable of thinking beyond his own selfish desires, perhaps Django would have understood that the commander's life wasn't the only one he'd held in his hands.

But it was too late—too late for the countless souls lost to the void. Too late for his own soul, destined to fade into the abyss of time and space as retribution for his actions.

He caught fragments of the holo-feeds as the guards dragged him down the corridors. His face flashed on every screen throughout the entire building.

". . . terrorist attack on a FLOW station . . ."

". . . associated with the insurrectionist group known as the Resurgence . . ."

". . . alleged to be related to the infamous mercenary, Marvin Alejandro, who disappeared eight years ago . . ."

". . . Sources suggest a plutonium blast disrupted the station's core systems, leaving no chance of survivors."

Django wasn't sure where the Syndicate had captured the photo of him that followed him down the hallway, or how they'd discovered the fragmented details of his life. In the image, one of his eyes was partially shut, making him appear like a drug-induced maniac.

He hadn't been drugged, but his actions proved he was undeniably a maniac.

It was as if he was witnessing someone else's nightmare

play out, but it was his own face that assumed the role of the villain.

Django strained against his cuffs. Frequency-jamming armbands had been fixed around his forearms.

The guards had yanked Django from the command center in a stupor, while he was still wrestling to comprehend the disaster unfolding before him.

After he had pressed the button, Aries had stepped aside, his expression void of emotion. "I'm sorry to have to do this, Django," the commander had uttered. "You've been immensely useful."

The statement had bewildered Django, his gaze still riveted on the stations and the void where one had been moments ago.

"But . . ." He'd faltered as he lost the strength in his legs to hold him upright, too shocked to cry, too shocked to do anything but look on in horror. "Why? You didn't have to do this!"

"Oh, you're mistaken there. Do you know what you just did? You've discredited the fringe reports that were showing support for the Resurgence. You've smeared their entire movement. With the loss of the FLOW station, the Syndicate will be forced to implement stricter rations. You've removed all barriers to taking down the Prefect and seizing control of this empire."

Commander Aries was a lunatic. How had Django failed to perceive the insanity lurking behind those cool eyes? He had always dismissed the stories his mother had used to tell him—tales of monsters lurking in the solar system. But it turned out, the monsters were indeed real. He had been working with the devil himself.

He'd betrayed his uncle. The Resurgence was doomed. Who would stand behind an organization willing to obliterate a FLOW station filled with innocent civilians? His face was linked to it all—the Resurgence, the explosion, and death itself.

He deserved to be locked away forever, though he suspected he would be tried and then jettisoned through an airlock. Even that would be far too light a sentence.

"You promised!" Django had hollered in blinding fury, lunging for the commander. Aries' men had seized him before he could get within arm's reach, holding him back as his shouts, sobs, and cries fell on unheeding ears. "You swore you'd free Eventide!"

Aries had simply smirked. "Don't worry, I may still have use for you."

"*Never!*" Django had shouted, resisting as the guards hauled him out of the room.

"We'll see." Aries' grin had stretched across his face. "I did indeed vow to *find* your girlfriend. And I always keep my promises."

It was this veiled threat that had shattered him. Django hadn't been able to find the words to hurl at the villain before him.

"We'll find Eventide," Aries had said, pointing to the largest of the holo-screens on the side panel of the room. Django's holographically projected face had floated beside a three-dimensional representation of the station's explosion. "But how will she regard you when she sees this? Do you believe she'll rush into your arms, thrilled by the lengths you went to for her freedom?" Aries had brandished his menacing grin, even more terrifying after the events that had unfolded. "Either way, if you want her to remain safe, you'll assist me again. Consider it our new arrangement."

A knee to the gut snapped Django back to reality, jolting him from the vicious loop that had been replaying in his mind since he'd exited the war room. The corridor the guards pulled him down was faintly lit with light orange LED strip lighting, casting an eerie glow on the rugged regolith surface of the walls. They were deep in Lunar's underground, far beneath the paneled hallways and metallic flooring of the cells he had occupied before. These cells were designed for their inhabitants to be forgotten.

They passed several stationed guards, all donning helmets with dark gray tinted visors, their identities concealed.

With a rough shove, Django found himself in a cell as barren as his hope. The cold metal of the bunk bit through his clothes, while the faint hum of life support systems served as the only sound in the all-encompassing silence. Django's light-headedness suggested they were only feeding minimal amounts of air through the system.

He stared at the blank wall, his eyes dimmed of their fire. The silence wasn't solitude but a relentless echo, taunting him with the nothingness that now lay ahead of him. The only thing remaining was the void that was his future.

A future barren of anything but the dread of what other atrocities Aries might use him to commit.

Django wasn't certain if the station he'd destroyed *was* the *Eclipse* or if it was one of the other eleven. There was nearly a ten percent chance he'd blown up his home. His sister Nova might have been on board that station. Had she died by his own hands?

Everyone on that station had someone who cared for them.

How many innocent people had met their untimely end today? Station guards following orders. Bartenders pouring vile glasses of ale. Handymen salvaging what they believed were relics from the time of Earth's past. Farmers harvesting their grains. Thousands had simply been going about their day, believing they were working toward Earth's recovery from an apocalypse that had occurred centuries ago.

They had all been a part of the station Django had called home. Now, they were gone.

When Django had left the *Eclipse*, he had been uncertain if he would ever see his home again. Now, he didn't even know if there was a home for him to return to.

And it was all his own fault.

AFTERWORD

Thank you for reading *Resurgence* and continuing on with Django, Mikka and Eventide on their journey.

As an independent author, reviews are really important. They help other readers—like you—discover my work.

If you liked the book, and have a couple of minutes to spare, it would be great if you could leave a short, honest review on Amazon, Goodreads, your bookish blog, social media or of course, on the book's retail page.

Thank you!

Watch for the fourth instalment of *The Fractured Orbit*, coming in 2024.

ACKNOWLEDGMENTS

Resurgence was originally the second half of Chimera, but as I mentioned in the Acknowledgements of the last book, the story ended up growing far past what a single book could contain.

When I finished Eclipse, I immediately knew how Django's story in this book would end, I just hadn't realized how much it would take to get him there. The result was a good 900 pages, not including the text that didn't make it into the final manuscript.

Thank you reader for continuing on this journey with me. This story would not be possible without you.

Shane Millar gave this book an initial beta read and pointed out where some of the flaws in the story were. You were a cheerleader for Eventide throughout, and you helped me to realize that I had to give her even more page time to do justice to her story.

I'd like to thank Pete Smith from Novel Approach Manuscript Services for providing a copy edit, and assisting with details and phrasings that I was at a loss for.

Covers by Christian continues to blow me away with his cover design, and I thank him for making these books look amazing.

I want to thank all of my author friends from my various writing circles who have provided feedback and encouragement. To the Rebel Author Slack group, thank you for your encouragement and motivation to set goals and stick to them. To my friends in the Dystopian Author League who are always willing to promote and lift each other up. The Write Better Fiction Discord group for letting me agonize about each step of the process of editing and completing this manuscript. And to all of the others who have offered words of support and encouragement along the way.

To my wife Nettie, who always supports of me when I need to head to a coffee shop on the weekends to write. Who encourages me when things don't go as planned, and who won't let me quit. This wouldn't have been possible without your unwavering belief in me.

ABOUT THE AUTHOR

Herman Steuernagel is a science fiction and fantasy author. His internationally best-selling debut Lies the Guardians Tell reached the top of the science fiction charts in multiple countries.

Herman grew up with a love of story and science fiction, watching Star Trek, The Next Generation with his father. As a teenager he fell in love with The Sword of Shannara by Terry Brooks, and The Wheel of Time series by Robert Jordan.

His currently published works are dystopian science fiction that highlight the struggle between humanity and the technology we keep, as well as the motivations that keep us fighting with each other.

Herman currently lives in British Columbia, Canada, While he's not working on a new book he can be found cycling, running and dreaming up new worlds.

9 781990 505133